THE PHOTOGRAPHER'S BOY

THE PHOTOGRAPHER'S BOY

A NOVEL

STEPHEN BATES

OPEN ROAD
INTEGRATED MEDIA
NEW YORK

978-1-4976-6106-6

This edition published in 2014 by Open Road Integrated Media, Inc.
345 Hudson Street
New York, NY 10014
www.openroadmedia.com

Verbal representations of such places, or scenes, may or may not have the virtue of accuracy; but photographic presentments of them will be accepted by posterity with an undoubting faith.

Alexander Gardner

Preface to *Gardner's Photographic Sketch Book of the War*, Volume 1, 1866.

PROLOGUE
1863

The corpse was perfect. The young man was lying on his back, head resting across a rock, like it was a pillow, arms at his side, the left leg splayed at an angle, dark hair tousled and wafting gently in the breeze. He must have been dead at least two days.

"Will you look at that?" Gardner bent over the body to get a closer look. "He's just right, the wee man. He'll do."

He returned to his tripod and the large, brassbound wooden box on top. The camera was standing a few feet away from the corpse and Gardner disappeared under the cape. "Oh yes," he added, muffled, "this will work very well. Fetch me a plate."

The youth, who had been watching with interest, wandered over to the covered wagon nearby. Its unhitched horse, grazing peacefully a little way off among more dead bodies, paused briefly to look up.

"And fetch Mr O'Sullivan" he called after him.

The preparation of photographic plates couldn't be rushed. O'Sullivan's lower legs and feet could be seen standing on a step at the back of the wagon, his top half swathed in canvas as he fiddled about with the chemicals in the small, makeshift, dark room. Gardner saw the wagon gently rocking as his colleague worked. It would take ten minutes before the lad would be carrying back the plate ready to be slid into the back of the camera.

Squinting against the sun, Gardner looked around. The battlefield was hazy, mist rising from the ground like a miasma following the overnight rain. The day was getting hot, the humidity beginning to stifle, the air solid. The sickly, sour smell of putrifaction was becoming pervasive as the bodies scattered across the field began to swell, bellies inflating in the heat, the buttons of uniforms popping open.

Smoke from camp fires hung in the distance, like grey foliage in the branches of the trees. The battle around Gettysburg had ended two days before and the troops were beginning to move off, but the foraging parties and burial details remained.

Gardner withdrew the sodden handkerchief he'd tied round his nose and mouth and mopped his face. He was a big man and was uncomfortably aware that pools of sweat had collected around his armpits, where the sleeves emerged from his vest. He'd removed his topcoat and hung it from the back of the wagon, but could feel the perspiration running down his back and eyelashes and big, black beard. He ran a finger round his shirt collar. Two days without clean clothes, or a wash, and his lips and mouth were the driest part of him.

The July weather was too hot for work. He should never have left Scotland. It wasn't like this there in summer. Fresh from the corpses, flies were crawling across his face, seeking sweat, and he flicked them with the side of his hand. He tied the handkerchief around his face again.

Everything in this distant part of the battlefield lay still, though men from burial parties could be seen moving methodically through the haze a half mile away, collecting bodies for burial, lining them in rows, picking up weapons and equipment and piling them in heaps. Indistinct voices and the occasional shout carried across the space. There were muffled shots as injured horses were killed.

Gardner's mind returned to his job. The soldiers were still some way off and he and O'Sullivan wouldn't be disturbed. There was work to be done, photographs to be taken, portraits of carnage to thrill people in homes and galleries of Washington and New York. But they would have to get a move on. The bodies were rotting in front of them, their faces blackening; soon the gases inside would start to explode. Ravenous from days of hiding from the armies, wild pigs had started emerging from the nearby woods to gnaw at the dead flesh, even in daylight.

'Poor fellow,' Gardner thought. 'No one deserves that.' Some mother's son, from Georgia, or Alabama who, a week ago, had been marching to glory with Lee's Army of Northern Virginia, now just carrion.

Corpses had to be picturesque to be affecting. That's what people liked best. They were the money pictures: stark, romantic, morbid and real. There wasn't much in mere landscapes. That's why they had raced to the battlefield. People didn't want prettiness. They wanted to see enemy dead. They liked the blood and guts. Death was the thing.

Whistling *The Dead March from Saul* Gardner looked down on the young man's unmarked corpse appraisingly. This one was good. The soldier had been handsome – no more than in his early twenties, slim and tanned, the hint of a small beard on his chin. He looked peaceful. Perhaps his end had been sudden, or perhaps he'd had time to compose himself for eternity and pull at his clothes. The brownish-grey tunic was unbuttoned from the bottom, opening up an expanse of grubby white shirt which had not yet burst apart. It was far better than the other bodies they'd seen. Too many had been contorted, legs drawn up, arms flung out, the mouths gaping open. But not this man. If his death had been as agonising as the others he didn't show it.

A possibility occurred to Gardner as he waited. The body was too good to use just once. Too nice for this piece of scrubby, rock-strewn ground. He deserved somewhere more appropriate. More...picturesque and affecting.

As he straightened up, the youth returned with the photographic plate in its case. "All prepared Mr Gardner," he said as, behind him, O'Sullivan hauled the stereoscopic camera with its double lens up the slope.

Gardner took the plate and disappeared under his cape. Yes, that would do nicely for the picture. The corpse came beautifully into view, floating upside down as if stuck to the landscape, its head turned slightly away. He pushed the plate into place, aimed the lens, removed the cap, counted up to ten to secure the exposure, and replaced the lens cap. Pulling the cover over the plate, he pushed it into the carrying case and handed it to the youth who ran back to the wagon with it.

"What do you think, Tim?" He asked O'Sullivan.

"He's a nice one, boss."

"Well, you take your stereoscopes as well. I think I might have an idea."

O'Sullivan took his exposure and trotted back to the wagon to develop the pictures. Meanwhile Gardner, the artist, turned back to contemplate his corpse. Looking away like that the head was a difficulty, he decided, and he bent down to touch the man's face. It was cold and as hard as the rock it lay on, like alabaster, but rigor mortis had receded and the photographer could flop it back the other way. Except that the rock, embedded deep in the ground, made the head fall back again. No good. Even if the face could be made to turn to the camera, the angle would make it look stilted. Gardner walked around the soldier, occasionally bending down to move the head or adjust a limb. If he was to straighten the leg he'd probably have to break it and that would not do: straight legs looked posed. He didn't want that.

The youth was back with another plate and Gardner moved his tripod. A slightly closer angle, perhaps? No, not great, but it would have to do. A barren shot with nothing to involve the viewer or arouse their emotions to shock and wonder. If you couldn't see the face it was just another anonymous body. But still too good to waste. A burial party was only a few hundred yards away. No time to lose. There had to be a more appropriate composition somewhere and, while the plate was being developed, Gardner wandered further up the slope to see if he could find a better location.

And there it was: a small enclosure. Two large rocks six feet apart, perhaps four feet high. Between them someone had piled a wall of slates and smaller rocks to seal it off. Maybe it had been done long ago, or maybe in the heat of battle for shelter by some sharp shooter?

Gardner's mind was raced with possibilities. Even though the body lay seventy yards away the young man could have done it. Yes, that might work. Poignant, even. A soldier walling himself in for protection, dying alone and at peace in the midst of battle. He saw how it could work poetically. They just needed to get the corpse to the wall. They could move the body on a blanket. No one would know and, if they did, it wouldn't matter. The young man was dead, he'd died here, or almost here. It was a very small licence. And a bigger truth about the loneliness of death.

Gardner scarcely thought of this, though he could have justified it to himself had he needed to. This was art; and sentiment, not cold fact. He was intoxicated with the thought of being at the battlefield first, before his rivals, while the bodies were warm. The stench of commerce and death was stimulating even as it reminded him to work fast and get away soon, before contamination, or competition, surrounded him. Or putrefaction ruined his compositions.

Gardner ran back down the slope to where the corpse, O'Sullivan and the youth were waiting.

"Tim! Alfred. Over here. I've got it. Fetch the blanket!"

Standing with his arms crossed, Alfred looked quizzically at his master.

What on earth did Gardner want a blanket for in this weather? Though he'd been rushing around all day hauling plates from the dark room to the camera, it was too hot to run to the wagon.

It had been a toss-up which was worse: being outside with the smells and the eyes of the dead upon you, or rummaging about in the dark room on the back of the wagon, sweating in the airless little canvas cave, suffocated by the reek of chemicals. Even standing outside they made him feel queasy, especially when the wagon swayed on its springs as the photographer shifted his weight on the step.

What was worse was if you got it wrong and the chemicals ran and ruined the plate or if you dropped the glass as you hurried to the camera. Then you could expect hard words and a clip on the head. Worst of all was what happened if you inhaled the fumes or sucked your fingers afterwards. Then you could end up as dead as these corpses. Mr Gardner said so.

They had been at it for five hours and must have exposed twenty plates already, moving from place to place. Almost all the pictures were of dead bodies. He'd been running all day, with no water. They hadn't eaten anything since early morning; he was beginning to feel sick and dizzy. And now the master wanted a blanket.

"Look lively!" said Gardner then, more gently, "we'll stop after a wee bit longer and eat."

The youth stumbled back with a folded tartan rug and the photographer pointed at the immaculate corpse, gesturing for him to lay out the rug beside it.

"Help me get the body on. We're going to shift it."

Alfred closed his eyes. All day he'd avoided looking too closely at bodies, concentrating on getting the glass plates just right and not on the photographs they'd reveal. He didn't want to touch a corpse, leastways not one with its eyes still open. The dead man was looking at him now, through its eyelashes, examining his shoes. He could smell the sweet, sickly odour, and took in the stubble on the chin. Gardner was already down by the corpses's feet, pushing them onto the rug, manoeuvring the buttocks. He was humming to himself.

"Grab him under the arms and lift. He don't weigh much. Tim, take the head."

The youth turned his face away and reached down, feeling the shoulders and fleshy armpits. He hadn't signed up for this. He was only an apprentice.

The corpse suddenly groaned. He could not be still alive, could he? Then it sagged in the middle. It took all three of them a moment to realise it was just an exhalation of air. It was like lifting a drunken man, not a dead one. Then there was a sort of tearing sound as the back of the uniform gave way and the terrible, gaping wound was revealed. They could see the white of a rib and the black stain behind his chest. That's what had killed him: a bullet or a shell fragment in the back, a big, grey slug of iron, ripping through the ribs, leaving a hole the size of a large apple. Either he'd been hit by an unlucky bullet from hundreds of yards away or by a random shot from a comrade's rifle, fired in excitement or terror. No one could see it from the front, but he was done for none the less. He must have dropped like a stone.

"Get him down, get him down!" shouted Gardner. "Damn the stain on the rug. We're going to carry him up to the rocks."

The youth looked up. The rocks were some way beyond the rise and their parcel heavy and floppy. Heaving and sweating, the three of them hauled the corpse up and into the little enclosure, laying it down by the end wall.

Now, said Gardner, bring the wagon closer and while you're about it, fetch that rifle which was lying near the soldier, for the composition.

As the youth stumbled back down the slope to catch the horse, the photographer bent over the corpse, adjusting the head to face where the camera would go. The body was much the same – still a little stiff to rearrange– but Gardner could see the picture, and he and O'Sullivan went down the slope to fetch their cameras.

Within a quarter of an hour they were ready, the two cameras next to each other just by the open end of the little enclosure, no more than fifteen feet from the corpse. To make sure, they'd be taking a glass plate composition and a stereoscope.

There wasn't a moment to lose. A burial party could be heard just beyond the crest, the men grunting and swearing as they laboured. They could commandeer the area any time. Gardner knew from his experience at other battlefields that burial parties could be funny about photographers. Sometimes they would stop and pose for the camera, grateful for the opportunity to rest. If asked nicely and given a dime they might even pose dead, lying on their backs in ghastly caricatures. Other times they'd curse photographers as scavenging ghouls and for getting in their way. Unpleasant work for both.

The plate, sticky with silver nitrate, was ready and Gardner was under the cape. Even upside down he could tell that the composition was good. He could almost feel the corpse breathing, see the bristles on the tanned, handsome face.

Now he had to get the timing right. He removed the lens cover. One, two... then, fingers trembling – because he knew what a good picture he'd made – Gardner pulled the plate clear, clipped it in its case and handed it to the youth.

"Don't drop it! Hurry."

An artistic triumph. The best picture today. And no one else had seen it. Pray God it wasn't ruined.

Beside him he could just hear O'Sullivan clearing his throat to gain his attention. As he emerged from the cape, Gardner blinked in the light. The sun was high now and a tall shadow flickered into view in front of him. He put his hand up above his eyes and squinted, foolishly aware that the gesture made him look furtive and uneasy.

The shadow turned into a man, high on horseback. It was an officer, wearing a dark blue uniform, the face in deep shadow under a broad-brimmed hat, making his features indistinct except for a long, waxed moustache.

"Good morning officer," Tim was saying ingratiatingly, "how are you today? Hot work..."

Thank God, thought Gardner, a Union man, not some damned rebel butternut soldier like that poor devil on the tartan rug.

The man on horseback leaned forward. "What the devil do you men think you are doing?" he said.

CHAPTER ONE

As soon as they saw the old house on the hill they knew that they must have it, despite the discouragement of the realtor. "No one's lived there for years," he'd said. "I'm not sure it's worth saving. It would take a heck of a lot to make anyone want to live here. It's been on our books for months. There might be a price to knock it down and start again with a nice new house, I suppose. If you want my opinion that's what should be done with it."

He was right. The old house on the rise running out of town was boarded up and high among the eaves they could see the shingles had slipped in places, leaving holes scattered across the roof. There were gaps in the floor of the porch running along the north side of the building. A rag of curtain blew through the remains of an upper window.

But there was something about it, Eugene and Isabelle Hofsettler agreed, that would suit them for their grand project. Maybe it was because they saw it on a crystal-clear Fall day, against a blue sky, with the nearby maples turning scarlet. Or maybe it was just that it was so quiet. There was a new estate of executive homes just on sale down the hill – the realtor had asked them if they'd really not rather look at one of those instead – all trimmed lawns and driveways sweeping up to triple garages, house fronts with fake pillars and porticoes as if they'd been there since before the Civil War. But that wasn't what they wanted at all.

Ever since they had known that they had to get out of New York following

9/11, they had been looking for somewhere of character and taste, genuinely old, not just pretending to be: a place which they – or their builders – could do up, which would anchor their lives at last. Maybe they could make it a chintzy, gingham-laden bed and breakfast home, with Victorian antiques, stripped floorboards and patchwork quilts. Or maybe it would just be their home, where Gene could have a study looking out towards the Berkshire hills and write the Great American Novel. Perhaps they could do both.

9/11 had just come too close to them. Isabelle had watched the first plane turn past Greenwich Village and hit the south tower from their apartment as she brewed herself a morning coffee. She'd left the building a short while later – so hurriedly that the television news was still playing in a weird simulation of the sight playing out through the apartment's picture window behind it. She had joined the grey, dust-covered office workers making their way up Seventh Avenue in the foggy half-light, the paper shards of office life drifting around them. Returning to the apartment later had been almost too much: the skyline view that she had so loved about the living room when they bought the apartment three years earlier had irrevocably changed, an everlasting reminder of what had been lost, a gap filled by sky where the towers had been. Even though the windows had been firmly closed too, a miasma seemed to hang about the rooms and grey dust covered the furniture. She could not bear the thought of the violation of their space. What the dust might contain was unthinkable. It had taken her days to wash the dust and smell off her body, out of her hair. The water had run grey down the plughole of the shower. It seemed to be everywhere, hanging like a pall over their lives, in their clothes and in their minds. They had been invaded and needed to get away.

On that terrible morning, Gene's was an even narrower escape. He'd had to catch an early flight from Newark to San Fransisco for a business trip. It had been a chapter of accidents all day: they'd overslept because the alarm clock was running slow and the cab was late to pick him up and he'd had to race down the New Jersey pike to get to the airport. In the distance, he'd looked across and seen the towers gleaming in the early morning sun and thought how beautiful they appeared. Then he'd looked at his watch again and urged the driver on. The man's good luck charms, hanging from the rear-view mirror, had jangled as they weaved through the traffic, the silver surfaces with their Arabic inscriptions catching the sunlight.

Little things like that stuck in the mind, like how when he finally got out at the drop-off zone, the African cab driver had grinned winningly and said: "Inshallah! Have a nice day." It was only later that he wondered what that had really meant.

He'd raced through the terminal to the gate. Luckily, he had made the flight often enough to know which it would be and they were just closing as he made it to the desk. "I am sorry, sir, we're just going," the attendant had said. "The next flight's leaving in a few minutes. You'll be good for that. Let's see... Gate A-17, United 93. It's pretty empty. We'll get you on that OK, it's boarding at eight." She'd started typing on her terminal.

What had made him insist, except for impatience and a loathing of waiting for anything, he never knew, but Gene had said no, he was here now, they hadn't shut the doors yet and he only had hand luggage. He could just sneak on. It would be OK. And, thank God, she'd said yes.

Later, when their flight had made an emergency landing in Nebraska as the skies across America closed down after the hijackings, they had been stunned to see what was happening on the airport television screens. And later still, as he and a few other passengers had pooled together to hire a car and drive all the way back to New York, radio going the whole time, all through the three days it took to drive home, he found out what had happened to United 93: lost with all lives in a field in Pennsylvania.

There had been a long time to think on the journey home. It made the goose-bumps stand up: two minutes later and he'd have been on that flight, one more hold-up on the pike, one more set of traffic lights on red, one car blocking a turning, another lorry unloading in the Village and he'd have been gone. Or, if he had been less insistent on getting on the earlier flight, run less fast through the terminal, or if the attendant had been more bloody-minded and made him wait. Or, indeed, he later felt, if he'd had to go through all the security checks they brought in later, he'd never have made it. Looking back, Inshallah indeed.

But it was too close for comfort. It seemed like a narrow escape. And it made them reassess their lives. Maybe it even saved their marriage: they'd been getting so fractious with each other with the stress of living in Manhattan, catching cabs, running for planes, making meetings. 9/11 was a break in their lives too.

So, here they were, in western Massachusetts, looking at old houses where they could work from home, maybe raise chickens and children, write books, run a B&B if that failed, and step aside from the rush of city life too. And now, in front of them, lay the perfect house. Built around 1880, the particulars said, a former family home in need of complete renovation and TLC. Weather-boarded, built in the Victorian gothic style, three storeys, with high gables and, so far as they could see because of the boards covering them, large windows.

There was even a porch running round the north side on which to sit in the evenings in their rocking chairs admiring the view. Out back there was a yard and a few overgrown shacks, patched with corrugated iron and old tin advertisements.

"It's like something out of Norman Rockwell," Anne had said. "Or *Psycho*" he'd retorted.

The realtor had unlocked the padlock and chain securing the front door, shoved his shoulder against it to force it open and with a grunt of disdain walked them out of the light and into the dark hallway. As he shone his torch around, they could see it was like walking back 100 years, as if it had never been touched. The curving wooden bannister of the staircase was intact and the patterned tiles on the floor were cracked but in place. Some of the plaster had fallen from the ceiling, but enough was still there to show the scrolls and and acanthus leaves that had decorated it.

They didn't need to go any further. "We'll take it," they had said.

Through the winter and the following Spring, the builders had made the place habitable, but there was still work to be done on March 1st 2002, which they'd determined was the day they would move in. The house was water-tight but some of the upper-storey rooms were still bare and musty. In one they had even found an ancient iron bedstead and a Victorian wardrobe, the glass mirror in its door cracked clean across. This could be a project for later: even all the stuff from their large apartment in the Village wasn't enough to fill a house this big.

They had their good days and their bad days, of course. Neither Gene nor Izzie had ever lived in the country and it was infuriating that things couldn't be done as fast as in town, and no Starbucks to hand when you just needed one. They missed their colleagues back in the office – emails weren't the same – and the buzz of chance meetings and after work drinks in a local bar.

New England folks were reserved too. When the newcomers told them they had bought the old house, locals just said drily that they had heard that already, or that they had known the place years ago when a family was living there. Gene and Izzie were not great church-goers, except at Christmas and anyway, which church to go to? The Episcopalians – God's frozen people in the old white church under the steeple on main street – or the Baptists with their hellfire sermons and their waving and clapping in the brick barn by the shopping mall? None really appealed. Izzie wasn't into baking, or quilt making and they did not play bridge. The Republicans had the golf club, Democrats owned the squash courts, and really Gene and Izzie's tennis was not good enough to display in front of people they didn't know. There was no one to invite round to a meal: what would they talk about after the introductions?

There was a Walmart, of course, even a deli of sorts. But go in and try asking for gigli or orechiette as Izzie did just once – "You know, like pasta..." – and the assistants would look at you as if you had stepped off a plane from Mars. Frankly, if you had to wait and order new books and CDs from the store, which could take *days* to arrive, or if the movie you wanted to see was just not coming to the multiplex, well, you might as well be living in the Victorian era, as well as a Victorian house. Izzie felt at a loose end, cut off, underwhelmed and isolated, especially when Gene was away on assignment for his magazine. There were whole days when she didn't speak to a soul.

But there was always the B&B idea. Gene tried to sell it to her as a cure for her blues. Once they had got the bedrooms sorted out and the antique shops raided for miles around for the essential trivia of lives gone-by: wash stands and jugs painted with flowers, mirrors and chests of drawers, embroidered cushions and pot-pourri bowls, he was sure she'd feel better.

And maybe that would be an escape from loneliness. Izzie had worked in public relations, admittedly for a film company, but would hospitality be that different? It would be like dressing a period film set, wouldn't it? She'd always liked baking muffins, hadn't she? Coffee, clean sheets, bowls of fruit – what was so hard about that, she reasoned to herself even as her heart sank.

As Spring drew on, there was a succession of removals men traipsing through with renovated bedsteads, new mattresses and chaise-longues, escritoires and rag mats to set off the polished floors; bathroom fitters installing replica baths with clawed feet and wash-basins on fluted pedestals. They were running through their savings quicker than they'd intended, so the first guests couldn't be too far away. They'd better come soon, and in droves.

What to put on the newly-wallpapered walls? There were reproductions of 19th Century Currier & Ives prints of stagecoaches stuck in snow and railroad trains crossing the Prairies to set off the tasteful patterns of pink roses climbing up trellises, and there were Audubon bird prints and Rockwell posters for the more modern rooms and hallways: *Shuffleton's Barber's Shop* and *Freedom from Want* created just the right atmosphere for a New England home. All they needed to be now was New Englanders.

The corrugated iron shacks in the yard had to go. But they were full of junk: rusting tools, parts for ancient, long defunct bicycles – there was even a wheel that had been twisted double as if it had been run over – garden implements, paint tins and cans containing liquids of uncertain provenance.

Gene did not know where to start when he pushed his way through the door one Saturday morning in an attempt to establish what was salvageable, what might be sold and what was be trash. No one could have been in there for years, he was beginning to think that they might just as well pay someone to come and raze the whole lot to the ground when he kicked his shin against an old, black trunk poking out from under some logs. He was about to kick it again in retribution when something made him stop, bend down and pull at the rope handle at one end of the trunk. Amazingly it held as he tugged. Damnation! It was heavy and he might have abandoned it for ever if a tea chest of old crockery hadn't slipped allowing the trunk to come free. As he straightened up, Gene realised the sweat was running in grimy rivulets down his face.

The trunk was clear now, a big rectangular tin box. Wiping the dust from the top, he could see the initials AB roughly painted long ago in white across the lid. It was locked, but having got this far Gene decided he must open it. It was heavy enough to have a body inside, he thought to himself and that triggered the fantasy in his mind of the Old Haunted House.

Prising open the lock was not hard with a crowbar and as the catch snapped there was the sound of glass breaking inside. Gene flung back the lid and saw that the trunk was full of large rectangular glass plates, some of them cracked right across.

He lifted one out and took it outside. As he swivelled it to catch the light he let out a gasp. Looming out of the shadows on the glass a man in uniform was staring back at him. It was a negative image and, by the look of it, of a soldier. Not a modern one though, a soldier from the 19th century. He knew enough history to think immediately of the Civil War.

Gene ran back inside to the box and pulled up another plate and another until he had half a dozen to carry outside. Sure enough, on the first, he could make out a line of troops on parade; on the next a group of soldiers and the one after that men standing around a cannon. The images were all shadowy and faded, black where white should have been and white where black: it was a considerable archive. There must be thirty plates in the box. They could not have been seen in decades, maybe not for a hundred years or more – maybe never since they were taken.

One other thing Gene knew: they must be valuable. People would want them and they would fetch a considerable sum. Enough to help finish the house, maybe. And to think he'd been wondering ten minutes earlier about bulldozing the lot.

As he ran to tell Izzie, Gene started laughing. "Come and look at what I've found," he was shouting. He'd discovered a treasure-trove. Inshallah! It was another of those 9/11 moments....but this time only in a good way.

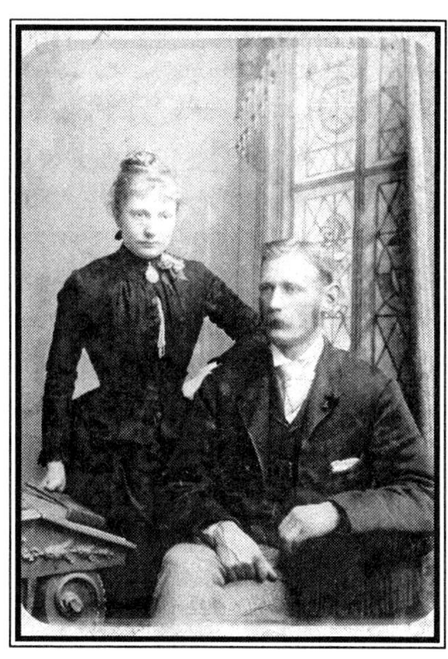

CHAPTER TWO

It was the late afternoon sun, pouring through the blinds of the bedroom window, sending a rectangle of light across the floor and into his eyes, that woke the old man.

He ached all over, but that was just age. When a man's so old most things, except one, get stiff, he thought. He did not want to get up yet, but knew his afternoon siesta was definitively over: he would not get back to sleep again.

The light tickled his eyes and, when he opened them, he could see a spiral of dust rising through the light in the still air of the bedroom. On the mantlepiece, the old heavy-cased clock, that he had had for 40 years, ticked on loudly. It never missed a beat, unlike him these days.

He turned his head away from the light and there, on the bedside cabinet, was his wedding photograph. It showed him as a young man, sitting smartly dressed in a chair beside a sloping desk on which – for some reason, as he had never been much of a reader – lay a book. Beside and behind him, her finger squeezed into the pages, stood Sarah Jane, his wife, all in black – a bleak colour for a wedding, but it had been the only formal dress she had had, as a serving maid. At her neck was a cameo brooch, loaned by her mistress for the day, and perched alongside on her shoulder a small posy of lilies-of-the-valley, tied with a ribbon. It was the only sign that the occasion was a celebration. Otherwise, she looked resigned to what lay ahead, lips pursed, her eyes fixed and staring, grim-faced. Not radiant in the least, no one could ever accuse her of being that.

He knew that scowl. She had always been an impatient, resentful woman, he thought, and if he closed his eyes and listened hard, he could still hear her voice scolding him, even though she was long dead now. Time and again she had told him how he should be saving his money, not drinking it away, spending it on his wife and child, on buying nice things, not indulging in selfish pleasures. Yes, those had been the words, engraved like a sampler inside his head. Selfish pleasures. He grunted.

It had never exactly been a love-match? Not love at all once they'd got married. Just gruelling. They'd got married on a legacy and because he had said he would. He grunted. As he thought of it now – it had never occurred to him before – in the photograph their gazes did not meet. He stared out of the picture to the left. She stared over his shoulder out of the picture to the right. They did not look happy, even on their wedding day.

The picture had his attention now and took him back more than 60 years to the day it was taken. He could remember it more clearly than most other days in his life, though whether that was because of the momentousness of the occasion, or simply because he saw the photograph every day glaring down on him as he awoke, he could not quite recall.

But he was wide awake now and staring at the photograph, as he had not done for years. It was all fake, of course: the little sloping desk, the stained glass window and the curtain, even the leatherbound book, all photographer's props, set up in a corner of the studio and used a thousand times.

He had been a handsome dog that day, he thought. A large man with broad shoulders, big strong hands and a handsome, firm featured face. Blonde hair. Sideboards reaching down to the edge of the jaw and a heavy moustache, not too drooping, quite well trimmed for once. Unlike today.

Thinking about it, he sucked on the bottom of the same moustache, grey now and stained and smelling of tobacco. The hair on top had gone, but he always covered that with a hat if he was out. The suit had been smart, he thought, though of course it wasn't a suit exactly: just a dark coat and vest with check trousers underneath, a stiff wing collar with a white necktie and a little flower in the buttonhole, that he had picked in the garden that morning. He remembered that. And remembered that the suit had gone straight back to the draper's afterwards.

The old man's appraisal turned back to his wife, dead now for, when was that? Ten years, no earlier, fifteen. When was it? Before the war in Europe. Nearer twenty, must have been.

He was looking at the picture intently now. There was a disparity in their sizes, which he had always known, but now seemed more obvious. That's why they had sat him down for the picture. Although she loomed over him in the photograph, it was an illusion. She'd always been small, eighteen inches shorter than him. But controlling. Oh yes, she'd had a ferocious temper. And tough, she would pummel him with her fists when she realised he'd been drinking. When their daughter, Mary, as a little girl, had innocently asked him why he had married such a funny *little* woman in her hearing, she had smacked her too, for insolence.

He'd been scared of his wife really in their fights. That was an admission he didn't like to make. Did he miss her? Not really: she'd receded as a memory until she was scarcely more than the photograph. But he could still remember what she sounded like: shrill. What had she seen in him? More to the point, what had he seen in her? Apart from being pregnant, of course, and that hadn't worked out, as it happened, leaving them stuck together. She'd always worried about money, worried that they never had enough, that they would not be able to afford to eat. It ate her up, consumed her: meant that they'd end up destitute on the street if he ever consoled himself with a drink. She was always frowning till the day she died. Well, that had never worried him. But they had survived, hadn't they? At least he'd survived anyway. He gulped and rolled onto his back.

As he did so, he saw the door of his room was open and a youth was standing next to the bed, staring at him. After a moment or so, he realised it was his grandson. How could he forget? The boy even looked like him, well, him as a young man with blonde hair, and no moustache. He remembered now: the child was...was Jim and he was sixteen years old. Or was he fifteen, or fourteen even? He couldn't quite remember. Just a year or two younger than he himself had been in the war.

"Oh, you're awake," the youth was saying. "I've been sent up to fetch you. Mom says, do you want some tea? She needs some potatoes digging up."

Jim's gaze flickered up from his grandfather's face, as it often did in this stuffy room, whose windows were never opened, to the wall above the bed and the rifle hanging there, gathering dust.

He gestured. "When you going to show me how to fire that, like you promised?"

It was a question the lad often asked. Frankly, the old man had never wanted to show it and had always put him off. Wait till you're older, he'd said.

More than once he'd caught the boy climbing up onto his bed when he was a child, scrambling in his dirty boots up over the pillow, to get a closer look and he'd had to warn him not to touch.

He did not even know whether the rifle would work. It had not been fired in sixty years, nor polished, nor greased. But today he could not think of an excuse any more: the lad was old enough now and all young men should fire a gun.

The grandfather sat up slowly and reached for the glass of water beside the wedding picture. It contained his false teeth, so he fished them out and pushed them into his mouth, manoeuvring them into place with his tongue. He felt almost human again and, sucking the water from the enamel, was suddenly resolved. So he said gruffly: "No time like the present."

Standing up in his stockinged feet, he reached for the gun, pulled it down and blew the dust off the trigger and the breech, coughing as he did so. Then he sat down again and reached for his boots, next to the chamber pot beneath the bed.He stared at the lad and handed him the gun. This was a serious moment. The weapon was heavy and the boy's eyes opened wide in shock. He almost dropped it as his knees buckled but steadied himself against the bed.

His grandfather laughed throatily, still clearing his pipes from the dust.

"Picked that up on the field of battle. Oh yes, it's been fired in anger. Handsome, ain't it?"

Jim nodded. He'd heard the story before, but not which battle, or whose the gun had been.

"Do you know what that is?" the old man said, "They call that a Sharps rifle. Good gun, accurate to 500 yards. Knock a man over flat and never knew what hit him."

The weapon was indeed handsome. It had a hexagonal barrel and a wooden stock and an elegant hammer mechanism, curved like the rearing head of a snake. Underneath the trigger a curving rod pulled the breech open for the bullet. The rifle must have been four feet long and weighed as much as a heavy baby.

The old man opened a bedside drawer and pulled out a small cardboard box, containing a handful of long gray-headed bullets and a tape of black primer pellets. Then he hitched up his galluses and straightened his trousers and the pair made their way together out of the back bedroom, along the corridor, down the staircase, stealthily past the open kitchen door so as not to alert Jim's mother and across the hallway to the front door with its glass window panel. Grandfather gestured to the boy to open it softly and Jim was through it, just in time to conceal the rifle from his mother as she emerged from the kitchen.

"Ah, there you are," she said. "I've got things for you to do, Father."

"Yes, I know, dear. Just taking Jim to dig the spuds. We'll be back in two shakes," he answered.

Before she could say any more, the old man had smiled at her, winked, picked up his old hat from the stand and walked into the bright rectangle of afternoon sun, shutting the door behind him. The grandfather never went outside without his hat. He felt undressed without it and he had worn it so long that the rim of the hat exactly matched the edge of the bald crown of his head. He didn't like people to see that shiny dome, glinting in the sunlight. The illusion that he still had a full head of fair hair, instead of just a fringe, was better.

The two of them crossed the porch, down the steps and walked across the yard to the barn beyond. As Jim blinked his eyes to get accustomed to the dark, his grandfather soaked the edge of a rag in oil dipped from a can and produced a lanyard with a weight on the end from a tin on a shelf. Then he ran the cloth down the barrel and around the stock and pulled it through the inside of the barrel several times. "There, good as new," he muttered to himself.

They emerged back into the light and walked over to a rough wooden fence marking the edge of the property. On the other side lay an open field. In the distance cows looked up from their grazing. The old man looked around. "Got to have a target," he said.

"Here boy, find some bottles we can set up."

While the youth was gone, he hobbled over to the fence. He reckoned one of the rails would do if it was flat enough for a bottle to stand on. He gave the wood a push and it stayed firm. They could rest the target on top and aim at that.

And then Jim was back, with an old can. The grandfather set it up on top of the rail. They paced back twenty yards, almost to the house, to give them a range.

Now, he said to the lad, the thing to do was to load the rifle properly. He placed a percussion cap on the nipple where the hammer would come down, then put a two inch bullet in the breech, panting slightly at the effort of opening it and cocking the mechanism, which was stiff after so long. "This is what you do," he said, drawing up the rifle to his right shoulder, "Aim along the barrel and...."

A tremendous explosion rocked the gun and made the old man stagger backwards, clouded in smoke. Across the field the cows stampeded in a rush towards the bottom of the hill. The can was untouched.

"Yes, well," the old man said, coughing as the smoke cleared and rubbing his shoulder furiously. "That's what you do. Now you have a go." And he loaded the gun again.

Jim took the weapon uncertainly from his grandfather and held it up to his shoulder. It was so heavy he could scarcely lift it and, once it was in place, he could see the far end of the barrel waving wildly around feet away in the distance, sometimes aligned with the can, more often shaking upwards to the sky.

"That's it," his grandfather was saying. "Hold her steady. No, you're waving it. Aim, boy, aim. You can't miss. Aim along the barrel and squeeze the trigger when you've got a bead. Don't jerk her..."

The boy scarcely heard. The gun was still wobbling. In the distance he could hear his grandfather urging him on amid bouts of coughing. It was too heavy. After a few moments, he determined he must fire as soon as the can hovered back into view, just to get rid of the damned thing. He wished he'd never asked to fire it.

There it was! And, with a tremendous bang, he fired. The rifle rammed back into his shoulder with a thump and the percussion knocked him off his feet into the dust. As his head hit the ground, clouds of smoke billowed, obscuring the view in front of him entirely.The sky circled overhead. There was a sudden silence, except for the banging open of the kitchen door. Now he could hear his mother in the distance, running from the house and yelling.

Then the smoke cleared and there was his grandfather examining the rail. The can had fallen off. He hadn't hit it, but the wood it stood on. Close enough. It quivered, shot neatly through. "Well, I'll be darned," said the old man. He walked back and smiled at Jim, helped him pick himself up and shrugged apologetically at his daughter.

"Got to teach him, Mary," he said. And to the youth: "Good shot, that. Bet you couldn't do it again if you tried."

Jim smiled. It seemed to him that just at that moment he had become someone to be reckoned with, in his grandfather's eyes at least.

"What have you done, Father?" the boy's mother cried, as she fussed around her son, patting his face, half to reassure herself and half to make sure he was conscious. And she hugged him. Jim was uncertain whether to be embarrassed or relieved. As she enfolded him in her arms, he could feel her soft skin and smell the warm, familiar scent of her body, the carbolic soap that he always associated with her. "Oh, my boy," she said.

His grandfather was explaining, gruffly: "He's got to learn one day and he hasn't got a father to teach him."

His mother turned angrily, but kept whatever it was she planned to say to herself. There was a silence. In the distance in the house, Jim could hear music on the radio. The Kentucky Serenaders were playing *Keep Your Sunny Side Up.*

Half way back to the house, his mother looked back. She still had a dishcloth in her hand. "You could have killed somebody, anybody. Don't you have any sense, father? That old thing could have exploded and blown your heads off," she said. " I don't want to have to clear up the mess. Think of the boy. Oh, Alfred!"

She only used her father's first name in times of stress or exasperation, Jim knew, so it must be serious.

"I hadn't thought of that," Alfred replied. "Anyway, it was all right." And, like a naughty schoolboy, he added, "Won't do it again."

Finally, she glared and sighed deeply. "Just you two be careful. I don't want to lose either of you. Especially you, Jim. Do you hear me Father?" And she flounced back into the kitchen.

CHAPTER THREE

The old man and Jim followed her into the house but it was an hour before they spoke again. By then the gun was back on the wall above the bed and the two were sitting on the porch, Alfred in a rocking chair, the lad on a swing seat, both gently swinging forward and back, looking out across the fields to the distant, wooded hills, now sinking into a purple evening haze as twilight fell. On the radio through the window in the parlour, the music had given way to vaudeville of fast-talking wise guys. The boy's shoulder still ached. It had a bruise as big as a dinner plate where the rifle had recoiled.

Usually, Jim enjoyed these moments in the evening, the sense of being alone with a grown-up. He was an only child, his father had died in a road accident when he was a baby and his grandfather was the only male companion he had. At this time of the evening there was always a repertoire of stories. "See these teeth?" the old man would say sometimes, out of nowhere, taking them out and placing them in the palm of his hand.

"Came off a man killed in battle during the war. Ain't they good?"

He popped them back in his mouth and swivelled them back into place, relishing and polishing with his tongue as he did so.

"Served me well, they have, nearly seventy years. Had my own taken out. Never had a day's trouble since."

Jim had seen the trick many times before, but it always disconcerted him. His grandfather would grin and bare the teeth which would seem to take on a life of their own. It was as if a dead man was peering out of his mouth, another person under the skin, long dead, who only looked out when his grandfather opened his lips and grinned.

"That was a common thing then when there weren't enough teeth to go round," Alfred was saying. "You'd get dentists taking them out after men died – go round the hospitals. You could pay a lot for good teeth like this. Don't know whose they were, mind. Could've been rebel teeth I've been using all these years." The thought made the old man chuckle.

In the kitchen, from where she stood peeling the potatoes for her men's evening meal, letting the shards fall into a large mixing bowl, Mary could hear the general rumble of their conversation, just enough to catch the odd word. He was telling the story of his teeth again. It mingled with the odd words coming out of the wireless set in the parlour, that she could hear through the open door. That was Jack Benny in his show, setting up a surreal, wisecracking, counterpoint to her father: if you don't mind, it doesn't matter...teeth...what's on next?

This evening, her mind was far away, thinking of the incident with the gun. How could her father have been so stupid, risking Jim's life like that? Didn't he realise Jim was all she had? Since Dan's death anyway.

She was still a handsome woman: tall and fair-haired like her father, with strong features, but there was something resigned in the lined face, the hair awry, hands knobbly and reddened with housework, the clothes worn and shabby. Life had shut her in. Her chance was gone, bowled over by the man going too fast in an automobile who had run into her husband, Jim's father, as he cycled home one night. It had been a great misfortune: in those days you could still pedal home in the dark most nights and never see a car, let alone one veering across the road. An accident in a thousand, they'd said: a driver unhurt, his car scarcely buckled and Jim's father stone dead in the ditch, his neck broken as he'd hit the hedge.

There had been no compensation. The driver had walked away, pleading Dan had swerved in front of him, not the other way round, even though the man's cronies had admitted he had been drinking in some bootleggers' shebbean somewhere. Nothing could be proved and there hadn't been the money to bring an action. The scenario played round and round in her mind, even though it had been fourteen years now since it happened. She sometimes saw the man in town, fit as a fiddle, just as Dan might have been, and he always averted his eyes from her gaze and crossed the street to avoid her. Mary was glad he felt guilty but it was small recompense. He'd never offered her compensation – that would have meant acknowledging some responsibility – even though he was one of the wealthiest men around, son of the local building contractor. He certainly had not been shamed into moving away.

She had stopped peeling the potatoes and was looking, without seeing, out of the kitchen window, across the yard, over the fence past the field to the woods beyond, now deep blue in the twilight. She had tried going back to her old profession as a school teacher but it hadn't worked. She'd been too depressed, too seized by grief for her loss, too distracted by having to bring up her young son single-handed, too resigned to moving back into her father's home, up the hill outside town, off the very road that Dan had been cycling along when he was hit by the car. She had to pass the spot every day she went into town. Cycle past it even, on the way to school. It had been too much.

Jim was her compensation. He was tall and growing handsome as his face thinned from its childhood plumpness. People said he looked like Alfred but she knew better. He looked much more like Dan, reincarnated, the way he glanced sideways at you when he spoke. She could not bear to let him go, although deep inside she knew she would have to one day, just not yet. That was why she was so cross that all that had been put so carelessly at risk. It was just so thoughtless. So *negligent.*

Amos'n'Andy was on the wireless now and supper was ready. She called the men in.

The old man was still a striking figure, tall, spare and almost gaunt. He only shaved on Sundays, so for most of the week his chin was stubbly. His fair hair had become peppery and his moustache was entirely gray except for a yellow stain between mouth and nostrils from the tobacco he had always smoked. His clothes seldom varied, white shirt without collar, unless it was a special occasion in which case he also wore a black tie, creased with age and secured to his chest with a silver pin. Mostly he wore a vest and his trousers, shiny with age, were held up with thick black, woollen galluses.

In the mornings they could hear him above their heads, wheezing about in his bedroom and coughing as he cleared his tubes for the day. There would be a slop of water, a gargle and an expectoration, the thud of his heavy boots on the floor and grunting while he tied up his laces before the creak of floorboards as he crossed the floor to come downstairs.

Then the kitchen door would fly open and, swaying slightly, the old man would appear. He always said the same thing: "Still here. One more day," as he sat down and waited to be fed.

Alfred seldom left the property except for morning strolls – his constitutionals, he called them – but when he did, when he "went on the prowl" as he said, it would be to visit old friends in the town, on his bicycle, to wet his whistle. He was kind of habitual about that. He had never been deterred by Prohibition, but then few men were thereabouts. Everyone knew where to get a drink when they wanted it.

"Oh, that Alfred. That Alfie Barker," Mary would say behind his back on happier days, affection mingled with annoyance as she shook her head and gave a forced smile, "he's incorrigible."

Never more so than after the whistle-wetting expeditions when he would come back, breathing hard, staggering slightly and leaning against his old bicycle like it was a crutch as he meandered up the road.

That was the noise that would wake the boy in his bedroom under the eaves – the sound of old songs being sung, sometimes imperfectly remembered, in the darkness outside. Then Jim would peer through the drapes and see the silhouette making its way up the moonlit lane, leaning the bike against the fence around the front of the house, picking it up when it fell over, saying: "Stay there then, darn it." Then he would be clambering over it to get through the gate.

At the foot of the steps leading up to the porch, the old man would throw his head back, open his arms wide as if to embrace the house and sing softly to himself. Sometimes it was *Home on the Range*, sometimes a more wistful song:

The years creep slowly by Lorena,
The snow is on the grass,
The sun's low down the sky, Lorena...
...But the heart throbs on as warmly now
As when the summer days were nigh.

There would be a sigh and a clatter as the boots came off on the porch, the sound of the key in the lock, the creak on the stairs as his grandfather made his way to his bedroom as quietly as he could. Then, often as not, his door would slam as he forgot himself.

Jim couldn't quite tell whether it was the song that was sad, or just grandfather's way of singing it. It was a sound he would always associate with his childhood and with the branches of the old tree in the yard gently tapping against the roof above his head.

So far as he knew, Jim thought they were a happy family, just the three of them. The deal was that she would cook and clean and look after her father and her son in return for the roof over her head. It was precisely the life she had married to get away from, except for the extra responsibility of a child; and this time there was no prospect of escape.

For Mary, there was no marriageable man in the vicinity, except those she met at church on Sundays, ageing bachelors and widowers with crooked teeth, bad breath and musty smells, who smiled ingratiatingly, stood slightly too close and breathed acridly over her when they spoke. They were her father's friends, not hers, decades older than she was. Marrying one of them would be to swap one jail for another. She would be a housekeeper and a nurse, not a wife and lover, not even really a companion, and she did not want that at all.

The house the family lived in had been bought new by Alfred Barker after his marriage, from his wife's savings. He had hoped to make a go of his business, setting up as a photographer, with a studio in the nearby town of Springbridge. The business had not been much to write home about, merely a rented room with photographic props, a desk, a chair, a wooden fence and scenery painted on sheets, out round the back of the local drug store. He had barely scraped a living, with family portraits and weddings and local worthies looking pompous, and none at all once cheap Kodak box cameras arrived and people could take their own snaps informally.

It had been a dull, quiet business and one he had been pleased to leave. He had had no aptitude for it, no artistry, he knew that. And not much charm or business skill, either: he had liked his clients as little as they had liked him and it had showed. He was too blunt with them. "Come along, come along," he'd say. "Shoulders back, chest out," as if they'd been in the Army. "And stand still, darn it!"

They simply stopped coming. His pictures were lifeless and stilted and sometimes barely in focus and in the end the business had defeated him.

Few of his photographs survived, though one which did was a framed picture of their house which hung at the top of the stairs. It was a large photograph, depicting the place newly built when they had first moved in. The photograph showed the building surrounded by bleak, open, white space, where trees now grew and in front of the steps leading up to the front door Alfred's wife Sarah Jane could be seen, arms folded. She was slightly out of focus but looked from the slump of her head as though she might be scowling. By contrast, the building itself was in perfect detail, every plank of the walls and shingle on the roof crystal clear, as if shown in an architect's drawing.

By the time Jim knew it however, the house was not so fine. It was delapidated by now, ramshackle the best word for it, with peeling paint and fading shutters on the dusty windows, the result of fifty years of neglect. There was not the money for improvements, or even maintenance beyond what grandfather could do himself and even that was difficult now he got dizzy going up ladders, so it had an air of neglect. It was the sort of place where lonely, unwelcoming people who don't do much entertaining live. Which was just how they were.

The ultimate treachery came when Mary bought a Box Brownie to take family pictures. Although Alfred had long since given up the business by then, he still retained his studio camera, a large wooden box with a brass lens and concertina-ed leather sides, standing on its tripod, with the cape dangling behind it, in a corner of his bedroom. That was the machine to use, he had said, and anything else was just snaps. You needed a professional to take proper photographs.

Mary had come home very excited with her purchase, waving the small, brown camera as if it was a trophy. She had spent her hard-saved housekeeping money on it and instantly demanded that Jim and Alfred should come outside to have their picture taken.

Alfred was not keen and came outside grumbling, his hat rammed straight on his head. "Take your hat off father, for heaven's sakes," she cried.

"No," firmly.

"Why ever not? We can't see your face."

"Good. This is how I am known. Who'd recognise me without it? Anyway, don't feel comfy," he said and held it down on his head by the brim, as if his daughter was about to wrench it off by force. Then he added: "Anyway, good photographers don't need artificial assistance. You don't want it *posed*." Then he added: "Proper photographs are taken in a studio by a professional artist, not larking about outside."

Mary sighed hard and took the picture: a stern affair, a little snap of a couple of inches with both Alfred and Jim staring suspiciously at the camera. The old man's face was almost entirely obscured by the shadow of his hat so that only the white tip of his nose and the bristle of his moustache was visible.

Alfred renewed the offensive afterwards. He looked at the little camera and snorted: "Call that a camera? There ain't no art to that. Won't amount to much, I shouldn't wonder. Why don't you start off taking trees and things – stuff that don't move – then you can move on to decent things later when you're some good.

"You should see the equipment we had to carry in the old days. A whole cartload. Heavy as lead – and develop it yourself. Now *that* was an art. You can't beat the wet plate process. Clear as a bell, as if you could talk to the person in the picture and he'd turn and answer right back! Not fuzzy like this – this rubbish. I don't think it's worth bothering with, frankly speaking."

With that, he stumped off back to his rocking chair on the porch, leaving Mary close to tears. He may have intended that – to patronise and belittle her efforts in his field, just as she had unconsciously tried, by buying the camera, to show her independence of him.

She decided not to show how much he had hurt her. "Why don't you take photographs any more then?" she shouted after him, across the yard. "Perhaps you could get them in focus next time round, with one of these."

But he just waved her away with a dismissive toss of his hand and resumed reading the paper. Caught between the two, Jim laughed nervously in embarrassment, not knowing what to do for the best. He knew he ought to go and comfort her, but that would have been a betrayal of the old man too and so he walked off down the yard instead. They just weren't a great family for emotion.

Mary wiped her eyes on her handkerchief and placed the camera carefully on the ground. "Damn thing," she murmered quietly and walked away, leaving the Box Brownie lying where she had left it. It had been a big deal for her to buy the camera, but she never took another photograph with it.

Jim noticed little of this tension, except when it burst out like this. What he did know was that they did not have much money, relying largely on his mother's widow's pension and grandfather's odd jobs and occasional excursions to take somber wedding photographs, wheezing as he hoist the camera on to his shoulder by the tripod and stowing three or four glass plates in a bag to carry in his other hand. There was no fuss about it, just as if it was as much of a chore as chopping logs. To Jim, his grandfather was remote and austere, but also a hero. Hadn't he fought in the great war between the states? That was why he was so old and why he still had his rifle hanging above his bed.

Their distance from the town had thrown the boy himself back on his own resources: to the books in the cabinet in the drawing room downstairs and to long walks in the woods where, as a child, brandishing a stick, he had fought solitary battles and sword fights against the low-hanging branches trunks of the trees. Other boys had friends and companions, sometimes now even girlfriends, whereas he just had himself, and the stories he told himself. The stick was straight enough to be a rifle too, depending on the tale at any given time. There he could be Ivanhoe, or General Custer, Teddy Roosevelt leading his men up San Juan Hill, or Sergeant York single-handedly knocking out the German trenches in the late war.

Whole days could pass this way in solitary fights. It made him dreamy and distant from other children. His mind would wander in class and the others would laugh at him when he didn't answer the school teacher because he was gazing out of the window. Childish, the teacher called him. He barely understood their annoyance because his mind was so full of sound and history.

The truth was, his imagination was always far away. Following the incident with the rifle it was often on the Civil War and stories of heroism and fighting in which his grandfather always played a part. On holiday mornings he would escape from the house before his mother caught him to do chores, run across the field and down the hill, giving the cows a wide berth, and into the trees beyond. There it was quiet and cool and dark and he could be alone with his thoughts and his fantasies and be at his happiest.

That one particular morning, he had been fighting a battle in the trees. Maybe it had been the battle of the Wilderness of 1864, a vicious fight conducted hand-to-hand in dense scrubland down south of Washington. The generals had been particularly hopeless that day and he'd had to give them their marching orders. Look to the front, soldier, look to the front. Pot that sniper! He struck a tree a sabre blow with the stick and in his mind's eye the enemy fell like wheat before the sickle in front of him.

"What are you doing there?"

The voice made him start and turn round. Peering over a fallen log across the clearing was a girl who he recognised from school, though he could not remember her name. He thought she was new. "You look awful funny," she said and giggled.

Jim flushed with embarrassment at having been caught. "I don't, so," he replied. "I was just playing...it was just the Civil War."

He realised he was really too old to be fighting imaginery enemies with a stick and talking to himself. Fifteen now and still in a world of his own from seventy years ago!

How lame his explanation sounded and how dreamy. He blushed, but instead of laughing some more, the girl looked impressed. "Oh," she said. "I know all about that from my grandpa. Can I play too?"

"No. It's not play, really."

She giggled: "Aw, go on. I bet I could fight you better than some old tree which can't answer back. Anyway, I know all the drill moves. I could show you. I won't laugh any more. Promise."

"No...no. It's alright. I don't play with girls." Damn, he thought, that sounded even worse.

It was too late anyhow. She had broken off a stick from the log, clambered over and was standing beside him grinning in triumph. She knew that his uncertainty meant she had won. "Have at you!" she said and poked him in the chest with the stick. "You're dead."

Jim lunged at her in retaliation, but she sidestepped, laughing and ran off as he floundered. Somehow, she had taken his breath away and his chest seemed stretched. He was gasping. Now she was running down a path through the woods and he was running after her, furious but also unexpectedly excited.

Rounding a corner in the path, he stopped short. She had disappeared. Then, "Coo-ee," from up a tree and the aggravating girl was grinning down at him from the branches. "I've run you ragged," she said.

He flushed more deeply and shook his head.

"What's your name anyhow? Mine's Annabelle-Lee," she said, jumping down. "Anyway, see ya."

They were standing in the clearing now, at the foot of the tree and she leaned over and kissed him. No one had ever done that except his mother. It was not much more than a peck, scarcely more than a brushing of cheeks, but it was amazing. He blushed again. Then she sauntered back down the path, grinning to herself without a glance to see the effect she'd had.

Jim gazed after her until she disappeared from view. He could not work it out: had she meant for him to chase her? Had she even meant for him to catch her? And what would he have done if he had?

She was tall and dark and dressed in a check shirt, jeans and sneakers and it was only after she had gone that he realised that, although he knew she had been pretty, he could not be quite sure how he would recognise her again. Nor had he asked Miss Annabelle-Lee *what* her full name was, or where she lived. How could he have been so stupid? And now it was too late. Damn, damn, damn. But he still wanted to know her better. He liked the feeling she gave him.

Alfred, Mary and Jim often listened to the radio in the parlour in the evenings. The large sturdy cabinet with its bakelite dials and its fretwork panelling brought the outside world into their home. It was their entertainment and their means of connecting with life beyond Springbridge, with places to which they never travelled, with folk who they would never meet and stars they would never see.

This particular evening it was Eddie Cantor, honking a song which suddenly caused Alfred to stare intensely at the radio and Mary to put down her darning: *When My Ship Comes In.*

"We'll have the cottage you've been wishing for,
We'll have those roses rambling round the door,
And maybe baby playing on the floor,
When my ship comes in
"You'll have the most expensive evening gown,
I'll have the finest dinner coat in town,
The finest families won't turn us down
When my ship comes in...."

When it finished, Alfred said: "Dammit, that's true! We will." Mary looked wistful: "Yes, that would be nice." But neither sounded as if they thought it was ever going to happen.

CHAPTER FOUR

There were times in his old age when a very particular memory came back to Alfred Barker. It could be triggered by the bright sunlight on a summer's day, or by the smell of trampled grass. Or, he could wake, sweating or shaking, in the middle of the night, transfixed by an image of a young man staring at him unexpectedly from a few inches away. The young man's eyes would be open, but he would be dead. Slowly, blood would trickle from a gaping wound which had just opened in the side of his head, where his right ear had been. At those times Grandfather could not sleep again, useless to try. Seventy years on and the picture would not go away. It would haunt him for the rest of the day. And still it kept coming back.

He could remember the incident as vividly – more so – as if it had just happened. He could not always remember things about the rest of his life, could not easily remember his childhood so far away and long ago, nor could he readily recall what he did yesterday. But he could remember this, before all others, the smells, the sights, the sounds. What happened before was like peering through a frosted glass and what happened since was often vague and cloudy too: ten years ago, twenty years, fifty. But not that day of high summer. July 21st 1861. The First Battle of Bull Run.

He had never been more frightened in his life than he was that day. He had never joined up for this. In fact, he shouldn't have been there at all, for his three month term of enlistment had already expired and they should have let him go home, except they wouldn't because of the coming battle. Not a few had deserted and most of the rest were moaning about what if they were killed when they had already done their bit?

All morning the regiment had been marching resentfully in the sticky heat of a Virginia summer, past fields and orchards where many men had taken upon themselves to fall out and gorge on ripening plums. Now, as they approached the battlefield and could hear the noise in the distance, the reality of war was striking home. They had spent the day drawing slowly closer, lost on dirt roads they and their officers had never seen before, surrounded by the chaos that lurks at the back of armies. There had been abandoned wagons, formations of troops drawn up without orders, whole regiments taking a rest, sitting down in the fields beside the road. Officers and messengers on horseback were milling aimlessly about and shouting at each other. Military bands were playing and bugles sounding. And, as it was a fine, sunny Sunday, there were also crowds of spectators who had driven out from Washington 20 miles away with their black butlers and their picnic hampers and their binoculars. They had been squealing with pleasure in the expectation of seeing a real, live battle which the Union army would surely win. Some of the rich old men in the barouches had stood up as the troops marched by, waving their straw hats in the air to impress the ladies and shouted: "On to Richmond, boys! It's thataway...."

This war was not how he had thought it would be. When Alfred, had joined up in New York three months before, he'd done so just because of the uniform and the idea of glory, not actually to fight. That's what had appealed in the regiment he had wanted to join: the 10th New York Volunteers were like the Zouaves of Africa, a smart blue collarless tunic with red piping round the edges and a curly red snake-like design running up from hip to breast, a red undershirt and a red fez with a blue tassel, baggy blue trousers and white canvas gaiters. The zouaves looked more like pirates than soldiers.

He did not get a uniform like that though. He did not have the social connections, or a patron, for an elite regiment like that. Alfred's enlistment had been much more mundane: what he got was an ill-fitting and flimsy serge blue jacket, a belt with US on the buckle and a kepi that kept sliding off the top of his head. It was a sloppy, unsoldierly, thin, cheapjack uniform. Instead of a zouave, he looked like a shop clerk as he found himself in a regiment of foot.

There had been no problem with him joining up at the recruiting office. They had not even asked him where he came from, or what his Mammy thought, not that she could have told them from three thousand miles away. He'd walked in off the sidewalk after seeing the big banner with the Stars and

Stripes hanging outside: "All for the Union – Enlist Today!" He had scarcely realised it was soldiering, or what the Union was for that matter. It was a job and there was pay and he would be fed, which was something when a man was down to his last fifty cents.

He was tall for his age, sixteen looking like twenty and the recruiting office down by Wall Street was keen for all the men it could get. The recruiting sergeant twirled his long moustaches, winked and smiled at him, told him he'd make a likely fellow and shook his hand. Alfred was fresh off the boat from Ireland, with no ties, no relatives, no friends and no work and there were no questions asked. The sergeant even gave him a silver dollar as a downpayment on wages and winked again like he was sharing a big secret man to man as he took his name and directed him towards a file of other recruits.

"You'll do laddie," he said, before, with his voice changing suddenly to a bark, he shouted at the recruits he had enlisted: "Look lively there."

And so Alfred found himself in the army to fight for a country he had never seen, in a regiment he had never heard of, recruited in a town he had lived in for less than a week, for a cause he did not understand, against people he had never met. Most of the other recruits were the same. Some scarcely spoke English and others spoke it with accents so strong that he could not understand a word they said. There were Irish and Scots, English, Germans and French as well as Yankees, men from Tipperary and the Bronx, Toulouse and Harlem. They were a shambles, for all their new uniforms, and there was no time to turn them into a disciplined, fighting unit.

So they had spent the past weeks marching up and down in the summer heat, learning to tell right feet from left, with straws slipped into the sides of their boots so that the dullest of them could tell which was which. Left, left, left...links, links, links...gauche, gauche, gauche...learning to march in step, look sharp and understand the sound of commands, even if they could not speak the language.

They had also been handed muskets to practice how to slope arms on the march and present them on the parade ground. They had been shown how to fix bayonets, but not how to fire the weapons. That would come later, the sergeants said, there would be plenty of time for that, if they ever arrived before the fighting finished and the war was over. One fight was all it would take.

It had been brutal too. The corporals carried willow canes with which they thrashed the backs of troops who turned the wrong way or were slow to come to attention. They were sworn and shouted at by incomprehensible men and bullied and kicked and pushed by sweating, blaspheming, red-faced drill orderlies.

The food was strange, foul-tasting and wormy, even for hungry men straight off the boat from the Atlantic crossing, and the bell tents in which they slept in the fields of Harlem were musty and dank and smelled of the summer body odour of exhausted, unwashed men pushed too close together. Their uniforms stank too of sweat. Every night more men slipped away in the darkness and never returned.

Alfred Barker stayed because he had nowhere else to go, but the regiment was depleted daily: nine hundred men had become seven hundred by the time in high summer they received orders to move and were marched to the train depot for the journey south.

Their troop train jerked and jolted slowly across the plains of New Jersey, through Philadelphia and down to the capital. It took two stifling days to get there. They were shunted into sidings to allow more important trains to pass and took a long detour round Baltimore because it was a nest of rebels. For Alfred, who had never been on a train before or travelled so fast, the journey started with excitement and anticipation but long before the end had come to be just hot, uncomfortable and awful tedious.

Then it had been another field, this time outside Washington. Alfred had scarcely seen an officer in all his weeks in the service, but one morning they were called to parade and stood to attention in the heat as the sun burned down and singed their necks.

After an hour or so, their colonel had ridden by, resplendent in a deep blue uniform with brass buttons, knee boots tight against the withers of his chestnut horse and a gold-braided kepi, topped with a plumed white feather, squashed on the top of his head. He was a large, heavy, city man, not shaped the least like a soldier at all, wearing spectacles, more like a banker than an officer. Beside him rode a man wearing a top hat and morning suit.

"There you are, congressman" Alfred could hear the colonel say. "The best of men."

The congressman leaned forward in his saddle, took a swig from his silver hipflask and handed it to the officer. "But are they ready colonel? Will they fight?"

"Oh surely Ely. They are full of enthusiasm. On to Richmond and all that. I'll lead them there myself. We'll cleanse the rebellion. Shall we lunch?"

And the two men had trotted off and that was the last Alfred or any of his comrades saw of their colonel until this morning as they moved towards the battle. Now the colonel had reappeared on his horse, waving his sword uncertainly in his white-gloved hand and, now and again, taking a deep gulp from a bottle. "Will you look at that?" the Irish sergeant had said, wonderingly.

"He's drunk."

And now, after all the weeks of waiting and drilling and marching and waiting some more, they were closing on the battle. The noise, of shouts and bugles and explosions was getting louder and beyond the hill clouds of smoke were shooting upwards. By the side of the lane, wounded men were lying unattended, groaning and leaning against the fences that fringed the fields.

Beyond them were the day-trippers from Washington on a Sunday outing, hoping to see the battle that the papers had all said was due. The men were standing up, straining to see what was happening through their spy-glasses, giving commentaries on what little they could see to their squealing womenfolk. They seemed oblivious to the wounded men nearby and turned their heads away when wounded soldiers approached their carriages begging water or food.

But they paid lively attention to the marching troops. As the regiment stumbled past the spectators cheered. They waved handkerchiefs and doffed their hats. Even Alfred's company received its own applause.

"Go get them, boys! Forwards men!" they shouted, and "Onwards to Richmond!" wherever that was. The colonel waved his sword cheerily at them and twisted heavily in his saddle. "Just watch us!" he cried back.

Alfred felt dizzy and sick, especially as he saw the wounded heading back towards them. The stream of bloodied soldiers limped aside to allow the fresh troops through.

Even worse were the casualties who could not move, men who had lost legs or with ripped open bellies, still alive, lying scattered about on the grass and crying out for help and water.

"Don't go there," one shouted to the troops still marching towards the sound of firing and "It's bloody murder!" cried another. "God help me!" said a third. "Oh mother, mother..."

Alfred began praying, as a good Catholic boy ought, but he was out of practice and all he could say, again and again under his breath as they pressed forward was: "Oh Christ, oh Christ, oh Christ." Beside him another boy was repeating: "Holy Mary, mother of God, pray for me now, pray for me now...and at the hour of my death."

"Steady up," shouted the sergeant. "Column of threes. Hold your lines. Hold your lines. Damn you!" They could barely hear him over the roar.

"Follow me, men!" shouted the colonel, waving his sword and, not waiting, disappearing into the smoke on his horse.

And now they were over the crest and their mouths dropped open as they saw the battle laid out across the fields in front of them. In later years, maps would show neatly-coloured rectangles and arrows to indicate the dispositions of the armies and their directions, but there was no neatness here. Groups of shouting men ran haphazardly about and lines of cannon fired, billowing smoke from which cannon balls bounded, knocking through thick-packed columns of soldiers like ninepins. The noise suddenly hit them like colliding with a solid wall. It disorientated and deafened them.

The troops were running now, down the slope, towards a gap in the field, next to a regiment in blue and, as they did so, Alfred could see an officer ordering the blue soldiers to turn about and present arms. They were fifty yards away.

"My God," he thought. "They're going to fire at us." And he flinched.

It saved his life. No one else around him had noticed, so the volley caught them side on, by surprise. The whole troop was buffeted, as if caught by a sudden gust of wind. As he ducked, Alfred sensed the rush of air and the man to his right stumbled and stopped in front of him. He thought the man must have tripped, but he fell over him and, even as he did so, realised he was already dead.

Now as Alfred lifted his head from the ground, he found himself staring into the man's open eyes and could see his glassy expression, mouth gaping in shock and a big, red, cavernous hole on the side of his head where his ear had been and from which the blood was just starting to bubble.

This was the figure that haunted his dreams, that wouldn't leave him alone and kept coming back to him many decades later.

They had been chatting on the march all morning, about Ireland and the places they knew and the ship crossing and the army. And now he was dead, a second ago. Far from home and in a fight he knew nothing about. Alfred didn't even know his name. And no one the dead man knew would ever know what happened to him either. It was as if he had never been alive.

As he stared into the man's face, Alfred could hear cries from his comrades. They were shouting at the other regiment to stop firing. The sound seemed far away. But even as they waved their arms there was a second volley and more men fell, the sergeant among them.

Lying prone and burying his head in the dead man's chest as the bullets passed over his head, Alfred could feel the reverberations as men fell. When he looked up again he only saw heaps of his comrades, some sprawled around as if asleep and others crawling away or screaming out for help, or water. Or God, or their mothers. In the distance, he could see the other regiment turn back to face their front and then, mercifully, his cap fell over his eyes.

Alfred was terrified. As he lay against the still-warm body, he sobbed. To get up would be madness. He would not last a second. He had never meant for this. He felt his chest beating fast and so loud it sounded like a drum. How could he escape from this nightmare?

Then, as if the sound of the battle had suddenly stopped, he heard the pounding of running feet nearby and shouts. "Run for your life!" the voices were saying and, "we're lost!" And, most frightening of all: "The black horse cavalry is coming!"

The pounding grew louder and he cautiously raised his head again. Running past all around him were soldiers in dark blue uniforms. In the distance, from the direction of the enemy, came the sounds of cheering. "We're whipped, boys! Run to save yourselves," someone shouted.

Now there seemed to be the sound of thousands of men running and Alfred decided it was now or never to join them. He got to his knees, then raised himself up and, leaving his musket and knapsack where they had fallen, but keeping holding of his kepi, he turned and joined the throng heading back up the hill down which he had charged a quarter of an hour earlier.

As he got to the top, he turned to look behind him and was nearly bowled over by the colonel, clinging now to the neck and mane of his frightened horse and making fast progress bolting up the slope. Both horse and man looked terrified, eyes staring, nostrils flaring.

"Colonel..."said Alfred. But the pair galloped past. "Out of my way," the colonel cried.

The stream of retreating men was becoming a flood and Alfred could see enemy soldiers, in brown, grey and blue already at the foot of the hill, starting to follow in more orderly fashion. His side's defeat was becoming a rout and he turned and rejoined the rush.

The country lanes were already becoming blocked. Wagons had overturned and the crowds of soldiers were streaming past on foot, or clambering over the fences to make their way back, running across the fields. Teamsters mounted on the horses that were pulling gun carriages were whipping their mounts in frenzy, vainly trying to push a way through the crowd. In their fury they lashed out too at all those around them, cursing and swearing for them to get out of their path.

And, stuck in the middle of the melee, were many of the picnic parties, still in their carriages, the women shrieking, the men shouting angrily for their way to be cleared. "Cowards! Cowards!" one man was crying, "Why don't you stand and fight?" As he did so, a teamster's whip caught the side of his head and he sank back into his seat, his wife screaming hysterically beside him. There was a blockage at the narrow bridge over the Bull Run creek where a wagon was stuck fast against the parapet, men tearing at the reins to tug the horses clear.

There would be no escape down this road, Alfred could see that. The knot in the lane was now so congested that he clambered through a gap in the fence and made his way across the field with hundreds of others. How sad, he thought, for the farmers that their crops had been squashed so flat just as they were ripening for the harvest. It had been a good crop too.

He had no idea where he was going, having no notion of this part of the world and only knowing that he should follow the crowd away from the fighting.

At the edge of the field was the creek. A crowd was poised on the bank, wondering how to cross and how deep the stream was. Alfred joined them just as one soldier and then several others dived in. There was a current and it caught them, tossing them away downstream. Then a civilian slipped or was pushed off the bank. Flailing in the water, he cried: "I can't swim. Help me." And then he too lost his footing and disappeared below the surface.

"Come on mate, let's go," shouted a soldier beside Alfred and the two of them jumped as the others hesitated. The water was deep and the bottom rocky but somehow, grabbing tree trunks and debris, they scrambled across. Looking back across the stream, Alfred could see the crowd surging and screaming as, along the field on top of the rise, rebel horsemen began to appear.

Alfred plunged on, following the bedraggled exodus of others who had made it over the creek. Gradually the crowd thinned out, or he outpaced them.

Eventually he found himself at the far edge of a meadow, bounded by a narrow stream and on the other side was the start of a wood. That would be a good place to rest and hide, he thought.

The stream was not deep this time and, as he waded across, the water felt so cool and clear and he was so thirsty that he stopped and scooped handfuls into his mouth and splashed it over his face. He thought he had never tasted anything so good and he was reluctant to leave it.

On the other side Alfred sat down behind some bramble bushes and took off his boots to empty them of water. As he did so, he realised he did not need to. The boots were already so sodden and the leather so poor that they were coming apart, the soles flapping open and the seams unstitched. The material seemed more like cardboard, crumbling to the touch and, as he pushed his boots off Alfred realised dully that that was exactly what it was. Just cardboard.

All was quiet now. It was like a summer's day back home in Ireland, though hotter and more sultry, and he suddenly felt tired. They had been marching all day and he had been running all afternoon. Exhaustion overtook him and he lay back in the soft grass and closed his eyes. The earth felt soft and comfortable.

Suddenly, he was woken by the sound of splashing and singing and, when he had adjusted his eyes and recollected where he was, he rolled over cautiously, peered through the bushes and saw a middle-aged man, stripped to his combinations, bathing in the brook.

The man was staggering and seemed to be chuckling to himself, as if he had taken drink. Alfred could not quite place him, but he looked familiar because of the curious bushy beard that inhabited the space under his chin and, as he pondered this, he became aware of a group of horsemen, dressed in gray, watching the man silently from the far bank.

"Well now, sir," said their leader after a while. He was a tall young officer with a fair beard; clearly amused. "What a pleasure to meet you, to be sure. It's Congressman Ely, isn't it?"

So that's who it was, thought Alfred. The gentleman from New York who had been riding with their colonel the other day and had urged them on to Richmond. In the stream the bathing man stopped and turned round with a start. There was a lengthy pause while he considered what to do. Flight or fight were clearly out of the question. So he smiled ingratiatingly instead, holding his wet hands uncertainly in front of him to shield his groin.

"Now boys, you don't want me," he said. "I'm a civilian. There's plenty of soldiers yonder you could be taking. I'm harmless to you. Leave me alone."

The bearded cavalryman laughed. He said: "Oh no, I think we do want you very much indeed Mr Ely, sir, Mr Congressman. I do beg your pardon, but we'd like you most particularly, especially after all the disagreeable things you've been saying about us in Washington. Hanging's too good for us, isn't it?"

"Boys–gentlemen–now that was a joke. Just politician's talk. Lies, gentlemen, lies. You know how it is. Get along on now. I am no use to you. You needn't worry about me."

"Oh, we'd like you, sir, just as you are. You'll look fine dressed in your combinations on Jeff Davis's mantlepiece in Richmond. Come on boys, take him up," said the cavalryman.

"I'll pay you. I'll speak up. My voice will be heard. We've been too hasty," the congressman sang out, desperate now. "Don't do this to me." His hands moved upwards, together, in supplication. He was almost crying; and suddenly quite sober. "Don't hurt me. I'll speak...."

But it was too late. Congresman Ely was being chivvied out of the water and surrounded by the enemy troops. Laughing, they prodded him up the bank with the flat of their sabres. And then the whole group wheeled away, back the way they had come, with him stumbling along, still protesting and wheedling and begging, in their midst.

It took some time for Alfred to realise that they had really gone and the coast was clear. Now he suddenly felt cold and shivering. Night was coming on and his uniform was still soaking wet. Then he spotted the congressman's clothes lying in a pile on the far bank of the stream. It seemed like a fair swap. After today's experience, he reasoned, he would not be needing the uniform again. He had done his bit. And the congressman was unlikely to come back for his clothes either.

So he took off the uniform and folded it neatly in a pile under the bush, as if leaving it in case someone else might want to take it up. Then he waded naked across the stream and tried Ely's suit on instead. It was of good quality gray tweed with a double-breasted frock coat, still with a handkerchief tucked into its breast pocket and neat, dark frogging round the collar and cuffs – the sort of clothes a gentleman might wear for a jaunt into the country on a Sunday. The suit was dry and fitted after a fashion, though it was too long and baggy around him. The boots were much too large, so he did not take those.

Best of all, in the inside pocket of the congressman's coat, he found ten dollars, which he kept as no more than his due for nearly getting his head blown off in the government's cause. He saw no reason to prolong his army career further. Although Alfred did not know it, one meeting was about to change his life forever.

And so, dressed in fine cloth, but out of his depth and shoeless, he set off again, through the woods, heading east.

CHAPTER FIVE
2002

Isabelle laid a white cloth over the kitchen table and Gene went back down the yard to the shack to extract the plates from the trunk. Holding each glass rectangle reverently between his fingers by the edges, he brought them up to the house one by one and laid them out.

As far as they were able, they divided the plates with their shadowy images into groups: portraits in one pile, landscapes in another and then a miscellany, plates of what looked like military equipment: men standing next to guns, guards on sentry duty next to a railroad engine and finally pictures of buildings and tents.

Quite a few of the plates were cracked across or had lost corners and some seemed to have blotches and stains erupting across them like weeds, or creeping damp. Counting them all, there were thirty three, more than half of them damaged.

They sat and looked at each other. "What are we to do with them?" asked Isabelle. "Do you think they're valuable?"

Gene shook his head. "God knows. They could be. They ought to be. It might be our lucky day. We'll have to find someone to value them."

The pictures were clearly old and showed soldiers, so it did not take Gene and Izzie long, sitting in front of their computer that evening, to track down that they were photographic plates from the Civil War era in the 1860s. They looked at each other in wonder: pictures that were 140 years old, or more, of living men and women who must now be more than a century dead and gone. They were from the very dawn of the age of photography, an invention then as new as the Internet was to Gene and Izzie, and just as revolutionary.

On the web sites one name kept cropping up: Mathew Brady, the man who had photographed the war and seemingly taken all the pictures of it. Could he have been responsible for their photographs and, if so, how did they end up in their shed?

Their website searches showed the Brady name and dates – circa 1822 to January 15th 1896 – and also spoke of his fame and celebrity. And also of the thousands of dollars originals of his photographs fetched at auction. The only difficulty was that the initials on the trunk were AB, not MB, definitely an A, not an M. Could they belong to Brady's little-known brother: Amos, or Andy? Or even his wife or sister: no, more Googling showed his wife's name was Juliet and, with the best will in the world, the A looked even less like a J than an M. Perhaps, the thought struck them, they had discovered a hitherto unknown Victorian photographer, AB, in which case they really had struck gold.

After that, they carefully placed the plates in the trunk which Gene had brought up from the garage once it was empty. On the following Monday, carefully wrapping a couple of the plates in a towel, they placed them in Gene's hard-sided tan briefcase and drove to the local antique dealer who had sold them most of the bric-a-brac for the house. He rather thought they might be worth a few dollars and promised to bring a friend to value them. "Of course, they won't be Brady's," he said, discouragingly. "And even if they were, they'd only be copies. Brady's pictures are all in the Congressional archives."

A few days later the dealer, George Montgomery Price, showed up at their house with his expert, whose card announced him to be Joshua Butterfield IV and whose affected nonchalance was belied by his eager, shining eyes. "Oh yes," he said, "oh yes. Oh my." He lifted each plate in turn, held it to the light and stared fixedly at it through magnifying spectacles.

It took him more than an hour to view all the plates and at the end he said as if making a definitive pronouncement: "That's quite a collection. I could offer you – ah – three hundred dollars for them."

There was something in his manner that made Izzie suspicious. His reticence had been too studied, his caution too deliberate, too far at odds with the look on his face. To her mind, she knew they had to be worth far more than that. Especially if they were Brady's.

"Oh no," Butterfield said. "These things are not quite a dime a dozen, but there are still thousands of them lying around and many of these, like the landscapes are, frankly, quite boring."

He leaned forward confidentially. "Do you know, ma'am, there were millions of these sorts of thing taken during the Civil War and you couldn't get a price for them afterwards? Not even Brady got much money and he wasn't the only photographer by any means. Whoever your AB was, he was no Mathew Brady. Just some hack photographer. Plates like his used to get used in greenhouses and all sorts, to shield the plants. Oh yes, ma'am, pictures are turning up all the time and in better condition than this."

They could do with the three hundred dollars, no doubt about it, towards a new roll-top bath in one of the en-suites, but the offer was just too low. Isabelle said: "What will you do with them if we sell them to you?"

Butterfield blew out his cheeks. He shrugged: "Well, I'd print them up, see if they had anything of value and then, probably, donate them somewhere if they weren't worth much. Maybe make garden cloches from them if necessary." And he chuckled benignly.

Gene was nodding sympathetically at this. Three hundred dollars would fix the leak in the main bathroom and get the glass plates off their hands. They could probably negotiate copies of the photographs too, for a nice album as a talking point for guests... "See that picture? Yes we actually found that here, in the shack out the back, after we moved in."

"No," said Izzie decisively. "They're not for sale. I have a feeling they're worth more than you're letting on and I think we need to think a bit harder about what to do with them. They are our little archive and I want to see what the pictures really look like before we decide."

"Alright, five hundred," said Butterfield. "And I'll take the trunk. And give you a set of the pictures..."

But it was no good, once Izzie had made up her mind. Gene could have told him that.

The week's *Springbridge Dispatch-Messenger* had a photograph on its front page (just under its masthead bearing the legend: "The paper that's more interested in our town than you are yourself") showing Gene and Izzie holding a large magnifying glass and gazing at one of the plates with a headline announcing: "Newcomers Strike Glass at Home".

The story read: "Incomers Eugene and Isabel (sic) Hofseter from Manhattan, NYC, thought they had a bargain when they bought the old Barker place off Jefferson road last Fall. But now it seems they may have gotten more than they bargained for as they have uncovered old photographs in a shack out back."

"Mrs Hofseter, 34, who formerly worked in the public relations industry, said: 'My husband found these glass plates with negatives on them in a trunk under a pile of junk. They seem to show views of 100 years or more ago and we want to know more about them. They may be valuable.'

"Her husband Eugene, 35, a writer for a top Manhattan magazine, said the glass plates had been valued at $500. It is thought they may show views of Springbridge as it was in the 19th Century, in which case they may be worth a great deal more to collectors, experts say.

"The only clue is that there are initials: AB painted on the trunk. But no one knows who AB might have been.

"Mr George Montgomery Price III, 56, who runs Bijou Memories downtown said he had seen the plates and believed them to be interesting relics of a bygone era. 'We won't know what they are worth until the Hofteters agree to having them properly examined, but my associates believe they could be of considerable value. I hope we may be able to make some arrangement, before they get further damaged,' he told the Dispatch-Messenger yesterday.

"The couple moved to the house, which they are renovating with the help of local contractors Turner and Sachatash, and may open later as a bed and breakfast facility. Henry Turner, 42, said: "The house is pretty and they are doing it up real nice for visitors. I am sure the pictures will look good once they are renovated too."

Izzie looked at Gene and giggled. "Well, they nearly spelled our name right and I don't know where the extra hundreds came from on the pictures, but at least that's put us in our place: Incomers. And our ages too!"

"Not sure we want folk knowing how much those pictures might be worth, or we might have some unwanted visitors," said Gene.

And, as if on cue, at that moment there was a shuffling sound outside and a knock. "What did I tell you? They're here already," he said.

Through the fake Victorian patterned glass of their brand new front door, they could see a figure as they looked down the hall.

It was a woman, and an elderly one. She had parked her ancient, black bicycle at the foot of the steps. As Gene opened the door, she had her back to him while she gazed at the view. "It really hasn't changed all that much," she said after a moment as she turned towards him. "I haven't been here in donkeys' years and it's just the same, excepting the new houses. I don't like them, do you?"

Smiling sweetly, she added: "You have done this old place up very nicely, dear. May I come in? You see, I've seen the paper and I may be able to help you with your photographs. And I think I know who AB was."

CHAPTER SIX: 1861

Darkness was falling fast now and the wood was thick. Alfred decided he had to make a move before the rebels returned and seized him too. It was heavy going and his feet were soon bruised and cut. He slithered across mossy trunks and branches lying on the ground and, occasionally, terrifyingly, he would hear the groans of wounded, exhausted men who had reached the shelter of the trees but could get no further. Once he thought a man reached out at him, but the fingers were only twigs, brushing his beardless face.

There was no light among the trees. Even as he became accustomed to the dark, he could scarcely see where he was going and feared he would have to stop and bed down with the dead and dying men there. But then, suddenly, the wood petered out and he was back on the road again.

The route was still crowded, though the stampede had stopped, replaced by the steady tramp of feet as the army, its followers, hangers-on and onlookers made their way back to Washington. A full moon shone wanly overhead, lighting the crowd's faces to a pallid grey. They looked sick with fear. Uniforms and weapons had been thrown off and discarded, leaving a thick litter of clothing and equipment in piles along the road. Here and there, civilians, their clothes disarranged, were limping back home too, arguing and squabbling as they went.

The defeat had abashed them all, so unexpected had it been. They were a tattered mob, surging along the dirt road, kicking up dust as they hobbled along. Above the mutter of voices, there was swearing and cursing of a sort Alfred had never heard before. He joined the flow. There was no other way for him to go.

Hour after hour the exhausted rabble stumbled on, unchecked and unmolested by the enemy troops. Gradually, as men fell out and lay down by the roadside, or peeled off down other paths, the way grew easier.

Then it started to rain. Alfred was limping badly now. He decided he needed shoes and paused by the corpse of a soldier lying against a fence. The boots the man was wearing appeared to be the right size, though almost any size would have done. His feet were splayed out, his arms flung back, mouth open, catching the rain drops, and his hair was on end, moisture dripping down onto his face. Clearly he'd never need his boots again. They looked good leather ones to someone going barefoot. The desperate boy knelt beside the body and, bending down, began to ease them from the dead man's feet.

Suddenly a sharp blow knocked him backwards into the dirt. The corpse had sat up and brought his hand slap down across the top of Alfred's head. "You leave my boots alone," it said. "Or you're a dead man."

"Well, that's what I thought *you* was," Alfred exclaimed as he picked himself up. "I'm sorry." And he beat a retreat.

"Not dead, just drunk," the soldier shouted after him. "Mind you tell the difference." And he lay back again, open mouthed in stupor.

Alfred limped on, still barefoot. He did not know where he was going, or what he would do when he got there and he had a suspicion that you weren't meant to leave the army of your own volition like he had, though plenty of others on the road seemed to have done so. Anyway, he'd certainly been abandoned and even his colonel had fled.

War in this country was a puzzle. Surely men did not turn and kill each other on the same side? Otherwise, who would you know you were fighting for, and who against? It was an impossible conundrum and one he could not unravel. Perhaps that is what it was like in America though. You could not tell friend from foe, or who to trust and who to fear. If you couldn't do that you were truly lost. And he was, both mentally and physically.

He was only sixteen years of age. He knew no one in America, no one within three thousand miles, except the companions he had left dead on the field behind him. He had nowhere to stay and no means of making his way in the world. He was quite alone, desolately, desperately so. He should never have left Ireland in search of his fortune. And he felt himself welling up inside.

The boy leaned against a fence post and sobbed, tears mingling with the rain already running down his face. He did not know what to do and the effort to think just added to his exhaustion.

"What's up, old man?" said a voice. "Hi, I am talking to you."

It took a moment for Alfred to realise that the question had been addressed to him and when he turned round, it was to see a small man, sitting up on a large wheeled wagon with a sort of tent contraption on its back, drawn by a sullen-looking horse.

The man was wearing a long white linen overall coat and a flat, wide-brimmed straw hat from which the rain was dripping. Alfred could see little of his face except for his pointed, dark beard. As he waited for a reply, the man took off the pair of small, round pince-nez he was wearing on a cord around his neck and started polishing them with a handkerchief, misting them with his breath.

The vision was so eerie and unexpected that Alfred wondered for a moment whether it was quite human, or supernatural. All he could do was stammer his name. "Alfred Barker, sir," he said, then added forlornly, "I don't know where I am."

The man on the wagon replaced his spectacles on his nose and adjusted the cord which secured them round his neck. Then he said: "Can I give you a lift? Look sharp and hop up beside me."

And that was how Alfred Barker met Mr Mathew Brady and found his future career.

The horse and wagon trudged on through the drizzle for an hour more. Then, as the sky lightened, they passed across a bridge over the Potomac river into the suburbs of Washington, past rows of large mansions and villas, with shutters barred across their windows and no lights showing. Their owners had either fled, or were cowering inside in imminent fear of an enemy invasion that day.

In the muddy, unpaved streets, groups of soldiers who had made it back from the battlefield milled aimlessly about with no one to take charge or give them orders. The rain had become a thick, warm mist now and dawn was breaking balefully over the city.

As a conversationalist, Brady was much more interested in monologue than dialogue. He chattered amiably on beside Alfred and when the lad, lulled by the motion of the cart, nodded off, he did not seem to notice. When the boy awoke again, Brady was still talking while giving the horse an occasional flick with his whip to emphasise what he was saying and to encourage it forward.

Brady had much to talk about. He was an artist, he said and he took photographic portraits. He was exceedingly famous, he informed the boy and had had all the eminent men of the day and all the crowned heads of Europe seeking him out to have their pictures made.

And now, damn it, he'd been to the battle, to assess the possibilities for the portraiture of war and had only lost his camera, his second wagon and his assistant in the flight at the end! It was really too, too bad. Some damned rebel was probably even now in possession of his second-best Woodward Solar Imperial camera. He had had to leave it and run as they suddenly swarmed forward.

In the flight, the other wagon had overturned on the road and lord knew what had happened to young Ned House, his assistant. He had salvaged one or two plates, but really this was too bad. He shuddered to think of the cost. How unfortunate. He just hoped that his rivals, Bell and Bryant, Smith and Ulke and McCarty and Seibert, had done no better. He had not seen them on the field, but they must have known about the battle, unless they were skulking in the city because it was Sunday. There was not a moment to loose! Damn it! Where was House? He had told him to stay with the wagon and preserve the remaining plates and equipment. Lord, he'd better not have been captured....

Alfred understood very little of all this chatter as he dozed and then woke with the rocking of the cart, to hear the famous man in the white coat still talking, and then he dozed again. Finally, he was jerked awake as his head went back and then fell forward when the wagon stopped outside a four storey building at the end of a parade of shops in a tree-lined avenue in the centre of the city. Brady leaped down, shouting, "We're here!" and strode across the sidewalk, under a pillared-portico to a door, which he rapped hard with his knuckles. "Come on, Gardner, wake up, man" he cried.

Stiffly, Alfred got down from the cart and followed Brady to the door. The boy was shivering now, from the cold and the rain and his teeth chattered as they waited while the bolt on the door was drawn back. It was opened by a large man with a shaggy black beard, his fierce appearance belied by kindly eyes. He was scratching his hair as if to rake its wildness into order.

"Mr Brady, sir," he said in a strong Scottish accent. "Thank God you're safe. I hear the news is bad."

"Very bad, Gardner. I've lost my camera and most of the plates and House managed to upend his wagon in a ditch last night. I don't know whether he is alive or dead, or captured or safe. It's a complete fiasco. And we lost the battle too.

"All I got out of the battle was this sword," Brady was saying, gesturing to a scabbard hung below his coat. "Never mind: it will come in useful, I dare say.

"Now, what I want you to do Gardner is take *my* portrait. 'Brady: Back from the Battle!' People will be interested in that."

Gardner tutted sympathetically and led the way inside and up a flight of stairs to a photographic gallery, with framed pictures lining the walls and ottoman settees and padded armchairs for visitors. To Alfred it seemed like a palace. He flopped onto one of the chairs; scarcely able to stand from tiredness.

Gardner looked inquiringly from the boy to Brady who shook his head dismissively. "He's a waif and stray I picked up on the way back. I think he may have the makings of an assistant, but he'll need some breakfast and a bed first. And probably some boots."

He turned to the boy and pointed to the large, framed photographic portraits lining the walls. "This is what I do, young man" he said. "Do you recognise these folk?"

Alfred shook his head. They all looked much alike, men striking upright poses, hands lightly resting on books placed on table tops, or fingers hitched into the lapels of morning coats. Sometimes beside them sat their wives, looking demure, or bored; or, for variation, the husband would be seated with the wife leaning.against his shoulder. None smiled: there were too many men of destiny here. But there was a most remarkable thing about the portraits: though the figures were still, caught in a moment of time by the photograph, they all looked most vividly and assuredly alive. The portraits were almost life-sized and to Alfred they seemed so fresh and so detailed that the famous personages might almost still be present in the room.

"Did you make these pictures? With your box?" he asked in wonder. The photographs had captured every crease and fold in the sitters' clothing, every blemish and pock-mark on their skin, every whisp of their beards and every dishevelled strand of their hair.

By now Brady was giving a guided tour of the portraits in the gallery, snapping his fingers impatiently to attract Alfred's attention and pointing floridly as he reached each one. It was a practised routine. He was not interested in the folds and creases, but in the fame of the celebrities he had caught and the poses they had struck.

"Here," he was saying, of a large photograph of a grim, portly man with his right hand thrust into his checkered waistcoat. "This is Senator Cass, the former Secretary of State. Surely you have heard of him?

Alfred shook his head. The senator in the portrait, glaring through gumboil eyes, looked as though he could reach out and smack the boy for his impertinence.

As the reached the end of the gallery, Brady stopped and opened the drawer of a desk, containing a series of little boxes. Picking one at random he opened it like a small book, to reveal, faintly, on a tarnished copper sheet, the portrait of a demure young woman in fine satin clothes.

"And here, this much smaller one, a Daguerreotype – ah – Miss Jennie Lind, the singer – the Swedish Nightingale. A voice like an angel! Worth a thousand dollars a night to sing for Barnum: paid in advance before she'd sung a note – imagine that! No? And here, Junius Booth, the late actor." He opened another small case and pointed to a sturdy looking elderly man with a mottled and broken-nosed face, scowling theatrically in a lace collar. "Ah, the Great Booth," he cried. "Playing Richard III. A remarkable man and a sad loss to the American stage...."

"Do you mean he's dead, sir?" Alfred found this hard to compute, with the man in the picture who had been evidently alive.

"Oh, quite dead, for several years now," said Brady, looking quizzically at Alfred. "Fortunately he has a number of sons carrying on his distinguished tradition of thespianism."

This all meant little to Alfred. He was finding Brady's high-flown way of speaking confusing. Anyway, he scarcely knew what an actor was. Or cared now.

"You must know this man. Surely." Brady was exasperated by the boy's ignorance. "It's my most famous portrait, damn it. Everyone's seen it. *It's the President, boy!* I took him before his great speech in New York. Harper's Weekly engraved it for its cover. He was known by it all over the country!"

And there he was. Mr Lincoln himself, standing at a table looking stiff and pensive, his left hand resting lightly on a book. A tall, clean-shaven man, with a high brow and unruly hair. He looked sad, to Alfred, but his jaw jutted, so he was resolute too. So that's who he had been fighting for, he thought. He had not known of him before, or what he looked like.

There was only one portrait Alfred recognised in the whole room and that was Congressman Ely, the man he had last seen in his combinations the night before, being led away from the stream by the Confederate cavalry. In his studio portrait however he looked serene and determined, with a grim smile on his lips and a glint in his eye. He sat next to a desk, casually relaxed, legs crossed, as if interrupted while writing a letter. And what transfixed Alfred was that the congressman was evidently wearing the same grey tweed suit as he had on at that very moment.

Old Alfred chuckled at the memory of that suit. Of course Brady had not spotted it. After the picture tour, he had given him over to Mr Gardner who'd fed him porridge and coffee – the first and so the best he'd ever tasted – and tucked him up under a rug on a couch in a back corner of the room, while Brady himself made ready for his portrait to be taken. He could remember it well: Brady standing in profile, still wearing the straw hat and duster coat, hands in pockets, pince-nez on nose, his gingery-brown beard jutting defiantly. "Brady The Photographer returned from Bull Run" they'd titled it and "Photo taken July 22nd 1861" in shaky writing along the bottom of the print, just so no one could mistake the immediacy of the image, or the importance of the man.

Later that day, Alfred had been put to work sweeping the floor in the gallery. No one, least of all Brady or Gardner had asked him whether he wanted to stay, or whether he was going to go home to his family. It just seemed obvious that he would remain and be employed by the photographer in his gallery.

The room where Alfred wanted to work was at the back of the building, where a group of assistants made prints from the glass plate negatives taken in the portrait gallery and ran off small cartes-de-visite for clients who had stopped by to have their pictures taken for a few cents.

For those you used a special camera with a multiple lens which took four portraits at a time – cheap stuff, not like the formal sittings of famous folk for the Imperial-sized portraits, feet across, that Mr Brady supervised himself, for which he could charge them seven hundred dollars each if he wished.

The cartes-de-visite men had been busy in those days, as so many people wanted their picture taken at the start of the war. Young soldiers in their fresh uniforms, fathers with sons, mothers with daughters, fashionable women for their beaux and sweethearts, politicians for their constituents: they all queued for their calling cards and they all got dressed up specially in their best clothes. Some of them even sat on the couch where Alfred had slept.

Many of them wanted the distinctive cachet of the signature too: Brady, engraved in the bottom left corner, Washington in the bottom right. Some were even disappointed when they were hustled through in a line to have their portrait taken by an assistant, not the great man himself.

He reserved his attentions for the famous. And – though it was never to be mentioned – the little man's eyesight was going and he could see barely well enough to focus the lens properly. These days, with pardonable vanity, Mr Brady preferred to be in photographs, rather than taking them.

Gardner and the others sniggered and grew resentful that all their photographs were published as if they had been taken by Brady himself. But it was the truth. For all his bluster and showmanship, Mr Brady was not the photographer he once had been.

But now, all those decades later, if he closed his eyes, Alfred could still sniff the chemicals. He could still remember those days.

They'd started him tidying the studio, rearranging the furniture for the portraits when the sitters came in. "Would you like this chair, sir? We call it our *Congressional* chair. This desk would suit remarkably well, sir....A sense of studiousness, don't you think?" the photographer would say, laying it on thick to flatter the guest and Alfred would have to move the props into place.

Then he would also be sent to work for the technicians, running to stock up their collodion and silver nitrate solutions in the big glass bottles. After that, when they saw that he was reliable, he'd been allowed to coat the plates in the dark room and prepare them for the studio.

It had all been so different in Mr Brady's day. That was a proper studio: the most famous in the world. Stand still long enough in the gallery and every celebrity and politician in the country and every famous visitor from abroad came through for their portrait. Brady would make sure they came to him, even if he had to pay them himself to do so.

And you would see them as they were, not just depict how they looked when posing for a portrait. There would be the fussy and the self-important and the proud; and the kind and considerate and polite.

There had been Edwin Stanton, the secretary of war, brusque and pompous, a large, portly, bearded man glaring behind his oval spectacles and making clear he had more important things to do – as indeed he had. General Tom Thumb, Barnum's famous midget, had come with his midget wife for a portrait on their wedding day, looking proud as Punch and placed beside one of the studio chairs to show how small they really were. Oh yes, they'd all come by.

Who would know who'd be there on any day? More than once it was the president himself, Mr Lincoln. Alfred had known who he was by now. So tall and erect, with a face ever more gaunt and lined. Stern-looking as he composed himself, but with a warm smile and a wry expression when relaxed and talking to Brady. And the eyes, sharp but genial. Oh yes, Alfred thought, he was a man without side, or arrogance.

Alfred could not say the president had actually spoken to him, or taken any notice of his presence, but on the occasion he best remembered Lincoln had been chatting to Mr Brady who, as usual, was fluttering around him like a dove with beating wings.

The president said: "Let's do a standing portrait this time. My feet joggle when you get me sitting down. I am like an old maid at a barn dance and all you see of my feet is a blur. They look like great paddles. You'd imagine I was moving them about and I know I don't. I'm confident of it."

Brady said: "Well, sir, perhaps they jerk with the throbbing of the arteries."

Then the president had sat down at a prop desk and crossed his legs to see; and they had wobbled. "I'll be blowed," he said. "Now that's very curious, isn't it? I'll have to keep my legs still if I am to have dainty feet in future. Yes, a standing portrait – but don't you make me look like some scrawny giant out of Barnum's circus."

"Oh, not at all, sir. You are quite right, of course. A statesman-like pose, I think...Hand on a book perhaps, or holding papers of state?"

And Lincoln had laughed. "What do you mean *like* a statesman, Brady? Ain't I one already? Get on with you and your soft-soap. Never knew a photographist who didn't make me look mad or boss-eyed before, so you'll always do for me. You can flatter me anytime."

Brady had been covered with confusion and pride. Of course he was. Comically, he had stood on a chair to adjust the president's collar upwards to make his neck less long, to straighten his tie and to lengthen the metal clamp which held his head steady.

Alfred, using the excuse that he would be needed to rush the plate back to the darkroom, had stood near the door to watch the president then put on his stern face and Brady open the camera lens and take the portrait. Serious faces were not so difficult when your head had been placed against the prongs of a metal brace to hold it straight. It was smiling that was hard for ten or fifteen seconds because your lips trembled and your head wobbled – and why would you smile in a formal portrait anyway? It was no laughing matter.

Mr Brady jumped around, all the time bowing and scraping. "It is always a great honour to have you with us, sir. We will always accommodate you, sir."

He'd seen the president live, thought Alfred in his old age. Not many still alive could say that, seventy years on. And he'd seen him dead too, in his coffin. And taken his photograph. No one still alive in all the world could say that either. Only him. And it was his secret.

CHAPTER SEVEN

The first thing Gene noticed about the elderly woman as she came through the door was her gloves. They were dainty yellow leather numbers, secured by a single button at the wrist. She was swinging a cyclist's safety helmet with racing stripes down the side in one hand, as if fresh from a time trial, and carrying a large old-fashioned leather handbag in the other and, most striking of all, she was wearing beige cropped pedal pusher pants. For some one who must have been in her seventies, he thought as she sashayed down the hall, she'd kept her figure well. She must have been quite good looking once.

Then she took off the headscarf she had evidently been wearing under the helmet and with a toss of her head let her long grey hair swirl down to her shoulders. It was a well-practised gesture. As she turned and grinned at him, he saw she was wearing bright red lipstick.

Izzie came to meet them from the kitchen, hand outstretched. "This is..." said Gene then realised they had not been introduced.

" Annabelle-Lee Morrow," the woman said, stretching her hand out to Izzie. " Enchant-*ay*...I am just so pleased to meet you. And to see your house." Looking around, she added: "I used to know it so well and it's like stepping back into yesterday even though I haven't been inside for decades."

Izzie led them both into the kitchen and the elderly woman sat straight-backed, even slightly imperiously in the big carvery chair at the end of the old wooden table they had placed in the centre of the room. As she pulled off her gloves, she looked up – Gene could have sworn it was seductively, if only for an instant – and said: "Well, this has certainly changed."

She graciously accepted a cup of tea and one of Izzie's fresh-baked blueberry muffins, eating it delicately, almost it seemed crumb by crumb, and then said: "I expect you wonder why I am here?

"The fact is, I used to know the folks who lived here many years ago – was quite sweet on a boy who lived here once, actually – and because of that I think I might know about your photographs. I can tell you who AB was anyway."

Miss Annabelle-Lee smiled , crossed her hands in her lap and looked expectantly from Izzie to Gene and back again. She seemed very little interested in them, which was disconcerting. It was as if she was waiting for a cue to start.

"You see, the man who lived here then – I am talking about back in the thirties, you understand, had been a photographer, I believe. AB stood for Alfred Barker. That was his name. It was his grandson I knew. We spent a wild summer...and then I went off to learn to be an actress in the movies, in Hollywood....oh well. That's enough about *that*...Anyway, I still have some photographs that Alfred Barker had taken way back and he gave me copies. I just thought they might be the same, or similar to the ones in your trunk and I've looked them out of my attic for you ."

She reached into the depths of her bag and pulled out a sheaf of papers which had been folded in half. On them were copies of photographs, each perhaps nine inches by seven. She smoothed them flat and laid them out one by one on the table, the creases running vertically down the centre of the prints. Then she delicately put a pair of large-rimmed spectacles on, ready for the inspection.

Gene gasped. The black and white images certainly looked familiar, though this time they were positives, not negatives. They were not good copies and were faded and scratched, but they certainly looked like the same pictures.

He went to the hallway where the trunk of glass plates was stored and brought back several of the portraits from the front of the box. By holding the plates up and shuffling the paper copies, they could see they matched and, what was even better, along the bottom margins of the photographs they could see titles in crabbed and creaky handwriting, some of them flowery and poetic.

Startlingly, one landscape of a field which in negative had looked as though it had boulders in it, could now be seen to have men's bodies laid out in a line instead, above a caption which read: "After the Angel of Death had passed over." Izzie wrinkled her nose, partly at the gruesomeness of the image and partly at the sentimentality of the words.

Another picture showed a uniformed general with a florid moustache and goatee beard, sitting on a chair in a field outside a large tent, surrounded by young men in uniform, to whom he was paying no attention whatsoever. His hat was at a rakish angle and his arms were folded defiantly across his chest as though he was not a man to be crossed. The caption underneath read "General Hancock and his staff."

A third had another general, a bulldog-faced, choleric-looking man with a moustache sweeping down from the sideburns that framed his face. He had a newspaper in his hand and was looking up furiously as if he had been startled by the photographer's intrusion during a moment's relaxation. One side of the picture seemed to show a small, fuzzy, ghost-like figure stealing out of shot. It was wearing a long linen duster coat and a straw hat and it was as if he was trying to get out of the way. The handwriting stated: "General Burnside at his headquarters."

The images that now lay before them, as if looming out of an ancient fog, took their breath away. Remove the uniforms and print up good new copies and these were young men you might encounter in the street or at the drive-thru any day.

For an hour they matched photographs to plates until there were separate piles stacked across the table. Mostly it was Gene who sorted out the images, while Izzie looked over his shoulder and Miss Annabelle-Lee (they could not think of her without the title) just smiled benignly and condescended to glance across with polite interest as the pictures were matched.

So these were Alfred Barker's pictures, not Mathew Brady's. Gene consulted his laptop and Googled the name. There was a professor in Nebraska, a landscape gardener in Oregon and an accountant in England, but no photographer, not even an historic one. It looked as though they had uncovered a new name.

At last, as Gene stood up and eased his back, she said: "I think I could manage a drink now."

Certainly, said Izzie, a soda? A juice? Another cup of tea? Then, seeing the old lady shake her head: err, something else, perhaps?

"Yes," the old lady said decisively. "Do you have something stronger by any chance? I think it's time for a Martini, don't you? To celebrate..."

They watched as the old lady downed the cocktail in one. Then she said: "I am so happy that the pictures match up. I am glad the plates weren't lost after all the care the old man took of them." And she flashed them a twinkling smile, which was shut off almost as soon as it arrived.

Izzie said: "Tell us about these pictures. Who was the old man?"

Miss Annabelle-Lee sat back in her chair, as if preparing to make the speech she had been rehearsing ever since she had read the newspaper and the flicker of an old memory had flooded back into her consciousness. She acted now like she was dredging up a distant recollection, but actually she had been thinking of little else since the previous day.

She had daydreamed of the past as she made her supper, found herself chuckling at a picture in her mind as she watched the evening news and, as she sat in her nightdress on the side of her bed, she had idly opened a drawer in the cabinet beside it and, from deep inside, below the Bible, the spare spectacles and the tubes of aspirins, had pulled out a small, creased photograph of a smiling blonde-haired young man in a white open-necked shirt standing next to a pretty dark-haired girl – herself – long ago.

She had propped it against a book on the bedside, next to her alarm clock, so that it was the last thing she saw that night and the first when she woke the next morning. Jim, she'd thought, oh Jim. He was the first and suddenly he seemed more vivid than any of her three husbands. She had used to think of him a lot but that had faded into a distant ache, except for now when the Dispatch-Messenger's little story had brought it all back.

"Well, I don't know," Miss Annabelle-Lee said to Gene and Izzie, lying. "I don't know that I do remember that much." The lie was because she wanted to spin it out, as if she didn't want to let go of the memories, but just spill them gently to this nice young couple. "The old man Alfred Barker was the grandfather, I believe. He and his daughter and his son...his son – what was his name? – Jim, I think. They lived here in this house together. I am talking back before the War of course, when I used to know them. That's the Second World War, naturally.

"The grandfather had been a photographer, I guess. And – hard to believe now, I know – he'd been in the Civil War, so I suppose he took the photographs. He must have been in his eighties or nineties when I knew him though. Just a bit older than I am now...."

She gazed past them through the window. "I got to know them through Jim, yes Jim – that was his name." She was in danger of overacting the memory bit now. "Alfred was a funny, crusty old soul. A bit smelly – I don't think he washed too regularly – but then everyone smelled a bit in those days, especially in summer, if they didn't make an effort. He didn't change his clothes often enough – I do remember that. I don't recall him taking photographs, except once, but I can remember him talking about the war and showing his photographs.

"He seemed to think they were precious, but Jim and I didn't take much account of them, as far as I can recall. We were just young and it was ancient history. And then one day the grandfather just gave me these pictures! I hadn't thought he had paid me any attention – just a girl and all – but he must have seen something. I don't know, maybe I reminded him of someone he had known. Perhaps that's what it was. Anyway, I don't know why he did it. And I don't know why I saved them either, all these years, cluttering up the place. Maybe it was to a purpose – to give them to you! That's what it must have been! And now I have, and they can clutter up your place instead of mine!"

Then she stood up briskly: "Well I must be going. I have a bridge game to go to and I mustn't keep my partners waiting." Gene and Izzie would not, they agreed later, have been surprised if she had said the game was poker.

Izzie told her she must come back, come to supper, come for tea, anything. They wanted to hear more about her career in Hollywood. All about her....Izzie sounded almost desperate: this was by far the most interesting person they had met since they moved here and she didn't want to let her go.

"Well, maybe I will come back," said Miss Annabelle-Lee as she made her way back down the hall. "Thank you for the muffin. And the drink. And the tea."

At the door she turned and took Izzie's hand and shook it earnestly. "I am so glad the photographs have gone to a good home. I am *really* pleased about that – like they're coming home. Yes. I will come back. Thank you and good-bye."

As she said the last few words she turned abruptly and started across the porch, pertly waving the fingers of her left hand over her shoulder as she did so. Gene and Izzie watched her as she mounted her bicycle and wobbled down the drive to the road, turning straight onto the highway without looking left or right. Nor did she look behind to give them a last wave.

What they did not know and could not see was that a tear was trickling down her cheek. She didn't like to show emotion in public. Damnation, she was thinking. Those damn memories had affected her more than she had realised. She hadn't told them all she knew, far from it, and she did not know whether she ever could. She was pedalling harder than she'd realised as she went down the road, harder than she'd ever tried to do for years, but she was not thinking of the road, or the traffic – at least not as it was in 2002.

"Damn," said Gene as they closed the front door. "We never asked how we'd get in touch with her again, or where she lives."

"Well, if she's for real, she shouldn't be hard to find," said Izzie. "How many eighty year-old Tour de France winners can there be in Springbridge?"

CHAPTER EIGHT

Annabelle-Lee was still thinking of Jim as she carried her bicycle through the front door of her small terraced house at home and parked it in the hallway and she would go on thinking about him all evening.

After that meeting in the woods, she had soon seen him again at school. In fact, she had spotted him before he saw her and he had looked startled when she confronted him in the corridor.

"Hello," she'd said. "How's the war going?"

And he had blushed red and just said, oh. He had not looked her in the face, but had stared past her at the wall. She could see she would have to make all the running, but there was something about him that made her want to do so. He was vulnerable and sad and lonely and she felt she could do something about that. And he was really quite good looking, with his blonde hair, blue eyes and long dark eyelashes. Maybe he could be interesting as a pet project and, if he turned out not to be so, well, nothing was lost.

"Do you want to walk me home one day?" she had said, straight out.

"Oh. No – I mean, yes. No I can't. I have to get home," he had stammered.

But after school, at the gates that afternoon, he had changed his mind and been waiting for her. There was something electric and vivacious about her that excited him. She had a direct manner and a funny way of speaking that he found interesting and charming. And she was pretty and, most amazing of all, she seemed to be interested in him for some unfathomable reason. So he carried her books and they walked in awkward silence, neither knowing quite how to start a conversation with the other. Eventually, she had said: "Do you like school?"

No, he'd said, he got teased and he just was not interested in most subjects, except history. He liked that. And then suddenly he said: "My grandfather fought in the Civil War, you know."

And she had said, so had hers. In fact, she had recently moved to Springbridge to live with him, her parents being abroad, missionaries in China. They had wanted to move her back home to safety and here she was. Our grandfathers should meet, she had said, they would have a lot to talk about.

Jim had thought so too and suddenly his conversational floodgates had opened. He was telling her all about the battle of Gettysburg for some reason, in considerable detail, a lot of it gruesome – more than she had wanted to know anyway. He had known the most arcane facts about it and could not stop telling her, as if she was at a public lecture, even as they stopped at her grandfather's gate. When she had told him she must go in now, he had seemed to be surprised to be interrupted in the middle of his interesting monologue and then blushed again in embarrassment and stammered apologies. She had found that rather endearing. He had asked if he could carry her books home again, and she had laughed and said yes. The truth was, she had been lonely for company too, being a stranger in town, from a foreign land.

Later on, Jim remembered that encounter rather differently. He would have insisted that he saw her first and volunteered to carry her books home. But he would have winced at the thought of the public lecture on the battle of Gettysburg. That would come back to him too, but with awful clarity and even years later he would blush at how boring he must have been in his teenage seriousness and how excruciatingly embarrassing. He must have bored her to tears! It was like a twist in his guts and he would find himself clenching his fists until the whites of his knuckles showed What, *what* must she have thought of him?

And yet, they met again the next day to walk home together, then the day after that, then every day. And at the lunch break they would eat their sandwiches and cookies together in the school yard. And she would make him laugh. He was still awkward and gauche and prone to blushing, but they made a pair together.

Then one weekend that summer, they had arranged to meet up in the woods and go for a walk. It had to be clandestine, of course and both slipped out of their homes early and made for the clearing by the fallen tree where they had first met.

Annabelle-Lee had been first to get there and she was sitting on the log swinging her legs when Jim arrived carrying his most treasured possession, a large volume entitled *Harper's Pictorial History of the Civil War*. It was a heavy book, made up of the articles and dispatches which Harper's Magazine had published during the war and, interspersing the gray acres of text, there were line drawings made by artists: battlefields and scenic views, portraits of generals and statesmen and maps of the campaigns. The artists could get close to the action, Jim explained carefully so as to protect Annabelle-Lee, because some of it was quite gruesome.

Then he showed her anyway: a full page picture of Confederates bayonetting helpless black Union soldiers, wild-eyed men slitting negro throats at the Fort Pillow massacre. It had always made his blood boil, but Annabelle looked at the picture quite calmly with only a polite show of interest.

It was a strange way of wooing. After a while, as they sat next to each other, their backs against the log and the book spread out before them, Annabelle-Lee suddenly looked Jim full in the face and said to him, quite seriously: "Would you like to kiss me?" Actually, she had no more experience of kissing, or being kissed, than he did, but she thought she'd like to try it.

Jim had looked shocked and blushed. He didn't know what to say. He knew kissing was what boyfriends and girlfriends did but it had never occurred to him why, particularly. At home, his mother would kiss him goodnight, but that wasn't this: it was just a polite peck on the cheek. This must be different, but he didn't know how.

There was a pause which made her think she had totally misjudged the situation and then he said: "If you like...yes, I would. Yes, we could...." But, when he still made no move, she reached across and kissed him, lengthily, full on the mouth, not a peck out of politeness, like her parents, or her grandfather would have kissed her. "Oh!" he said. "Oh!" Then they kissed again.

Jim thought, oh boy, this *is* different. This sort of kissing lasted and their mouths formed a seal together. He caught his breath and found himself breathless. He felt tingling and his heart was pounding. He put his arm towards her waist and she did not object. Was this the right way to do it? And then they were embracing and hugging each other close and her arms were around his neck and she wasn't complaining. And then they were kissing again and he didn't want it to stop.

Then, as they kissed a third time, there was a rustling in the undergrowth and a cough. They pushed each other apart in shock and embarrassment and there was Jim's grandfather, leaning against his walking stick, watching them.

Strangely, he did not seem particularly cross. "Errrm," he said. "I am not sure you should be doing that. Jim, you be careful. You too, young lady. Not unless you're his intended. You're not old enough. That sort of thing can lead to...things. Now, don't let me catch you again."

Then he chuckled, gave a wink and resumed his morning stroll, giving a nearby bush a swish with his stick and calling back over his shoulder: "You hear me? You be careful. And you watch out for that book: I don't want it torn."

But Alfred was still smiling as he made his way slowly back up the field to the house. He sat down heavily at the kitchen table, undid his vest, and told Mary what he'd seen.

She was shocked: "My Jim? I hope you stopped him right there. I can't believe it."

"Of course I stopped him. I told him – no telling where it might end." Then he added: "Probably good for him though. He don't have many friends, does he? Maybe this will sharpen him up, put some lead in his pencil, eh?"

"Father, don't speak like that! How could you? What was the girl like, who was she, could you see? Oh my God!"

"I didn't notice. Probably no better than she should be. Anyway, I don't expect any harm's been done. It was only kissing. Not the other thing. Don't 'spect he knows about that yet, unless you've told him, 'cos I ain't. He's a sensible lad...They had my old Civil War book with them – that ought to kill any passion. Heh?"

Back in the woods after being discovered, Jim and Annabelle-Lee sat up and straightened their clothes, all passion spent. Jim said: "I guess I'll walk you home. Probably better not go back to my place yet. My Mom'll kill me."

He picked up the book and they slowly made their way, mostly in silence, back into town to Annabelle-Lee's house.

It was a grand brick building, two storeys high with a red-tiled roof, set back from the road behind a neatly-cut lawn and at the front there was a wide porch running the length of shady side of the building, set behind white wooden pillars. On the porch there was a swing seat and on the seat was sitting Colonel George Quincy Putnam, Annabelle's grandfather, reading a newspaper.

They had not bargained for him being there. The colonel was easily the richest man in town, owner of the local newspaper, landlord of most of the shops and offices, head of the largest local law firm and chairman of the biggest lumber company in the county. He had a finger in most local pies and what he didn't know wasn't knowledge. Most days there was a queue of folks waiting outside his office for a consultation on their affairs, advice on their disputes or an appointment about local matters. People joked that a leaf did not fall on Main Street without his permission and that Springbridge should really be renamed Putnamville in recognition of his services. They also murmered about his fearsome temper and warned that he was not a man to cross or thwart.

The colonel, a thin, distinguished-looking man with sweeping white moustaches, looked up and smiled to see his granddaughter, but the smile faded when he saw she was with a young man. "Hello," he said, "Who's this?"

"Grandfather, this is Jim – James – he's from school. He was showing me his book about the Civil War..."

The old man perked up. She knew the way to pique his interest and he peered through his spectacles. "Ah. The Harper's history. Where did you get that from?"

They were beside him now on the stoop. Jim silently offered the old man the book and he began leafing rapidly through the pages until he found what he was looking for. He stopped at a picture showing a battlefield: houses burning in the distance, troops milling about, soldiers checking the dead and injured and carting a man off on a stretcher. "There – battle of Fair Oaks Farm. 1862. I was there: 'course it didn't look a bit as clean as that..."

Jim's eyes opened wide. "You ought to meet my grandfather, Alfred Barker," he said. "He fought in the war too."

"Barker? Barker? I don't recognise the name. What regiment was he in?" And then light dawned: "Do you mean the photographer chap? Who used to have the studio in town? He was never in the war. At least, not fighting it. No boy, you can't count him among the honoured veterans. I know of him and I know that." The colonel snapped the book shut and handed it silently back, as though it was tainted.

Jim turned and ran home, not even stopping to say goodbye to Annabelle. He felt furious and humiliated but scared too. And he could weep to think he must have lost Annabelle's friendship. After what had happened that morning, that would be too terrible for words.

By the time he got home he was red in the face and crying. He burst through the front door and ran straight up the stairs. His mother said: "Jim I want a word with you..." as she emerged from the kitchen on hearing the sound. But all that could be heard at that moment was his bedroom door slamming upstairs.

CHAPTER NINE

Jim flung himself on his bed in embarrassment and humiliation. He could not understand what the colonel had said – surely his grandfather had been a hero in the Civil War? He had fought in it and his rifle hung above his bed, as plain as a pikestaff. There could be no mistake. His girlfriend though would probably never want to see him again. She would have been poisoned against him by her grandfather. She would of course despise him and his family, because they were poor and because it seemed they were not as they said they were.. It was a gulf which could never, ever be bridged. He could feel the tears running down his reddened cheeks and his sobs jerked his body until he gasped.

After a while there was a gentle knock on the door. "Go away," he cried, but instead the door was quietly opened and his grandfather stood on the threshold. "What's the matter, old chap?" he said.

Jim sat up slowly and wiped his nose and eyes on his handkerchief. Then he told his grandfather what had happened, culminating in an accusatory: "So you weren't ever there, in the war. You weren't a hero at all."

Alfred sat down beside him on the bed and tried to put an arm around his shoulders. It was the first gesture of touch or comfort he had ever offered the boy, but Jim squirmed away.

They sat in silence for a while and then Alfred said: "That damned old man. It's not right what the Colonel says. I was there. I seen it all. Just didn't fight is all. I was doing a job of work, not killing people. Vital work, telling them, the public – showing them – what war is like. We were pioneers, see, people like me. No one had taken photographs like them before, ever. I can show you, if you like, one day....

"Putnam just wants to govern this town and rule everything that goes on here. He don't even allow that people can have other opinions from his own ideas. Well, he ain't going to have it all his own way, sorry Jim when you're sweet on his girl, but he ain't."

Silence descended again. Jim's snuffles gradually subsided, though his eyes remained red. Finally, his grandfather said: "All right. Come with me."

They went down the corridor, past the old framed photograph of their house when it was newly built and into his grandfather's room. Alfred pointed to a box under his bed and said: "Could you haul that old trunk out for me?"

It was a large black tin box with AB painted on the top. Now the old man collapsed down onto his knees beside it and, coughing from the dust that had been stirred up from the lid, he pulled out a key from his vest pocket and opened it up. Inside were the rows of photographic glass plates and, squashed in along the side, a buff manilla envelope of photographs.

"Here," he said, putting on his spectacles. "I took these pictures. They're mine, from the war. I took them for Mr Brady and Mr Gardner. They're my treasure."

Jim pored over the photographs of the generals and encampments, the landscapes and the troops.They were like some he had seen in books, but the reproductions were not good and some of them were blotched and hazy, slightly out of focus and taken at a slant. He said softly: "So you *were* there."

His grandfather bristled: "Of course I was. Did you ever doubt it? Never thought I'd have to prove it, to my own grandson."

Jim shuffled through the prints. Even though they were faded to a light brown colour and the images on them were shadowy, he could see there were pictures taken on battlefields. Several showed dead men, lying scattered across misty fields. Others showed buildings: the Capitol in Washington with its dome unfinished, a street scene with small blurred figures caught in the act of crossing the road, a clapperboard church with a great hole in the side. The prints had short inscriptions on strips of paper pasted along the bottom, all written in the old man's handwriting; several were quite poetical.

One of the pictures showed President Lincoln, pictured in a studio, looking careworn, deep lines etched on his face, under his dark eyes and, grimly, around his mouth. Alfred stared intently at the picture as Jim looked at it, almost as if he was willing the president back to life. The boy could sense his grandfather's hot, musty breath as the old man leaned over his shoulder.

"*You* took President Lincoln's portrait?" he asked, unable to conceal the incredulity in his voice.

"Yes, well. I was certainly there. I prepared the plate so I as good as took it. I was in the room. I think Mr Gardner actually operated the camera. But I helped. It's almost as if I took it."

The old man had the print in his hands now. They trembled slightly. He hauled himself up creakily from the trunk and sat back on the bed, sighing deeply. He said: "I wish I could have taken a portrait as good as Mr Gardner. He could *see* a composition somehow and I just couldn't. If I'd taken a picture of Mr Lincoln, I'd probably have got it in focus but, I don't know, I'd somehow have missed the majesty of the man. He'd just of been a man, not a president. Not *the* president."

He was talking almost to himself. "That's what always fascinated me, Jim, you see, the artistry. That's what I wanted to do but I just wasn't much good at it myself. Oh, I mastered the technicalities alright, eventually, but really I was never more than a journeyman photographer. A photographer's boy, really. I couldn't see the composition, see? Mr Gardner, or Mr O'Sullivan, or Mr Brady himself, could go out and compose a portrait or a scene and fix it like an artist and it would be brilliant in its detail. I could take a picture, but it just wouldn't be the same. I'd get the thing in the middle all right, but somehow it did not live. It was not poetical. It was mundane. Well, I set up in business later in Springbridge. I could take people's pictures, but I wasn't much good at it really. It was not that I was not interested – I was fascinated by the technicalities – but I just could not see the character in their faces, or, in the war, spot the event to make it memorable. No artistry, you see. That's the truth of it."

Jim said: "Why did you take photographs of all those dead bodies, grandad?"

Alfred looked puzzled. "It was just that the public liked them. Couldn't get enough of them. They thrilled them and thrills are good for business. We had queues around the block when we had pictures of stiffs.

"Those photographs brought people into the gallery and then they bought them and not just the pictures, but *stereos*. You slid them into a little viewer and that merged two pictures in one and it looked like they was coming out of the frame at you. Oh yes, that was very popular. If you'd been there and seen the actual bodies, you didn't want to see them again but I guess they went down well in New York or Boston. Whenever we got to a battlefield just after an action we made a beeline for the dead. Anyway, if we saw a body we had to take its picture because those were the photographs that sold best, for some reason.

It wasn't ghoulishness – it was just business."

Then he said: "I have something else to show you. It's the rarest thing in the world." And he reached into the trunk and brought out a photograph and its glass plate, which had been kept separately from the rest, wrapped around with a piece of ragged cloth.

"Here," he said. "What do you think of this? You asked if I knew President Lincoln. Well, I did – both dead and alive. What do you think this is?"

He passed Jim the glass plate that he had drawn out. The shadowy image seemed to show a figure lying down with other figures looking at it. It did not seem to make much of a composition.

Then Alfred silently passed over the paper photograph. Now Jim could see what it was: a picture of a man in his coffin with two soldiers looking down reverently at him. A Stars and Stripes flag hung limply behind them. And it was not just any man. Jim could see it was Abraham Lincoln. He gasped.

His grandfather was beaming with pride. "That's a unique picture, Jim. It's the president after he'd been killed. There's not another like it in the world. And no one has seen it for 70 years. I've got the only plate and I've got the print, so it's all mine. No one else in the world knows about it."

"Where did you get it?"

"I took it, of course. At least, Mr Gardner and me. In the White House, the morning after it happened. But they never let us show it to anyone and I've kept it to myself all these years."

Alfred looked sideways at him and said defensively: "It's a historic document anyhow. And now everyone's dead, I kind of think it might be worth something to sell. I am sure people'd like to buy it now if I can only work out how to do it. Do you think it might be worth a few dollars to us?"

Then he said with great seriousness: "No one must know. I don't want the FBI coming after me and locking me up. I am going to spring it on the world one day. And sell it. But meantime don't speak of it. At all."

At that moment, they could hear Jim's mother calling from downstairs that supper was ready. Alfred put his finger to his lips to enjoin silence and he added in case he had not made himself quite clear, or that the walls were listening: "Now Jim, not a word to anyone, you hear? Not to your Mom. Not to your young lady friend. This is our secret and you've got to keep it." And he wrapped the plate and the photograph back in its cloth and placed them carefully back in the box.

CHAPTER TEN

"So who is she, this young lady of yours, Jim?" his mother asked as she cut up a slice of chicken pie when they were sitting around the kitchen dining table. "Father says he saw you together in the woods."

Jim blushed. "She's just a girl at school Mom," he said.

"And a pretty one," said Alfred with a wink.

"But who is she? Who are her people?" Mary persisted.

Jim was reluctant to tell his mother too much in case she waded in in some futile and embarrassing way. He was embarrassed anyway, to have been found out and in despair because he thought he must have lost Annabelle's friendship and so whatever his mother thought was irrelevant.

"Her grandfather's Colonel Putnam. That's who she lives with. She's just someone I know and she's very kind and nice. Don't press it, please Ma."

There was a slight intake of breath at the mention of the colonel's name. "I see," said Mary. "I guess I'd better go and see him at once. I am not sure you should be seeing her. They're too good for the likes of us. I think you should keep away Jim. I don't want you getting in too deep and getting hurt."

" 'Ornery old buzzard," said Alfred. "That man's never done me a good turn in his life."

"I'll go and see him straight after supper...." Mary said. "And I'll say it's not your fault."

Jim was horrified. "No Mom, please no. Don't. Don't embarrass me.

There's no need. It's nothing. Just don't....please, no."

But his pleading did not do any good and an hour later, Mary and Jim were ringing the doorbell of the big house downtown, standing on the same porch where he had shown the colonel the book that afternoon. A black maid opened the door and led them into the hall. "Don't sit down," hissed Mary, so they stood uncomfortably, rocking on their heels on the highly polished wood floor under a large oil portrait of the colonel in his younger days glaring defiantly out at the world. The ticking of a grandfather clock at the foot of the staircase by the far end of the hall was the only noise.

After several minutes, which seemed to run the length of hours, a door opened and the colonel came out. "Yes?" he said, making little attempt at a welcome.

Mary bobbed slightly. "Excuse me, sir, good evening. I've come about my son, here, Jim – James."

"Ah yes. I met him today. What of it?"

"Well sir, he's come to apologise for seeing your granddaughter without your permission. It won't happen again, sir, and he knows it was wrong. That's what I have come to say."

The colonel said: "I see," and there was a long silence. He turned to look appraisingly at Jim: "Well, young man and what do you have to say for yourself?"

Jim had been looking at the clock and from that his eyes strayed up the staircase and, at the top of that, silently, Annabelle-Lee had materialised. She put her finger to her lips and shook her head.

"Well, sir? I am waiting."

Jim shook his head vigorously and lowered his eyes, but what he said was: "I am very sorry for seeing your granddaughter without permission." Up the stairs, he could sense rather than see that Annabelle was shaking her head too. Then something made him add: "We were only discussing schoolwork, and, and, the Civil War, like in the book I showed you."

"Yes," said the colonel testily, "And telling her lies about your grandfather's heroism, no doubt. The man's a scoundrel – he's not a hero. His word is not to be trusted, frankly and you'd do well to remember that. He wasn't in the war at all – he was just a rascally photographer, a camp follower, a hanger-on. A parasite. I know who he is." His voice was rising now.

Then suddenly there were two voices. It was Mary's turn and her voice was rising too, in outrage. "How dare you, sir! That is my father you are talking about and I won't have it. He's as good a man as anyone in this town and not only did he fight in the Civil War, but he was present at just about every battle in it. He is no fraud and you have no right to speak like that."

Mary's face was as red as the artificial cherries on her hat and they were wobbling too. Out of the corner of his eye, Jim could see that the maid had sidled out of the kitchen at the end of the hall following the sound of the raised voices.

"I'll speak how I wish in my own house, madam," the colonel was shouting now. "And I won't be addressed like this! The fact is, your father is a fraud...a...a... tradesman. Little better than a black. And I won't have Annabelle mixing with you, or your son!"

Jim could see the maid flinch at the colonel's words and, at the top of the stairs could sense Annabelle scowling and gesturing angrily in the direction of her grandfather's back.

"That's fine," his mother shouted back. "My son is a good and honourable boy, who's been well brought up and he won't mix where he's not wanted. We live in the Land of the Free, sir, where everyone is as good and equal as the next man, or woman, whatever you pretend. He'll grow up to spit in your eye. Come along, Jim, the air in here is fractious and I can see our politeness is spurned. I wish we had not come here to be insulted."

She turned on her heel, but before the colonel could reply, she pointed in his face and said, coldly now: "Not every man who claims a fancy rank for himself fought in that war, though many pretend. My father can prove he was there by the photographs he took. I doubt that everyone who says they're a veteran could do the same. Good night to you."

With that, Mary swept out under full steam, trailing Jim in her wake and leaving the colonel spluttering behind her. As he followed, Jim looked up to see Annabelle smiling broadly and clapping noiselessly. At the foot of the stairs, the maid slammed the door rather too loudly for her own good as she made her way back to the servants' quarters.

Outside, in the cool night air, Mary leaned against the gate post to regain her breath and her composure. She was shaking. Jim reached for her hand and squeezed it. "You were wonderful Mom. You told him a thing or two."

She looked at her son and smiled. "Oh God, Jim," she said. "I'm sorry. I went there to apologise, not to argue and I didn't mean to do it. It doesn't do to offend him. But I won't have that old man insulting us and deriding your grandfather. Nobody does that without me fighting back. I won't have it. Alfred's got his faults, God knows, but no one despises him and gets away with it, however high and mighty they are round here.

"I am sorry Jim. It's cost you your girlfriend. But I couldn't help it....Now,

I'll just get my breath back and we'll go home."

Inside the house, the colonel was smarting. He looked up and saw Annabelle grinning and gestured at her angrily: "Get back to your room," he said.

But inside the colonel was shaking too. The encounter had rattled him. Inside his own home too. He went to a cabinet in the parlour and poured himself a large whiskey. He noticed his hand was shaking so that the decanter rattled against the edge of his glass tumbler. "Why did I have to get into that?" he thought. "There was no need. I didn't need to lose my temper. I shouldn't have in front of a lady. I was provoked." The boy was clearly not suitable for Annabelle. But he should not have been so brusque, That was taking protectiveness too far. Then he said aloud: "Oh God! Oh God! Blast it. Damn!" and drained the glass in one.

CHAPTER ELEVEN

Jim was more distracted than ever in school, especially as he tried to avoid Annabelle for fear of what she might say to him.The knowledge that her grandfather disapproved of him and his whole family caused him to despair and if he saw her in the distance, he hung his head and turned in the opposite direction.

There were daily humiliations in lessons. His grades were bad and getting worse and he just wanted to leave school and find a job, any job if there was one to be had in the tide of the Depression when grown men were out of work. There had even been the shame of his mother being called in to see the high school's principal in his panelled office. "James just isn't working," he had said. "He really needs to buck his ideas up. Or perhaps he is just wasting his time, and ours?"

"Oh no," Mary had replied. "I want him to stay and get an education. He will need the grades for a job. I'd like him to try for a teacher, or a job in a bank... he's a good boy and he's bright. He's just dreamy. You need him to concentrate." And she had glared meaningfully at Jim.

Then there came the day when the class was discussing Abraham Lincoln and the Civil War in history and Jim had wrenched himself away from looking out of the window long enough to say to nobody in particular: "My grandfather knew Abraham Lincoln. He took his photograph.."

This was news greeted with ribald disbelief by the rest of the class. "Are you sure of that James?" the teacher had said. "I don't think that can be true."

"It's just fantasy, sir," one of the other pupils cried. "He's always dreaming.

"No, it's true," Jim had insisted, growing red as usual. "In the White House at the end of the war. After he'd been shot..." And he realised he had said too much and could go no further.

The class rang with mirth as the teacher rebuffed that idea: "Now I know that's not true James. No one takes photographs of dead men! Especially presidents! What nonsense. There are no such photographs otherwise we'd have seen them in the textbooks. Just quit making things up...You are being absurd. Don't try to make yourself look bigger than you are. We're not impressed, are we class?"

No sir, they had loyally chorused, making Jim feel more isolated and humiliated than ever.

Even the portrait of Abraham Lincoln looking sternly down on the class from above the teacher's desk seemed to view Jim's claim with disdain. No one believed it was true and Jim had to acknowledge to himself that he would not have done so either, had he not seen the photograph for himself – and it was the one thing he could not share with anyone else.

After the class, the teacher called on Jim to stay behind as the others sloped out with their books. He was a kindly man, but he said: "Look James, I can't have this. First of all you are day-dreaming in class and now you come up with a cock and bull story about your grandfather. You've got to click out of this, otherwise you'll just end up a bum. Do you understand? You have got to knuckle down and concentrate and give up on lying. When are you going to make something of your life? "

The words stung. Jim bit his tongue. He wanted to say it was all true, but that would just open a whole new argument and he had been sworn to secrecy. So, even at the cost of being thought a liar, he stayed true to his grandfather and just said: "Yes, sir," and scuttled out.

One day in high summer, some weeks after the Lincoln humiliation and a couple of months since the encounter with the colonel, Alfred, Mary and Jim were having breakfast when there was a knock on the front door. Jim was sent to see who it was. It was Annabelle. "Can you come out with me today?" she asked simply, as if they'd never been apart.

There was no need of a second invitation before Jim had his jacket on and was heading out the door, with a hurried "bye" to his mother, shouted back across the hall before she had a chance to put a stop to it.

They walked down the lane, away from town and cut across the edge of a wheat field. "What have you been up to?" asked Annabelle. "I've missed you."

Jim said: "I thought you didn't want to see me any more, what with your grandfather and all."

"And *your* mother," she said. "That was quite some storm. Phew! I wouldn't like to get on the wrong end of her hairbrush!

"Anyway, I've decided to do what I want to do, not always what Grandfather says. And I have decided I want to see you. I like you." She laughed winningly and his heart skipped.

They made their way by a circuitous route to the log in the clearing and sat down on the shady side of it. If Alfred took his morning walk this way, they would not be so immediately visible to him as the last time.

"Are you pleased to see me Jim?"

"You bet," he said and he leaned across and kissed her and reached his arms around her. It was a long embrace, making up for lost time. Her dress was soft and silk-like and he found his hands softly stroking it. Gently, she took his hand in hers and placed it over her right breast. He felt himself quite breathless once more, his skin as charged as if an electric current ran through it.

When they finally dragged themselves apart, they sat back and giggled conspiratorially. They were free from adult rules and restrictions at least for now. They dozed and they hugged and they laughed – carefully, in case anyone could overhear – and spent an idyllic morning together, before Jim reluctantly walked Annabelle nearly to her home. They untwined their hands before they got to the town and walked apart when they got to places where people could see them and then he left her, down the street and round the corner from where she lived. With a light heart, Jim headed home too. It was as if a cloud had been lifted from just above his head.

The days that summer followed a similar pattern. If the adults knew what was happening they did not let on and decided not to try and stop them. As they watched the two heads bobbing down the edge of the cornfield that morning, Mary called Alfred over. "He's seeing that girl again," she said.

Alfred, still holding the newspaper he had been reading, said: "Good. Do him good to have a friend. Knowing Jim, it'll be innocent."

"Well," said Mary more doubtfully. "I guess so. I am certainly not going to apologise to her grandfather again. Jim's quite good enough for his granddaughter. Let him find out and put a stop to it for himself, if he wants to. I'm not going to."

"Good for you," said Alfred. "Old buzzard..."

As far as any of them knew, later, the colonel who prided himself on knowing everything, never did find out what his granddaughter was up to.

It was one morning after they had gone swimming in a distant pool and were drying themselves on a rock nearby that Anabelle asked Jim what he was going to do with his life.

Jim hadn't really given it much thought, but he had been thinking of his grandfather's photographs and so he said impulsively: "I'd like to be a photographer."

"Ooh, exciting – like your grandfather," Annabelle said. "But what sort?"

"A war photographer," he replied, not really knowing if such a specialist existed. Like his grandfather, but also like the men who had taken photographs of the Spanish Civil War that he had seen in an old copy of Time magazine which he had leafed through while waiting at the barber's shop a few days before. "What do you want to be?" he asked.

"I want to act in films, to be a movie star. Have you seen, they're auditioning all over for someone to play Scarlett O'Hara for *Gone with the Wind* in Hollywood. Not just big stars – anyone. I'd sure like that part. I bet I could play it. Or any part really. " And they both laughed: she at the audacity of her ambition and he, nervously, at the thought that she might actually get it – she really might – and be taken away from him.

On a rare afternoon when Mary was out in town and Alfred had wandered out to spend time with one of his drinking companions, so that he had the house to himself, Jim invited Annabelle inside for the first time. They crept up the stairs, noiselessly attempting to avoid every creaking step as if one of the adults would come through the door at any moment and went into Jim's room where they sat on his bed.

Jim hauled the family's old wind-up gramophone, with the curved horn, upstairs and they listened to his five records in turn, in between bouts of kissing and cuddling and dancing. There was an old, scratched recording of a Dixieland band playing jazz and the Paul Whiteman Orchestra with Bix Beiderbecke on trumpet and Bing Crosby crooning *Louisiana* and *Because My Baby Don't Mean Maybe Now* and even the record that was Alfred's favourite, of Count John McCormack singing *Jeanie with the Light Brown Hair*. The record had just started on *I Hear You Calling Me* when the bedroom door opened and there was Jim's grandfather, returned early from his jaunt and swaying slightly in the breeze. The music had been loud enough to hear throughout the house, which was what prevented them from hearing him coming up the stairs. He frowned as they quickly sat up and smoothed down their rumpled clothes.

Alfred said: "Arr. In the house too."

"It's my fault," said Annabelle quickly. "I wanted to listen to Jim's records and we thought it would be alright....It's John McCormack: he's lovely, isn't he? Do you like him?"

Alfred softened: "Yus, yus indeed. It takes me back to the old days at home...." His accent had softened into an Irish brogue.

Then she said impulsively, changing the subject: "I believe Mr Barker that you were a photographer. Jim has told me about your collection. I'd really love to see them. Would you be a dear and show them to me please?"

Alfred blinked, taken aback and working out what had brought the request about out of the blue. "Of course, my dear," he said, his accent snapping back. But he looked quizzically at Jim as if to say, you haven't told her about the Lincoln picture, have you? Jim shook his head.

They padded down the corridor to the old man's room and once more the trunk was pulled out and Alfred drew out his key and opened it up. The manilla envelope sat on top of the plates now and, without troubling to take one of the glass negatives out to show her, Alfred instead just pulled out the photographic prints. Jim noticed he did not draw out the dead Lincoln.

Annabelle gave pleasing exclamations of interest and excitement as the old man produced each picture and gave a little description of what it showed. In doing so, she won his heart.

"Wow, Mr Barker," she said when he had finished. "That is amazing, that you were there and took these. They are *good.* You shouldn't hide them away." And then she saw the old camera on its tripod in the corner of the bedroom. "You wouldn't take *my* picture, would you, some day? It would be so much better than any I could have taken anywhere. It would mean so much to me. Oh, please say you will." She fluttered her eyelashes in a way that was alluring to both Jim and his grandfather.

"Oh," said Alfred, simpering. "It would be a great pleasure, my dear. We must arrange an appointment. I need time to assemble the chemicals and find a suitable glass plate. I will make it an imperial size, just like the old days. A *very* great pleasure indeed."

"That is so kind," said Anabelle, more businesslike now. "I need a good picture for my publicity shots and an authentic photograph like the olden days would be great."

They settled on a week later and, on the appointed morning, fortunately a day of bright sunshine, she turned up promptly immediately after breakfast, fully made-up and dressed in her best cotton summer frock.

Alfred had made an effort too, Jim noticed, putting on a collar to go with his shirt – an all-but unique occurrence for a weekday – and a tie to go under the collar. He had washed and shaved and cleaned his nails, dusted his hat and trimmed the whisps of hair sticking out from under the brim, so that altogether he looked quite presentable, apart from the egg stain on his trousers. The old man had spent the previous days turning his clothes closet into a temporary darkroom too, lining the sock drawer with bottles of chemicals, abstracting Mary's tin pan for cooking Sunday joints of meat to serve as a rinsing tray and hanging a string and clothes pegs across the gap between the bar from which his trousers usually hung and the hook on the wall opposite from which he suspended his two neckties. He was ready.

"Now my dear," he said, blushing pink. "I have two plates to take your picture. Would you prefer to be outside in the sun, or in the parlour, or the hall?"

Jim watched all this, not without a slight pang of jealousy that his place was being usurped, but he could hardly complain about the care his grandfather was taking. Anabelle had opted for an inside portrait and had been seated with infinite care in one of the chairs in the parlour, Alfred fussing around her, reaching out and fastidiously adjusting her dress, smoothing it across her knees with just a little too much exaggerated care and touching her chin with great delicacy to achieve just the right tilt. Then he disappeared upstairs to prepare the plate, before clattering back a few minutes later, puffing slightly, slotting it into place and leaning forward to do the adjustments once more. When he was satisfied he retreated under the camera cape, said in a muffled voice: "Chin up... smile! That's nice," and reached out to remove the lens cap. One, two, three, four..to fifteen, before replacing the cap. Wait there, he said, and with a deep breath, gathered himself and turned to hustle back up the stairs to develop the plate.

When he returned it was with a triumphant air and a beautiful portrait. Miss Annabelle-Lee looked every inch a gracious young woman, with flawless skin and a radiant smile.

"Good," she said, appraising it carefully. "That will be a perfect publicity shot. I would like four copies please: one for me, one for grandfather – to show him how good you are – and two for MGM. They are casting for Scarlett O'Hara and I'd like to send them to Mr Selznick."

CHAPTER TWELVE

Alfred Barker, at not quite seventeen, could not believe his luck. He had escaped unharmed from the Army and his brief encounter with the enemy rebels and had, by a fluke of chance, ended up with a more congenial, warm and comfortable job than he could ever have dreamed of a few weeks before when he landed off the boat from Ireland in New York City. The privations of sleeping in the attic high above the Brady Gallery on Pennsylvania Avenue in the heart of Washington were as nothing to the farm he had left in County Tipperary, or the crossing that had tossed him and his fellow immigrants about in the hold of the ship that had taken ten weeks to carry them to New York that Spring, or his weeks in the regiment of foot.

He even began, as the stress of the recollection of the battle began to leave him, to believe he might have found his true metier in life: as a photographer for the great Mathew Brady. He graduated from sweeping the floor of the gallery, dusting the pillars and props of the studio and moving them into place for portraits, to polishing the brass door knocker and cleaning the windows to make them gleam and entice clients inside.

Then his personable manner and soft accent meant he was promoted to the more prestigious job of welcoming customers as they came through the door and leading them to the waiting room. Not the likes of the president, of course, nor important men such as senators, celebrities and generals, but certainly captains and their wives from the lower ranks. Once he had even had to escort in the colonel whose regiment he had joined and who he had last seen clinging to the mane of his horse as he galloped off the battlefield at Bull Run. The man, naturally, did not recognise him.

For all Mr Brady's vanity, Alfred loved the man for having rescued him and given him a job. Mr Brady was a small, dapper figure, self-consciously looking like an artist, and a showman. His long red curly hair, drooping moustache and trimmed beard framed his pallid complexion and the blue tinted lenses of his spectacles gave him an exotic aspect, as did his neat clothes, the linen shirts, the doeskin pants, the soft merino vests and the long handkerchief that spilled from his coat cuff. He even smelled sweet, unlike most men in those hot and steamy days, a fragrance of lavender water and cologne and a breath made fresh by sucking peppermints. It was the gestures that made Alfred smile though, the angle of his hand to his wrist and the way his long fingers extended as he set sitters to their poses.

What was most marvellous to Alfred was how precisely the portraits reflected the clients' characters, as well as how they wished themselves to look for posterity: General Winfield Scott, too old and fat to get on a horse any more, his uniform heavy with braid and his hand thrust into the edge of his coat as if he thought himself a new Napoleon; or Andrew Johnson, the bumptious senator from Tennessee – the only politician from the South to stay loyal to the Union – who arrived drunk and slumped in his seat as he tried to look impressive. Brady caught them alright in a way that Alfred later never could.

In the gallery, he ached to be shown how to make the portraits and badgered the photographers. Eventually it worked. "Right, sonny," said Jim Gibson, one of the picture men, one afternoon when trade was slack and he had nothing better to do. "The next person who comes through the door is yours. I'll guide you through."

Gibson was a genial young man, Scottish like Mr Gardner, who had got him the job on the strength of being a compatriot. Gibson was fiercely ambitious to get on.

He led Alfred into the back office and picked up a sheet of plate glass, not much bigger than a page of a book. "First you skim round the edges to make sure it's smooth. You use one of these small wet-stones for that. Otherwise you can cut your fingers to buggery." He looked sideways at his apprentice. "That's a technical term we use.

"Then you wipe the plate clean with this cloth. No stains, no finger marks, no smears, no gaps. Understand? Otherwise the picture will never take."

Alfred nodded. He had seen the care the staff in the print factory at the back of the studio took in preparing the glass, polishing it until it gleamed like a shop window in the morning.

"Right, now we go into the darkroom to apply the gloop," said Gibson. "That's another technical term, for collodion, gun cotton and alcohol. Here we go."

Inside the airless box of the room, lit only by the filter of a small orange screen covering a window, the photographer uncorked a bottle of dark, syrupy liquid like thin treacle and told Alfred to hold the plate flat at its edges. Then he poured a thick puddle several inches across onto the middle of the glass and instructed the boy to tilt it back and fro until the whole plate was evenly covered, with no rippling, or puddles. Once that was done, the residue was tipped back into the bottle.

" Now, here's the business," said Gibson. "It gets coated with silver nitrate to make the image." He slipped the plate into an enclosed tray. "And now we wait five minutes for it to take to the plate."

They stood and waited. It seemed to take an age. "Once it's ready you have ten minutes to take the exposure before it loses its stickiness. If it goes dry it's no use, you have to start again because it won't work. There, that should be about it. See if there is anyone waiting for a portrait."

The waiting room was empty. "Right," said Gibson. "We won't waste it. I'll take your picture, show you how it's done. Into the studio, quick before anyone sees us. Let's hope no one walks in."

Alfred was suddenly nervous. He didn't want to be caught by Mr Brady, sitting in the sitters' armchair. He had never had his picture taken, scarcely knew what he looked like because he'd never owned a mirror, except from catching fleeting glimpses of himself in the waiting room glass before leading guests up to the studio. He would even have had some difficulty describing himself, apart from his clothes. He believed he was tall, knew he was fair haired and people back home had said he looked like his mother, but for himself he could not tell. The thought of being fixed for all time in a photograph rather scared him. It was all right for the high-ups, but not for the likes of him.

So he said: "Mr Gibson, I could take *your* picture instead. To see how it's done."

"Get away w'you. You just watch and learn. It's not every boy who gets his picture taken in Brady's," Gibson said. "Anyway, I don't like the idea for myself. I'm superstitious. So you just sit there."

Alfred did as he was told, sitting in the congressional chair with the padded seat and the heavily carved curled-scroll arm-rests that was used for all the seated portraits taken in the studio. The back wall was plain and white, the floor was covered with a square-patterned carpet and the light shone in from a large skylight window in the ceiling behind the camera.

Gibson hastened round behind Alfred and moved a metal clamp, adjusting its height so that its prongs, like a pitchfork's, held the sides of his head in place. Then he bustled to the back of the camera, tossed the cape over his head and reached out to remove the lens cover at the front while he adjusted the focus, moving the tripod back an inch or so to do so.

"Now," he said. "Don't move. No time to lose. I'll just get the plate."

A few moments later he was back with the glass in a covered wooden frame, which he slid into place at the back of the camera's wooden box. "Don't move, not a muscle," Gibson said again, wagging his finger. Then he headed back underneath and slid out the front of the frame so that the plate was exposed. Immediately, his hand snaked out from under the cover and he delicately removed the lens cap once more. Alfred could hear him counting: "One, two, three...five...ten...fifteen. Done. Good." And the lens cap was replaced, then the cover of the frame and Gibson emerged from under the cloth.

"Come on youngster, back to the darkroom," he was almost running now. "Good job the light's good today. Can't let it dry out."

In the gloom of the darkroom, Gibson opened the frame once more and pulled out the plate which, as far as Alfred could tell, had nothing on it. Then magic happened. Gibson lowered the glass into a tray of watery developer liquid – "salts and water, boy. Ferrous sulphate. Now watch," – and as he gently swished the plate about a ghostly image started to emerge. In a little while it grew darker and darker still and Alfred recognised what must be his face looming through the liquid in negative, black face, white hair and a startled expression. Now details were forming. He could see the tangles in his hair, the button he had forgotten to do up that morning, even the bitten finger nails of the hand he had placed in front of his breast.

"This is the most lethal bit," Gibson was explaining, his Scottish accent coming out in his seriousness. "You have to fix the image with cyanide. Verr-y poisonous. It can kill you. Don't breathe it in and don't whatever you do leave it on your hands while you go and eat an apple. You've got to clean your fingers off." And he waved his own fingers in Alfred's face. They were still black, the boy noticed from the silver nitrate. He thought they looked like a negroe's and said so with a laugh.

But Gibson wasn't laughing. He said abruptly: "Don't kid about that sort of thing. It's dangerous. You don't want to make jokes. It's no laughing matter to me."

Then he rinsed the plate off in water and dried it over a burning candle before varnishing it. Then a copy could be run off on albumen paper, treated with egg white and dried in the sunlight on the roof. Gibson took the plate and put it into a new, open frame then he led the way out of the darkroom, up the stairs past the attic bedrooms and onto the flat roof at the back of the building where dozens of pictures were drying in the sun.

"It's a nice day. Good drying weather," said Gibson. "It won't take long."

And so it was that Alfred was given his first-ever photograph, a rectangular print, seven inches by nine, on stiff paper coated with albumen from egg whites. It wasn't half-bad: a black and white image which looked so vivid it was as if he was staring up from the paper, every spot and blemish and the smut on his nose clear to see, his skin as textured as in life, his hand and finger nails as grubby, his shirt as creased.

He could see it was definitely him, from the perplexed expression and tangled, unbrushed hair, dark against the background rather than fair, to the buckle of his belt, too tightly fixed around the top of his too-big pants. It was a very fair portrait and he stared at it open-mouthed. This was what he'd look like forever, to anyone who ever saw it.

Gibson stood beside him, appraising his art. "Pretty good, eh boy? Though I say it myself. You keep it and don't tell Mr Brady or Mr Gardner or they'll want to charge you. That would cost you five hundred dollars if Brady took it. Better hide it so they don't see it, I guess."

He winked. "And that's how you take a photograph. Simple: step by step. Think you could do it next time? Try doing that outdoors, perched on the back step of a what's-it wagon, wrapped up in canvas, sweating like a pig, fiddling for chemicals in the dark and getting buzzed by mosquitoes" And he laughed.

Alfred hid the photograph under his mattress in the attic, where in time it became creased and torn. He eventually mislaid it and regretted not taking better care. He should have sent a copy home to Ireland, or framed it so that years later as he grew old he could have seen what a handsome young dog he'd been once upon a time in his prime.

CHAPTER THIRTEEN

The framed picture of what she always thought of as her Scarlett O'Hara portrait still hung over Miss Annabelle-Lee's bed all those years later, having survived several homes and moves from New England to the West Coast and back again. It had faded slightly from black and white to a mellow sepia but, she had to concede, it was indisputably the best and most glamorous picture that had ever been taken of her. How quaint that it had been taken not by some Hollywood glamour photographer, but by some wheezy, smelly old octogenarian back here in Springbridge, a man more used to taking dead corpses than live starlets. Alfred Barker sure could take a good photograph though – she had to give him that. Like Dorian Gray, she'd aged but the picture in her bedroom had stayed young and handsome.

She had not been chosen to play Scarlett. She had been far too young and inexperienced for that, of course she had. But she had been to the audition in Boston and, with much determination on her part and a certain degree of influence and a little money from her grandfather, they had given her a role in the film and, on the strength of that, the following Spring she had taken the cross-continental railroad to Hollywood, at the age of 18.

"Colonel Puttnam's granddaughter to star in Civil War Epic" the Springbridge Dispatch-Messenger had said, understandably proclaiming the proprietor's interests, but of course that was not quite how it turned out. She was ultimately to play Third Girl from the left in the Atlanta bazaar sequence and had even

been given a coquettish line of dialogue to say, if you could call it that: "Fiddle-de-dee, that Rhett Butler!" But alas it had been cut and, unless you knew exactly where to look in the dance scene, for half a second, some way behind Clark Gable and consequently out of focus, you would not have realised she was there at all.

She had not regretted using Alfred Barker in order to obtain the photograph, not in the least. It was just a case of employing a man with a skill ot perform a service for her. There was nothing wrong in that. He had done it from the goodness of his heart and for the love of her grandson – whom she had herself loved, chastely, all that summer. Alfred had not charged her for his services and she didn't mind that, because he had got something out of it too: a chance to show off what he was still capable of when he put his mind to it and to prove to the colonel that he was not just some hack tradesman.

Annabelle wondered whether the original glass plate negative of her portrait had survived. She had rather hoped it had – she could have said to the Hofsettlers: "Ooh look – that's *me! What* a surprise!" But it had not been in the trunk.

They were showing one of Annabelle-Lee's other old movies on the television that night after her return from seeing Gene and Izzie. She had played a young girl in *Going My Way* – of course she'd had a stage name, not her real one – and she turned it on for old times' sake, just to catch a glimpse of what she had once looked like, during her fleeting on-screen appearance. I had nice legs then, she thought. And she realised that is how she must have looked, only less glamorous, a few years earlier when she had known Jim and that set her off again.

They had not lost their friendship at all that summer, after the photograph was taken, quite the reverse. They had continued to go out secretly: he waiting down the road from her house for her and leaving her fifty yards away at the end of the evening, by the house next but one along so that the colonel would not see.

Jim would spruce up and wear a tie and tell his mother he was going to choir practice and she'd wear her summer dress and say to her grandfather she was going to play records with her best friend Dolores. *Choir* practice, eh? Mary had thought, so *that's* what they call it these days. Then they would slope off to see a movie like *It happened One Night* or *Swingtime* at the Springbridge Kino-Excelsior, or just go for a walk, taking care that the colonel's friends did not see them.

On the way back there was a side alley between the barber's shop and the hardware store where they could furtively hug and kiss unobserved in the shadows, and she would let Jim fondle her breasts and run his hand along the outline of her bottom outside her skirt, but no further.

She'd liked that, thought Miss Annabelle-Lee, sipping her regular night time slug of Bourbon whiskey. It was all so pure and innocent then, not like later. They didn't know any better of course, but there would be a time soon when it was not enough, for either him, or her.

For his part, Jim kept his grandfather's secret about the photograph of the dead president, though for the life of him he could not really see it was so vital. Surely the FBI had more important work to do, catching public enemies and master criminals? Mr Stanton, the man who had ordered the picture to be destroyed, was long dead and so was everyone else connected with it, so would it really still be a state secret? Would Mr J Edgar Hoover creep up to their house with his G-men and their tommy-guns and demand it back before hauling the old boy off to jail, or, worse, shoot him down like he was John Dillinger or Ma Barker and her boys?

He and Alfred were connoisseurs of true crime stories in the newspapers. Would grandfather topple out of his bedroom window like Babyface Nelson at Little Bohemia and try to leg it across the fields like Pretty Boy Floyd, only to be gunned down in a hail of fire, leaving his mother, like Mrs Conkle, the Ohio farmer's wife who had given Floyd his last meal, to pose for pictures in the Springbridge Dispatch-Messenger with the dirty supper plates he'd left behind?

Well, you couldn't rule it out, he supposed, and anyway, he had given his grandfather his word of honour and that could never be broken, not even to Annabelle-Lee. So, for the moment, the glass plate remained safely wrapped up in the tin trunk under Alfred's bed.

CHAPTER FOURTEEN

Alfred instinctively liked the fearsome Mr Gardner, who managed the gallery in Mr Brady's frequent absences in New York, where he had another studio on Broadway.

Mr Gardner was a big, round-faced, middle-aged man with long, thick, black hair and a wild beard and he could have a temper when roused. "God damn it to tarnation!" he would roar if a plate was ruined, or smashed – just as much if it was his fault as anyone else's – and his whole body would shake and his hands clench into fists. He was a terrible man for swearing and shaking, Alfred decided. It did not last long, but while it did, watch out. Then the passion would seep away, almost before your eyes, the lip would purse, the foot would stamp and the breathing would become heavy. Then, "Darn and Saize it!" and a sigh and a return to the business in hand, as if honours were even between his temper and his temperament.

Alexander Gardner was certainly not someone to stand in the way of. Even at the sunniest of times he was a commanding figure with a booming voice and a strong Scottish accent. But he also had a twinkle in his eye and, actually, a geniality and gentleness of nature as his normal disposition. Alfred sometimes wondered whether he would have minded about his photograph and whether he should tell him, but the boss's stern look when he disapproved, advised him better not

Then there was Timothy H. O'Sullivan, Irish, like Alfred, young and slight, making up for and disguising his youth with a big, bushy moustache, and of course James Gibson, also young and a Scot, ambitious and reckless. Whenever he saw Alfred, he would grin conspiratorially and wink. That was good and made the lad feel part of the team. When his fingers too became stained black with silver nitrate like theirs it was like a badge of membership.

There were other photographers too of course: David Woodbury, Silas Holmes, Dick McCormick and Ned House – who had had to walk home from Bull Run without his camera or the wagon, and finally got back two days later – but it was the three big Celts that Alfred was drawn to and they seemed to accept him as a fellow foreigner. He followed them round like an anxious puppy. "We Caledonians must stick together," Mr Gardner would say. "Along with you Hibernians, of course."

In the days now Alfred would sometimes be allowed to take the carte de visite photographs of the soldiers and civilians who called at the gallery, if the other photographers were all busy, or absent. It was a mechanical job, using a big multiple lens camera which took four photographs at once. They cost twenty-five cents – far removed from the hundreds of dollars Brady could charge for his big Imperial portraits – and you got Brady's name stamped in the bottom corner. But they were routine affairs. You scarcely needed even to focus the camera since the clients all stood in the same place, against the same backdrop and the camera didn't need to move. This was just as well, as Alfred found focusing difficult, what with the image being upside down and in colour when you peered through the back of the camera.

But the best times were after the last clients had left and the daylight had faded when Mr Gardner and the others would get out the Scotch whisky bottle, pull up the studio chairs and have a gossip about the day and the war and, as often as not, Mr Brady. Alfred would squeeze into a corner and sit on a table or the floor, drawing his legs up to be as inconspicuous as possible.

"What I don't understand," said Jim Gibson on one of these evenings after the bottle had gone round several times. "Is how Brady gets the credit for our photographs? It's always a Brady photograph, never a Gardner or an O'Sullivan, or a Gibson. We might as well not even exist and he's not even there, but they're still his pictures."

"Now Jim," Gardner had replied. "It's his business and his equipment and his money that keeps us here so he's entitled to claim the credit. And he's the one with the fame, who people come to see. Whoever's heard of Alex Gardner, or Tim O'Sullivan, or even you Jim?"

"But I wouldn't mind if he took some photographs but we all know he's as blind as a bat and can't see to focus. It's just too bad."

"He does take pictures..."

"Yeah, but he turns up late and then he wants to be in them himself. You look at any picture he's supposed to have taken and like as not you'll see him standing in it. That's why Ned goes along. There'll be a line of generals and him popping up in the middle of it."

"Like a bloody leprechaun!" sniggered O'Sullivan. "It's true – you can't keep him out. People are starting to notice and what does he say to them? That he's honouring them with his presence in the picture! He's everywhere." The snigger turned into a hacking cough.

Gibson said: "What I say is that we ought to branch out on our own. He'd be nothing without us. Who goes to the front? We do! Who sleeps under the wagon when we're out in the lines? We do! Who has to eat the muck in country hotels, when we have time to get any? Who keeps on chivvying us to get back quick and get the pictures out? And all the time he's fawning round some politician or other and giving them a free sitting, for the publicity....I tell you we could clean up here, he wouldn't see us for dust. We could be making a hundred dollars a week."

Gardner poured himself some more whisky and took out his pipe, filling it slowly to give himself time to think. When it was well lit, he said ponderously: "Now Jim, that's treason talk. It's a good job there's only us to hear it. Your secret's safe with us isn't it –eh, youngster?" This last, pointing the stem of his pipe at Alfred. "I'd keep quiet about it if I was you....Let's hear no more about it."

And the talk turned to gossip about the generals and the army, the vanity of the man they called Little Mac – George McClellan, who had been the young head of the army until he had fallen foul of the president – and the arrogance of "Fighting Joe" Hooker, whose ambitions outweighed his abilities.

Gardner chuckled. "Little Mac wanted me to take him in a Napoleonic pose: he's quite the young Bonaparte and knows it. He said to me in the studio, 'My left profile's my best one, so make sure you catch it. And he didn't want to sit down because he said it made him look smaller! He's nothing but a spit...."

O'Sullivan said: "Joe Hooker's as bad. There are women all round his headquarters and he takes what he wants. They're calling them Hooker's whores. They're like a rash and some of 'em'll give you one too. Fighting Joe – you know how he got that? Because he sent a wire to Washington saying he was in a battle: Fighting – *dash* – Joe Hooker. Only the wire office left the dash out. The joke is – he *don't* fight!"

And so the night wore on, with chat and scandal and jokes and laughter and, towards the end, the old songs of home: *Flowers of the Forest*, sung softly and chokingly by big Alex Gardner and Jim Gibson and *My Love Nell*, sung as a duet by Alfred and Tim O'Sullivan, then they all sang *Lorena* before they went sniffling up the stairs, thinking sadly of the homelands they would never see again and the folk they'd left behind them.

One bright morning early that fall of '62, Washington woke to hear that the Confederates had crossed the Potomac river only twenty miles upstream of the capital and were heading north into Maryland to incite the population to rebellion there.

Slowly, three days later, the columns of marching men started out after them, mile after mile, accompanied by brass bands playing *Yankee Doodle*, squadrons of cavalry and gun teams jolting along as they dragged their cannon after them. In the rear followed supply wagons, provisions merchants, ammunition trains and surgeons and the other detritus of an army, heading for the big fight that all knew must come soon.

And, alongside them, next to the reporters and sketch artists, rumbled the photographers. Alexander Gardner and James Gibson had harnessed up their what's-it wagon outside the studio and followed the rest up the dusty road out of the city, heading into the wooded hills of Maryland where it was predicted that Bobby Lee and a whole rebel army would be waiting for them.

CHAPTER FIFTEEN

The next time Izzie spotted Mizz Annabelle, as she'd taken to thinking of her, was by chance a week later when she popped into The Age of Innocence Cafe in Springbridge to buy a cheesecake and have a cup of tea after a morning's shopping around the antique shops and the farmers' market. Annabelle-Lee was sitting at a corner table by herself, nursing an espresso and she gestured Izzie to come and join her. "My," she said, "That's quite a cake."

Izzie said that they were having friends up from New York for a couple of days to test the main guest bedroom before they started advertising it later in the Spring. "I am so glad I saw you," she said. "I needed to find a way of getting in touch because I want to know more about the family you knew at our house – the photographer and the boy you were sweet on."

"Well, I've been thinking back to those days quite a lot," the old lady confided, "And in my opinion, the most interesting person in that household was the mother. The men in that house didn't give her a lot of time, you know – men didn't in those days – and treated her like a servant, so she didn't have much chance to develop her talents: too busy tidying up the place for them.

"But she was real feisty. I saw her go for my grandfather once in the hallway of our house and tear him off a lot of strips. That took some courage because he was a powerful man in this town and had a lot of influence. I watched it happen through the banisters at the top of our stairs. She was defending her menfolk. Grandpa was in the wrong, as he was about so many things.

"Looking back now, I'd say she was stuck there in that house. Her husband had left her or – something – anyway, he wasn't there and she couldn't break away to have a life for herself: that took some doing in those days if you were a mother on your own. In fact, you could say it was her example that made me determined to get out of Springbridge myself and the first thing I did when I was old enough was – whoosh – get out of town and go to Hollywood. I always remember her saying to me in the kitchen there when I told them I was leaving: 'Good for you! I wish I could come too.' And I do believe she meant it. Well, I don't know what happened to her, but I guess she never did, except the one time I knew about, probably never again got out of state."

Izzie said: "You got about as far away as you could, if you got to Hollywood...." She wanted to coax some movie memories out of the old lady, such as, what were the stars like to work with and who else did she know. She had Googled her name on the Internet to find out who she had acted with, but the entry was frustratingly short – and it said she had died eight years earlier.

"Oh dear, I didn't get far in Hollywood. Just a few movies and a handful of lines. I never did get a studio contract. Blink and you'd miss my whole career. You can catch me in shows on the Movie Channel at two o'clock in the morning, if you really want to know, dear – but you won't recognise me. I was pretty back then.

"No, I gave up and married a car dealer who promised me the earth and boy, was that a deal! The biggest Chrysler dealership in Pomona and all he wanted to do was get inside my panties! He wanted to have a starlet and frankly, by that time, if you will pardon the expression, I wanted to be made love to too – and not just by Errol Flynn! I was lonely out there and tired of being good when no one else was. All the men used to have those little moustaches in those days, didn't they and – trust me – I fell for one of them. He turned out to be about as sexy as a windshield wiper.

"What's a well-brought up New England girl to do? The bastard – excuse me – wouldn't even let me borrow a car off the lot to go for auditions, so that was the end of *that!* I'd have been better staying here with Jim, playing summer stock, but I wasn't to know, was I? And look where I've ended up – back here and no Jim... My other two husbands were not so hot either," she added.

Izzie pressed her luck: "Did you – with Errol?" but Annabelle-Lee waved her hand dismissively. "Oh sure, but every girl in Hollywood who was half-way presentable did. And quite a few who weren't. It lasted about two minutes – and that was just the sex." Both of them were well aware of the customers at all the neighbouring tables craning to hear.

Miss Annabelle-Lee laughed throatily and turned to give a little wave to everyone and flash them a smile. "And as for Clark Gable – had every girl on the lot! Anyway," she said, leaning forward much more quietly and patting Izzie's hand. "Don't you fall in the same trap, my dear."

"Oh no, Eugene's not like that...."

"I don't mean your husband, dear, I mean getting trapped out here. Don't fall for it. Make sure you have your own life, just like he has his. Don't be like Jim's mother and wake up in ten years' time and all you're doing is ironing sheets for the guest bedroom and baking muffins for breakfast..."

"We may want to start a family before it's too late."

Miss Annabelle-Lee grimaced: "I guess I never wanted that for myself. Maybe I did when I was eighteen and with Jim. I wanted babies then, but not as much as I wanted a career...not enough. They'd be retired too by now – biggest Toyota dealer in Amherst! Best attorney in the Berkshires! Most exciting accountant in Stockbridge! – and I'd be a grandmother: my God!"

Then she said: "Be careful of that house, dear. I don't think it's been a happy home. We nearly had an escape of course: summer of '38. Our little trip to Gettysburg. That was pretty wild. I must tell you about that one time. Would you like to come to tea some day?"

At home that day with Izzie out, Gene was inspecting the bills. It was a chore he hated but he knew it had to be done, particularly if they were going to start a bed and breakfast business in the house. It was true that he was much keener on that idea than Isabelle. He could see her point of view: she didn't want strangers tramping through their home and their lives, didn't want to become a housekeeper rather than write books, or resume her city career. But some things had to be done, some trade-off for their new life in the country away from the dangers of the Big City; and if they were to keep their heads above water financially that's what they would have to do.

He could see the thing much more clearly and positively than she could, he knew that. He'd help when he wasn't flying off on assignment for the magazine, so it was not as if she would be on her own. And they would employ a girl from the town to help with the chores, clean the rooms, make the breakfasts if need be. The sooner the better really, now the bills were really mounting up. Surely Izzie would see sense about that? Of course she would!

It wasn't just the utility bills and the builders' bills – they were necessary, though inevitably more costly than they had bargained for and if you were restoring a historic house there were some things you could not skimp on, like the sash windows and the engraved glass in the front door, at a pinch even the roll-topped iron baths in the guest suites. But had they really needed to buy an early 19th Century escritoire for a house not built until half a century after that sort of furniture had gone out of fashion? What about the horsehair stuffed chaise longue in the lounge, so hard and uncomfortable and actually so rickety that no one could really sit on it? Or the polished mahogany sideboard with its great pillars and scrolls and original bevelled glass back mirror that was so heavy that it had taken five men to lever it into position on the ground floor (and the men had not come cheap either).

Whose idea was all that stuff? Who'd gone out and bought it with scarcely a word to him? Izzie, of course – oh, she'd enjoyed that spree in pursuit of her ideas about her new life as a lady of leisure. And who'd gone meekly along with it, he thought bitterly. Yes, he had. He should have kept a tighter rein on it, but then so should she.

As he looked at the receipts from Bijou Memories and the other antique shops they had raided, it seemed to Gene that the proprietors must have seen them coming and added an extra nought or two to their prices every time they had walked through the door. Hey – that would pay for those damn shopkeepers' skiing vacations in the White Mountains next winter! Wealthy New Yorkers, eh? – they'd buy anything at any price. Sure they would! Yeah – right.

He almost did not like to add up the figures and did so only roughly in his head: maybe twenty thousand dollars more than they had planned for? Rule of thumb on rough estimates: double it....

There was no doubt about it, they were nearing their limit and would soon pass it. Not only the capital from the sale of their Manhattan apartment and their savings had been eaten up, but their credit cards were maxing out too. In a couple of months – less if they went on like this – they'd be broke. The more he thought about it, sitting looking at the bills, or lying awake in bed at nights, the more frantic he became.

Something drastic needed to be done. There would have to be a showdown with Izzie about her extravagance. They would have to open the B&B as soon as possible (but that would cost money with advertising and what-not, though they could try the Internet as well – but would anyone see it there?) And, even just to tide them over, they'd have to start realising their assets. The more he thought about it, the more sense it made. They could scarcely sell the escritoire so soon after buying it and hope to make a profit, but there were those photographs...the five hundred dollars they had been offered for them by that friend of Price, the Bijou Memories man, was certainly generous.

It would keep them afloat for a month, two if they exercised real economy, just while they got themselves under way and back on an even keel. He didn't want them anyway – they were nothing to him, were they? Izzie's attachment to them was just sentimental. She'd see that. Gene felt he almost didn't need to ask her. It was so obvious. Anyway, needs must.

There, on his desk, amidst the bills was the business card that Joshua Butterfield IV had left behind in case they changed their minds about the photos. It said he was proprietor and managing director of The Cannons' Roar Emporium of Lexington, 19th Century Antiques: Militaria a Speciality. That seemed about right and Gene was reaching for his phone almost before he realised he was doing so.

CHAPTER SIXTEEN

Back at the Washington studio on Pennsylvania Avenue, they waited for the news of fighting for several days after the army and Alex Gardner left, but mostly there was silence from the front. No one in the whole city could concentrate. The clerks and officials went about their business, gossiping over their ledgers about the rumours they had heard from the telegraph office, housewives swapped stories on the sidewalks that the rebels might arrive at any minute and many of their black servants began to think about how they might best slip away northwards, beyond the clutches of the Confederates. In the White House, Mr Lincoln was engaged in constant meetings about what to do next – there wasn't one person in Washington, including the hordes of rebel spies, who didn't have a notion what to tell him – and in the barbers' chairs and the shops and offices no one could talk of anything else.

In the previous fights, at Bull Run and elsewhere close by, the Confederates had held back from venturing into the capital after they had won, even when they could see its buildings shimmering in the distance, but this time for sure, if McClellan didn't stop him, General Lee and his wild, whooping Southerners would be in the streets within a couple of days. And then General Lee would be able to reclaim his mansion across the river on the hill at Arlington and do just what he wanted with them all. The war would be lost and they would be a defeated people in a diminished and divided nation.

Dispatch riders clattered up and down the avenue outside the Brady gallery, their horses' hooves kicking up dust in the sunshine and, sure enough, one rode up to the door late in the afternoon with a telegram routed through the military department. Tim O'Sullivan tore it open.

"It's from Alex," he said, for once forgetting the dignity due to his boss. "He's with the headquarters staff and he wants me there right away, with spare plates."

Alfred seized his chance and pleaded earnestly: "Let me come too. I can help." Now he wouldn't be fighting, he was keen to see a fight. "I can wash, or hold the horses, or prepare the glass...I'll make myself useful and won't get in the way. Promise."

"All right. You'd better not. We'll take Simon too. Tell him to get the wagon ready.You get the collodion and the other stuff. Make sure it's all stocked up. And get the stereo plates for that camera. We'll leave within the hour.

"And Alfred," he added, making the boy swell with pride: "Good lad."

Simon was one of Brady's black servants. A big, strapping man with a wide grin, who habitually wore an old army kepi that he had foraged from somewhere to make himself look more official, he was one of the studio's teamsters, employed in the stables out back to look after the horses and wagons and make sure everything was made ready at short notice. The gossip was that he was an escaped slave who had come north in search of his freedom. Alfred never knew Simon's second name, because it was never used, but he had been told that it was the same as his former master's, back in the south.

When he heard where they were going, a shadow crossed Simon's face as he loaded up the wagon. Eventually, he said: "Oh master, that's fine, I guess, but you'll keep me safe from being captured won't you? I want to stay with Mr Brady." Alfred had never been called master before. It didn't seem quite right to him, being as how Simon was a good twenty years older than he was.

It was twilight as they rolled down the avenue towards the Hagerstown pike on the way north. All three of them were squashed together on the box at the front of the wagon, while on the small flatbed behind them sat a large superstructure covered by a tarpaulin, wrapped round with rope.

At the edge of the city, sentries guarding the road nervously clutched at their rifles as the wagon, bouncing on its high wheels, went through the cordon. They had decided they would get as far as they could before dusk fell and then find a field to camp in before making an early start the next morning.

Alfred remembered the next day as a golden one: a brilliant hot September forenoon with a clear blue sky above, birds singing and farmers pausing to watch them go past as they harvested their crops in the fields. The road was busy with traffic: messengers on horseback galloping past them, forward to the army or back toward Washington, units of troops trudging on and gun limbers bouncing past, their horses' bridles glinting and rattling in the sun and their crews swearing and gasping as they jolted over the holes in the road.

Gradually, as the wooded hills on the far horizon grew more distinct, they could hear a distant sound like far away thunder and then could see whisps of smoke curdling upwards in great puffs. "There's fighting up ahead," said Tim. "Come on."

The road was getting thicker with troops and more congested, just like it had been at Bull Run and it needed all Simon's skill to thread the wagon through the gaps. "What is it?" Alfred heard one soldier cry. "Photographers – let us through!" shouted Tim, and then to Alfred more quietly: "Now you know why we call it a what's-it wagon. Come on boys, clear the way. Important transport!" And, astonishingly, the path cleared.

It took them several hours yet to find the army headquarters, in a large brick, porticoed farmhouse on a bluff above a valley. As they drove up, an infantryman on sentry duty pointed them to a nearby field on top of the rise, where a number of tents had been set up and men in civilian clothes were milling about. And in the middle of a group stood Mr Gardner and Jim Gibson.

As soon as he saw them, Gardner bustled over. Without waiting for pleasantries, he said: "Thank goodness you've come. We've got a battle brewing here boys. That stuff over yonder's just skirmishing. We'll have the real fight soon. Did you bring the plates and supplies?

"You haven't missed anything yet. It's been a crazy few days but McClellan thinks he's got Bobby Lee where he wants him, over there. And, do you know, the damndest thing – the rebs dropped their battle plans in a field, wrapped round some cigars and we've got 'em! If we can't win now we never will. Best smoke ever! I think Little Mac's given one of the stogies to the soldier who found them and is going to hand round the rest when we've won..."

"When can we start taking pictures, boss?" Tim asked.

"Not yet, old man. We are not allowed further forward than this and the front line's down by the creek a couple of miles off. Lee's over the other side. We've got the jump on him this time. Now we just have to sit put and wait. I reckon it will be tomorrow."

Just then, General McClellan rode up with his staff and Alfred got a good look at him for the first time. Now back in charge of the army, he was indeed a small man with dark hair and a big moustache, but even that could not disguise the fact that he was young, no more than thirty, Alfred guessed. He didn't look short of confidence though and his chest was puffed out like a turkey cock's.

The men who had been standing about, gathered round him as he reined in his horse and they took out their notebooks and pencils. "Gentlemen," the general said, his words evidently well rehearsed. "I am glad to see you. We stand here on the brink of a great battle, one which will decide the war. Tell your readers it is my army's responsibility to save the Union, as the politicians cannot. I shall do my best and I am confident that I shall prevail. Tell your readers that – and remember to spell my name correctly!"

"Tell us the story of how you found the rebel orders again, general," said one of the reporters.

McClellan chuckled. "Boys, those are the most beautiful cigars I ever seen. They were so nicely wrapped in the orders of the day and dropped in a field just where we could find them! Well, I don't know any general who has had such good fortune in modern times! McClellan's luck! If I can't beat Bobby Lee now, you can pack me up and send me home to New Jersey!"

"Three cheers for the general!" shouted a voice and Alfred turned to see it was Pinkerton, the army's chief spy, wheeling his horse about near the back of the crowd. And all the journalists raised their hats in unison as they hurrahed.

That night the two Brady wagons were parked beside each other in the field, next to the reporters' tents and Simon foraged some branches and shrubbery to make a fire around which everybody gathered. The field was on top of a hill and stretching out across the valley in front of them they could see the army's campfires burning for several miles in each direction. Further away in the darkness other lights flickered in the distance: the fires of the rebel army.

Mr Gardner stood up, whiskey in hand, the breeze ruffling his wayward hair and gazed out over the valley. Then he flung his head back, stretched his arms wide and declaimed: "From camp to camp, through the foul womb of night, the hum of either army stilly sounds. Fire answers fire and through their flames, each battle sees the the other's umbered face and – err – steed threatens steed... piercing the night's dull ear...and, um, give dreadful note of preparation. Etc, etc," ending feebly as his memory faltered: "That's Henry V. Shakespeare, aye?"

One of the reporters gave a slow, ironic clap. "A little touch of Gardner in the night, eh – what, Alex?"

"What's he that wishes so? Ah, Forbes – I might have known it! Oh for a muse of fire!" And they both collapsed in giggles and passed the bottle round again.

As he fell asleep that night, wrapped in a blanket on the ground between the what's-it wagon's wheels, Alfred was anxious and excited, waiting to see the battle, fearful about its outcome – and relieved he would not be in the fight this time. In the distance he could hear snatches of singing and shouting and the bustle of preparations down the hill, punctuated much closer at hand by the snores and grunts and whistles of Mr Gardner, tucked up under the next wagon, fast asleep.

Alfred woke cold and stiff early the next morning, to hear gunfire and see smoke already rising in the distance. As his eyes grew accustomed to the light and he recollected where he was, through the spokes of the wagon wheel he saw Gardner and Gibson standing in discussion, looking towards the action. Gardner was saying: "Jim, there's nothing to be done. We can't go down there with all the equipment. It's too dangerous and how on earth could we ever take a picture in the middle of a battle? They won't stand still for us, you know. We've just got to wait till it's over."

Gibson replied: "When the sun comes up we might be able to get a picture from here, don't you think? Or down the hill a little way, if there's not too much smoke. No one's ever got a picture of a battle going on before."

"Well, I don't know," said Gardner and he sat down heavily on the grass. All around, Alfred could see scores of others, all gazing westwards towards the gunfire a mile off. There were reporters, artists unfolding the cases which carried their pencils ready to start drawing, officers with binoculars and telescopes, teamsters, and beside them whole families of local folk, who had driven from their farms and villages to watch, farmers and their wives and children, all gathered together with their picnics as if to view a spectacle in the theatre.

The hill top was an ideal vantage point: out of range of the guns, but not out of sight of the action, which unfolded before them as if on a distant carpet. Through the smoke, whole units of troops were marching, or running and men on horseback and gun carriages could be seen careering about. The firing had started to their right and, as the morning wore on, proceeded in front of them before rolling out as a rumbling roar on the left. Hour after hour, all day and into the evening the noise and the far-off shouting continued, the smoke getting thicker until there were only occasional glimpses, a flag here, the glint from a sword there.

The man who had quoted Shakespeare with Mr Gardner wandered over, grinning. "Hard pounding, Alex! Pursuing the bubble reputation, even in the cannon's mouth!" he exclaimed.

"Oh Edwin, do give over. This is too frustrating for words. How do you think it's going?"

"Who knows? But isn't this a glorious spot for a view of the action? I do believe this is the most picturesque battle of the war. What a spectacle! We can see the whole thing! Look at the crowd...."

All day the rumours flew. The rebels were drawing back; they'd been wiped out; the Union men were charging; they had taken the bridge across the creek... and then the twilight came on and night fell and the orange flames from the cannon finally faltered and fell silent.

The farmers and their families packed up their baskets, harnessed up their horses and turned for home as if heading back from a harvest supper, the officers wandered off and only the journalists were left, writing their copy on sheets of paper by the light of their campfires, all ready to beg, or borrow, access to a telegraph line to send their stories to New York, Washington and Chicago.

Although he had done nothing for most of the day, Alfred had discovered that even battles get wearying, battering the senses, leaving his ears ringing and his eyes raw from the smoke. He returned to his perch under the wagon and fell instantly asleep.

If anything, the following day was even worse. There had been drizzle overnight, making the ground wet, but the sun rose to burn it off and, as it did so, both sides lay in the same places where they had finished the day before, as if too exhausted to resume the fight.

A great stillness hung over the battlefield. As they looked out from the hill, the photographers could see the flotsam of the day before: clumps of colour, blue and brown, scattered across the fields of what had once been wheat ready for harvesting. It looked now as if the fields had a new harvest. Occasionally, far off, a wounded horse could be heard whinnying and later in the afternoon troops could be seen down below walking out into the meadows waving white flags as they looked for the wounded.

All day they waited for the cannonade to start again, but it never did.

Gardner and Gibson paced the hillside impatiently, arguing endlessly about whether it was safe to go forward and start work. "I can't lose you Jim, you can't go," Alfred heard Gardner say. "What if you're down there with the wagon and suddenly all hell starts up again? Even if it's quiet, you might get potshots taken at you and everything – from our side as much as the other. The enemy's still in the field. I can't let you risk it."

And so the day passed, frustrating and anxious, but tedious too. The photographers ached to start working before any rivals made it up the road from Washington. It had been a huge battle, they could tell that, and both sides were like exhausted boxers, lying against the ropes, winded but wary, eyeing each other just in case the fight started up once more. Meanwhile, in the space between the two sides, amongst the heaps of bodies, wounded and dying men and horses cried out for help.

Then, overnight, the rebel army stole away, through the deserted streets of the little town of Sharpsburg and back across the Potomac river into Virginia, leaving the field to the Union troops, who scarcely noticed their departure and were too shattered to follow. And now, at last, the photographers could descend from their hill and get to work.

The first Alfred knew was when in his deep sleep at first light he felt a kick against his boots. "Come on, wake up boy! We've got to get started," Mr Gardner was shouting. "No time to lose now. The field is ours!"

Within an hour the wagons were rattling down the hill into a scene of devastation. Army scouts had told them to head for a little church at the far edge of the fields, but to get there they had to cross a plain of corpses. Hundreds of bodies were scattered about, some in clumps, others singly, some twisted, holding hands up beseechingly to the sky in the moment of their death, others lying peacefully as if they had fallen quietly asleep. Burial parties were already moving across the fields of trampled wheat, sorting out the dead: Union men to identify and bury first, Confederates later to be shovelled into mass pits.

The photographers tied their handkerchiefs over their noses but that was not enough to exclude the smell of death and the first odours of decay. Their wagons bounced over the ground steering a narrow course between the shell holes and the corpses. "My God," said O'Sullivan repeatedly and crossed himself.

They could not stop here as there were too many people about and the dead were mostly Union men. Alfred had never seen so many bodies before, not even in the middle of the battle of Bull Run. Whole fields of men seemed to have been mowed down. He held his hand to his mouth in shock. Beside him, steering the way, Simon was slumped in his seat, shaking his head.

As they were crossing the battlefield, an elderly farmer, approached their wagons. He was very distraught and addressed himself to Gardner, almost pleading. "Who's in charge? Who's in charge here? This is my land. Look at it, sir."

Gardner eyed him beadily: "Search me," he said. "I am a photographist. I can't help you, you need military men – officers. You'll have to find them."

The farmer scarcely heard. He started wailing: "I'm ruined. Twenty years building this farm and it's all wrecked. My house is ransacked and burned down flat. There's no harvest left. We have nothing any more. What am I to do? We need compensation." He rose in his saddle as if to demonstrate the scale of his loss.

Just then, two officers rode up. "Are you being disturbed by this man, Mr Gardner?" one asked. Gardner shrugged: "He's the farmer whose land you've just fought over."

The senior officer turned and said: "Your name, sir?"

The old man took off his hat respectfully. "Mumma, sir. Samuel Mumma. That's my farm over yonder. All gone, all gone. I have eight children and a wife...I need help. Someone must pay me for this." He pointed to where the smouldering ruins of a once-large house were standing a short distance off. All that was left upright was a chimney stack and some outbuildings.

The younger officer consulted a map from his pocket. "That's right: Mumma," he said, turning to the older officer. "Not our damage, sir. It was the rebels. They were at his farm."

The senior officer leaned forward in his saddle. "Well Mr Mumma, it appears your claim is not against us, but the enemy government in Richmond. It is to them that you must make your claim for redress. It was not our men who damaged your property but General Lee's men, so you have no claim on us."

"But what am I to do? I can't go to Richmond," cried the old man, looking anguished, head swivelling desperately between the officers and the photographers. "Winter's coming. I have no harvest and no shelter. Eight children, eight children and a wife, sir."

"I cannot help that. You must make what shift you can. It is not the government's fault or our responsibility that the rebels chose to fight on your land. Good day to you, sir."

The farmer turned away in despair and trotted off. Gardner nodded to the officers, smiled ingratiatingly and said conversationally: "Poor fellow, eh? Accident of fate: hard luck that the fight took place on his land, not some other wretch's a mile away. Tragedy of war – did you catch his name? We must get a photograph of his farm."

The officers wheeled their horses away. The older officer said: "Don't worry about him. They're all damn rebels round here – that's probably why they chose his farmhouse: getting fattened up for the fight on his biscuits and beef. If that man's not got money stashed away for a rainy day he's not much of a farmer. See how much he likes the cause when he's paid out in rebel dollars." And they rode off.

"We must get on – no time for chatting," said Gardner to the others. "Drive on boys."

After half an hour or so, the photographers came in sight of a small, white-walled building on the edge of a copse. It was pock-marked with holes and from inside could be heard the groans of wounded men. A doctor was standing at the door, his shoulders hunched as he smoked a cigar. Gardner hailed him: "Where's the church?"

The man looked up, uninterested, his eyes dull and glazed. He did not answer, just nodded.

"Is this the church?" Gardner asked again, more forcefully.

Now he got an answer. "Yes, this is it," the man said. "If you can call it a church. Some Kraut sect called the Dunkers have it, though I don't expect they'll want it any more. They're pacifists, I believe. Don't look inside. You won't want to see it. I've got men dying in there and there's nothing can be done about it."

A little way off, across the road, there was a deserted gun carriage and a line of bodies, with dead horses lying about. Gardner and Jim Gibson got down from their wagon and went to look for a few moments before shouting back to the others: "Get the camera. They're rebels."

Gardner added: "Bring the stereoscope. Alfred: start preparing the plates – the ten by fours!"

It made a good composition: the simple, unadorned little church in the background and in front of it the raddled bodies and the gun carriage, so good that they took it three times, scarcely moving the camera. Alfred wrapped himself around with the tarpaulin and concentrated on spreading the collodion, so he would not have to think about what the glass would shortly depict. In the distance, muffled, he could hear Mr Gardner saying: "Good...good...excellent."

After they had been on the spot for half an hour or so, a troop of artillerymen trotted up, thirty or forty men on horses, hauling several gun carriages behind them. "You want to head up the road here a bit," their captain called. "You'll see some sights up there."

And so they did, scarcely more than 200 yards up the pike, beyond the end of the woods, the track was fringed by a wooden rail fence and scattered along it into the distance lay a line of men. They looked as though they had been trying to shelter and been caught by a volley of bullets between the gaps. There must have been several dozen men, lying in clumps, their eyes open, their mouths gaping wide, their heads turned towards each other as if in conversation while preparing for sleep.

Gardner caught his breath and looked at Gibson. "Oh, the poor wee men," he said. "Whatever were they thinking of? Come on: there's a rich harvest here." And he jumped down from the wagon.

They spent a long time working their way along the roadside with the stereoscopic camera. There were long shots and close-ups, panoramic views and pictures of the tangled bodies so intimate that their families, back home in Louisiana might have recognised them. It was gruelling work. The day was getting hot and as he sought refuge from the sights outside under the tarpaulin, Alfred could feel the sweat trickling down his nose. He had to hold his head back and work at arm's length so as not to drip perspiration onto the plates, but as he did so he could feel the flies crawling across his face. He did not like to think where they must have been shortly before and he could not swat them for fear of dropping the plates or smearing the photographic chemicals across his face. Instead he blew out of the side of his mouth, hoping that the jets of foetid air he emitted would drive them off. But it did not do so and he had to keep working, feeding the obsessive demands of the cameramen even as the insects crawled into his eyes and across his nostrils.

He thought he must faint at any moment and at last, having a few moments to spare, he emerged from the tarpaulin to breathe. He inhaled huge gulps of air, but as he did so became aware of the stench outside, the sweet, sickly odour of the deteriorating corpses, human and animal, lying all around them as far as the eye could see, bodies now two days old and swelling in the sun. He ducked back under the tarpaulin and the whole cycle began again.

At length, Gardner was satisfied. They had reached the end of the line of bodies and turned the wagons back towards the centre of the battlefield, sated with death and satisfied with the images they had produced so far.

Alfred could not quite understand why they needed pictures of dead bodies. They were pretty horrible and grotesque and surely not the sort of thing to show people who could not see them for themselves. If you were taking photographs of the battlefield at Antietam Creek that day, it was hard to avoid getting bodies in the pictures.Why would you want to buy a copy to look at in your pleasant parlour in New York City? What would you say to your men friends: "Come and look at my terrible pictures of the battle?"

In his mind, Gardner was turning over the captions which would sell these gruesome pictures to the Northern public. They had a truth as a description of what had happened but they had to have a moral purpose too: to evoke a sentiment and provoke a thought beyond revulsion. He found himself thinking, the Devil's highway..no, fence of death...no...harvest, harvest of death.... cut down...cut down by the scythe....no, before the scythe...no, that did not make sense....a hornet's nest of bullets, a rain of death? Hmm, something like that. And as the wagon lurched over the ground, its wheels slipping on the flattened wheat and dipping into the dark brownish puddles that had formed in the hollows between the stalks, he found himself muttering aloud: "Terrible, terrible. Oh God." But whether that was because of the sights they had seen, or his efforts at composition, he was not clear.

Just then, two soldiers in shirt sleeves, leaning on shovels, hailed them from the side of the path. "Hey men! You men photographers? You ought to get a look over there. That'll bust your camera," one shouted, pointing towards a burial party some way off.

The wagons veered towards the group. The men were standing on the banks of a little sunken lane, staring dully downwards. It seemed full of bodies, yard upon yard, stretching up an incline to the top of a slope a hundred yards or more off. They were not scattered randomly as over the rest of the battlefield, but knee deep all the way, close enough to hug each other, tangled together like a lumpen floor.

Gardner turned around. His companions looked stunned and white-faced. "Get the cameras down boys," he said.

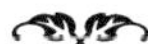

The pictures of the Dead of Antietam caused a sensation when they were shown in New York a month after the battle. There were queues down the street, all along Broadway, from Brady's National Portrait Gallery at number 785; men of business in their suits and top hats, their wives and sweethearts in their crinolines, clinging excitedly to their arms and chattering about what they were about to see. This was bringing the thrill of war home without the bother of traipsing round a messy battlefield hundreds of miles away and holding a handkerchief to one's nose as one surveyed the bodies.

Alfred was sent up from Washington to help control the crowd. It was his job to greet parties and guide them up the stairs and into the studio, then chivvy them through to the exit to keep the stream of visitors moving forward.

"Oh yes, ma'am," he would say. "Yes, I was there when these photographs were made. They are very like...yes, terrible scenes. Poor men, poor men."

Mr Brady had not exactly advertised the show – a small placard in the gallery window announced the arrival of the war views – but they had had wide circulation. If you subscribed to Harper's Magazine you could see the woodcut drawings made from the photographs: sanitised and prettified maybe, but still images of death. The New York Times and Atlantic Monthly both wrote up the exhibition. They were astonished by it.

It amazed Alfred and appalled him too that the ghouls should gather in such numbers. They had seen bodies, loved ones, parents, aunts, brothers and sisters, children and babies in their own families, laid out in bed or in coffins, but those had been peaceable, waxy, cold and wrapped in shrouds, not writhing and frozen in extremis in the fields of Maryland.

As the crowd bent over the photographs, Alfred could hear the gasps as the gawpers caught their breath. They took out their spectacles and bent their heads low. He saw them crane and twist their necks to try and get a sight of the faces of the dead men and tut and cluck as they gazed. The men's jaws grew firm and some of the women dabbed their eyes, looking round surreptitiously as they did so to see whether anyone had noticed their onrush of sentiment. One or two had to be led to a corner to sit down and compose themselves and once or twice smelling salts had to be wafted under the noses of women who found themselves quite overcome.

What did they think they were going to see? thought Alfred. It was not as though they did not know or could not guess. And these corpses were southerners: they would not know them or, if they did, could never recognise them in their mangled state. If a loved one had died, you would not come: the imagination would be enough without the sight of what had happened to others. No, what these people wanted was sensation, a thrill. What was it the New York Times had said? "Mr Brady has done something to bring home to us the terrible reality and earnestness of war. If he has not brought bodies and laid them in our door-yards and along streets, he has done something very like it."

And there was Mr Brady now, fluttering among the crowd, his hand pointing upwards, wrist cocked, handkerchief fluttering from his sleeve. He was almost worse. He had not been at Antietam, yet he acted as if he had taken the photographs himself.

Alfred wanted to shout out: "He does not know! He wasn't there! It was Mr Gardner and Mr Gibson! And me! This is what we saw, not him!"

Brady was saying to a small group who had surrounded him. "Yes, quite terrible. It was...most affecting. These young men – mothers' sons, brothers, fathers – cut off in an instant. Buried far from home, with their relatives waiting, waiting for a letter that never comes, for news that they will never hear. A loved one's body flung into a trench, far from all who love and mourn them! This, ladies and gentlemen, *this* is the tragic reality of modern war." And he sighed deeply, the sound taken up and echoed by the women in the group. "Oh Mr Brady, how brave you are," one cried.

Brady turned away and saw Alfred looking hard at him. He raised his hand like a plaster saint in a Catholic church and shook his head almost imperceptibly as if to say, "I know...I know – but what can I do?" Then aloud, businesslike again: "Come along Alfred, move the ladies and gentlemen along."

CHAPTER SEVENTEEN

One early summer evening on the porch outside their home, Jim was reading the newspaper to his grandfather. Alfred liked that: now, in his old age his eyesight was not what it was and anyway the sound of the boy's voice was soothing and made the bad news of the Great Depression and the march of the dictators in Europe and Abyssinia and the Japanese in Manchuria seem somehow further away.

In the distance that night the "raddio" as he liked to call it was playing music in the parlour and from the kitchen came the welcome sound of his daughter making supper. Mary was singing along with Nelson Eddy, so that meant she was in a good mood. Alfred sat back comfortably in his rocking chair and watched the sun sinking beyond the hills to the west.

"Here's something that will interest you, Grandad," said Jim as he turned a page. "There's going to be a reunion at Gettysburg this summer. Listen."

He began to read and, as he did so, Alfred's mind returned once more to his expedition with Alexander Gardner, the summer after the battle of Antietam. He could remember it as clearly as yesterday, clearer maybe, given that most days were the same now. They had rushed hot-foot from Washington, when news that a great battle was taking place had reached the capital, just as they had to Antietam ten months earlier, in order that they might make the first pictures from the scene and get them on show to the public.

"The paper says it's going to be a last get-together of the veterans of the Blue and the Gray," Jim was saying, half reading the news story. "It says: 'Though sundered in the after-years, three quarters of a century on, the old men who fought the greatest war in our nation's history are being invited back one last time, to commemorate the greatest battle of that war on its anniversary. United at last, the former foes will meet in peace....It is understood that President Roosevelt will attend....'

Alfred snorted: "Meet in peace? Who are they kidding? Those rebels are as wrong now as they were then! It was a damn rotten cause! Best thing they can do is pipe down."

But he was scarcely listening by now to the newspaper's purple prose. He was thinking once more of those days photographing bodies in the July heat. He was recalling the prickly humidity and the smells.

The battle at Gettysburg, in Pennsylvania seventy miles north of Washington, had lasted three days in early July 1863. It was the biggest battle of the war and the northern, Union, army finally prevailed but there had been heavy losses on both sides. Never again would the rebels get so close to breaking through. Thousands had been killed before the rebels retreated back south to lick their wounds.

Jim looked up from the newspaper as his grandfather chuckled, but the old man waved for him to go on. Alfred had never been back to the little town of Gettysburg since 1863, nor even thought about it much. How many of the veterans could be left? They must all be at least in their nineties after 75 years. But it would be kind-of fun to see them all again. All good old boys together now. Men of his own age; men who'd understand him and had the same aches and pains as he did.

He snapped back to attention: "How much?" he said.

The boy scanned down the paper. "It says it's free to veterans, grandad. You can take an attendant to help you and they're building a tent city to put you up. The railroad companies are charging two cents a mile for fares...."

"It's too much...how much? That would be...how much do you reckon?"

"No more than six or seven dollars, we could run to that....It says you have to get a regimental certificate, or a note or something, from the governor to prove you're a veteran."

Well, that might be a problem, Alfred thought, considering he'd only served one day in battle and not at Gettysburg. But he'd sure like to go. Perhaps he could bluff his way in? He looked old enough and that's because he was. Stuff and nonsense having to get a chit from the governor at his age!

But he did not wish to seem too keen to the boy, so he grunted noncommittally. "Seven dollars. No. Lot of money. And there's your food.... No, ain't interested. What else is in the paper?"

But he *was* interested. If they were holding the reunion on the anniversary, that would be the start of July. Less than a month away. There was no time to loose. He could go. He could take Jim...Errr, fourteen dollars, say twenty: the cost was mounting up rapidly.

Perhaps best not. They really could not afford it. And yet, now or never. He just could not get the idea out of his mind. It was like one of those damn Eddie Cantor songs on the radio: *"You were meant for me...it was meant to be."* Something like that.

Lying in bed that evening, staring at the ceiling, Alfred knew he had to go. Too many times he had not done things because they would be too expensive, or too difficult. That sort of thinking had closed down his life too often. He thought of the roads not taken, the girls not kissed, the opportunities in business and in life not seized. Too late for regrets now. Well, he'd damn well go. Yes, he would.

Jim knew the old man had to go too. And if he was going, his grandson would definitely be going too. He'd make sure of that. It would be an adventure, a chance to escape for a few days from this house, from this dump of a small town in which nothing unexpected ever happened. It would be like Annabelle-Lee escaping to the movies! It would prove to her that he could do something exciting too. He could do that. He could escape. And, better still, it would prove to him that his grandfather was the hero he had always believed him to be. It never occurred to him in his excitement that Annabelle might want to go too.

"I think you ought to go, Father," Mary said to him at breakfast the following morning. She thought she would go too, as his helper. It would be a good change from this house and its endless work. A chance to see other places, meet other people, not just the middle-aged men with pomaded hair and teeth like tombstones who smiled at her in church each week. At the very least it would mean a week without doing dishes and cooking meals and washing her menfolk's clothes and sweeping the house and all the other chores. That had to be worth the twenty dollars they could not otherwise afford to spend.

That meant all three of them were in favour of the trip. Well, that was it. After the meal, Alfred pushed back his chair and said: "Jim, let's go straight down to the railroad station and see about those tickets."

They set off right away. Most mornings the lad made the journey into town to go to school reluctantly, dragging his feet, but not today. He could not remember when he had last been out of the district. They might see New

York...Washington....President Franklin Delano Roosevelt himself! And a battlefield of that great war between the states that had run like a river through his childhood imagination, as clear as if he himself had seen it happen.

At the station, Alfred took charge, proceeding to a vacant ticket window and leaning down against the counter to address the plump clerk in shirtsleeves who sat on the other side.

"I want two return tickets to Gettysburg, young man," Alfred said, in his best proprietorial fashion.

"Bit late, aren't you?" the clerk answered facetiously, chuckling at his joke. "Afraid you'll miss the battle?"

Alfred drew himself up and just said in dignified fashion: "Not this time."

Sensing his joke had fallen flat, the clerk answered uncertainly: "I mean, the war's over."

"So I believe. Now would you just run along and find out about the tickets. I understand there is a veterans' discount."

There was a muttered conversation behind the counter between the clerk and his colleagues and then he turned back to confirm that, yes, the fare was two cents a mile travelled, but that proof was needed of veteran status in order to qualify. "Do you not have some certificate or regimental letter? Something to show you're a veteran?" he asked.

"Young man, does it look like I'm an imposter?"

"No sir, but the company rules state..."

At that point there was an eruption further back in the booking hall. "He *is* an imposter!" It was the colonel, immaculate in a white linen suit, silk shirt and tie and looking as cool as icecream. "This man is not a veteran. He did not fight in the war. If he has to go, let him pay the full fare like any other."

Alfred leaned against the ticket office counter and said urgently, quietly, to the clerk: "Don't give me your rules. Are you going to give me a ticket or not?"

"No sir, I cannot, not without the proof."

Alfred turned to the other customers waiting in line. His spread his arms wide in an appeal for support, shouting: "Can you see what's happening? I am being denied my rights here. I am prepared to pay the rate, but they won't give me a ticket back to Gettysburg."

But if he hoped for sympathy, there was none. The man behind Jim and Alfred in the queue said: "Listen, old man, you've got your answer. Now, can you get out of the way and let someone else buy a ticket?"

Grandfather stepped aside reluctantly, but he leaned over the man's shoulder as he got to the ticket window and bellowed: "I wouldn't travel with this railroad now, if you paid me."

"No danger of that," said the clerk, turning to the next passenger.

"Come, Jim, we'll find some other way," said Alfred and stumped towards the door, passing the colonel as he did so. "A nice morning's work you've done," he said.

"No more than my duty," replied the colonel.

Outside in the street, Jim looked at his grandfather, puzzled. "Why can't you just show him some proof?" he asked. "You could show him your photographs."

"Because I just can't, boy. Not to some jumped-up functionary," said Grandfather, banging his walking stick on the ground. "What proof are photographs anyway? I don't have to tell him anything. I'll get to Gettysburg if I have to walk all the way. Anyway. I've got a better idea." And he started stumping towards home.

CHAPTER EIGHTEEN

"You did *what?*" said Izzie aghast, when Gene dropped lightly into the conversation that he had accepted Butterfield's offer to buy the photographs. "Without consulting me? Well, you just can't. You'd better tell him the deal's off."

Gene had been expecting this and had rehearsed in his mind what he was going to say about their (he meant her, of course) extravagance and the need to make savings and how this was an opportunity to get rid of some clutter that they didn't need before the first guests arrived to stay.

It cut no ice. Izzie put her foot down. It was the scorn with which she did it that was worst. "You just can't do these things without talking to me about it first. I have an equal share in all this as you do. Who's the one who's going to be doing all the work in this bed and breakfast scheme? Anyway, I don't agree to sell the photographs, at least not to that man, not now.

"If he's offering five hundred, you can bet they're worth a thousand. I want to keep them. Don't you see they're a talking point if we get some good prints made and hang them up?"

He said: "They're just some old pictures. We can get some more...nicer ones...happier. I don't want some creepy pictures of old dead men on the wall. All those battlefield pictures – people won't want to look at them. *I* don't want to look at them. I don't care how historic they are – they're just horrible. They'll give the guests nightmares!"

She parried: "Yes, but they're authentic. They're what our ancestors looked at..."

"They didn't stick them on the walls, for God's sake!"

"Now you're losing it. People want to see these things these days. There's a thriving Civil War market. You want us to make a go of this business – well here's a ready-made customer base."

Gene knew she had him there. He was the one pressing the Bed and Breakfast idea, but he had not really envisaged what sort of customers they might attract. He didn't really want those re-enactor guys who wore big beards and dressed up in authentic uniforms and carried muskets in order to refight old battles. He'd more imagined the Tanglewood crowd, coming for the open air symphony concerts and folk festivals in the summer, in so far as he had imagined any sort of clientele at all. The truth was, the B&B scheme was just an idea of his: something to earn income out of their house. He'd not given much thought at all about how it would be run, who might come, or even, actually, how much to charge them – just as much as possible really.

The same thought was occurring to Izzie even as she said it. Civil War re-enactors! She'd read an article somewhere about how they were divided between amateurs and the real hardcore: men who grew their hair long and only wore authentic uniforms in the original sweaty, itchy materials down to their underpants and, when they went cavorting on manoeuvres, slept in the sort of tents and only ate the sort of rancid food that the men of 1861 would have done, so that they got the full gastro-enteric experience. She wrinkled her nose at the thought of it: they would not want to stay in a B&B would they? Not really? Not unless they were really sick...then she would be like Melanie in *Gone with the Wind...*

But she sensed an opening, to rub home the point. "Listen Gene, if I am to go along with this business idea, I've got to have some say in it. I am not going to be the little old servant lady, like the woman who used to live here. Anyway, I think we should make a feature of those photos and the historical connection. We don't have to put the gory ones on the walls – they could be in an album or something for people to look at if they wanted to. We haven't got a name for this place yet, have we? How about The Photographer's House? That would draw them in, wouldn't it? It's kind-of heritagey."

They had not thought of a name but he did not want to concede anything his wife might suggest in this particular argument. "No," he said. "That's too – too – specific. I was thinking..." (what was he thinking?) "...something like High Gables. Or Hofsettlers'. Something like that."

"Why? Half the houses round here have got high gables. You've got to stand out in this job. Give them a unique selling point. And we've got a precise one here: the old photographer."

"No. I don't think it's any good," he said stubbornly.

Izzie exploded: "*Christ!* We can't even agree on a name! How do you think we're going to run this place, like this?"

"Well, if that's your attitude, we might as well pack up and go home to New York."

"You said it!"

This was getting them nowhere. They agreed a truce, to talk about it more calmly in the morning. At 3am that night they were both awake, though neither would admit it to the other. Two sets of eyes, both staring unhappily out into the darkness.

Izzie was thinking: "This is not going to work. This is not good. What would Alfred Barker have thought if he could see us like this?" She imagined him sitting at the end of their bed, chortling as he took his hobnail boots off. Would he have been like that? Not having known him, or even knowing what he had looked like she rather thought he would.

Into her mind then came a vision of Mary, carrying a pail of dirty water for some reason out of the kitchen into the yard. She had no idea what Mary had looked like either, but she thought: "That's going to be my lot: my future. Cleaning and cooking, cooking and cleaning. Just drudgery." For guests, all dressed in grubby grey woolly combinations, wet with summer sweat, that they had been wearing for weeks. She shuddered and turned her face to the wall.

On his side of the bed, Gene was thinking, desperately: "We've got to make this work. She's got to see that. We can't be defeated before we've even started. I'll help out, when I am not away. It won't be so bad. Most guests are nice, civilised people. They are hardly going to be rapists and mad ax-men are they?" And he turned his mind to working out how to find the money to pay for the pre-launch publicity, and the adverts and the website and the hired help and the sign outside and a parking lot and provisions for the first breakfasts. Would they offer evening meals? He rather thought they should. What would Izzie say to that? It didn't bear thinking about. One step at a time. And he too shuddered and turned his face to the opposite wall.

CHAPTER NINETEEN

"We'll go by car. We shall become *automobilists*," Alfred explained to Jim while they walked home following their rebuff at the railroad station, matter-of-factly as if it was all settled already. "Old man Trumper's got one he could let us have.

Jim shook his head in disbelief. "But we can't drive, Grandpa," he said.

"I can't, but you could. You could learn. It can't be that difficult, when you see the morons who do. Just a matter of pulling levers and pushing pedals, I believe. And steering, of course."

"But it's hundreds of miles to Pennsylvania..."

"Pooh, a little practice and you'll be fine. Your trouble is you're just too nervous. It's your mother's fault. She's spoiled you. No ambition.You need to get about more. We'll go round and see Trumper after supper."

Old Man Trumper emerged from the barn at the back of his tumbledown house to greet them as they came up the track. He and Grandfather were friends – perhaps the only one each of them had, as most people in town tended to shy away from them both. With Alfred it was his prickliness and the brusque barriers he placed in front of affability. With Trumper, it was the unmistakeable smell of a long unwashed body which contributed to a certain unsociability.

Simeon Trumper was a bachelor, living in the house he had once shared with his mother and had inherited from her after her death years before. His interests ran to mechanical things, but not to tidiness or personal hygiene. He habitually wore old dungarees and a dirty check shirt, to go with his greasy face and tousled hair, his bloodshot eyes, unshaven chin and yellow snaggle-teeth.

The local rumour amongst Jim's school friends was that he had his own private still for brewing hooch hidden outside on his property somewhere, but no one, except possibly Alfred, had ever seen it, or sampled its products. He could well have hidden anything out the back, safe from it ever being found among the old car engines, cartwheels, a long-rusted plow, stacks of lumber, old paint pots and garden tools, all tangled together among the nettles and briars.

Certainly though, on the nights when he went whistle-wetting, it was to Trumper's that Alfred rattled on his bicycle, pedalling as if into a stiff wind. And, whatever it was they drank together, it certainly had an effect on the old man on the way home.

Trumper wiped his hands on his dungarees in a polite but unsuccessful effort to clean them, or at least to show willing that he had done so. He greeted grandfather warmly and Jim less so and led them back into the barn.

It was a sloping, wooden-slatted place that had seen sturdier times and was full of the souvenirs of Trumper's scavenging: old tyres and metal rods and miscellaneous cogs and sprockets and stacks of planks and odd-sized timber and hammers and brushes and all sorts of junk.

"What do you want to see the car for?" he said. "It ain't gone in years."

If there had been any hope that Old Man Trumper owned a car of even moderately modern vintage that would actually go, it was in vain. He led Alfred and Jim to the back of the shed where, buried under a tarpaulin and a stack of odds and ends there was a large object of indeterminate shape. Trumer lifted off the pots, some brackets and a small chicken coop before pulling at the covering and underneath there was undoubtedly an ancient motor vehicle of sorts.

It was a Model T Ford, somewhat battered, rusted and very dusty, cobwebs clinging to its crevices and corners and the remains of a bird's nest – to judge by the surrounding droppings – sitting squarely on its sagging black canvas roof. It had not been driven for a very long time. The spindly wheels had been taken off and placed nearby, leaving the chassis resting high on wooden blocks.

"There," said Old ManTrumper proudly. "What do you think of her? Of course she ain't been out of the shed in a while, but she's under cover. She could do with a little bit of a clean-up, but otherwise she's sound. Ain't you, old girl?" And he gave the side panel a hefty thump, leaving a dent the size of his hand behind.

"That looks just what we want, Trumpy," Alfred said, appraising the car with his pipe clamped resolutely in his teeth as if he was an expert.

. "Could you get it ready in a couple of days for us? Jim's going to drive me to Gettysburg."

"Is he now?" said Trumper, rubbing his stubbly chin. "That's sure a place I'd like to go..."

"Well come too. The more the merrier. You could drive as it's your car."

Trumper shrank away from that idea. "Oh no. Your lad would be fine. I haven't driven in years – never gone that far – but I'll show him how...Fact is, it gives me the shakes to drive. I'm not so confident any more as I was. I'll sure come along with you. But I won't drive."

"Suit yourself," said Alfred. You'll be most welcome to keep me company. And" he added meaningfully, "you can help with the cost. We'll leave by the end of the week. Reckon you'll have it ready by then?"

Old Man Trumper reckoned he would and they shook hands on it. Jim could sense that both men were secretly enthused by the idea of the trip, however hard they tried not to show it.

But as they walked home, Jim said to his grandfather: "You know Mr Trumper can't come. What will Mom say? She can't stand him."

"Never you mind about that. You leave your mother to me," said his grandfather. "Keep it to yourself, but I have a kind of a feeling that she won't be coming with us after all. Anyway, there won't be room for her, not with that tin box."

"You are taking the pictures?"

"Of course: that's the main reason for the visit. We could not take them by train, could we? I want to sell

copies as souvenirs! Especially the dead Lincoln."

It was almost impossible to hide their true plans from Mary, but grandfather managed it pretty well. She thought they would all be leaving by rail in three days' time – that was the impression he had given her anyway. But Jim and he knew that, if all went well, they would be driving off in Trumper's flivver the night before.

"Can't have a woman with us, Jim," Alfred said confidentially. "She'd only get in the way. And she wouldn't enjoy it."

Nevertheless, Jim told their plans to Annabelle, never expecting her response. "How exciting," she said. "Can I come too? I could help to drive if you showed me."

Jim was appalled. "Oh no. It's just me and my grandfather and Old Man Trumper." Then, seeing her reproachful look, he had to think quickly for a more appropriate response: "Anyway, what would *your* grandfather say?"

"He won't know – he's going to the reunion too, by train. Your way sounds much more exciting: can't I come, really?"

"No, you absolutely can't," said Jim, but to Annabelle, that seemed to leave open a possibility that she might, if she played her cards right.

Thirty-six hours after their visit to Old Man Trumper, Jim and his grandfather slipped out of the house after breakfast and made their way back to the barn. Trumper had been as good as his promise. The car still stood where it had, but the wheels were back in place and it had been cleaned up and polished until its bodywork had at least returned to a dull black. Its padded leather seats were dusted, its hinged windshield wiped over and folded down, the brass radiator and headlights shone and the car's canvas roof had been washed, patched and folded back on itself behind the rear passenger seats. It certainly looked more road-worthy than before. Trumper had evidently been tinkering with the engine. His hands, blackened with oil, showed that.

"Help me push her out," he said to Jim and he lifted the handbrake lever They pushed the car forward, out of the barn door and into the yard where it came to a stop, its front wheels resting behind two bricks. The three men circled the car admiringly.

The vehicle now sat high on its wheels. It had two low doors to enclose the front bench-seat where the driver and front passenger sat and the two low-slung doors behind for the passenger seats had no side windows. It was quite a climb up to the running boards to get aboard too.

"That was some job you gave me! What do you think?" Trumper said. "She polishes up good, don't she? A 1911 Tourer. Good little runner....I got her for fifty dollars in 1923 and she went well enough before I put her in store after mother died. I've managed to turn the engine over last night and put a gallon of gasoline in the tank, so she's about ready to go."

"A whole gallon, eh?" said Grandfather. "Ten cents' worth – I'm glad you didn't splash out."

"That'll get us 20 miles," said Trumper defensively. "Then a dollar should take us most of the way to Pennsylvania on a full tank. Do you want to get up, young man, and give her a go?"

Jim scrambled up into the driver's seat with some nervousness. The wheel on its long stalk thrust itself high towards his chest, so that steering it would be like carrying a tray of food. At his feet were three pedals and on his lefthand side, between him and the door was the handbrake lever. Through the holes where the pedals and levers fitted he could see right through to the ground beneath. The steering wheel itself also had two levers attached to the central column. The wooden dashboard had a small box fixed to it and three switches.

Alfred scrambled up into the seat behind and Trumper stood in front of the car ready to turn the starting handle.

"Now, I'll start her up," he said. "And when she's going forward, you've got to step on the left pedal for the clutch and engage the lefthand stick on the wheel. See?"

Jim didn't see, but by then Trumper was cranking the handle vigorously and, miraculously, the engine fired grumpily. As it turned over, he kicked the bricks away and jumped agilely up into the passenger seat beside the driver.

"Work the levers," he bellowed, "Work the levers!" And he leaned across Jim and pushed the stalk on the steering wheel.

The car lurched forward, belching and popping and Jim shouted in panic: "What do I do now?"

"Press the left pedal. Lift the throttle stick – this one, this one, on the right," said Trumper, calm now. "And the left lever, to fire the spark plugs. Now down on the pedal – the left one, *the left one* – to go faster."

The engine made a roaring noise as the car jerked through the open gate and Jim hauled on the steering wheel to turn the car left towards town. It shuddered and obeyed and as they went down the hill, gained in speed.

"How do I stop it?" cried Jim above the ticking and wheezing of the engine.

"I'll tell you when," Trumper shouted back.

"This is fun," cried Alfred from the back, holding on to his hat. "Wee-hee. Go faster."

The car was bouncing along now, taking the bumps in the road in its stride and emitting a plume of white smoke from its exhaust and a loud tapping from its engine. It only stalled three times and each time Trumper hopped out to crank the engine again.

In the town, Jim stopped the car, more or less at Trumper's command, by taking his foot off the clutch and hitting first the central pedal and then the foot brake on the right, so that it stalled. The three of them stumbled down from the car, shaking slightly from the vibration and noise, and staggered into the drug store to regroup and discuss tactics.

The first person they saw there was Annabelle, drinking a milkshake at the counter. Her eyes sparkled and she said: "Wow! Was that you making all that noise coming down the street? It looks fantastic. Hello Mr Barker, how are you today?"

Alfred and Jim both blushed and the old man touched the brim of his hat in greeting. "Why, hello little lady," he said. "What do you think of the car?

Jim's going to drive us to Gettysburg for the reunion in it."

Annabelle didn't let on she already knew. "Gosh," she said. "How wonderful. Can I come too?"

Alfred beamed and said: "Well, I don't know. What would your grandfather say?"

"Oh, he's all in favour. He's going too, by train."

"Really....*really?* Well, I don't know. What do you think Jim?"

"No," said Old Man Trumper hurriedly.

"I wasn't asking you. Jim?"

"I thought you said no women, Grandad..."

"Oh, I don't think I did. Not a general exemption. My dear, I think you'd be very welcome to come with us. Good. That's settled then."

Later that evening as they sat on the porch, when Jim queried the decision, which seemed to have overruled the majority vote, Alfred looked at him and said: "Hostage. If we're looking after her, her grandfather can't make trouble for us....Anyway, she'll be company for you. Don't want too many old timers on board, do we?"

The next morning after breakfast, the four of them reconvened in Old Man Trumper's shack. Alfred said: "Now Jim's learned to drive, I think we should leave as soon as possible tonight. The rate that old jalopy goes we won't reach Gettysburg by Christmas otherwise. We'll travel light, like in the old days. Just a bedroll and a change of clothes. Maybe some provisions."

"Definitely," said Trumper, licking his lips.

"Think you can do it boy?" Jim hadn't the heart, or the courage, to say no, so he just nodded.

"Is that alright Annabelle?"

"OK. Grandfather leaves tomorrow, so I will say I am staying with a girlfriend over night. That will give me an excuse to take my things with me. I won't be able to leave before after dinnertime though. Can you teach me to drive it too?"

The old men looked horrified. Trumper said no, certainly not, not ladylike. But Annabelle had a kind of glint in her eye that made Jim think that was not going to do as a final answer.

They agreed to meet Trumper outside the grocery store that evening and drove home, parking in the yard. Mary came out to greet them, wiping her hands on her apron. "What have you got there?" she said.

"Old Trumper's loaned us his car," explained Alfred simply.

Mary's nose wrinkled at the thought. "Why?"

Alfred and Jim realised they had made a tactical mistake in bringing the car home. They looked at each other guiltily, hoping the other would answer.

Alfred spoke first: "Well, the fact is Mary...the fact is, we thought Jim could drive us to Gettysburg, instead of the train. Cheaper."

To their surprise, instead of scolding, Mary roared with laughter. "Boys!" she said. "Jim can't drive that thing all the way. It's hundreds of miles.We'll never get there in that. No, we'll go by train. Jim can drive me to the station this evening and I'll get the tickets, since you made such a bad job of it."

Then she added: "Doubt whether that old thing would get us much further than the station anyway."

After supper Mary and Alfred clambered into the back of the Model T and Jim bent over the starting handle out at the front, as he had seen Trumper do. Cranking left-handed, remembering to keep the thumb under the starting handle, was hard but eventually he got the rhythm and managed to remember to let go before the handle whipped back at him. Turn it right-handed and the handle could snap your wrist, or your thumb in two as it spun back on itself.

The car rumbled down to the station and Mary got out to make her way to the ticket office. Jim thought idly how handsome she looked. She had got dressed up for the occasion of a trip in a car – and was wearing her brown linen coat and the straw hat with the cherries which she had worn for her confrontation with the colonel. The heels of her shoes clicked smartly on the sidewalk as she crossed into the station. He was proud of her.

"Just get the one ticket for yourself, Mary!" Alfred called after her. "We can string along for ourselves."

But as they waited with the engine running, Jim saw his grandfather suddenly get up in the back seat and start waving furiously. In the distance, Trumper could be seen staggering from the general store with a large paper bag.

"Trumpy! Quick! Come on!" shouted Grandfather. "Climb aboard! We're off. Get going Jim!"

Jim turned, startled: "But Mom..."

"No time to waste, boy. We can't wait for her. Let's go. Now."

Scarcely knowing what he was doing and responding automatically to the command of his grandfather, Jim complied. Trumper, looking baffled, had climbed onto the running board and as the car jerked forward, fell onto the front passenger seat, his legs dangling out of the side of the car. His head rested on Jim's lap. "Hello Jim," he said looking up, smiling benignly. Jim caught the smell of alcohol wafting upwards.

The car turned across the wide main street and started back the way they had come. They had arranged to pick up Annabelle outside their house. She would be waiting for them there out of sight.

"Come on boy, faster. Don't let your mother see...."

As the car bounced up the road, Jim looked back and could just see his mother emerge from the railroad station, putting her purse in her handbag. He had not realised that his grandfather had planned to abandon her in town.

Mary looked up to see the car disappearing down the street in a cloud of dust. "Wait for me!" she cried in desperation. Her voice echoed and she began to run after them."Wait for me!"

But it was too late. Her men folk had left her behind.

CHAPTER TWENTY

"Well, that was some departure," said Izzie as she heard the story from Miss Annabelle-Lee over tea in the old lady's kitchen. Annabelle had invited her over to show her the Scarlett O'Hara portrait above her bed, but actually to prove to Izzie that she had really once been an actress and they had sat downstairs and gossiped about Hollywood in the 1940s and the stars she had known.

Izzie thought that, handsome as Mizz Anabelle still was, with her high cheekbones and carefully-applied makeup, even as her perfume wafted across the table with every nod of her head, it was hard to imagine her ever making love to the screen legends of the 1930s. Clark Gable, Errol Flynn...they had remained young, pickled in aspic in their movies, whereas the woman sitting opposite her was now a little old lady, even if a glamorous one. That's if she was telling the truth of course, about her Hollywood lovers. *If.* But she certainly seemed to know all about them and their foibles.

Afterwards, Annabelle would wonder how the Model T and the trip to Gettysburg had come up. That seemed a different part of her life again, entirely. Perhaps it had been the sight of Izzie's smart metallic red Ford Mustang drawing up smoothly outside, that brought to her mind how she herself had skipped aboard the old car sixty-four years before. Or maybe it was because she was in the mood to chat that afternoon because it was raining and her bridge partner had called off.

She remembered how she had lied to her grandfather then slipped out to wait for Jim and the others at his house. When the car rattled to a halt, Alfred and his drinking partner had hustled down to pick up the tin trunk which, with much wheezing and puffing they had managed to hoist aboard into the footwell of the back seat.

"It's too heavy, Granddad," Jim had said. "Nonsense," said Alfred. "I've taken out most of the plates. These are just the Gettysburg ones I'm taking – and the special one, of course. I've put the rest in another trunk in the shack. It's the Gettysburg pictures they'll want to see. They're the ones that will sell down there."

Annabelle's valise had gone on top of the trunk and there was also a bag of clothes shared between Jim and his grandfather and a paperbag containing a bottle of whiskey and a spare shirt that was all Trumper's luggage. He had not seemed to need more clothes, or perhaps he had just not thought of bringing any.

"I don't know what made us think we could do it in that old thing," Annabelle said now, gazing at the raindrops running hard down her kitchen window. "If it had been weather like this we'd have been soaked to the skin in no time: no side windows, you see. No windshield wipers either."

"What did the colonel say?"

"Oh, I didn't tell *him*, or the maid. Just said I was going to stay with my friend Dolores and would probably stay over a few days while he was away at the reunion. I used to do that and he didn't seem to mind, you see. He was a busy man and looking after me was a chore. He used to leave it to the maids, really and then we'd meet at supper most evenings – and even then we'd quite often eat in silence because he would be reading his papers and making notes. He left me to my own devices and that suited both of us just fine."

"But what if there'd been an accident and you'd been hurt getting to Gettysburg?"

"Do you know, none of us ever thought of that? At least I didn't – I just thought it would be a hoot. A chance to get away for a few days on an adventure. I guess we all did. Looking back, I would think young Jim was probably the only one of us who worried about that sort of thing: that was Jim all over. His grandfather was just worried about getting to the reunion and the other old boy – well, I think he was too drunk to notice most of the time.

"But Jim – no Jim, looking back on it, I think he was worried about just about everything, all the time, and he had to drive, poor boy. It must have been like steering a kicking mule."

Izzie had left her desire for the movie gossip behind now. She wanted to know about the car.

Annabelle said: "My dear, thrilling wasn't the word for it. It was a crazy, noisy, lumbering old thing. I couldn't ride in it now and I don't know how the two old men could do it then. The seats were nice, high padded leather, like sitting in an armchair perched on a platform, but really ten miles would have been enough. Not a bit like your shiny red car, dear. Isn't it funny how they both have the same name, with the same squiggly signature on the front?"

"Did you never drive?"

"Oh no, dear. That's to say, yes of course: I *could* drive. I learned on the old Model T, actually. But later I always had a man to drive *me*. What is it about men? The poor dears, they always like to drive, don't they? So, later on, I always let them."

Annabelle watched the rain again. "But I wouldn't mind a little drive in your car one day...perhaps not as far as Gettysburg though..."

CHAPTER TWENTY-ONE

The moment Mary emerged from the station and looked up as she heard the Model T spluttering and wheezing, she guessed what must have happened. She had been double-crossed by her own father. No wonder he only wanted her to buy one ticket.

The car was going so slowly that she found herself running up the road after it. She could almost touch its rear fender and she was screaming: "Where are you going? Father…Father come back! Jim, don't leave me!"

There was no possibility that they could not hear her, even over the noise of the engine, but as she ran, it started to pick up speed and pull away from her. By the time it reached the corner of main street and the turning towards their home, it was leaving her behind in a cloud of dust and smoke.

She stopped in the middle of the road and let out a cry of despair and anger, before, looking round, she saw onlookers staring at her and giggling. Mary straightened up, glared back at them defiantly and said: "Oh bother!" before patting down her coat and heading across to the obscurity of the drugstore with as much dignity as she could achieve.

As she revived herself with a glass of milk at the counter, she was already forming a plan. Mary was damned if she was going to be left behind, abandoned by her menfolk. Well, if they would not take her to Gettysburg, she would go of her own accord. She had the train ticket. She could find her own way. And when she got there, she would give them a piece of her mind. She was seething now, already working out what she would say. Alfred and his crony Trumper were probably to blame, insofar as Trumper was capable of formulating any coherent plan at all. They were corrupting Jim, teaching him all the wrong lessons in life. And she would make sure they knew it!

She would go tomorrow. It would be an adventure – almost a holiday for once, she told herself, free of the need to keep house for a few days. She had some savings which she could draw from the bank in town in the morning: thirty dollars would be enough, probably. And Mary smiled as she drank her milk and thought how good it would be to get away – and of the look on Alfred and Jim's faces when she caught up with them.

A mile away, at their house, everything was hurriedly stowed aboard and, with Jim at the wheel, Old Man Trumper beside him to give advice and Alfred and Annabelle-Lee sitting high behind them in the back, the Model T was turned right out of the gate, heading south. The tin box sat in the foot well in front of the passenger banquette with Alfred's feet resting on top of it as added protection.

Jim was still smarting at the way they had abandoned his mother. He had imagined that it would be a more gentle parting, the grandfather telling her there was not room for her to go when they were sitting round the kitchen table after dinner, not just leaving her humiliatingly in front of everyone in the middle of the street. What must folk have thought?

He felt his eyes pricking, but did not want to cry in front of Annabelle. So, instead, he gripped the steering wheel tighter and gazed hard ahead at the road, concentrating to block out the noise and evade the traffic. Hunched as he was, his grandfather slapped him on the back, sending the car slewing forward. "Good work, boy," he said. "We sure showed a clean getaway, eh?"

Jim said: "Oh, grandad: did you have to do it like that?"

His grandfather was leaning against the back of the front seat, his mouth only a few inches from Jim's ear. "What do you mean, boy? We had to make a break for it, otherwise we'd never have got away. She'd have insisted on coming and that would have been no fun at all. Anyway she'll get over it. And we'll make it up to her – bring her something back from Gettysburg, a little souvenir perhaps, or some candy."

Even though they were only a little way from home, Jim had no idea where they were heading, or even whether they were going in the right direction. At the next opening, almost on a whim, he turned right into what looked like a road, but was no more than a track through an open gate. They found themselves driving into a field. The car came to rest against a large grass tussock.

"Perfect," said Trumper, tumbling out of the car as soon as it paused. "Now if you'll just wait here a moment..." and he vanished behind a tree. As they waited for him to board again, it occurred to Jim that not only did they not know where they were going but darkness was coming on and they had nowhere to stay. Not only that, but they did not have any lights on the car either.

Jim turned to Alfred and asked where they were going to sleep. "Good point," he said, flummoxed. "Well, it's a golden night to be out under the stars."

Old man Trumper, hearing this as he clambered back into the car, pointed to a dark object on the other side of the field. "There's a barn there. I think it's the Bradley place hereabouts and he won't mind us bedding down. We can stop here."

Which was how the four of them came to be staggering across the field in the twilight to bed down in a barn less than three miles from their warm beds at home, scarcely closer to Gettysburg than when they had started out. Jim was not sorry. The trip so far had upset and exhausted him enough for one day, maybe for good, and it had only been going half an hour.

The barn door was closed but not locked and inside by the light of a match they could just make out piles of straw. Alfred said: "I don't think we need undress tonight. No ablutions before daylight. Young lady, I think you should sleep over there in the far corner. And we gentlemen will be over here, so we do not succumb to temptation, eh Trumpy?"

Trumper snorted: "I think she's safe enough with me. It's your grandson you need to worry about." It was a good job that they could not see Jim blushing red in the darkness.

They collapsed onto the straw and shortly Jim could hear the old men wheezing and snoring in the darkness. It had been a long day for them too. He was on the verge of dropping off to sleep as well when he heard a rustling beside him. He was instantly awake.

It was Annabelle. "Are you asleep yet?" she whispered.

"No."

"Good. Then can I come and snuggle up beside you? I don't want to be on my own right over there. I'm scared."

He did not mind in the least. But in a few moments, they both fell fast asleep, like Babes in a Barn in each other's arms. Jim's last sensation was of the scent of Annabelle's body mingling sensuously with the dusty smell of the hay.

Jim's night was nevertheless a disturbed one, not because of her proximity, which was warm and comforting in itself, but because his dreams were troubled by images of his mother being left behind as they accelerated away and the memory of her scream as she realised what was happening. The worst dream had him reversing the car to pick her up and running her over with a bump, so she lay squashed in the road. "Good work boy," his grandfather had seemed to say and he slapped him on the shoulder. That is what they had done to her, in effect.

When Jim woke up the following morning it was because the sun was shining through a gap in the roof directly into his eyes. It was already hot and as he stirred he realised that Annabelle had already moved away to her side of the barn. Suddenly, the sunlight was closed off and his grandfather was standing over him, blocking the light. "Jim, listen to me. I've got some money with me. It's in my sock. Don't tell old Trumpy," Alfred said a stage whisper that, had he not still been snoring lightly, Trumper must have heard. "It's thirty dollars. That should be more than enough to see us through.

"That's good," Jim said, turning over. He had eight dollars and thirty cents, five of which had come from the teapot on the mantelpiece where they always kept emergency reserves and the rest was savings.

"Jim, Jim," Alfred added, after a pause. "Thanks for coming with me on this, boy. Good of you to help an old boy along. Much appreciated…"

Then he added: "Come on, let's go." The old man was already dressed, or perhaps he had never undressed, and he was moving over to shake Trumper awake too.

Jim was still troubled.The dream remained fresh in his mind. He asked: "Grandad, did you leave Mom a note?"

Alfred thought about it. "Hell, no," he said, under his breath. Then, louder: "Dammit, I meant to and clean forgot."

"Oh, you promised," Jim exclaimed. "We'll have to go back and tell her where we're going."

Alfred shook his head: "No, no. We'll write. Send her a card from the next stop. Can't be held up any further."

Within a few minutes all four of them were staggering out into a bright dawn, blinking and yawning in the sun, to find the car had come to rest a few feet short of a water trough. Had Jim driven further forward they would have hit it in the dark and the trip would have finished before it even began. Alfred and Trumper scarcely seemed to notice and were examining the luggage to make sure it was still intact.

Annabelle stood beside the car picking straw out of her hair and stretching. "Oh boy," she said. "That was quite a night. I've never done that before.What's for breakfast?"

Jim's first task was to reverse the car. There was no escape from learning this manoeuvre now if they were to leave the field and avoid slewing into the trough. Trumper gave him a hazy idea of how to move the car backwards by manipulating the foot pedal and the shift and the old man then plodded mechanically round the front of the car to bend down and start cranking the starting handle. He still seemed nine parts asleep as he did so.

The car choked and coughed into life and slid forward. Jim realised they were closing fast on the bog surrounding the trough and the Model T was threatening to pin Trumper against it. The old man started hollering and waving. Suddenly, just as there seemed to be no hope, it halted as if considering its position, juddered and started moving backwards onto firmer ground and up towards the entrance to the field. Trumper flung himself aboard. Alfred, peering steadfastly ahead as if not deigning to notice the way they were going, gave a gentle whoop. "Comc on, let's get weaving," he said.

Somehow the car steered through the gateway at a rush, and lurched out onto the road, turning right towards Connecticut.

It was a beautiful, morning of high summer as they headed south, down tree-lined roads, over little wooden bridges crossing streams and past woodland pastures where chestnut-colored horses ran beside the fences. There was no traffic, only an occasional farmhand sauntering to work, pausing to gaze at the noisy vision grinding past. Cresting a hill, they suddenly saw what seemed to be the whole of New England spread out before them: a blanket of woods and hills stretching into the distance, under a cloudless blue sky, occasional wisps of smoke from little houses far below and white church spires pointing heavenwards.

About fifteen miles south of Springbridge, in unknown territory to them all, they came to another little town. As they drove down the main street, men in country overalls could be seen making their way into a roadside diner. They caught the scent of bacon and eggs in the air. It smelled good and made them realize how hungry they were.

Alfred said: "Stop. I'd say it was time for re-vittaling," and when Jim had parked the car against the curb, they walked stiff-legged inside.

An immediate hush fell as the waitress, then the cook and all the customers, turned to look at the strangers, clearly unused to such surprises. In silence they mounted the stools along the counter – a bit of an effort on Alfred's part but he managed it surprisingly well.

They ordered ham, eggs and coffee. As she took the order, the waitress smiled. "You boys aren't from round here," she said, eyeing Alfred. "No ma'am, we're from Springbridge," he replied, as if it was the other side of the moon.

"Really? I was there once," she said like it was some distant city rather than the next place up the road.

Alfred became conversational. "Yes we're heading for the great reunion at Gettysburg," he said proudly. He was visibly relaxing the further they got from home and the greater the distance he had put between himself and anyone who might know him.

The cook, a big and greasy man, turned from his griddle tray, wiped his hand on his apron and extended it across the counter with a smile. "Sir, I am honored to meet you. Aren't we boys?" he said. "My father was in the war – 20th Massachusetts – but he's no longer with us, or he'd have been hitching along with you." Alfred shifted nervously.

"Hey, what do you think of this?" the man continued, turning to the other customers. They grunted vague approval. An elderly couple smiled, nodded gently into their plates and raised a hand as if to wave in their general direction. "You must have this meal on the house, sir," he said.

Before Alfred could answer, Trumper had grabbed a plate of pancakes from the counter and shoveled them towards his mouth. "We're goin' too. Thank you. Much obliged," he said as the first mouthful hit his lips.

"I am indeed grateful to you, sir. It is a fine gesture," said Alfred, swelling in confidence and courtliness with every syllable. "This here's my grandson. I am going to show him where real heroes fought to give him freedom." He clapped his hand on Jim's shoulder. "And this," he said, touching Annabelle lightly on the shoulder, "is my grandson's intended."

Annabelle and Jim both opened their mouths in surprise and then closed them again. If it got them free pancakes and eggs, then that was alright. But Annabelle still muttered under her breath: "I am NOT his intended."

The cook looked at the four of them, as if to work out how much food his generosity might cost him and then nervously smiled as he prepared to do his patriotic duty. "Were you in a Massachusetts regiment sir? Where did you serve?" he asked Alfred.

"Alas no. I wasn't from this state back then," Alfred replied ambiguously and he launched into a tale not about being a photographer's assistant at all, but about a gallant officer. "I had the honor to serve my country in several theaters during the conflict. Bull Run in 1861, Antietam in '62, Gettysburg '63...right up to the surrender at Appomattox in eighteen hundred and sixty-five," he said. "Emerged without a scratch though we had some hot times. Yes sir, thank you for the bacon. Another egg? Of course, please..."

Jim could not believe what Grandfather was saying and kept his head down, concentrating on his pancakes and syrup. "Of course, I knew the late president and General Grant. They were great men, oh yes...and friends." The boasting went on way above his grandson's level.

At last, with a final piece of toast and sup of coffee, Alfred decided he had had enough and tapping Trumper, who was still eating, he rose to his feet.

"My dear friends. Thank you for breakfast...thank you for honoring the memory of our great Civil War. Thank you for your generosity. I take it on behalf of all my gallant comrades who never came back," he said and with a final gesture that started like a wave and finished by sweeping a couple more pieces of toast unobtrusively off the counter and into his pocket, he turned towards the door. The cook looked bemused and sentimental, finally lost for words, and the other customers watched open-mouthed, food poised on their forks halfway from their plates.

At the door, Alfred lifted his hat, ignoring the piece of straw that descended gently from his head. He pronounced: "Farewell!" as if taking a curtain call and skipped outside.

When they were beside their car, Annabelle said sweetly, to no one in particular: "Do you think I might have a go at driving the car sometime? I am sure I could."

Alfred stared at her. "A girl driving?" he said. "A girl? Oh no, my dear, I don't think that would be possible, do you? Far too difficult. Why, even I can't drive"

Annabelle pursed her lips: "I have been watching. I am sure I could, once I got used to it." But she obediently clambered into the back again.

As they made off from the diner, the old man sat back with a happy sigh and changed the subject. "What nice people," he said. "Why ever didn't I settle here instead of Springbridge? I can't imagine. I thought that went rather well, didn't you?"

Jim was outraged. "Grandfather, why did you say all those things? You knew they weren't true. You didn't need to say all that."

Alfred was peeved and a little irritated. "Why not? I was at all those battles. We didn't have to trouble all those people back there with details. Especially not when we were singing for our supper. Or breakfast in this case," he said.

And so, as the morning warmed up, they drove on down the valley and over the state line, past neat clapperboard farms and ancient trees casting shadows across the pavement, through sleepy little villages and between open meadows waving with ripening corn. Mr Trumper nodded drowsily in the front passenger seat and from the back Jim could hear his grandfather humming a gentle tune. He was exuding happiness and freedom and he at least knew where he was going.

For lunch they stopped at a drug store for a soda and a sandwich, then, a little further on, Alfred insisted that they should stop for a while so that he could have his afternoon nap, as if he was at home. Jim pulled over onto a patch of gravel beside the road, on the edge of a bank leading down to a meadow through which ran a clear stream. It was an idyllic place on that perfect day.

As the other two old men stretched themselves and lay down under the shade of a tree on the bank, Jim and Annabelle took off their shoes and socks and went down to wade in the stream. Jim was becoming vaguely conscious that he had not washed since the previous morning and splashed the water on his face, noticing for the first time that stubble was beginning to grow there. Annabelle noticed too and pointed it out: "You're all spikey to kiss now," she said and, grinning, splashed water up onto his shirt. "Big boy!"

Jim hated that, even as he felt his excitement rising, and he splashed across to her. Then he picked her up bodily and tossed her into the creek. She screamed and slopped back to the bank. The game was over.

"Look at my clothes," she said. "You idiot!" And she dodged around the far side of the Model T to change. When she reemerged she draped the wet things over the canvas awning, took up her book – *Gone with the Wind* of course – and, pouting, went and sat a little way along the bank.

Jim settled beside his grandfather, somewhat confused. The old man had taken his jacket off and was lying on his side resting his head on one hand. "I should not worry," he said quietly. "That's just girls."

They lay in silence for a while and then Alfred said: "I had a girlfriend once."

Jim looked at him: "Yes, granddad, you had grandma. The little woman in the photograph by your bed."

"Oh no, not her. Before Sarah Jane. No, no I had to marry her. The one I am thinking of was lovely to me...."

He struggled to sit upright and, gazing across the stream into the middle distance, began to recall a new story that Jim had not heard before, though the old man was largely speaking to himself as if the boy was not there.

"No, this girl was called Faith. She was tall and beautiful, a big-boned country girl, as kind and gentle as you could ever wish. Sweet, with a smile as wide and generous as Christmas. She found her way in to Washington and she was a maid in Mr Gardner's house. She wore a little uniform with a lace cap and all….

"Well, I met her one day when I was sent to get something that he had left at home and she opened the door and smiled at me and that was it. Oh I fell for her all right…"

As he sat by the stream, suddenly the fog of memory cleared and Alfred could remember everything clearly. The hot afternoon in Washington in the war, him walking down the sidewalks of the dust covered streets, whistling happily for having escaped from mixing nitrate in the darkroom for an hour. When could it have been? It must have been that Fall, after they came back from Antietam – yes, that was it because he'd boasted to her about being at the battle and offered to show her the gruesome pictures on one of her afternoons off. And she'd wrinkled her nose and said no, she didn't want to see such things.

Well, that day when he'd first met her, he had dawdled, chatted to some soldiers outside the gallery and dodged a carriage to cross the street – he could remember that: the black driver in his livery uniform and top hat flicking the whip at him to chivvy him out of the way.

Then, there he was, outside the terraced house, with the porch and the big bay window with the maid peering out when she heard the bell. She had given him Mr Gardner's valise that he had been sent to collect. It contained overnight things and a clean shirt and he kept it by the door in case he was called away in a hurry. She knew where it was and handed it straight over with a smile so radiant that it had taken his breath away and he had taken his billycock hat off and smoothed his greasy hair with his hand and taken a risk and asked her out for a walk one evening when she came off duty and she'd said yes! Oh my, that was Faith.

Alfred turned to Jim and said: "You know when you know immediately that someone's for you? Like you and that young lady? Well, that was Faith and me."

Clear in his memory was a Sunday walk with Faith. They'd gone down to the Potomac and promenaded with all the swells along towards the basin, walking through the red and golden leaves of the Fall. They had had so much in common. She was Irish – well, her folks were, Sullivans from County Tipperarey, like his, but settled in Baltimore. She was too good to be a housemaid. It had been one of those hot October days and they had sat down under a cherry tree and held hands and kissed.

"Couldn't have been much older than you then Jim," Alfred observed. "I'd never done that before. So you see, I know what it's like. Well, I used to anyway."

"What happened Grandad?"

"We went out all that winter – well, at least once a month when she got time off. I wanted to propose and make her mine and I asked Mr Gardner and he said no – he was her employer, see? Didn't want to lose her, did he? He forbade me to see her on pain of losing my job and I didn't want that to happen. And in the end she went off anyway – went to work in Mrs Surratt's boarding house of all places, I believe. That's what I was told. The woman they hanged for helping the people who killed the president after the war. Well, that was a damned thing for her to do, wasn't it? Lost touch after all that...shame, really."

Jim wanted to ask more, but it was obvious that his grandfather was ending the conversation. He shook his head and struggled to his feet, leaning on his walking stick and muttering: "The damned things you remember. What brought that up? Wonder what made me think of that?" Then, more loudly: "Come on. We ought to get a move on. Wake up, Trumpy!" And he banged his stick impatiently on the ground.

The four of them made their way back to the car where Annabelle plucked her now dry clothes off the hood and smiled at Jim. "That was a nice, sad story," she said.

It was late afternoon as they turned the car back onto the highway, leaving the meadow and stream behind, peopled by the ghosts of three-quarters of a century before.

All day they had encountered scarcely any traffic but now they were well over the state line the number of cars was a little heavier. Mostly they whistled past with a wave of the driver's hand, but by now Jim was getting more confident of the car. It still had a tendency to bounce and swerve on its spindly wheels when it hit bumps in the road, especially if his hands were not tight on the steering wheel, but it was now reaching speeds of more than twenty miles an hour on the downhill slopes, sufficient for Jim's grandfather to murmur periodically: "Whoa, boy, slow down...too fast, too fast."

As evening fell they passed through Danbury. Jim suggested that they should stop to find somewhere to sleep but Alfred would not hear of it. He wanted to press on, but then the road entered a sandy, deserted stretch, weaving through a forest of pine trees. It began to look as though they would have to spend a second night in a barn.

Jim was beginning to worry with dusk drawing on that he would soon not be able to see the road, driving without lights, but Old Trumper had a solution.

They stopped and the old man reached into a wooden box strapped to the back of the car, pulling out two ancient hurricane lights. One was draped over the radiator cap at the front of the hood and the other hung at the back from a hook. The front lamp certainly didn't throw much light and what it did swayed about with the motion of the car – but it would do for the time being. They could drive on further.

CHAPTER TWENTY-TWO

Gene had not paid much attention when he returned home to find Isabelle's red Mustang not in the drive. She was probably out buying more bloody antiques they couldn't afford, he thought resentfully as he headed up to the kitchen door after parking their Volvo estate on the patch of bare ground where the shack where he had found the tin trunk had been. It had been flattened and covered with cinders and would do as a guest car park in due course. The pictures though remained a sore point between them, still sitting in their trunk in the hallway, and he guessed she might be out meeting folks in town, seeking consolation in their sympathy.

Meanwhile he had some good news. A friend of his from the magazine where he worked in New York had agreed to design a website for their bed and breakfast to attract visitors and he had also dropped in on the Dispatch-Messenger and arranged a display advertisement to run for the next four weeks. Plus, he had picked up a box of brochures from the printers: a thousand glossy copies folded three ways so that a colour photograph of their door filled the front fold and then you opened it, cleverly, just like going inside, to see pictures of the bedrooms and the lounge. There was also a blurb he had written and, on the back, a photograph of him and Izzie standing smiling, arms around each other, on the porch, above the caption: "A Warm Welcome Awaits You from Eugene and Isabelle Hofsettler..." and the address and contact numbers underneath. A bit pompous or even twee? Maybe, but it was a case of casting their bread upon the waters… He would take a few copies around to the local tourist office and drop some more off at the Shaker Village and Tanglewood and the local gallery – anywhere where people might see it really.

They had compromised on the name. It would be The Photographer's House after all, even though they had not yet found somewhere to print up copies of Alfred Barker's more acceptable pictures, nor tracked down an old 19th Century wooden camera with a cape and a tripod to place as a talking point in the hall. The name was a concession to Izzie's sensibilities, but one Gene had felt able to make, magnanimously, particularly as he had not been able to come up with anything better. "Once the home of the renowned early photographer of the Civil War, Alfred Barker…" the blurb had said, hopeful that potential guests would think of course they had heard of him alongside the great Brady. "Lovingly restored by Gene and Isabelle…" he had liked that touch: "expensively restored" or "extravagantly restored" might have been nearer the mark, but best not to gild the lily.

These really must be the last expenses before they opened, but he thought Izzie would be pleased at how the brochures had come out as he came through the kitchen door.

Then his eyes fell on a note on the table and his blood ran cold. After their row, she couldn't have, could she? He snatched the paper. "Taking Miss Annabelle-Lee to Gettysburg in the car," it said, "Back in a few days. Love Izzie XXX PS: I need to get away for a bit. See you soon."

This really was too bad when they were so busy. She was needed here, he needed her here, right now. Gene rang Izzie's mobile immediately. An electronic message said unemotionally: "The mobile number you have called may be switched off. Please try later." Exasperated and a little scared by the shock of her absence, he hurled his own cellphone against the wall and it was only as it shattered and fell to the floor in shards sending its sim card and battery skidding under the cooker that he realised what a stupid, impulsive thing that had been to do.

Izzie glanced at her cellphone. She saw there had been a call from Gene an hour before, but when she tried to answer it the electronic message just said that his number was unobtainable: "Please try later." Perhaps he had taken umbrage: she was not looking forward to their conversation.

"Never mind, dear," said Annabelle. "Let him sleep on it."

CHAPTER TWENTY-THREE

After they had spent the night at a dingy country roadhouse, the next day was another fine one as the Model T and its occupants rattled down towards the turnpike. Jim knew it would be a tougher drive than the previous day. They would be turning west and driving towards New York before too long. There would be no escaping the great city even if they could have found a way round it, for his grandfather had made clear, with sublime indifference to his lack of driving experience, that he wanted to see the place again. Old Man Trumper thought it would be a good idea as well and so did Annabelle, excited at seeing Manhattan and all its skyscrapers. Jim was just fearful of what they might find and whether the big cars of New York would blast them out of the way.

Soon they were on the 'pike, where the traffic was much heavier. The car could still get away with rattling along at twenty miles an hour, although it must have seemed absurdly quaint to the limousines and saloons overtaking them.

And then, as noon approached, they breasted a small incline and ahead in the distance, Manhattan shimmered in the heat, its skyscrapers touching the sky at the far end of the island like a petrified forest. It was an awesome sight. Alfred spontaneously broke into his rendition of *How you goin' to keep 'em down on the farm, now that they've seen Paree?* at the top of his voice in sheer excitement.

An hour later and they were descending into the city through the neat suburban bungalows and houses of the Bronx, each surrounded by little garden yards. Then they were across the river onto the island, into Harlem. Here was a different world to the country folk: people filled the streets, dressed smartly, going about their business.

The traffic was very heavy and slow moving by now and Jim kept having to brake and ease the clutch, fearing all the time that he would stall the car. He sat on the edge of his seat and held the steering wheel in the sweating palms of his hands, anxiously eyeing the cars that drew up alongside and trying not to acknowledge the amused smiles of their occupants.

"Hey, mac. How d'you pedal that thing?" someone shouted. He smiled weakly and beside him Mr Trumper woke up, hearing the noise but not what was said, and waved cheerily as if he was some sort of celebrity. The streets were wide, open boulevards, running straight as far as the eye could see. Like paths through a canyon, they were surrounded on all sides by the sheer cliffs of tall buildings. The streets were wide as fields. Cars all around them were driving two abreast, weaving between lanes without a care as they did so. Jim was petrified that one would hit them and wondered, if they had a smash, whether some fellow in this city full of gangsters would shoot them for damaging his car. He was also feeling increasingly anxious, not least because he had no idea where they were going. Alfred gazed around him in bemusement. Little, muttered sounds of astonishment and wonder came from the back of the car. "This sure has changed. I've no idea where we are. It's all new," he said helpfully.

One moment they were easing forward through the traffic, the next the Model T was stuck alone in the middle of an intersection with cars bearing down on them from both directions. He had not noticed that the bronze traffic signal on the previous corner had changed color. In fact, he had not noticed it at all as it was not something he had ever encountered in his brief driving experience.

In trying to reverse out of danger, Jim stalled the engine. There was nothing he could do and Trumper could not be expected to leap out into the traffic to crank the handle. Instead the old man sank lower in the seat and pressed his hat down on his head as if drawing the shades on any involvement with the outside world.

They braced themselves for the shock of a collision but it never came. Horns blared all around them and cars piled up on each side, lining up to get past, their drivers leaning out with angry shouts, but no one hit them. After what seemed like hours, Jim clambered gingerly out and turned the starter handle himself. Nothing happened. "Hi kid, get that garbage out of the way," someone shouted.

Tingling with embarrassment, he realized there was nothing for it but to push. But with Alfred, Annabelle and Trumper still on board, the car was far too heavy for him to move by himself. By then cars were lining up again because the lights had changed once more. "Give me a hand," Jim cried, but neither of the old men seemed to hear. They appeared to be chatting amiably about some matter of local consequence as if they were sitting on a park bench at home.

As Jim leaned desperately against the back of the car, sweating hard and praying for the end, a large shadow fell across him. Looking up he saw a policeman holding a nightstick.

"You'd better get this thing out of here," he said unnecessarily. "Before I book you for obstructin' the highway."

Jim was close to tears. "I am trying. It's too heavy. I need help," he said.

Annabelle piped up, simpering: "Oh officer, can you help Jim to push?"

The policeman peered into the car. Pointing at Alfred and Trumper with his baton he said: "You. Get out now and help." And, standing on the running board and leaning over, he added: "You'll also find taking the brake off helps."

The four of them pushed the car out of the flow to the side of the road and, with a final flurry of horns and shouts, the congestion cleared in moments. Jim was regretting he had ever seen New York. It was the noisiest, most frightening place he had ever been in.

When the men climbed back into the car, they found Annabelle sitting in the driver's seat. They had not noticed that it was she who had steered the car into the kerbside for them. "You see," she said. "I can drive. Now let me take the wheel…."

Jim was too exhausted to argue. He was secretly glad someone else wanted to drive the car through Manhattan. She was in possession of the steering wheel. But he did notice Annabelle's grin of triumph when he slumped beside her.

"Where are you boys headin'?" said the policeman, "'Cause at this rate I don't think you'll get there. We don't want our nice clean streets cluttered up with old wrecks like this. Where're you from anyway?"

Alfred raised his hat courteously and said: "I am so sorry officer. It won't happen again. My grandson is a little inexperienced at city driving. He is taking us to the reunion at Gettysburg and I just wanted one last look at the city in whose regiment I was honored to once serve. I had no idea New York had changed so much since I was last here."

Alfred was trying hard and as the policeman was folding his arms, he added: "Can I ask you sir, are you Irish? Finest people in the world. I had the honor to serve in the 69th militia under Colonel Corcoran." As Jim listened, his accent began subtly to change to a brogue. "I have Irish roots myself, sorr."

The policeman's demeanor began to change. He unfolded his arms, sheathed his nightstick and began to grin. He put the accent on too. "Is that roight now? Well I never. Moy own grandfather fought wid the 69th at Bull Run," he said.

"Ah, I was there myself," replied Alfred. He couldn't resist it. "Tell me, what was your man's name? Is he going to the reunion? Can we offer him a lift?"

"Sadly no. He died a while back," said the policeman and Jim thought he detected a slight sigh of relief from his grandfather. "He was caught at the battle and put in prison with all the other men who were made prisoners of war. They didn't have such a good time of it as the officers. My grandda fought for one day and then spent three years in Pinckney Prison so he didn't have much to be grateful for."

Alfred looked sorrowful. "Indeed no. I don't wonder your grandfather had unhappy memories."

"Oh, I didn't say that," said the policeman. Alfred was clearly having difficulty keeping up with the ideological turns in the conversation. "No, he was proud to have served his country against those filthy heathen Protestants. Even if it did mean all them coloreds comin' up here and taking all the jobs afterwards. Thank God we keep them out of the force."

With that, the policeman eyed the car, peered inside and then bent down at the front to give the starting handle an experimental turn. It started at once. "You'd better all git going. I hope you find what you're lookin' for," he said, grinning. "And don't try that phony Irish accent on anyone else, y'hear?"

Alfred looked affronted and was just about to insist that he had indeed fought with the regiment – which was, after all, briefly true – but he decided it was not a good time to risk further confrontation with one of New York's Finest and clambered back aboard.

By now the afternoon was well advanced and they were some way towards the foot of the island, approaching Chinatown and the Bowery. The buildings were lower now, but grimmer, built from a deep red stone and with metal staircases descending from the upper floors on the outside. As they peered down one grimy side street, a sign stuck out from one of the houses. It said: Putain Hotel in illuminated letters – or actually Pain Hel, since several of the lights were missing. "There – that will do us real well," said Alfred.

Annabelle parked the Model T neatly outside and Jim was sent to ask about rooms. She came too. They cautiously made their way up the steps, leaving Alfred and Trumper sitting in the car guarding the belongings. The hotel looked unpromising from the outside and even less prepossessing inside. It was a tall narrow building with dark walls and dirty windows with gray shades and underdrapes. Its only concessions to brightness were battered and faded red awnings over the entrance and first floor windows but these were streaked with dirt. The front doorway was scuffed and dotted with litter.

The lobby was dark and cool like the inside of a cave; emphasised by the brown and cream paint on the walls and maroon, tin-plate sheeting on the ceiling. It smelled sour and musty as if no one had cleaned the place for a while. A fan lazily swept overhead and eventually, from a still deeper cave behind the desk, a middle-aged man in shirt sleeves emerged. Behind him there was the sound of a ball game playing on the radio.

He looked them up and down suspiciously, not bothering to do up his waistcoat-vest and wiping the back of his hand across his mouth and moustache as if he had just been eating something. "What do ya want?" he said brusquely.

Annabelle spoke up. "Hello, sir," she said brightly. "We are seeking rooms. Do you have two available?"

Still keeping his eye on them, the man opened the ledger on the desk. "How long do you want them for. By the hour or what?" he said.

Both of them knew that was odd. Didn't you rent a room overnight? This time it was Jim's turn. "If you please sir, until tomorrow. There's four of us. My grandfather and me and a family friend…er, all men. And one single for my friend here,"he said.

"Ya don't want two doubles?" the man seemed surprised. Then he shook his head as if he had suddenly understood. "Oh yeah? Out-of-towners, huh? Well make sure your grandfather ain't too frisky with you. This is a clean house. Room 104. Three dollars: double bed: one of ya's sleeping on the floor. And 112, single, two dollars, unless the third in 104 wants a cuddle," he said. "That's the closest I can do for you. You OK today, little lady?" And he leered.

"Oh yes, thank you," said Annabelle. "Are the sheets here clean?"

The man guffawed. "Clean as the last person who slept in them. And he left half an hour ago."

"Well, I trust they have been cleaned since then. And the room fumigated by someone more hygienically inclined than you yourself," she replied, smiling so sweetly that it was not until after she had turned away that the man realised the slight.

He glared at Jim: "Hey you. Five dollars. Now."

Jim signed the register. Despite the hotel's drabness, the book was full of famous names: Tom Mix was a regular, so was Charlie Chaplin and Rudolph

Valentino – how come he had signed in only the day before? It occurred to Jim that they might not be real names and, puzzled, he took the ancient keys tossed onto the counter by the man who was already retreating back into his inner cave. There seemed no indication where the rooms might be but there was a narrow flight of stairs at the far end of the lobby and Jim and Annabelle took those.

Upstairs, the corridor was even gloomier, with the smallest possible naked light bulb glowering from the ceiling. It was a bleak, narrow, unwelcoming place, a long alleyway lined on each side with brown painted doors. Even the linoleum on the floor was cracked and faded and there was a smell of damp. The rooms had numbers in the hundreds, though not all the cheap metal numerals were still on the doors. They groped along the corridor, past doors behind which occasional laughter and low adult voices could be heard, until Jim found what he took to be their room. It certainly looked like 104 but when he tried to push the key in the lock it stuck. As he attempted to jiggle it free there was the alarming sound of footsteps inside and a man in his undershirt flung open the door, wrenching the doorknob and the key from the boy's hand.

"What the devil do you want?" he said. Behind him Jim could see a woman lying in the bed, even though it was still the afternoon.

"Please sir, is this 104?" he asked timidly.

"No, the hell it isn't. It's 109. Clear off." The man said and slammed the door again. As he did so Jim caught the sound of the woman's voice saying: "Come back to bed, honey."

Annabelle said: "There's something strange about this place. It's not like somewhere I've ever stayed before."

They cautiously made their way back along the corridor until, by feel, Jim traced out the figure that appeared to be the right number. He put the key in the lock, turned it easily and went in.

The room was as gloomy as the corridor. A gray under-drape shivered against a window that seemed almost as dingy as the rest of the room. Peering out, they saw it looked directly onto a brick wall only a few feet away. As their eyes grew accustomed to the gloom, Jim's spirits sank. The room was filthy, the air heavy with the sour smell of unwashed bodies and the decoration a drab floral wallpaper. Along the longest wall was a double bed with an iron bedstead. In the small remaining space there was a solitary brown armchair with ripped upholstery. Across one corner hung a drape concealing a small hanging bar and some metal coat-hangers. A chipped empty pitcher and basin stood on a rickety card table. It was the sort of place to commit suicide in and, judging by the dark stains on the bedspread, it seemed possible that was what some previous guest had done. Jim and Annabelle looked at each other and sighed.

They crept out along the corridor and found Room 112. Annabelle unlocked the door and went in. It was much smaller, scarcely wider than a cupboard, and with the narrow single bed, there was just space to stand upright alongside it. On the wall a sampler said: "God is Love. All Others Pay Cash". Through the window the same grim wall could be seen opposite, blocking any view, or sunlight. The bed itself had an indentation in the middle, as if someone had just got out of it and left the room.

"Well," said Annabelle dubiously. "If it's just for one night: put it down to adventure, I suppose."

They made their way downstairs, Jim half resolved to reclaim their five dollars, but there was no sign of the man behind the desk. All that could be heard was the sound of the baseball game commentary and some gruff male voices chatting and laughing together. His courage to try and gain the man's attention failed him. Yes, put it down to experience, he thought. They went outside and were immediately blinded by the afternoon sunshine.

Down in the car, Alfred was growing impatient, tapping his fingers on the top of the front seat upholstery. In the front, Mr Trumper had acquired another bottle, wrapped in a brown paper bag, and was taking surreptitious swigs from it.

"What kept you?" Alfred said irritably.

"Oh Grandpa, it's not a very nice place," Jim said.

"Looks fine to me," he retorted, as if his original judgment and taste in spotting it had been questioned. "I very much doubt we'll find somewhere finer, or cheaper. Come on Trumpy, let's be going inside."

They pushed Trumper out of the car and gave him their bundles of clothes to hold, while Jim carried his grandfather's camera and tripod. Alfred started to haul the package of glass plates to the edge of the footwell so they could be lifted onto the sidewalk.

Trumper paused for a moment to consider, then placed their clothes carefully on the ground. After that, he flung up the hood cover, unscrewed a small round metal object from the engine and held it aloft, smiling. "Won't get far without this," he said as he slammed the hood shut. "Or this," he added as he detached the starting handle and added it to his bundles. The car was pretty open to the elements, but who would want to steal it when there were so many more up-to-date models along the roadside? Alfred waited impatiently for Trumper to dump the clothes in the entrance to the lobby and then the two of them lifted the plates between them and staggered up the steps together as if they were carrying a body.

Up in the room, Jim's grandfather resumed the benign bonhomie he had exercised almost all trip so far, despite the fact that there was now a rhythmic bouncing sound coming from the other side of the wall. He roared with laughter, loudly enough to interrupt the bouncing for a moment. "A cat house! My word. What larks! I think your education is proceeding apace young James," he exclaimed.

While he and Trumper sat on the bed chortling to themselves about something, seemingly oblivious to the stains, Jim was sent down the corridor with the empty pitcher to find some water. Eventually he found a bathroom, almost as grubby and bleak as the bedroom. While he was filling the pitcher, a figure slid into the room behind him.

He thought he had closed the door and wheeled round, surprised at being disturbed. It was a large middle-aged woman in a pink silk bathrobe. He supposed she must be planning to take a bath. This sure was a strange place where people walked around in their night attire in broad daylight. He had a brief impression of lipstick and rouge, but found his eyes lingering unconsciously on her extensive cleavage.

"Can I help you dearie?" she said aggressively.

Jim stammered, blushing red yet again: "Oh, no, sorry. I didn't realize you were in here, ma'am. I didn't mean to interrupt. I didn't know. I'm sorry."

"I wasn't in here and you didn't interrupt, but you can get out now if you like," she said more equably and he hurried out of the room in confusion.

Both Trumper and his grandfather were still lying on the bed but this time with both heads thrown back, their mouths wide open, snoring gently. Jim sat in the chair a while to contemplate what to do and then, nervously, resolved to take a stroll out and see something of the great city. He extracted the roomkey and tiptoed quietly along to Annabelle's room.

She was sitting on the bed with her knees drawn up, reading her book. Jim sat at her feet and said: "You know what I think this is? I think this might be a whore house!"

"Well, that took you a while. I guessed it when the man downstairs said they rented by the hour."

Then she put her book down, clambered along the bed and gave him a kiss. "Poor innocent boy."

Jim leaned his head towards her and brushing her cheek with his hand made to kiss her properly. But she pushed him away, saying: "No Jim. Not here.

I don't want to do it in a place like this. It's not nice."

Instead they got up and, locking the door behind them, set out to explore the big city. They crept along the hall, down the stairs and past the man at the desk. He was still listening to the game, leaning on the counter, his face resting against his fist and he scarcely registered their presence.

Jim's first aim was to buy a postcard to send a note home to his mother, so he stopped and asked where he could buy one. The greasy clerk, interrupted once more, seemed none too pleased. "Cards, what sort of cards do you want?" he said. Then a sly grin spread across his face. "If you want postcards, I got nice ones, of my sister…" and he pulled a creased picture of a woman in a bathing costume out from his vest pocket.

"No, no," Jim said, beating a retreat. "It doesn't matter. I'll find something else." And he stumbled out through the door. Behind him Annabelle was saying: "I don't believe that's your sister. She looks far too clean for that."

Outside the heat seemed to radiate off the sidewalk and shimmer on the surface of the road, as if given a concentrated focus by the tall buildings on either side. Jim was conscious of looking like a country boy to the city folk, had they gazed at him as consciously as he felt sure they must be doing, but beside him Annabelle thrust her arm into his, smiled engagingly and plunged off down the sidewalk as if she had lived there all her life. Jim had vaguely resolved to see the Statue of Liberty or maybe the Empire State, but he did not like to ask for directions from the people brushing past them in their city suits and straw boaters for fear of getting a rebuff. They mooched along, gazing around them, him idly pretending he was looking for a particular address and inwardly astonished at the range of provisions piled outside the shops on the sidewalk and she looking as poised and elegant, he thought, as a mannequin model. He was so proud of her it made him gasp for breath.

There were vegetables and foodstuffs they would never have seen in a lifetime in Springbridge. Signs and hoardings hung from every building. But what really fascinated and astonished Jim was the noise of all the voices and arguments in every doorway, the gesticulations in even the most inconsequential of conversations and, most of all, the range of languages spoken. The city seemed alive with shouting, shoving and argument.

They returned to the hotel, Jim too anxious of the crowd to try and see the sights. In the corridor Alfred was prowling outside their room in a state of agitation and excitement. "Son, you've brought us to some place here. Do you know what it is?" he asked, answering himself: "It's a whorehouse. Didn't you realize? Well, there's a thing. Now, Annabelle you need to be especially careful.

You lock yourself in and don't let anyone in."

"I reckon I can take care of myself," she said and headed towards her room. Jim rather reckoned that was true.

CHAPTER TWENTY-FOUR

The old man was fully rested now. "Well Jim," said Alfred. "I rather think it's time we went out to see the sights that the Big City has to offer. Would you care to come with us young lady?"

Annabelle needed no second introduction but in their bedroom Old Trumper was still snoring gently. Alfred prodded him unceremoniously, saying they were going out to view the sights. Trumper turned over but made no attempt to join them.

Alfred really wanted to see the Empire State building. He had heard tell of it, but could not quite believe it could be true: one of the wonders of the modern age: the tallest, grandest, most breath-taking building in the world. "I think we might hire a cab, don't you?" he said in expansive mood, eyeing their old car sitting by the kerbside. And he stepped straight out into the path of a yellow car, holding up his hand and shouting.

The car braked and they could see it was a taxi. He got in and Jim and Annabelle followed. Alfred sat back in the seat, his arms outstretched along the upholstery and said in a lordly way: "The Empire State building if you please, my good man." The driver in his peaked cap looked back quizzically and, finally deciding no insult was intended, edged forward into the traffic.

A haze rose off the streets. The air seemed to smell of gas and tar and the noise was louder than anything Jim had ever heard before. He looked out of the window at the people hurrying in their business suits with a kind of wonder.

The hustle and rush of the men seemed to be the essence of commerce and the languid stroll of the women the epitome of elegance and wealth.

Nearly every doorway had a commissionaire in uniform and the noise and shouting, whistles and car horns, were deafening. Everything seemed heightened and more vivid. The colors were brighter, the noise louder, the movement more rapid. This sure beat the country.

Alfred was uttering small cries of astonishment as he too peered out: "Well, will you just look at that? Good Lord. Goodness me. You wouldn't believe it. Gosh this has changed. What a place."

"You guys new in town?" said the driver, glancing at them in his rear view mirror with a vulpine New York smile.

"Oh no," Alfred said hastily. "I've been here many times before. It's just it's changed a bit recently. But I've got my bearings."

"When were you last here?" said the driver, rolling the gum across from one side of his mouth to the other. "Oh, just a year or two back," the old man lied. "It's just all these buildings...so high these days. It's hard to keep up..."

"It's all right Grandpa, I won't give you the fifty cent tour. I want to get home tonight," said the driver. "I guess you really haven't been around for a bit after all."

Alfred admitted as much. "Not this century. But I fought with a New York regiment in the late, great, war. My grandson here's taking me to the reunion at Gettysburg and we thought we'd fit in some sight-seeing on the way."

"Well, you just be careful," said the driver. "Here we are – and don't go up too fast. That'll be a dollar." Leaning out of his window he undid the rear door with a practised flick of his wrist.

Grandfather huffed a bit at the cost of this but he handed over the money and a one cent tip. The driver looked at it. "Don't invite me to your next party," he said and the car roared off. Alfred was puzzled. "What a nice man," he said. "But what party could he have meant?"

They stood outside the entrance to the Empire State, which dwarfed all the other buildings. It seemed to soar forever into the sky, like a great gray pencil or Jack's beanstalk. It was enormous. In a day of wonders, this was the most extraordinary sight yet.

"Come on now," Alfred said and marched inside, through the great shiny chrome doors, through the paneled halls and towards the public elevator.

"Sir, we're closing in a few minutes," said a uniformed man at a desk.

"That's alright. We only need a few minutes...on our way to Gettysburg," Alfred said shamelessly and headed for the doors.

The elevator was in itself a new experience, carrying them soaring upwards in its paneled box, with a bored lift boy in uniform sitting reading a newspaper in a corner by the control panel. Alfred, holding onto his hat in case it might get blown away even in an enclosed space, tried to engage him in conversation. "This is a wonderful thing," he said. "Do you never feel sea sick to be going up and down all day?"

"No," said the youth and turned the page of his paper.

"It must be wonderful to be employed in such a building…."

The boy did not answer. He was engaged in the *Dick Tracy* cartoon strip.

"Hurtling up and down?"

By now the lift boy was reading *Ripley's Believe It Or Not* column.

"Tallest building in the world? A great American achievement!"

The boy deigned to answer: "Yupp. An' we're going up at 1,200 feet a minute."

"My God," said Alfred and edged against the elevator wall. They were all transfixed by the dial above the doors with its arrow moving steadily towards the right. Then they were at the observation deck.

Moving out onto the concourse, they gasped. New York was laid out far below, glittering in the afternoon light. Out in the river tiny boats and great liners shimmered on the water and down on the streets, already in shadow, specks of people and minuscule limousines silently and slowly made their way like insects. Up there all was silent, as if they were suspended above a picture, disconnected from the world far below. Alfred grasped the brim of his hat against the wind and looked out agape over the sheer drop beyond the balustrade.

Finally, he said: "Isn't America wonderful? Aren't you proud to belong to this great, shining country? This Empire State must reflect out across the whole world. They can see it from Europe, I shouldn't wonder. This is...a beacon to all men." His voice was full of emotion and wonder and a tear trickled down his cheek

"It's mighty fine, Grandfather," was all Jim could say. The wind was getting up and he and Annabelle flattened themselves against the wall of the building. Jim looked up at the storeys above, heading up to the great mast from which he had seen King Kong swinging in the movie and it made him dizzy, as if he might be flung out into eternity at any moment. Beside him, Annabelle stood with her eyes tight closed and her teeth chattering with the cold. She held tight to Jim's arm. "Let's go down," she whispered. "Oh please. I can't stand heights."

A few minutes later they were back down at ground level, reeling out of the building breathless and exhilarated, as if they had stood on a high mountain.

Jim felt as though they had viewed all the kingdoms of the world in a moment of time, just like the Bible says the Devil showed Jesus in the Wilderness.

CHAPTER TWENTY-FIVE

The photographers smelled the battlefield of Gettysburg long before they ever saw it. They knew the battle had been a huge one that had lasted days and, miles short of their destination, the discarded refuse of the big fight was already littering the route and the fields around. As they headed north they found the road increasingly choked with traffic, carts moving north, stragglers heading south. Some men were moving seemingly in a daze, others staggering, their wounds dressed with handkerchiefs and torn bedsheets. These were Union men.

There had been rain overnight but it was a hot, dull day and the atmosphere was stifling.Three miles south of the battlefield, in the still air they could already smell the musty aroma of gunpowder and sense the smoke hanging in the trees. Soon there would be the sour smell of the putrifying corpses of men and horses, wafting gently south.

An hour of plodding through this and, in a gap in the woods that lined the road, Gardner signalled a halt for a break. He and Tim O'Sullivan got down from the wagon to stretch their legs and, in the debris by the side of the road, Gardner picked up a discarded rifle, its bayonet still attached. Climbing back on board with it he smiled at Alfred and said: "This will do nicely for a prop."

"What do you mean?" said Alfred.

"In case one of our subjects needs one," Gardner replied enigmatically.

"Hi there. Do you know where the battle is?" a clergyman had ridden up. "I am heading there to offer succour to our brave men," he said, raising his wide-brimmed hat to reveal the white clerical bands which had been in shadow before.

The man thrust out his right hand and Gardner shook it unenthusiastically. "Charles H. Keener," he said. "Christian Commission. From Baltimore."

"I believe the fight was at Gettysburg," said Gardner. "Up along the pike. You can tag along if you wish.

They moved off, up the road with Mr Keener bobbing along on his horse beside the darkroom wagon, earnestly attempting to draw Gardner into conversation. Instead, with every attempt, the Scotsman grew more taciturn.

"Are you with the celebrated Mr Brady?" he asked, eyeing the lettering on the canvas hood of the wagon.

"No."

"Well, I thought everyone was with Mr Brady."

"No. We were, but we've branched out on our own, my colleagues and me."

"Are you going to take photographs of the battle?"

"Looks like it."

Keener fell silent. Then: "Will you take my photograph, to show the folks back in Baltimore what I am doing?"

"No."

"Why?"

"Can't spare the glass plates. We need 'em for important subjects, not vanity ones." Then Gardner relented a little and passed the man his carte de visite photograph, the one with him posing next to his camera. "Look, if you want a picture taken, you will be welcome to make an appointment when we get back to Washington," he said.

A few minutes later they crested a low rise and suddenly there, spread out before them, was the valley of the battlefield. It was a wide, panoramic view of destruction.

"My God!" murmered Gardner.

The road ahead of them ran through fields of flattened corn edged with beaten-down fences running to the far distance where they could see the cluster of houses that was the town of Gettysburg. To the left was a line of trees marking the edge of a wood and to the right a line of small hills covered in scrubby vegetation and young pine trees.

But it was the fields themselves that caught their attention. They were covered in dead bodies across a stretch maybe a mile wide. Alfred was getting used to this now, the men laid out singly and in groups and lines, on their backs with their legs together, at attention; and beside them and all around the swollen bodies of horses, fat to bursting like great brown balloons, their legs still splayed in the air as if they had just toppled sideways as they galloped. They looked like monstrous rocking-horses that had fallen over, Alfred thought.

Across the field, burial parties were moving, men in shirtsleeves and galluses carrying picks and shovels, handkerchiefs tied over their noses to protect them from the smell. Shallow pits were being dug, only a foot or two deep, as if the ground was too hard to make a greater effort worthwhile, and the bodies were being placed in them, still in their uniforms, without coffins or even shrouds, and quickly covered over. Some had rough wooden headboards, ripped from the ends of amunition boxes, to mark their graves, but most did not. The priority was to get the bodies covered over before they rotted and spread disease. They could be exhumed again and reburied deeper later.

Smoke still rose from burned out farm houses and barns. Everywhere were signs of the battle's destruction, broken gun carriages and shattered cannons, rifles that had been dropped or thrown away, knapsacks and ammunition boxes, water canteens and bandages. Scraps of paper fluttered on the ground like small ghosts. Alfred thought for a moment that they looked like the souls of the departed, vainly seeking the bodies they had left, but in reality they were just torn pieces of newspaper, printed notices and even letters from home.

Mr Keener looked horrified and put his hand to his mouth. He uttered little bleats: "Oh...oh...I never, never...expected this."

Gardner grunted. "Well sir, that's what war is. Now, if you will excuse us, we have work to do. The day is getting late. We have photographs to make of the horrors of war. And I dare say you have souls to save. Good day to you."

The wagon rumbled down the pike and turned off left through a gap in the split rail fence into an area of battered fruit trees, the first field they came to which still had bodies in it. The light was already beginning to fade and there would be no more than an hour for taking photographs that evening.

"Alex, these are Union men," said Tim O'Sullivan, examining one of the bodies. "Are you sure we should be picturing them? Their relatives might see."

Gardner shook his head. "No, they won't be able to tell. They won't see their faces. We haven't had dead Northern men before...This'll bring it home. Sorrow of war and all that. They're probably all Krauts and Swedes anyway... Alfred – start preparing the plates. Hurry up now!"

Alfred turned back towards the wagon and almost slipped over a corpse he had not seen. It was less a body and more a piece of meat. Although still clothed, the Confederate soldier's stomach had been ripped open as if excavated, rib cage and entrails showing, from the ends of his shirt to his open trousers. His left arm had disappeared, leaving the shoulderbone sticking out and his face had all but gone, as if gnawed away.

The boy cried out as he tried to avoid stepping into the man. Gardner and O'Sullivan turned round. "We'll have that," said Gardner. "Get me the rifle, Alfred." And he stooped and gingerly picked up a man's hand, neatly severed above the wrist, that was nestling nearby in the stubble and dropped it beside the corpse. He laid the rifle reverently across the body's knees, next to the disembodied hand.

The corpse did not make pretty viewing. There were times when Alfred wondered how much more shocking their pictures could get. This one was beyond decency. Who could want to see that? Who would want to buy a print except a ghoul? And who but a ghoul would make a photograph of it?

He coated the glass plate in the wagon's dark room, secured it in its frame and returned to the group gathered around the body, taking care to look where he was stepping now. They had set the camera up for a close-up picture. Alfred heard Gibson say, appraisingly. "I don't know whether it was a shell did that, Alex. Could have been the hogs come out of the woods, ripping him up...or even rats. He's been lying there a couple of days, they've had time."

"I think we'll say it's a shell," said Gardner, disappearing under the camera cloth. Then, muffled: "We don't want to outrage decency."

Alfred could not bear to watch. He stumbled back to the wagon, disappeared around the far side. And retched.

"You feelin' bad?" it was Simon, the black teamster. He was sitting on the ground with his back resting against one of the wagon's wheels.

"No," Alfred lied, then: "It's just horrible. I don't know..."

Simon said: "Mr Alfred, I've been thinking about all these bodies. You know, when I was a child down in Virginia, I always thought that when we black boys died and went to Heaven, we'd turn white. From God's justice, see? Become like white men."

Then he thought some more. "Thing is, seeing all these bodies now, that ain't true. All these white folks turns black." Simon shook his head: "Ain't that the damndest thing?"

"Are you alright Alfred?" It was Gardner, peering round the back of the what's-it wagon. "You looked a bit peaky just now. We do need you to do the fetching and carrying, you know."

Alfred scrambled to his feet. "Yes, sir, Mr Gardner, sir. It was just that body, made me feel queer."

Gardner grunted: "Yepp, pretty ripe one."

Alfred took his chance: "The thing is, sir, I don't know why you took it. It's not as if you could ever show it to the public."

Gardner was looming over him now, his beard bristling. He was not going to take kindly to this and started wagging his finger in Alfred's face. "Now see here, Barker: it's not for you, you wee man, to question what I do, or you can walk back to Washington and goodbye to you. You do not presume to question me, or the others, about our work, y'hear?"

He was working himself up now and Alfred cringed. "We are not taking these pictures for commercial advantage. We are taking them because they are a contemporary record of this war, this fearful struggle...the greatest event in this nation's history. We have at our hands one of the greatest inventions of the modern era and we have a duty to use it, to show people for all time a mirror of these events.

"That is what we are doing, and don't you forget it. You should be proud of it and of your part in our profession. This is our historic mission. We have a moral purpose: to show the reality of war, not its drums and trumpets, but its dreadful details! Not just for people now, but for people yet to come. In a hundred years people will be looking at these pictures and gasping, long after we're all dead. It is a noble – a sacred purrpose. Think, by showing this we can stop a calamity such as war from everr happening again!" His Scottish accent was coming out now, as if he was a Presbyterian preacher.

Gardner turned to go. "Plus, they will make money. People will want to see them. Now, will you get along and bring me the next plate, boy." It was a command, not a question.

An hour later, as the light faded, the wagons turned down the hill towards the little town on the horizon. They passed clumps of the dead, still lying where they had fallen three days before. Not all were as disfigured as the Confederate corpse. Many were lying peacefully on their backs, some almost as if they had been poleaxed while standing at attention, others with their arms flung out above their heads, more as though they had been wounded and composed themselves for the sleep of death, with their hands together in prayer. Their bodies were swelling, bursting open their trouser flies and snapping off their tunic buttons. Most had lost their shoes, leaving their feet just in their woollen socks, solid footwear always precious and worth pilfering by the living.

As the horse plodded along across the fields, Alfred thought: "Maybe Mr Gardner's right. Maybe it is history we're recording and that's why we have to get here early, before it goes, not wait like Mr Brady and take pretty pictures later, when it is all neat and tidy and the only corpses are living soldiers you can get to lie down for you and pose." And he felt a surge of pride to be one of the chroniclers, like some medieval monkish scribe.

Soon they had pulled onto the pike road, rattling slowly past troops of soldiers marching to their posts or to their bivouacs. They were young men, Alfred's age, tanned by the summer sun and scrawny with all the route marching they had done. Their eyes were hollowed and fearful, and the slump of their shoulders showed how exhausted they were. These were youngsters in need of a bath and a long sleep and knowing they had little chance of getting either.

As they passed one group, Jim Gibson stood up from his seat and shouted: "Are you New York boys?"

A soldier called back: "Yessir. 140th."

Gibson whooped: "My God! You're the ones I'm looking for. Do you know Hugh McGraw?"

The soldiers muttered among themselves, then one approached the wagon: "Do you mean the lieutenant?"

Gibson was excited: "Yes, that must be him. Good old Hugh, to be an officer! We were at school together in Brooklyn. Where are you boys camped? I can't wait to see his face when I tap him on the shoulder."

The soldier was standing beside the wooden footrest of the wagon now, looking up at Gibson. He said: "He's not with us any more, sir. He was wounded in the second day's fight and I don't know where he is right now. I don't think it was serious though, from what I hear, so you might find him down in the hospital, I guess..."

Gibson had gone white. "Oh my God. Thank you, soldier," he said. "I'll go find him."

They pitched the wagons on open ground near the edge of the town and Gibson could barely wait to start looking for his friend. "Wait a bit," said Gardner, "We'll come too," Alfred and Tim O'Sullivan tagged along as well and they headed towards a line of tents in a field nearby.

The large tents with their awnings had been erected in the shade of a grove of trees. Kerosine lanterns hung from the tent poles, lighting the interiors. There was an air of bustle about the tents, with medical orderlies and doctors in army uniforms moving purposefully, carrying surgical equipment, bandages and blankets. An intense smell hung in the air and from under the canvas the groans and shouts of wounded men could be heard.

A surgeon was standing outside one tent, smoking a cheroot. He was wearing a dark-stained leather apron and in his left hand, he held a saw. Gibson bounded up to him. "Excuse me, can you tell me where the wounded of the

140th New York are?" he said. "I am looking for a friend."

The doctor shrugged. "I don't know. I just cut 'em up and send 'em off. I don't care where they come from," he said. "I've done twenty-six amputations today and there's more yet. We've got thousands of men to treat here – those that survive that long anyway." He gestured to a bucket from which a bloodied arm was sticking out. And then he took a gulp from his hip flask.

The photographers went on down the line, asking for McGraw at each tent. At last Gardner saw someone he recognised, emerging from under an awning. "Keener!" he called. "Over here!" It was the clergyman from the Christian Commission who had accompanied them earlier in the day on the road from Emmitsburg.

"Why, Mr Gardner, this is a surprise," Keener said, coldly. "I thought you had work to do."

"Yes, we do. The fact is we're looking for a friend of my colleague here, Mr Gibson, who was wounded in the fight. Can you help us find him? Lieutenant McGraw from New York."

Keener pointed to an orderly who was carrying a sheaf of papers. "That man can probably help you. He's got names. Meanwhile I am busy saving souls. Good night to you." He turned and walked away.

McGraw turned out to be in the last tent of a row when they finally found them. He was lying in a bed, covered by a blanket and was barely conscious. The mound under the blanket where his legs were was narrow.

Gibson bent low over his bed, whispering urgently: "Hello Hugh, Hugh. It's me, Jim Gibson, come to visit. How are you?"

The young man struggled to rise in the bed and they could see by the lamplight that his face was covered in globules of sweat. "Is that you Jim? Oh thank God. I'm not so good, I'm afraid. They've taken my leg off."

Gibson put his hand over his mouth in shock. "Hugh, I'm so sorry. What happened?"

McGraw fell back against his pillow. "Damn fool," he said. "I put my knee in the way of a bullet in the fight. It carried the bone away, so there was nothing for it. Got a bit of a fever now..."

Gibson was searching for words of comfort. "Oh Hugh, it's not so bad. There's plenty skipping around with wooden legs. It gets you out of the war anyhow."

The lieutenant closed his eyes. "I don't think so. The doctors were good and quick, but I don't think anything can save me. It's these shivers."

"Can we get you anything?"

McGraw smiled: "No. You being here's enough. It's good of you to come. Will you write to my folks for me? Let them know...Dr McGraw, Brooklyn. Thank you. Thank you."

Alfred was sent to fill up McGraw's water canteen and when he brought it back Gardner topped it up with whiskey from his hip flask. Then they crept away from the tent, with McGraw's thanks still ringing in their ears.

Jim Gibson was sobbing. "He was such a good runner," he said. "And now he'll never play baseball again. Damn this bloody war!"

Gardner put an arm round his shoulder. "Now, now Jim. He'll get well. They do, you know. Not like those poor men we photograph lying out there. We'll keep an eye out for him..."

Gardner was as good as his word. A few days later, after the team split up, with O'Sullivan and Gibson following the army and the others returning to Washington, Alexander Gardner sent them a telegram: "I have just got back from Gettysburg," it said. "Tell Jim that McGraw is dead. I will write."

CHAPTER TWENTY-SIX

The knock on the engraved glass panel of the front door was so hearty that Gene thought it must break. "Coming, coming," he called as he rushed down the hall, hoping that the sound of his voice would preempt another assault. It did not: as he opened it, the pounding was beginning again.

"Oh hullo," said the spitting image of Abraham Lincoln. "I didn't think anyone had heard us."

Gene blinked at the apparition. Not only was the man tall and bony, with a beard hugging the contours of his prominent chin, but he was also wearing a frock coat and carrying a stovepipe hat. By his side was a much smaller, stouter middle-aged woman wearing a crinoline.

Gene took a pace back. "I can see you think we strangely attired," the man said aimiably. "I am not really Abraham Lincoln," he added unnecessarily. "My wife and I are visiting for the Lincoln Lookalikes' Convention. We are, you see, dedicated members of the Association of Lincoln Presenters."

"I see," said Gene, not doing so. He wondered vaguely whether the Lookalikes were some obscure religious sect, proselytizing door-to-door like the Jehovah's Witnesses.

The man stuck out his hand and said: "I am sorry, I have you at a disadvantage. We saw your brochure in the shopping mall and stopped by in case you had rooms to let tonight. We would esteem it a favor, if you have. And we pay modern prices."

They stepped over the threshold, taking advantage of Gene's retreat. The man was still talking: "My name is Henry Adams McMeikle the Third, but you can call me Abe if it's easier. This is my wife Pollyanna Nunley McMeikle. As you can see, she is Mrs Lincoln. We work together. But fortunately she hasn't gone off her head yet! Ha! Ha!."

"No," said the woman sourly. "You're still alive."

Gene said: "You go round places dressed like that?"

The man replied: "Well, all over Milwaukee, anyway. Not down South, oviously. We open fairs and supermarkets. And automobile dealerships – but only if they're Lincolns! Haw! Haw! We're very well known in Wisconsin. There's hundreds of us about in the ALP and every year we hold a convention. And this year it's here in Springbridge, at the Holiday Inn, only we booked too late. If you go down Main Street, you'll see a load of folks just like us right now. It's full of Abraham Lincolns! So, anyway, do you have any rooms?" This Abe had a way of looming too close with breath so bad that Gene rocked slightly back.

They were in the hallway now, so it was too late to keep them out. Gene started to frame in his mind the words to say that they weren't open yet, the season had not begun and they weren't ready. They really had not wanted re-enactors, but this was just too bizarre: opening a bed and breakfast with a Civil War theme and the first guest was Abraham Lincoln and his wife. At the very least he could take their photograph for publicity purposes. And, after all, he had been saying to Izzie, hadn't he, that they needed to open real soon. This would show her that he could cope on his own. He must not be stiff and stuffy with them.

So he said: "Well, we're only just opening for the season and my wife's away, so I am afraid you will have to put up with me looking after you, but if you're happy with that, I'll show you your room and get it aired and ready. How long will you be staying?"

"Well, if we like it, three nights," said Lincoln. "How much is it?"

Gene thought quickly. He and Izzie had not discussed this yet in detail and so they had not costed what they were offering. "Ah, three nights? Shall we say one hundred and fifty dollars? All in?"

Abe said quickly: "Done! That's very good: the Holiday Inn's charging the conventioners eighty a night. Do you take Mastercard? No? Oh never mind – not if you don't object to having my face on all the bills...."

After that, all day, Gene kept seeing President Lincolns. When he drove into town to collect supplies for the next morning's breakfast, there they were, milling about on Main Street in their black suits and top hats: tall ones, short ones (short ones? –Lincoln convertibles, Gene thought, and smiled), burly ones and beanpole ones, even a black one, all with their little beards and some with their wives. In the car park behind Walmart, you could tell which their cars were: mostly Lincolns – of course – but with vanity plates bearing legends like ABE L 1, ABES R US and even 4 SCORE 7. Sheesh, that man sure had crept into the national consciousness, Gene murmered to himself.

Then, back home, it was like Abe had rushed up from town and got in before him. There in the sitting room were Abe and Mrs Abe sitting on either side of the fireplace, like animatronic versions of the originals, surrounded by the Victorian antiques Izzie had bought. Abe was reading a volume entitled *Lincoln's Greatest Speeches And What They Mean For America Today* and Mrs Abe was thumbing through *The National Enquirer*, a trifle resentfully, Gene thought. No mention of the Lincolns in there, but plenty about Madonna, he guessed.

As he went to bed upstairs that evening, Gene could not resist pausing to listen outside their door. There was a creaking sound as if Mr Abe was striding about the room and the low rumbling noise of Mrs Abe complaining. He put his ear close to the door: this must have been what the White House sounded like in 1863. Mrs Abe was saying: "Have you seen the sanitary facilities here, Henry? They don't seem to have a working shower. We gotta get in to the Holiday Inn tomorrow...."

Gene was affronted. What was wrong with them? The room had an en suite bathroom with a rolltop bath! Admittedly he hadn't got round to fixing the shower yet, but it was clean and they could have a soak in the tub if they wanted. They were surrounded with Victoriana for God's sake! The real Mrs Lincoln wouldn't have worried so. You let people into your home and all they do is complain!

In the morning, still vaguely resentful, but conscious of the one hundred and fifty bucks in his pocket which he did not want to let go, Gene got up early to prepare breakfast. No muffins – he had not tried to bake them – but there were croissants, bought the previous evening, and Corn Flakes and smooth orange juice made from concentrate out of a carton (probably just how they'd like it, he thought bitterly).

He was waiting for them as they came downstairs, already dressed in costume and ready for the convention. "Good morning," Gene said. "How did you sleep?"

Abe nodded ruefully: "Not well," he said. "The bed's too soft. And too short: I kept getting my feet hooked up in the bedframe."

"And there's no television in the room!" exclaimed Mrs Abe. "I really wanted to catch *The Sopranos.*"

Gene bristled. "I am so sorry," he said. "We are trying to recreate the authentic feel of a Victorian home here..."

"I get that all day," said Mrs Abe. "I want to get back to real life in the evenings when I take this stuff off."

Then she made her way over to the sideboard where the buffet was laid out. "Where's the fruit anyway?" she demanded.

"Oh sorry. I forgot that. I'll just fetch it," said Gene and rushed back from the kitchen with the bowl of fruit: apples, oranges, bananas and strawberries that he had bought the night before.

"Don't you have paw-paw?" said Mrs Abe.

"Err, no. They were fresh out," Gene replied. Paw-paw? What was wrong with this woman?

She clicked her tongue. "Henry and I always have muffins," she said. "And waffles," said Mr Abe.

"I am sorry to let you down," said Gene.

After breakfast he stood in the hall as Mr and Mrs Abe brought their cases downstairs (Gene was damned if he was going to help them). Mr Abe said: "I am sorry. We've decided not to stay. This establishment does not meet our requirements."

Gene counted out a hundred dollars. "Here you go," he said. "I wish you better luck at the Best Western, or wherever you end up. I believe there is a Budget Inn in Vermont that might suit you."

Mrs Abe glared at him and he was glad. He stood on the porch and waved as their ancient Lincoln (registration plate: ABENME) swept down the drive. Fifty dollars, he thought, for that and he'd spent twenty-five on buying their breakfast. Then, when he went upstairs to tidy their bedroom, he discovered that Abe and Mrs Abe had cleared out all the Molton Brown toiletries. He sat down to do the math at the kitchen table, chewing on a slightly stale croissant and cold leftover coffee as he did so. He reckoned that having the Lincolns to stay had made him a profit of exactly nine dollars and eighty-five cents. Better not tell Izzie.

And he hadn't even got their photograph! Nor told them the story of the Photographer's House and why it was called that....Well, probably just as well: they'd only have charged him for the commercial exploitation of their image. Things could only get better.

CHAPTER TWENTY-SEVEN

Alfred was up and about early, before the others were awake. He was so used to the comforting contours of the mattress on his bed back home in Springbridge that he was finding the nights away from home a trial – that and the fact that he was so excited by a pilgrimage he had never expected to make. As he felt for his boots under the hotel bed, he could scarcely believe what they were doing. "Gettysburg, well, well, after seventy five years," he muttered to himself.

Three-quarters of a century and yet it felt like yesterday, actually more vivid than yesterday, or any number of days, or decades, since. He didn't even have to close his eyes to remember what it looked and felt like. It was almost as if the sweat was still trickling down his back. He could feel that, even as he could not feel what it was like to be seventeen again. Well, feelings were all relative. He still felt like Alfred Barker, a few aches and pains but he was still the same person, same fears and hopes. And this trip was like a tonic to him: it had given him a purpose in life. He felt livelier than at any time since he was a young man! He could do anything again – well, as he struggled to pull his boots on, almost anything.

"Come on – wake up Jim! Trumpy – shift yourself!" he cried, shaking the old man on the other side of the bed. There was not a moment to miss. His hat was already on his head, his vest buttoned and his collarless shirt done up fast to the stud. He had not shaved but it was clear that he could wait no longer to be off.

"Time to get under way. We've got to be over the 'Jersey shore today if we're ever going to get to Gettysburg. Let's get something to eat and get going," he said.

Jim was sent to rouse Annabelle and found her already dressed and sitting on the bed, reading *Gone with the Wind.* She too was bouncing with excitement. "I couldn't sleep," she said. "There's just so much to take in."

They all stumbled out of the hotel and crossed the road to a diner. Jim still felt full, or perhaps just queasy, but Simeon Trumper was soon stuffing himself with pancakes and maple syrup and Alfred was ruminating over a piece of toast and coffee. "Some things get better," he said, eyeing the meal with satisfaction.

Afterwards, they loaded up, ready to set off, while Alfred remonstrated with the clerk about the outrageous expense for the rooms. The old car started easily once Trumper had remembered to screw in the part he had removed the day before and which he found, with some surprise, in his pocket.

Alfred insisted that he wanted to see Broadway again and, leaning out, accosted a stranger to ask how they might find it. Jim laboriously turned the car in an enormous circle across the street. It stalled only once as they steered right around Washington Square to head towards the great white way.

It was still early but the traffic was already heavy as they drove into the canyon of the street. Jim became aware that his grandfather was leaning far out over the side of the car, trying to read the numbers. Then, at the corner of Broadway and Tenth, he suddenly shouted for them to stop.

Thinking something had fallen out, Jim applied the brakes so hard that the baggage in the back hurled forward, the box of plates thumping against the back of the front seat. There had been no time to draw to a halt; the car just stopped in the middle of the street. The traffic came squealing to a stop behind them and Jim could hear the other vehicles sounding their horns, their drivers swearing, as Alfred hopped lightly out of the back and picked his way fastidiously through the traffic to the sidewalk.

There he gazed up at a large office building, pushing back his hat in wonder. They joined him as soon as Simeon had cranked the engine to restart it and the car had been maneuvered to the kerb.

"What did you want to do that for?" Jim asked, but his grandfather scarcely troubled to reply.

Still looking upwards, he said: "It was here. Number 785. This is where Mr Brady had his studio in this city. Nothing like this in my day...all gone now." And he sighed deeply.

They returned to the car and slowly, reluctantly, Alfred rejoined them.

"How sad," he said. "Well, best drive on. What are you waiting for?"

It was already becoming a hot day. Thinking it best to stick to a road that at least was heading straight in one direction, Jim stayed with Broadway even though the road was becoming steadily busier and truck drivers were staring at them again. Simeon waved cheerfully back at them and Alfred raised his hat, as if taking part in a triumphal procession.

Onwards they went, past Times Square and the great advertising hoardings, astonishing to a country boy like Jim, then, further north still, past department stores and hotels overshadowed by the high cliff walls of buildings. It was breath-taking and threatening. Jim concentrated hard just to keep the car rolling forward. "Don't break down, don't break down," he kept whispering to himself, as if half-hoping the car would hear and obey.

Eventually there was a sign to make a left. Then, stretching far across the river, the George Washington Bridge soared high over to the Jersey shore. They were on their way again. Jim had never been on a road so big and wide and elevated. The great river glistened in the morning sun far below and once again a sense of exhilaration seized them all. Mr Trumper started singing *"Happy Days are Here Again"*, a smile broadening across his sallow face, with Annabelle joining in the choruses from the back, beating out the time on her lap as if she was cradling a pair of drums, and Jim could sense his grandfather waving his hands in pure joy, as if conducting a silent orchestra.

They all laughed for pleasure. Behind them lay the big city, its skyscrapers still pointing heavenwards, glittering in the sun, but Jim could only feel that they had escaped its clutches astonishingly unscathed. He breathed a sigh of relief and could feel the tension ebb from his body. They were safe again and would soon be back in the country.

Over the bridge and on the other side, they rolled along, singing cheerily now about being in the money as they passed first through the suburb of Fort Lee and then suddenly out on the highway into open marshland with not a house in sight. It was now that the car first spluttered and then rolled gently to a stop. They had somehow missed their way while they were singing and were on a small road in the middle of nowhere. And the sun was getting hot.

In the far distance the tops of the skyscrapers were still just visible over a flat landscape of high reeds and grasses. Otherwise the road stretched straight into the distance and the landscape was dull and featureless. A few cars passed but not many and the only sound was that of crickets and insects in the bushes. It seemed to Jim that their long-feared catastrophe had arrived. If it had happened on Broadway he would have been mortified, but happening out here was even worse.

"Get out Trumpy and see what's the matter," Alfred ordered from the back. After a few moments' contemplation, Simeon hauled himself out, grumbling under his breath. Taking off his jacket and vest, he undid his tie, spat on his hands, bent down and turned the starting handle. Nothing. He tried again and it was as if the car had expired. There was not even a splutter. Still muttering, he lifted the hood, waved away the steam, reached inside and then withdrew his hand hurriedly as it touched something hot.

"God dammit," he said, thrusting the hand into the other armpit and hopping about. Then he sat down on the running board and thought a little. "When did you last fill her up with gas?" he asked.

"I haven't," said Alfred.

"Well that accounts for it then," said Trumper, exasperated. "I only put a dollar's worth in when I got her going. She won't run on air you know. We're lucky to have got this far."

"Trumper," Alfred said sternly, wagging his finger. "I hold you personally responsible for this difficulty. How were we supposed to know about all this nonsense? You're the mechanic – that's why you're here. If we need gas someone had better go and get us some."

Sighing deeply, Trumper retrieved a tin can from the back of the car and, after a moment's reflection about which way to go, started trudging down the road ahead, coat slung over his shoulder. "And don't think I'm going to pay for it," Alfred shouted after him.

As the figure disappeared into the distance, shimmering in the haze thrown up by the road, there was nothing for the rest to do but to sit and wait. Jim and Annabelle chose the running board on the shady side of the car and took their ease. Alfred levered himself down onto the grass verge by the side of the highway and sat dangling his feet over the edge of the embankment towards the drainage ditch below. After a while he took off his hat and started fanning himself with it. "You know, I can't get over Mr Brady's gallery not being there any more," he said.

"That was such a grand place. Best spot in town. Right opposite Barnum's circus. I can see it now. Four storeys high and Brady's Gallery on the front in big letters. It was higher and grander than all the buildings round – 'course you wouldn't see it today, it'd be so small, but back then it was just the place. You should've seen the fine ladies and gentlemen flocking there. Brady lost it all in the end, but that was after the war...

There was a far-away look in his eyes and as he peered across the ditch to the waving reeds beyond, mopping his brow now with his handkerchief. "I don't suppose that damn' fool Trumper thought to provide us with anything for whistle-wetting, do you?" he said at last. Jim looked in the car and found a half-empty whiskey bottle that Simeon had somehow overlooked. Grandfather grunted and helped himself to a sip.

He looked down the road. It was now past midday and very hot. He undid his vest and loosened his collar button. "Where's that Trumper got to?" he said. "God dammit I think he's left us in the lurch."

Just then, far off down the road, a speck appeared in the distance. As they looked it became a figure and, after a few moments, it became Trumper. He was hauling the can of gas along with both hands, struggling and bouncing it along the ground. It was evidently very heavy and he was very drunk.

Alfred rose to his full height and pointed at him with his walking stick. "Trumper, where have you been? We've been crying out for you. You had no right to leave us like that. And look at you. You're in a disgraceful state. How dare you come back like this?"

Old Trumper, white and sweating, leaned hard against the shady side of the car, opening his mouth though few words came. "Long...walk. Shattering... small drink. Came as fast as I could. Heavy," he said helplessly.

"Well, never mind that now," said Alfred, brushing aside his excuses. "Fill the tank and get us started. We've nearly wasted the day, thanks to you."

Breathing hard and mopping his face with a filthy old handkerchief smelling of gasoline, Trumper draped his coat over the hood of the car and began to unscrew the cap of the can. Swaying slightly and spraying gas from the top, he then lurched towards the tank of the Model T. With great effort he hauled it up and started pouring the gas in, though more ran down the sides than into the tank. Eventually, the job was done and he sat down heavily on the running board, completely exhausted.

"Get up. You can't lie down there. You've got to crank the engine. Do come on, man," Alfred insisted.

Jim clambered into the driving seat while Trumper obeyed the instruction. He turned the starting handle and, after a few preliminary splutters, the engine burst into life. They were on their way again.

The road was straight and very long and it was more than a mile before they came to any houses. Finally, some way beyond, there was the gas station that Trumper had eventually reached and next to it the wooden roadside shack where he had wet his whistle. It was so dilapidated it seemed to be held up only by its tin Coca Cola signs.

They stopped to fill the tank with gas and the attendant smiled as he primed the pump and started pouring. He was an old black man with no teeth and he nodded amiably at Trumper, sitting sweating and shivering in the front seat. "Reckon he'm all done in after his stroll. He come in here orderin' me about, 'bout a couple of hours ago so I reckon he's had quite a walk round the old plantation by now," he chuckled.

"Yes, he's a naughty man, but don't you say anything bad," said Alfred, reluctantly consenting to pay for filling the tank.

They drove on into Newark and stopped at the first roadside diner. It took an effort to get Trumper out of the car. His shivers had become shakes and for once he couldn't eat and didn't want to drink, not even a sip of water.

All afternoon they drove through the suburbs of New Jersey, Elizabeth, Rabway. New Brunswick, North Brunswick, East Brunswick, down the pike towards Trenton and Philadelphia.

Trumper, whose head had been nodding, suddenly slumped over across Jim as he was driving. The car stalled and, as he pushed him back upright, he could see that the old man was really sick. His forehead was cold and clammy and wet with sweat. "I don't think we can go on. We've got to find a doctor. He's not very well," Jim said, turning to his grandfather.

"What's that? What's the matter with him?" said Alfred grumpily. "Nonsense, it's his own fault. He's just oozing whiskey. Come on. We've got to get on or we'll never get to Gettysburg."

"But I think he's dying. We can't have that," Jim said.

Alfred leaned over the seat and peered into Trumper's pallid face. "God dammit – I knew it was a mistake bringing him," he said.

Jim restarted the car and leapt aboard. Eventually a roadhouse loomed into sight and he pulled over into the yard. In the back, Alfred was still huffing about the expense and inconvenience.

It was a dreary, rundown place with small wooden chalets around a cinder track courtyard that was completely deserted. The first chalet doubled as an office and had a painted sign outside telling them they would get a warm welcome at the Bide-A-While Wayside Inn, Jim stopped the car and went inside.

He discovered that the welcome was not as warm as predicted. The office was painted a dusty orange color and decorated only with an old calendar of a Hollywood movie star and some ageing flypapers dangling from the ceiling. An electric fan whirred in a corner, pushing the air through a stifling atmosphere of heat and stale cigarette smoke.

He rang the bell on the counter and eventually an elderly woman appeared from a back room, limping heavily and leaning on a stick. Jim had interrupted her lunch and she was wiping her mouth with a handkerchief.

Before serving him she paused to do up the top buttons of her housecoat, through which a vast amount of cleavage was showing.

"Yes?" she said impatiently, anxious to return to her meal and resume listening to the radio which he could hear in the distance. It was playing Al Jolson. She brightened slightly to learn that two chalets were required, handing out the keys and taking a dollar for each. Then her glance fell on Trumper, who had been supported from the car with Alfred on one side and Annabelle under his shoulder on the other. He was leaning against the door post looking gray.

The woman said: "What's wrong with him? He don't look too good to me. He ain't contagious is he?"

Jim said, unconvincingly: "No, no, just a touch of the sun. He's fine really."

"Malingerer," said Alfred, glaring at him.

"Are you sure he's got malingerer?" the woman said. "I don't want no fever round here. We'll have to fumigate the rooms. Perhaps you should take him to a doctor instead."

Annabelle said: "That's a very good suggestion, ma'am. Do you know one around here?"

So it was that an hour or so later, a doctor arrived at the chalet to diagnose Mr Trumper with heat stroke and a touch of alcohol and insist that he should stay in bed for several days. Alfred was outraged at this latest perfidy, but there was little he could do. Not even he wanted a dead man on his hands. There was still a week to get to Gettysburg and they were more than half way there.

The following day, Alfred handed over two more dollars to the roadhouse woman and he and Jim sat on a swing seat outside the chalets, watching the outside world, while Trumper slept.

Alfred fished in his pocket and produced a small plain cardboard packet. He cleared his throat and said quietly: "I thought you ought to have this, Jim"

Jim looked at it, baffled, and said: "What is it?"

"It's, it's – ahem – a – err – prophylactic. It's for when you are with your young lady and things are getting kind-of intimate between you, Jim, if you get my meaning. I bought it from one of those ladies in the hotel in New York. Better to be safe than sorry."

Jim still looked puzzled. "It's a rubber, boy! Haven't you ever heard of one of those? You wear it. It stops her having babies, or giving you something you don't want."

There was a long silence and then he added, his speech coming out in an embarrassed rush: "I feel kind of responsible for you, in loco whatever it is... and seeing how you're getting on so famously together, I – well – I thought it might come in useful. Not that I approve, mind, no, not at all. But I know what young men are. We had a lot of that sort of thing in the Civil War...a lot of, um, sickness; and babbies – and getting rid of those babbies too. And that's not nice.

"You shouldn't do it. No, not at all. Might save you some trouble though. It's proper rubber and you can always use it again if you wash it out carefully. Well, there it is and there you are."

Alfred cleared his throat and stared straight ahead towards the far horizon. "Don't tell anyone," he added.

There was silence while Jim carefully placed the packet in his pocket, then he asked: "Have you written a note to mother?"

His grandfather replied: "Tarnation, no! Damn. I keep forgetting...but she'll be alright, boy."

Jim could not tell whether this was just absent-mindedness or indifference on his part. There was nothing for it, he would have to write to her himself.

As Alfred wandered off down the yard for his constitutional, Jim went and found Annabelle in her chalet. She was reading as usual, but looked up and smiled when he came in. They sat on the bed together and risked a kiss now that they were alone. Shyly, Jim drew the packet from his pocket and showed it to her. He did not tell her that his grandfather had given it to him, preferring that she might think he had bought it from one of the whores at the hotel for himself, like a man of the world.

She wrinkled her nose in distaste. "I don't think I want to try that, Jim," she said. "When I give myself to someone, I want it to be for real...someone I've chosen. Until then, no. I'm not ready yet."

Jim replaced the condom in his pocket. He understood, or thought he did. But he also thought it might come in useful one day.

After a while, they decided to go and see how Trumper was. They found him sitting up in bed feeling sorry for himself, still pasty white but no longer shaking quite as hard. "You couldn't get me a drink, could you? I think I still have some whiskey in the car," he said.

"No, Mr Trumper. Grandfather's drunk it, but I could get you some water if you like," Jim replied. The old man pulled a face and decided not to bother.

"This trip's becoming a nightmare. I never thought it would be quite like this," he said. "I thought it would be high times and crackers and beer all the way. I didn't suppose it would come over all serious and be such a rush. That's not my idea of a vacation."

Jim said self-righteously: "It's not a vacation to Grandfather or me. This is a trip into our past. I don't know what you're doing on it but it is important to us."

"It's important to me too," said Trumper, raising himself slightly. "I've said I'll get you there and I will. I'm not going to buckle this time. Your grandfather's my only friend and I want to see him right, otherwise I couldn't look him in the eye again.

" He's the only one who's stuck by me and asked me to do something, so I want to prove I can. Besides, I've got a reason to go to Gettysburg too. I've never been there and I want to go now before it's too late."

He said this unexpectedly long speech so vehemently that they were startled. "Why?" Jim asked.

"Oh, I have my reasons. Let's just say I want to go with your grandpappy and stand by him. I owe a lot to your grandfather. There's no one else in my life. Now – one more day and I'll be right as rain to go on," he said.

Back in Springbridge Simeon Trumper was the town lush. Nobody knew quite what he lived off, except for the dollars he earned by doing odd jobs around the place; mending fences and replacing roof tiles when they fell off in storms.

"That's very good of you Mr Trumper," said Annabelle. "We know you won't let us down. We're so grateful to you for coming with us. Now, you lie down and have a good sleep and we'll see how you are in the morning. There's no rush, dear." And she bent down and kissed him gently on the forehead.

Old Trumper gulped and the colour flushed back into his cheeks. "Oh shucks miss. No one's done that since my old mom died," he said. "I'd do anything for you."

Outside the chalet, Jim looked at her with admiration. "Did you expect him to turn into a handsome prince?" he asked.

Annabelle looked at him straight. "Get on with you. What does a little care matter?" she said. "All that old man needs is a bit of appreciation and if it takes a peck on the face to get him up so we can get on, I'm happy to do it. That will get him up quicker than whiskey or hard words. You want to get to Gettysburg don't you?"

By that evening, Trumper was taking nourishment. He ate some soup they brought him from the diner down the road, though he drew the line at a bottle of Coca-Cola. Annabelle's medicine was working.

Jim went to see the woman in her office and asked for some paper to he could write to his mother to let her know where they were. The woman couldn't manage that, but she did have a postcard of the Bide-A-While wayside inn. It was old and faded yellow and showed the inn in fresher times, though there were no people in the picture. Even so, it did not look like an enticing place to stay. But it would do for a postcard.

Jim only had a pencil and that would have to do too. This is what he eventually wrote:

New Jersey,

Friday, I think.

Dearest Mom,

We are here, on the way to Gettysburg for the reunion. Grandfather made me do it. Mr Trumper is here too. I am sorry you was left in the lurch and hope you got Home OK. Back Soon. Don't worry. We are safe and Alright.

All my love. Your loving son,

Jim

XXX

He thought it best not to mention Annabelle. Or Mr Trumper's illness. He did not know that his mother had by now arrived in Philadelphia.

Jim returned to the inn's office with the card. The fat woman had been replaced by a thin man.

"Do you know where I can buy a stamp and post this?" Jim asked.

He grinned. "Well sir, young man," he said, taking the card and scrutinising the address and the note as well. "I guess that's just a cent stamp you'll be wanting. I'll make sure we post that for you. You just leave it to me."

He showed no sign of giving it back and Jim thought better of asking directions for the post office to buy a stamp. It was too late now, so he fetched out a cent and gave it to the man. He pocketed it, tapped the card on his fingers and put it in his pocket. "I'll see this gets through," he said. Jim hoped he was as good as his word.

In the morning, Alfred was once again awake first, prodding them both to make the effort to move. Trumper awoke, sat up and said the most surprising thing: "I must find a barber." He dressed hurriedly and disappeared down the road towards the main street in the little town where they had stopped.

When he returned half an hour later the greasy stubble had gone from his chin. For the first time all trip, Alfred looked on him benignly. "Good, Trumper," he said. "Good man. You look much better. Now, all aboard."

Annabelle emerged from her chalet and immediately noticed the difference. She smiled at the old man and gave him a peck on the cheek. "Oh, Mr Trumper:

you look a different man. Was that for me?" she said.

"Oh garn," said Trumper bashfully and blushed.

"Yes, come along. No time for dalliance," said Alfred. "We've got to get on." Jim thought he detected a sliver of jealousy in his grandfather's manner.

CHAPTER TWENTY-EIGHT

The morning after Jim and his grandfather had left Springbridge in the Model T, Mary was up early to leave too. She had packed spare clothing and washing things in a gladstone bag, shone her sensible shoes, rammed her straw hat with the cherries on her head and put on a raincoat in case of bad weather, locked up the house and resolutely made her way down to the railroad station.

She had been pondering whether to go through with this all night, but every time a voice inside her warned that it would be a difficult and dangerous trip another told her that she really needed to do it. She had to show her menfolk that she was not some doormat to be walked over, expected to be at their beck and call, but ignored when her wishes were in conflict with theirs. Worst of all was the humiliation of being left standing in the dust as they took off in the car the previous evening, in front of half the town. Well, Mary had had enough of it: the worm had turned, she told herself as she strode down the road. She needed to make the trip for herself, her own sense of self-worth, her own *independence.* If she did not do it now, she never would and she would regret it always. And it would be an adventure.

On the platform at the station there was only one other person waiting for a train at this hour. Colonel Putnam, resplendent in a white linen summer suit and boater was standing between his two leather suitcases, He turned to stare at her without warmth, but he clearly recognised her and after a moment's pause that was long enough to seem ironical he touched the rim of his hat to her in the most perfunctory of politenesses before turning to read his newspaper.

That's all right, thought Mary, I don't have to sit with him. She wondered idly where he was going and when the train came she got into a different carriage.

The journey would be a long one, she knew, changing at New York, then Washington and up to Gettysburg and taking all day about it. Mary was minded to stay overnight in the capital as she had not got as far as thinking about where to stay once she arrived at the little town in Pennsylvania. She had been too cross to think that far ahead, but she had at least thought to make some sandwiches and pack a bottle of her homemade lemonade for the ride.

The train rumbled gently down through western Massachusetts, over the line into Connecticut and then slowly, stopping at every town, into New York. Mary had brought a novel with her – Elinor Glyn's latest, *Romantic Adventure,* had seemed appropriate, though she had also tucked Glyn's *The Wrinkle Book or How to Keep Looking Young* into her bag – but she found it hard to concentrate on reading. The sun kept flickering across the pages, then the shadows of trees, making the text difficult to see, but the journey was also so interesting, passing through new places she had only vaguely heard of, that she kept gazing out of the window or eyeing the passengers who boarded the train at each stop.

Eventually they rattled into the Grand Central Terminus and Mary found herself on the central concourse, bewildered by the immensity of the building with its great vaulted roof painted with stars, its majestic staircases and by the rush and bustle of the crowd. Ahead of her, she spotted the straw boater of the colonel bobbing through the crush and decided to follow him, at least until he had found his way out of the place. She emerged through the swing doors right behind him, just in time to hear him tell a cab driver: "Penn Station," before getting in. That was where she had to go too, but there was no question of sharing his taxi, or taking one of her own. And so she hauled her bag down eight blocks on the hard sidewalks, under the blazing afternoon sun and across Manhattan, past Macy's department store, which she paused to look wonderingly at, but did not dare to enter, and into the maw of the great station for the onward journey to Washington.

By the time she flopped into her seat on board the train, Mary was utterly exhausted from the tension of the trip, the excitement of all the new experiences that had crowded around her that day and the laborious exercise of her walk between the stations in the heat. As the train rumbled out, she fell fast asleep.

She was woken with a start by someone tapping her urgently on the shoulder and for a few moments as her eyes grew accustomed to the light, she had no idea where she was. The figure standing over her was a clergyman in a dog collar and dark suit, his round, pink face registering concern as he gazed into her eyes. "Are you alright, my dear?" he asked anxiously. "You were so fast asleep and I did not wish you to miss your stop. I am sorry to have woken you."

She smiled at him. He seemed almost cherubic: no danger there, so she said: "Thank you, sir. I am going through to Washington, so I won't miss my stop, but I am grateful for your concern."

He raised his trilby. "It is no trouble at all. I was just worried for you. Travelling is such a tiring business these days, isn't it? May I join you, as there's a seat free?"

Mary nodded and shuffled along, picking up her book to make space. The clergyman raised his hat again and smiled, showing an acreage of white teeth. "I am the Reverend William Godley, so pleased to make your acquaintance. An appropriate name for a clergyman, isn't it? Oddly, I'm Godley!" And he chuckled. It was obviously a well-practised joke. "So much nicer to have a companion on a long journey. I always find it so pleasant to meet people and learn their stories as we go. Ah – a fan of Miss Glyn, I see! Do you know *Love's Hour*, by any chance?"

By now the clergyman was sitting beside her, slightly too close, as men of the cloth so often did in her experience, breathing peppermint fumes over her. They chatted in a desultory fashion about where they were going and what they would be doing when they got there. Godley was heading south to Savannah, he said, but what *fun* to be going to Gettysburg, how he envied her!

Despite her instinctive wariness of strange men, Mary found herself warming to the minister. He was funny and charming and made her laugh – how long was it since a nice man got her to do that? He had a fund of good stories about his experiences as a missionary in Panama and little jokes that he tried out on her, asking her opinion about whether they were fit for inclusion in his sermons. She could scarcely credit that he asked her opinions as if he valued them and actually listened to her answers: that made her feel important for once. He really was very beguiling and, yes, rather attractive: no man had paid her that much attention for many years. And he was a man of the cloth, so that was good. She could almost wish that he was coming on to Gettysburg too.

He grew serious in talking about his faith and asking her about hers and gently, almost before she knew it, he was holding her hand in his and stroking it. What he had to say about Jesus's imperative to love was really most instructive and touching. She was beginning to feel quite light-headed: it was almost as if she had known this man all her life, not just for an hour.

A little voice inside her said be careful, watch out, but it was growing fainter. Now she was becoming drowsy again. "Rest your head on my shoulder, my dear," Godley was saying soothingly and her eyes closed.

Suddenly, her head fell back against the banquette and she woke up again with a start. Godley was still beside her, but she felt queasy, as if something had happened that she was not aware of. He quickly withdrew his hands from her lap and sat upright himself. Instinctively, Mary patted her pockets to make sure nothing was missing. He smiled at her and said: "It is alright my dear, it's all right."

Mary edged away slightly and reached for her book. "I am sorry," she said. "I don't know why I am so tired."

Godley gestured deprecatingly that it was nothing, quite understandable, and reached in his pocket for a New Testament, which he started to read.

A few minutes later, he tapped her on the knee and she bucked away, alarmed. "Pray, don't distress yourself," he said. "I merely wondered whether that was your purse down there on the floor? I've just noticed it."

Mary looked down and there, by her feet, was a woman's brown leather purse. She bent down and picked it up and it seemed full of money, much more than she had. "Why no. Someone must have dropped it," she said. "Oh dear."

There was no one nearby to whom it could have belonged – she was the only woman in the carriage – and Mr Godley said: "We must hand it in when we get to Washington, if no one claims it earlier." He riffled through the notes: "There must be a great deal of money here. It is bound to have a reward for the finder. This may be your lucky day, Mary!"

Mary blushed. "I couldn't possibly take a reward," she said. "You saw it – it's yours by right. You take it."

Godley shook his head and smiled. "No, no, I couldn't possibly do that – anyway, I am heading on to Savannah, with no time to hand it in. Err, tell you what – we could share the reward, couldn't we? I am sure for something like this, it would be substantial – fifty dollars at least.

" How would it be – tell me, oh Mary, my dear, if you approve – if you gave me a small donation for my parish fund, say twenty or twenty-five dollars, and then took this purse and reclaimed the whole amount of the reward? It may even be a hundred dollars – who knows? – and you'd be eighty better off. Nothing could give me greater pleasure to think of that for you!"

Mary was thrilled by the idea. How generous he was! A donation would make a considerable hole in her thirty dollars' savings, but it would be worth it and for a good cause. Perhaps she could visit his church one day. "You shall be rewarded twentyfold," he murmered. She reached for her purse.

"Don't give him that!" said a stern voice, suddenly. "It's a swindle and a hornswoggle."

Mary looked up to see Colonel Putnam standing in the gap between the seats. She had not noticed that he had been sitting on the banquette behind them. The Rev. Godley grabbed the purse from Mary's lap and was about to put it in his pocket when the colonel brought his cane down on his hands and flicked the purse away across the carriage. "What do you think you are doing, preying on a defenceless woman?" the colonel barked.

Mary put her hand to her mouth. "But he's a clergyman," she said. Godley said nothing.

The colonel picked up the purse and handed it to her. "I should take a good look at those bank notes," he said. "You may be surprised." Turning to Godley he said: "If they are what I think they are, you are despicable. And if you are a real clergyman I shall eat my hat. Oh good, we're stopping: I think this is where you leave the train, don't you?"

Mary was pulling out the notes from the purse. The first one was a dollar bill, the rest, carefully cut to size, were rectangles of newspaper. Godley seized the purse a second time, opened the carriage door without a word and jumped out onto the platform.

Mary burst into tears, in shock and surprise. She felt humiliated to have been taken in, the more so for having been rescued by the colonel. He handed her a handkerchief from his top pocket and watched as she dabbed her eyes.

"You have to be careful. The wallet drop is one of the oldest tricks in the book. You would not have got much reward for that purse. He wanted to skin you. I overheard him making up to you and knew he was up to no good," said Putnam, not unkindly.

"Thank you for saving me."

"It's just I can't bear to see a woman cheated; I won't have it happening to myself and I won't see it happening even to you. Let's say we're quits. Take care madam and good day to you."

Mary was wide awake now, but she could not concentrate, for thinking how narrow an escape she had had. As she put *Romantic Adventure* away in her bag, Mary noticed how much her hand was shaking.

CHAPTER TWENTY-NINE

It was late afternoon as the Model T and its passengers entered the outskirts of Philadelphia. The streets were quiet, with only the occasional dog stirring as it lay on the sidewalk. It was a mean and impoverished neighborhood of bleak, brick tenements. There was glass on the street and some windows were boarded up. Decay was everywhere round. Old furniture lay in the yards and on the sidewalks. Several children were playing around an old horse fountain, squealing with excitement and laughter as they splashed each other with the water, but the atmosphere was heavy and threatening.

As they pulled out onto a main boulevard, looking for somewhere cheap to stay the night, Alfred suddenly became agitated.

"Did you see what street this is? Did that just say Henry Street to you?" he asked. "We must look for number 1067...that's where we'll stay."

Jim had no idea that his grandfather knew Philadelphia, or had ever been there, or that there would be an address that he would suddenly recognize. As they approached the number, the old man craned forward, making little "yes" noises under his breath.

1067 Henry Street was a large residential villa, with steep gables, a brick portico and a porch at the front. From the upper level a small Stars and Stripes fluttered from a flagstaff pointing diagonally out of the wall. By the front drive a small white sign said: "Brittan's Guest House: Respectable Visitors Only."

Alfred was out of the car in a flash and up the steps, ringing the bell. An elderly woman answered the door and he flung his arms around her with a cry of "Faith!"

Something told Jim he had intended to bring them there all along.

Startled, the woman pushed Alfred back. Then she peered more closely with the aid of the light coming from behind her in the hall. "Alfred? Is it really you? Well, what a time to come visiting. What do you call this?" she said.

"Faith, I thought we'd look you up after all this time. Didn't I say that if I was ever coming this way I'd drop by?" he said.

"Yes but that was a very long time ago," the old woman said. "I didn't expect to have to wait all this time to see you again. Good job I got married instead. You're lucky I'm not dead." And, with that, she peered suspiciously over Alfred's shoulder at Trumper, Jim and Annabelle, standing discreetly on the path outside.

"Oh, you must meet my companions, Faith. Here Jim, this is my grandson, my only grandchild – bet you never thought I'd have one of them? Ain't he handsome? Ain't he like me – like I used to be? And this here's Mr Simeon Trumper who's along for the ride. And this is young Annabelle, my son's intended. We're going to Gettysburg, Faithie, for the commemorations. Do you want to come along?" he said, adding: "Boys, this is my Faith, Miss – Mrs – Faith Brittan, the sweetest woman of my life. And she still lives here. What do you think of that?"

Annabelle said, loudly and grumpily: "I AM NOT JIM'S INTENDED."

Jim echoed her: "Grandad, she is not my intended," But nobody paid any attention.

Then something the old lady had said stuck in Alfred's mind and he added incredulously: "You got married? "

Mrs Brittan did not entirely welcome their surprise visit so late in the evening but she gestured for them to come up and they stepped into the lighted hall. Before, she had appeared a shadowy presence, silhouetted against the doorway, but, once inside, they could see that she was still a handsome woman. She had a fine face set off by high cheekbones, surrounded by fading, fairish-colored hair swept back into a bun. She was wearing a long cotton print dress to her ankles and at her neck was a lace collar with an oval silver brooch attached to it. There was a haughty and forbidding expression lurking behind her oval spectacle frames, but now she was getting used to the idea, she seemed increasingly pleased by Alfred's unexpected arrival.

"Of course I got married," she said. "I couldn't wait for you any more. Anyway, you needn't worry. It didn't last. He's long dead. I'm all alone and I'm still here."

Jim gazed around the hallway, growing accustomed to the brightness of the light. And there, unmistakably, on the wall, was a framed portrait photograph of his grandfather as a young man. It was heavily retouched, but there was the fair moustache and the slightly lugubrious face of the person he remembered from the wedding photograph in his bedroom at home. It was a copy of the photograph Jim Gibson had taken of Alfred in Brady's studio seventy years before.

Alfred let out a long, low groan as he saw it. "Oh, Faith, you've kept it all these years…God, there I am, when I was young. You three – that's what I used to look like."

Faith looked around at the group and sighed deeply. "Oh, Alfred. Why didn't you let me know you'd be coming? I could have got things ready for you. I suppose you'll want to stay the night now because, if you do, you're in luck, as always. I do have some rooms free."

They followed in single file into the parlor at the end of the hall. The room was evidently her nest. It had plaster ornaments and brass knick-knacks on every polished surface. All the armchairs had crocheted antimacassars hanging over their backs to ward off the marks made by greasy hair and the pictures on the wall were all devotional: *The Light of the World*, Jesus Christ knocking on the garden gate in one, leading sheep across a pasture in another, bearing his breast to show a flaming heart in a third, all lit by the subdued flare of gas lamps; making the atmosphere in the room heavy.

The elderly couple sat down in the armchairs, facing each other. Alfred spoke first: "Oh Faith. I've missed you so much all these years," he said. "Where did the time go? How have you been keeping? What's the news?" It was if he was returning after only a short visit away. The huskiness of his voice showed his emotion.

"You're right. Your grandson does look like you used to do," she replied inconsequentially and looking at Jim, added: "Don't turn out like your grandfather, boy. At least not so far as women are concerned. Now, do you all want to stay? I suppose you'll need feeding."

She got up purposefully and bustled into the kitchen, as if to give herself something to do. Alfred turned to the rest, a great smile beaming across his face. "Isn't she still lovely? Best woman I ever knew, till I met your grandmother of course. Well, actually, still the best woman I ever knew. I never should've let her go."

Trumper grinned at him and said he would go and help prepare the victuals.

Annabelle went too, leaving Jim alone with his grandfather. The boy looked across at him questioningly.

"I suppose you wouldn't really have known about Faith," he said, "Except what I told you the other day about us being sweet for a time when I was young in Washington. No reason you should – it was all a long time ago and I've always told myself that if ever I got near Philly again I'd seek her out. Never thought I would though. That's why I wanted to come this way. Lucky she's still at the same address. And here we are – well!"

Annabelle came back into the room carrying a wooden breadboard and a loaf and stopped to listen. "Why didn't you marry her grandfather?" she said.

He waved his hand as if to bat the question away. He did not wish to address it now. "Oh. It was all a long time ago. No good dwelling on it," he said impatiently.

Faith came back into the room bearing a plate of cold meats, some pickles and tomatoes, followed by Trumper, dolefully, carrying a tray of plates, cutlery, some glasses and a pitcher of water. They all settled down to eat.

The conversation over supper began slowly and stiltedly, with Annabelle, Trumper and Jim just witnesses as the elderly couple swapped life histories about what they had done since they last saw each other. Alfred told her about the photographic business and she told him about her marriage, which had turned out to be a short one. When her husband died in a typhoid epidemic, she had opened the boarding house and been there ever since. Then Alfred sketched out a brief and expurgated history of his life, pausing briefly to speak dismissively of his wife: "...but she's long dead, anyhow," and at slightly longer length about Mary, his only child: "Jim-there's mother…"

Mrs Brittan turned to Jim and said: "I bet he never told you about me did he? Here I've been all these years waiting for him to come back and not even a letter until tonight.

"Before he gives you some cheap version, let me tell you that that man there was the love of my life. We met when I was Mrs Gardner's housemaid and he was a young cameratist. He was so handsome and charming and unfortunately he knew it too. Well, in those days, especially if you were a bit pretty, you weren't allowed to so much as look at a man."

Alfred broke in with a chuckle: "I saw this vision, like an angel, standing there looking at me shyly and I was determined to make her acquaintance. Oh well."

"Got any more pickles?" said Trumper, breaking in.

They ignored him. Alfred said: "Courting wasn't like it would be now with all you fast youngsters. You had to wait to be introduced and then chaperoned if you were going out together. She had beautiful long golden hair – you wouldn't believe it now, would you? Smartest, sweetest creature I ever saw. We walked out together on her days off. Do you remember Faithie?"

Mrs Brittan said: "Why wouldn't he believe I had golden hair? I wasn't born ninety you know." But she was smiling as she said it.

Jim asked: "How do you manage here Mrs Brittan? Are you alone? It must be a lot of work when you have guests to stay."

She replied: "It's no trouble, I've done it for an age and I don't get so many guests nowadays as I did, but I have men to come in and help me. There's old Lionel, the house servant, who's been with me for years. Thinks he knows it all, but he don't – tell the truth he don't know lickety-spit about running anything. And then there's Martin who comes in to sweep the yard: he isn't good for much else. So I ain't alone and don't want for help."

Then she leaned forward and reached for Alfred's hand across the table: "Could've done with a man all these years though, to help out and keep me warm."

Alfred withdrew his hand gently, pretending he had not noticed what she was doing and stretching past her for a tomato instead, which he proceeded to chew noisily to cover his confusion. "Now you know, it wouldn't have worked out," he said at last.

She said:"We could've made it work together. I set my heart on him. I thought we'd be married after the war, but I couldn't ever snare him."

"We got on well enough. It just wasn't the right time…"

"When would it ever have been?"

"I was busy. I wouldn't have been a good husband for you, my dear. I was never there."

"That at least is true. But then, eventually you did get married to someone you'd known five minutes. And all I got was a note to tell me!"

They were bickering like an old married couple now. Alfred sighed: "Well, at least I told you. Why drag this up? Oh Faithie, it was the biggest mistake I ever made. There has been a lot of time to regret it, believe you me."

Jim said: "What was all that about?"

"Well," said Mrs Brittan with some finality. "We wanted to get married but my boss, Mr Gardner said we was too young and couldn't. And I then thought, if I left him and went to work somewhere else, then we could. So I went to work about the unluckiest place I could have chosen, Mrs Surratt's boarding house and then Mr Gardner had his revenge by stopping Alfred seeing me! So we didn't get to meet, and we didn't meet and Jim kept getting sent out of town on assignments in the war and I think it was all to thwart me.

"And then came Mr Lincoln's assassination and all hell broke loose. Just to have worked for the Surratts was like death in Washington after that and so I ended up going home. And Alfred didn't follow me, did you dear? He got tangled up with someone else instead and in the end, that was that."

"I don't want to talk about that," said Alfred stubbornly.

"Does your family know about what happened?"

"They know all they need to know."

There was a silence, broken only by the noise of Trumper eating. The rest of them stared at their plates.

"Why are you here anyhow? What has brought you to Philadelphia? It's not me surely," said Mrs Brittan at last.

Alfred said: "Yes, no, well…Yes it was of course, but, we're going to Gettysburg for the great reunion. Have you heard about it Faithie? The president's going to be there and all…and I thought, one last trip, out of New England…show Jim here where it all happened. And look you up…Faithie, why don't you come with us?"

She sounded flattered to be asked. "Oh I don't know. I am very old. I can't be gallivanting around the country. You haven't given me any time. I can't just drop everything…I have a business to run here."

"But it would only be for a few days. You'd be back in a week or so. Gettysburg's not far from here…it would be fun. Just like old times."

Then she said: "Alfred, do you remember Ford's Theatre?"

There was a sudden chill in the room. Trumper put down his spoon, Annabelle gasped and Jim stared at his grandfather. That was where President Lincoln had been shot. Everyone knew that.

There was a choking sound from Alfred. "Oh, I'll say. You couldn't forget that. Yes. We were there that night. That's how I got my famous photograph, Jim" he said sadly.

"Faith and I were there that night, at the theater, to see the play. Mr Gardner and I had been chasing all over Virginia to catch up with the Confederate surrender at Appomatox and we were too late so we came back to Washington and Faith and I went to the show."

Jim cried: "But what happened? What did you see Grandpa?"

"Well, it was our first night off together for months – got allowed out specially to meet because the war was over – and we bought tickets for the pit earlier that day, before we knew the president would be there. It was a spur of the moment thing, like it was for him. It was going to be one of the last nights for the show and we didn't know if we would get the chance to see it again. It wasn't till we were going to the theater that we saw the boys with the bills in the street saying Mr Lincoln would be there – trying to drum up trade, 'honored by the presence of the president' – that sort of thing.

"He wasn't there though. They waited for him, but he didn't come. We kept on looking up at his box by the side of the stage, but it was empty. So eventually they started the show, this comedy, Our American Cousin, with an English cast. It was a big hit. Do you remember Faithie?"

She said: "Oh yes. It was such a wonderful evening. The war was just over. No more killing. And spring was coming. It was April. April 1865. The war finished just a week… And Alfred was back. It was such a big thing for us to go to the theater – I'd hardly ever done it before in my whole life. Good Friday too – my parents wouldn't have allowed me to go to the theatre that night if they'd known. But the excitement of seeing the president…And we'd just won the war!"

The old couple were falling over themselves to remember now. In the glow of the flickering lamp, in Mrs Brittan's back parlor in Philadelphia, they could all almost imagine they were in Ford's Theatre, the gas lights shining on stage and a new era just beginning. And these two old people had been there that night!

Alfred started up again: "The show hadn't been going more than twenty minutes or so and suddenly there's a commotion at the back and everyone whispered: 'He's coming. He's coming!' and we all looked back, craning our necks to see. And everything stopped. The actors on the stage stopped and then everyone started cheering and clapping and stamping their feet. The actors started applauding and the orchestra struck up 'Hail to the Chief' and we all stood up, whooping and hollering."

Mrs Brittan said: "Do you remember, Alfred, the president stood at the front of the box and acknowledged the crowd? And do you remember, he saw you? He saw you down in the lower seats and gave you a special wave and a bow of the head. Do you remember? I was so proud of you then! He recognized you from Mr Brady's studio! I'll never forget it."

"I didn't like to say," said Alfred modestly, for once. "Yes he did. I am almost sure he did.

"Well, the audience sat down and the show started up again. It wasn't much of a play to me. Some comic caper: I can scarcely remember it because of what happened later. It was not very funny though, I don't think. But we were all watching and all of a sudden there was a laugh and a little sound like a door slamming. I thought it was on stage at first. Then there was a great cloud of smoke coming out of the president's box and a shout and there's this man – Booth, the famous actor – climbing down the flag at the front of the box and jumping onto the stage.

"I'd smelled that smoke before, in battle, but I was just rigid. We all were. Thought it might be something added into the play – some sort of jape or high spirits. I wasn't so surprised – I recognized Booth because he'd been in to Brady's to have his portrait taken and for a moment I thought he must be in the cast, with the other actors.

"John Wilkes Booth. Handsomest man in Washington and the highest paid. I didn't even know he was a damn rebel, though apparently he'd been boasting about it all round town. He hadn't gone off to fight though. I thought he was just putting on some jest, some practical joke for the president.

Faith butted in: "Oh, I knew him from Mrs Surratt's. He thought he was *it*. You'd answer the door and let him in and he'd flash you a smile and chuck you under the chin and say: 'How are you today, my pretty little thing?' and give you a smile and try to put his hand round your waist. Oh mercy, I wish I'd reached up and put his eyes out right there, killing our president! Vain, vain man: you'd see him admiring himself in front of the mirror in the hall there before he went upstairs to plot and scheme with the rest.

"How Mrs Surratt didn't know, like she claimed after, I'll never understand. 'Course she knew! She had to know – her son John was in the plot up to his ears till he escaped…He was a bad lot and so was she."

Alfred did not like being interrupted. He held his hand up: "Anyway. There he was, in the president's box, Booth, surrounded by smoke like Lucifer.Then he tried jumping as if he was some, what d'you call it? Some spring-heeled Jack. But as he leapt onto the stage, he caught his foot in the flag draped over the box and fell with a bump. I've always thought the good old Stars and Stripes had the last laugh on him! And he shouted something – no one could tell what it was – and pushed the actor on stage out of the way, then rushed off limping. He'd cracked his ankle.

"Then, I've never forgotten it, a second later there was this terrible scream from the president's box. Mrs Lincoln. She just screamed and screamed and all hell broke loose. 'Follow that man! Don't let him escape!' they shouted from the audience. And then: "Is there a doctor in the house? For pity's sake," from the box.

"There's Major Rathbone from the president's party inside the box trying to break open the door that Booth had jammed shut. Pandemonium! Men rushing here and there, curtain coming down. The women – and men too – weeping.

'Leave the theater! Leave the theater!' Oh, just terrible, terrible. One minute laughing and the next tragedy and tears.

"One minute you're watching the play without a care in the world and the next the president's been shot."

Mrs Brittan was sitting sobbing now at the memory, dabbing her eyes. It was as if she was reliving something that had happened only days before. "Yes, yes, that was it. I didn't even hear the gun go off or see the smoke. There was just suddenly this man on stage and everything went quiet and then the scream. It was so loud...

"I thought we would be trampled under foot. The whole audience was surging around screaming and shouting and looking up at the box. Alfred said: 'It's Booth, the actor, I recognize him' and a man next to us took up the shout: 'It was the actors, the actors!' It looked as if they'd kill the players. 'Burn the damn theater down!' someone shouted. 'No, no, let us get out first!' Then we were all pushed out.

"Outside, everyone tumbled into the street in the cold and the fog and there was screaming and people praying and crossing themselves and others shouting that there was an insurrection and the rebels were coming. It was so frightening. We thought they'd murder everyone.

"Then they brought the president out, carried between some soldiers, with the surgeon holding his head and his legs brushing along the ground – no stretcher or chair to carry him. There was an officer forcing his way through the crush with his sword. The road was all muddy and bumpy and slippery – how they got him through the crowd without dropping him in a hole, I don't know. People were shouting to get him to the White House and the surgeon – a very young man – says: 'No – he would never make it. He'll die on the way. We'll just get him across the road. Clear the path!' "

Alfred broke in: "I knew one of the doctors, Dr Taft, from taking his portrait earlier and I introduced myself, asking how the president was. And he just shook his head and said: 'There's no hope for him. The wound is mortal. I put my finger right into it. It was a bullet in the head. He's barely alive now and he won't live till morning.' When we all heard this we just burst out weeping. We didn't know what to think."

"What did you do Grandfather?" Jim asked.

"I didn't know what to do. I knew I should take Faithie home, or that I should send for Mr Gardner to bring his camera, or go and get mine, but we didn't want to go. I just kept remembering how kind he'd been. They carried the president into the boarding house across the street and turfed a young soldier out of his room to make way for him. There was a huge crowd outside and I said to Faith to wait and I ran home to get my equipment, just in case. Fortunately it wasn't too far and I ran all the way – young and fit then.

"I came back half an hour later with rugs and a little nip of something in a bottle and my camera and tripod and box of chemicals. God knows what I thought I could do, but I didn't send for Mr Gardner. Must've just forgot...

"All the high-ups were arriving by then. Ministers and friends and generals and Mrs Lincoln, over from the theater, and the actors and the president's son and surgeons and doctors. God knows how they all got in the house, let alone in the room. 'Out of my way, clear the way," shouts Senator Sumner, leading in the president's son. Imagine that – your father's been shot!

"Then there's old Gideon Welles, the Navy Minister, bustling in, his brown wig all askew and his white beard shaking. And they even brought the vice president, Johnson, who fell up the stairs to the front door, drunk as usual. But he didn't stay long – Mrs Lincoln ordered him out of the room. She couldn't stand him, least of all that night, so he left in a hurry. 'Someone will pay for this,' he was saying. 'Someone will pay,' but we couldn't tell whether it was the rebels he meant or the people who sent him away.

"You should have seen the crowd. Blacks, whites, all quiet, all weeping and praying. Oh yes, that man was loved. Longest night I ever knew. Then it started raining – do you remember Faith? – heavy, freezing rain, tumbling down on us all.

"Like heaven itself was weeping," said Mrs Brittan, nodding her head.

"About daybreak there's suddenly a commotion and Mr Gardner drives up with the whats-it wagon. 'What the devil are you doing here? Why didn't you send for me Alfred?' he shouts above the crowd. I thought I'd be in trouble, but he didn't seem to notice. It was a big scoop.

"'The whole city's in uproar, Alfred,' he says to me. 'They've murdered Mr Seward in his bed at home and the rebels might be here at any moment to finish off the rest.' That wasn't quite right. Mr Seward fell under the bed, but they'd cut him to the quick, took half his face off and damn-near did for him. If there had been an insurrection, almost all the cabinet was in that boarding house staring at Mr Lincoln and we'd have had a ringside seat at the fighting.

"Then Mr Welles came out to get some air and walk round the block and Mr Gardner, who knew him well, went up to him and asked what the news was. Welles looked at him as if he was a complete stranger, all distracted like, and said: 'No hope I fear. Who are you?' 'Gardner, sir, the photographer.' 'Oh, of course, my apologies Mr Gardner, how is Mr Brady? Is he here? Forgive me, it has been a trying night and will get worse by morning.' He walked on, then he turned and pointed and said: 'Mr Gardner, do you have your apparatus? Good. Well, be on hand. It may be needed later.' That's what he said.

"Now Mr Gardner was not going to let this scoop go to anyone else, still less tell Brady, who was our rival now. We waited in the rain, trying to shelter by the wagon. And then, at nearly half-past seven in the morning, a soldier ran out and said: "He's dead, he's gone," and a great howl of grief went up from everyone. Then the young surgeon who'd held the president's head left – just walked off into the rain, all alone.

"Then in a while, the bigwigs started to leave and Mr Welles came out again, looking round. He spied Mr Gardner and called him over for a word. Well, Mr G. came back and said: 'I may be wanted at the White House, Alfred. You're to stay here and see what's what, then bring the wagon over. We may have some photography to do.'

"So I stayed put as everyone drifted away in the dawn. They brought Mrs Lincoln out and she was still crying and bawling. I've never forgotten it: 'Why didn't they tell me he was dying? Why did he have to die?' she's screaming. Then, she looks over at the theater across the road and says: 'That dreadful house! That dreadful house!' and so they got her away in a carriage, half fainting.

"After that, the troops lined up and they brought the president out in a long coffin, under a flag this time, and, with slow drums beating, they took him away.

"I was left standing outside the house on my own, debating whether to follow, when the owner, Mr Petersen, came out holding a pillow soaked in blood. Do you know what he did? He shook it at the cortege going up the road! 'Look at this!' he says to no one in particular. 'Ruined! Quite ruined! I didn't ask to have the president here and now who's going to pay for it? And they're calling my boarding house a tenement!' And he stumps back inside the house leaving the front door open.

"Well, I saw my chance and ran in after him, just in time to see him hurl the pillow out of the back window. And then I realized where I was – in the room, the very room where the president had just died. Petersen turned and said: 'What are you doing here?' and I said: 'Mr Gardner's studio, sir. Forgive me, but may I take a photograph?' And Petersen looks at me all suspiciously and says: 'Of me? What do you want one of me for now? How much is it going to cost?' The man was an idiot! I think he'd been drinking too.

"So I said, quick as a flash: 'Nothing, nothing. It will be a historic photograph of you, proprietor of the house where Mr Lincoln died. Your name will go down in history!' And the fool looked all proud of himself and said: 'Really? Of course – come in.' 'Course, I didn't want him. I wanted the room. But if the price of that was his portrait too, I'd take it.

"I got the camera and coated the plate in the wagon, like I'd done so often in the war, put it in its case and rushed inside to find one of the other lodgers already taking a photograph of the room! Well, I couldn't have that – he might have sold it to Brady! He was a foreigner and he turns to me, all innocent, and says: 'Ah, I see a professional, what would you advise for the exposure?' So I told him, but just a little bit wrong: too short for the light, I thought.

"Now the room was very small and dark, just an ordinary little back bedroom really, with pictures on the walls and pretty wallpaper. The bed was a big heavy wooden thing with its counterpane all still on, rumpled over as if someone had just slept on it, and another pillow, still in place, covered in blood down to the stuffing. And just a little wooden chair beside the bed.

"I didn't waste any time in case old Petersen changed his mind. Just set up in a corner to get as much in as possible, took the exposure – just enough light by then with a long count – and rushed out to the wagon."

Jim said: "I don't recall seeing that picture Grandpa." There was a deep intake of breath like a sigh from Mrs Brittan who had been listening intently all the time.

Alfred said grimly: "No, well you wouldn't have. That's where I made my big mistake. As I was rushing out Mr Petersen starts to stop me: 'Excuse me young man,' he says. 'When will you take my portrait?' And instead of saying that I'd be back in a minute or that he could call at the studio, I just brushed him aside – got what I'd wanted, too excited, see? – and said: 'Oh don't bother me now. I'm too busy.' Fool! Fool!

"Now I got down to the wagon and I am just developing the picture, in great excitement, when suddenly, behind me, the door opens and it's Petersen standing there, letting all the light flood in. 'Now see here,' he said. 'You promised me a free portrait…'

'Get out! Get out of here!' I shouted, slamming the door. But of course it was too late. The picture was ruined. For want of some politeness! What a time to learn that lesson.

"There was nothing for it. I stood there seething for a minute or two, then I came outside the wagon. 'Mr Petersen, you have just ruined my picture,' I said. 'Now I shall have to go back and take another one. 'Oh no,' he says. 'I see your game – it will be twenty dollars in my hand to step over my threshold again. And a free portrait.' I just didn't have the money, you see, of course. There were other people banging on the door by then, asking to be let in to see the room.

"No chance of going back. The moment was gone. Of course Petersen made a killing from all the souvenirs after that, when he woke up to what a gold mine he was sitting on. They snipped up the drapes, scraped off the wallpaper, even sold off the mustard plasters the doctors used to keep the president warm. They let the tenant sleep on in the bed a night or two and then broke that up too. I often wonder whether that other man with the camera got a picture out of it – never seen one."

Jim said to Mrs Brittan: "What were you doing all this while?" She smiled and said sadly: "I stood there waiting with Alfred just until they said Mr Lincoln was dead. Then I said: 'Alfred, shall we go now?' And he just ignored me, like he would so often. Him and Mr Gardner, they were just standing there discussing what to do. 'Oh go home if you want,' he said, all distracted, 'Just don't bother me now. Can't you see I'm busy?' That was Alfred all over when he was on the case. So I walked back to the Surratts' house on my own, through the rain, soaked through, crying all the way. It was such a shock, that terrible night, even when you'd seen sudden death in the war. One minute the president was there, waving at Alfred, the next he was gone.

"Then, when I got back to the Surratts' there was a guard on the place already and I got arrested…but that's another story. They soon realised I knew nothing and let me go."

Alfred nodded impatiently. "It was no place for a woman that night. We had work to do. Anyway, I made my way over to the White House to find Mr Gardner. The whole city was up and swarming with murderous crowds by now, looking for a southerner to hang from a sour apple tree. But I drove up in the what's-it wagon, right up to the front door. The whole place in uproar; no sentries on the door, nothing. I just walked in with no one to stop me and there, sitting on a bench in the hallway was Mr Gardner, looking all dignified, like an undertaker.

"'They're tidying up the body, Alfred,' he said. 'We're to stay in case we're needed.' Now this wasn't as strange as it might be because Mr Gardner was often called in to photograph corpses for the government records. A few weeks later we were sent down the river to picture John Wilkes Booth after they'd shot him down, just in case anyone queried whether the government'd really got him. And of course we took portraits of the assassins when they hanged them later in the courtyard of the Old Arsenal Prison. So we expected it. 'Get the camera, Alfred," says Mr G, 'but keep it discreet. Park the wagon out of sight round the back where it won't be noticed.'

"We sat there most of the day, me sleeping a bit because I was so tired by now. Then in the late afternoon, just as the light was starting to fade, Mr Welles bustled past and Mr Gardner stood up. 'Ah! Gardner!' he says, 'yes, we need you now. Be so good as to follow me and bring your camera and all you need. Hurry man.'

"Well Mr Gardner wasn't going to trust me to prepare the plates with collodion at a moment like this, so he hastened out to the wagon and then rushed back. Mr Welles is still waiting, looking at his watch. 'We don't have much time and, I can tell you, there's been some debate about whether you should take the portrait, but I think it's needed,' he said. 'God's grace, Mrs Lincoln isn't about.'

"We didn't know quite what a risk Mr Welles was taking – there wasn't any agreement to do this, quite the reverse. I think he might have wanted it for his own collection, not the government's records at all. We fairly rushed up the stairs with the wet plates.

"And there, up in some corner guest room, bare and chill, lay the president in his coffin. A more desolate sight I don't ever hope to see. They'd done an autopsy by then – lifted his brain out of his skull to find the bullet and it dropped on the floor. The surgeon showed it to me. It was no bigger than a fingernail. 'Look at this,' he says. 'This is the damn thing that's ended all our hopes today.'

"They had embalmed the president, combed his hair for once, shaped a strange quizzical smile on his face as if he couldn't understand the joke and dressed him all up in his best black suit and a little bow tie. He looked like we'd often seen him in the studio – not embalmed then of course – just a little puzzled and with a big black bruise on his face where the bullet had gone. They'd not been able to paint that over.

"I don't mind telling you, I cried just to see him like that there. He'd just been alive – nodded to me in the theater the night before. And now he was gone forever. I couldn't just break down though – I had a job to do, so I just sobbed quietly. I guess everyone did that day…

"'Come on, come on, no time to lose,' says Mr Gardner. I think he was snuffling a bit too and said it to cover his embarrassment at being unmanly. God knows why, everyone in that room was sobbing or at least blinking hard.

"He'd just brought up two plates and we took the one picture and I'd just got it back in the case to take downstairs and develop and that's when they heard Mr Stanton coming. Stanton! I've never seen a man look so angry or so black.

I could hear him shouting from down the stairs: 'Gardner! Good God – who let you in? I'll have them court-martialed. How dare you! Who gave you orders? Good God, there's to be no photographs of the president. Who said you could do this? I'll have you shot! You're under arrest!

"Well, by that time I'm down in the wagon processing the plate, and I could hear the kerfuffle outside. There's Mr Gardner saying: "I am so sorry. I cannot apologize enough. We understood – I understood – that we were required here on official business, to take a historical record. I am so sorry that there has been this misunderstanding." And that's when we did the switch! Stanton didn't even look at it. Mr Welles had slid quietly away. Here was Mr Gardner giving over the biggest souvenir of all, when all Washington was dipping for momentoes! 'Get out of here,' says Stanton, 'And we'll say no more about it.'

"Only he didn't of course! He switched the plates! 'That was a narrow scrape,' was all he said. And that's the plate, the self-same one that's in my box.'Course we couldn't use it, but I guess Mr Gardner thought that one day we just might…"

Annabelle said quietly: "And you have still got that picture?"

"In the box," said Alfred. "Yes, I'm taking it to Gettysburg to sell some prints. Can't do any harm now….It's been under your legs in the trunk all trip."

She turned to Jim: "Why didn't you tell me?" Before he could answer, Alfred said: "Now, now. He was keeping a secret for me. I asked him not to tell anyone. But now you know it, I'll show you if you want, in the morning. But it's precious so don't go blabbing."

CHAPTER THIRTY

"Alfred was a nice old boy. I warmed to him during that trip," said Miss Annabelle as Isabelle's red Mustang drove down the Jersey Pike towards Philadelphia. "He was very courtly in an old world way, but pretty antediluvian in his attitudes – I guess we all were in those days – and he would keep thinking that I was going to marry his grandson."

The two women had enjoyed themselves on the trip so far. Izzie found the old woman surprisingly congenial company. Instead of having to have things explained to her, Annabelle was alert and knew what was going on in the world. The difficulty was getting her to hold onto a line of conversation right through. She kept wandering off at tangents and refusing to be steered back on course. Izzie felt she was getting snatches of story, but disconnected, like a piece of dialogue only half-heard.

The threads of her thought had to be unraveled like a ball of wool and then rewound in some sort of order, with the missing bits added in later. It was even difficult sometimes to tell which decade she was talking about and then to work out whether a tale that began in one year was concluded in the same one, or another. In one era, out the other, murmered Izzie to herself as she concentrated on the road.

"I do like that Michael Jackson," Annabelle had said as Thriller was played on the car radio. "But I wish he'd leave his face alone. Can we have it louder?" And they had hit the Merritt Parkway with the sunroof down and the music playing. Just like Thelma and Louise, Izzie thought, but without the cliff.

In New York, they had had to go to Macy's, of course, so Annabelle could buy herself some shocking pink glossy lipstick, view the summer fashions and get some large, red-framed sunglasses, that made her look like an elderly owl.

They had even found, by luck, the hotel where she had stayed in 1938. To exterior appearances, it was the same building and still a hotel, but now it had been cleaned up and prettified, with clean awnings and sparkling windows. The lobby was no longer fly-blown and smokey, but had become an atrium of chrome, glass and deep brown wood paneling. The music seeping out into the air was no longer Duke Ellington and Paul Whiteman, but muzak. They sat down to rest on a leather settee and were approached, obsequiously by a manager. "Can I help you ladies?" he asked. Annabelle had looked up and smiled sweetly at him: "Do you have anything for two dollars?" she asked. "That is how much my room cost last time I was here."

And now they were heading across New Jersey and Annabelle was telling the story of how they had found Faith Brittan and persuaded her to accompany them to Gettysburg.

Izzie had put the roof up so she could hear what the old woman was saying, though the prattling monologue was drifting in and out of her consciousness as she focused on the road.

Annabelle said: "Goodness knows what old Mrs Brittan thought of us landing on her doorstep unannounced in the middle of the night. Now that I am her age, I don't think I'd take too kindly to it, but she took it in her stride. I think she must have been hankering to see Alfred again one more time after all those years."

Izzie said: "Did you ever discover why they didn't get married?"

"Yes, I asked her that, but she wouldn't tell me. I only found out much later. Jim told me. It was the usual thing, of course. Alfred got her pregnant and in those days that meant disgrace. I don't know the details and I don't know what happened to the baby, whether she had it or not – I guess not – but she was packed off home and Alfred went off on his merry way, as men did and do. It's always the same old story, isn't it? Men get away with it." And she sighed, and was silent.

A little while later, Annabelle said: "Anyway, I did get a sight of the grandfather's famous picture the next morning. He was very proud of it, you know, but I didn't think it was up to much myself.

"We went up to his room and he unlocked the trunk and pulled out this glass plate, all wrapped up in an old towel. Then he pulled out the paper copy of the print and said something like: 'There, young lady: what do you think of that?'

"To me it was just this body lying in a coffin. Oh, to be sure you could see it was Mr Lincoln, with his beard and all, but that was about all there was to it. Nothing to get excited about. I didn't think it would be worth much, to be honest. It wasn't the photograph, I suppose but what it showed. But who'd want to buy that? It was scarcely a thing of beauty."

Izzie snapped back to attention. "I don't remember seeing that picture in the trunk," she said.

"Well, you wouldn't have," said Annabelle.

And then she went off on another tangent. "I don't know why Alfred thought I'd marry Jim," she said, almost to herself. "I don't think I ever would have. I thought I needed someone more exciting and dynamic, I suppose. Goodness knows, I got that wrong. He was a good boy and sweet on me. I just wanted something more... Did I tell you, we took old Mrs Brittan on with us to Gettysburg? She came but it didn't end happily....Oh look, that place looks nice for a stop."

When they paused the car for a break, there were no messages on Izzie's cellphone. She said: "I wonder how Gene's getting on? I really ought to ring him, to see whether his phone's on again. I haven't been able to get through on the landline at home either."

"I am sure he's fine. He's got your number, hasn't he?" said Annabelle. "I'm enjoying this trip, aren't you? It's good to see what's changed."

But when Izzie tried Gene's cellphone, the message still said unobtainable. Their home number was on answer-phone too. All she got was her own voice speaking back to her: "Eugene and Isabelle Hofsettler can't come to the phone right now. Please leave a message after the tone...."

Izzie was getting really worried now. It wasn't like Gene. She felt as hopelessly out of touch with him as if they had been back in the age before telephones. At this rate, she'd have to send him a postcard.

The reason Gene was not in when Izzie called was because that morning he had had a call from George Montgomery Price at the antiques shop. "Hi Gene – howya doin'?" he had said. "I think I got something you might be interested in – one of those old cameras, just in. Ya wanna come and have a look?"

Gene was in the car and speeding down to Bijou Memories within minutes. There, sitting in pride of place in the middle of the shop waiting for him, was a large, ancient camera sitting on a five foot high tripod. It looked perfect: a large, square, polished wooden box with leather concertinaed sides, maybe a foot across and a foot deep with a large brass lens with a diameter of several inches sticking out from the front. At the back there was the sliding mechanism to push the plate into place and, best of all, attached to the back was a large, black cape.

Gene circled the camera several times, then poked his head under the cape and looked through the back. Price was standing upside down in front of him. He thought that, through the mustiness, he could even smell a lingering odour of chemicals, but perhaps that was just his imagination. He knew they must have it for the guest house.

Price was saying: "What do you think? It's a genuine Woodward Improved Solar Camera, circa 1870. It's as authentic as you'll get. Very nice, very good condition. Look at that brasswork round the lens..."

Gene could not disguise that he was impressed. "Where did you get it?" he said.

"You're not going to believe this, but a guy from round here, clearing out his father's house, name of Trumper. I guess they'd inherited it or something from some ancestor. It had been sitting up in their loft for decades. I said to him straight away that I knew someone who was looking out for one just like this. And now I've matched you up."

"How much?"

"Well, I could get twelve maybe fifteen hundred in Boston for it, but Eugene, you're a good customer and I know you'll give it a good home....I'll let you have it for a thousand."

Ten minutes later it was being placed carefully in the back of Gene's estate wagon. He had beaten Price down to nine hundred and fifty, but both of them knew he had to have it. "We just won't eat for a week," said Gene, more seriously than he let on. This must absolutely be the last purchase, he thought. Their credit cards were maxing out.

There was one more surprise when he got home as he screwed the wooden box back onto the tripod, ready to take its place in the hall. He had not noticed it in the shop, but there, in very small black letters incised into the wood at the back of the box long ago, were the initials AB.

There could be no doubt about it. The camera must have been Alfred's. "Welcome home, old chap," said Gene stroking the top of the box. What a find.

It was going to be a busy day. Actually, the reason why he had not contacted Izzie, apart from the fact that he had smashed his cellphone, was that he had been too busy to make time to call her. He was going to be interviewing potential staff to help with the bed and breakfast business that morning and they would be there at any time. He rather wanted to prove he could run things without his wife if she was going to disappear without notice.

It did not go well. The only two applicants following his advertisement in the Dispatch-Messenger had been two sisters. Gene had barely finished erecting the camera when they were at the front door and he opened it to find them lounging proprietorially outside. Both were wearing satin Boston Bruins baseball jackets, hands stuck in the side pockets, skin-tight jeans and sneakers. Their hair was peroxide blonde and they were chewing gum.

This is not going to go well, thought Gene, but needs must: at least they had turned up. He estimated they were about eighteen. There was only meant to be a job for one, but it looked as though he might be stuck with both as a job lot. "Hello," he said. "Have you come about the job – err jobs?"

"Hi," said the taller girl. "'Sright. Whatja want us for?"

They went into the kitchen where Gene sat on one side of the table and the girls on the other. Gene was used to interviewing people as a journalist, for stories, but not for jobs. He pulled out a pen and a sheet of paper. In what he hoped was a businesslike manner, he said: "Let's start with your names and addresses. Are you sisters?" He had to admit, the older one was quite attractive, in a sluttish sort of way. Mind on the job, he thought.

"I'm Shardonnay, with an S an' two Ns. An' this is Champayn, with a C," the older one said.

"My word," said Gene, trying to lighten the mood. "Your parents must have been going through the vineyards of France. Do you have a brother at home called Beau-jolais?"

The girls looked blank. "Nah, he's called Bud," said the younger one.

Could they make beds, he asked. They thought they might. Dust and clean rooms after guests? Yeah. How about serve breakfast and wait on tables? Sure. Were they punctual? They looked baffled, as if he'd suggested they kept time by the sundial. Duh, yeah.

References? Nah, but everyone knew them, di'nt they?

"Let me show you what we'll want you to do," he said and led them on a tour of the house, up the stairs and into what he now liked to think of as the Lincolns' bedroom.

"Coo," said Shardonnay, looking around. "You got a lot of old stuff."

"Oh no," said Gene, suddenly wary. "Not really, it's just old family things.

Junk really – sentimental value only to my wife and me." Then, as he saw Champayn idly pick up a Victorian ornament of a shepherd girl and her swain that had set them back two hundred dollars at Bijou Memories, he cried: "Don't touch that!"

"Nah, it's real cool," the girl said, waving it around to show her sister. "Aw, sweet," said Shardonnay.

Downstairs in the guest sitting room, he had forgotten that he had laid out the glass plates and the accompanying prints the night before while making his decision about which to have printed up and framed to put around the house. The girls gasped when they saw the line of pictures all along the skirting board.

"That's a funny place to put that old pictures stuff," said Shardonnay. She bent low to peer at them. "This one's got dead guys too."

"Wow! Cool!" said Champayn. "I'm cool with that."

The girls started examining the photographs more closely, squealing with excitement as they saw more mangled corpses. The Dead of Antietam still had the power to shock. "Grue*some*!" they chorused, fascinated.

Gene said hurriedly: "Yeah. They're photographs taken during the Civil War by the man who lived in this house. We found them in a shack round the back and I am planning to have some of them framed to put on the walls."

They stared at him uncomprehendingly. "Old photos? You could get new ones," said Champayn.

"No, no, we don't want new ones. That's why we're calling this place The Photographer's House, because of him. The Civil War – you've heard of that? Haven't you?"

The two girls looked at each other and shrugged. "Oh yeah," said Shardonnay. "That's the one where we fought them Chinese guys in the jungle wasn't it?"

"No," said her sister. "You're thinkin' of the Alamo. When we beat the English – you remember, we saw that program on the TV."

Gene decided now was not the time for a history lesson. What was that about most children not being able to place the Civil War in the right century these days? He'd always thought that those sorts of ignorance surveys were a joke until now.

He led them out into the hall and pointed out the camera. "He took those photographs on this," he said, proudly.

"It's kinda big, isn't it? You couldn't stick one of those in your pocket!" said Champayn and they both giggled.

"So, do you think you two can handle what we do here? There's quite a lot of responsibility and you must turn up on time, every day, clean and tidy. Can you do that?" Gene asked. "We don't want anything broken either."

"Yeah, course. We want the money," girls chorused.

Shardonnay said: "And we're cool with having dead dudes on the walls." They giggled again. "Awesome!" said Champayn.

Sighing, he agreed to take them both on, on a fortnight's trial, when there were guests. And as he shut the door behind them, he just hoped he had done the right thing.

CHAPTER THIRTY-ONE

Mrs Brittan showed her guests up to rooms at the top of her house, leading the way slowly and rheumatically up the stairs to the third floor by the light of the oil lamp that she carried. Annabelle had one room under the eaves and Jim found himself sharing an attic bedroom with his grandfather and Trumper.

Outside on the landing, Alfred said good night to Faith. "I am so glad I've found you again," he told her and made a clumsy lunge to kiss her good night. She pushed him away, but good naturedly and with a smile. "Oh get on with you. It's far too late for that, in all senses," she said. Leaning against the balustrade, she shook her head and said wistfully: "How did you come back into my life? And why now?"

"Oh Faithie, we lost each other for too long. I am so glad you didn't move away from here, otherwise I'd never have found you again."

"Well, now you have, what do you want to do about it?"

"I don't know. Maybe start again?"

She snorted: "No, no, we missed our chance years ago. We're too settled and fixed in our ways. I couldn't live with you now."

He said: "Why not? You could come to live in Springbridge, if you wanted…"

She shook her head. "You move out of my life for decades and then you turn up one night and say it's all forgotten. Oh no, that wouldn't work."

"Come with us to Gettysburg anyhow. And then see…"

Faith lifted the oil lamp and looked him in the face appraisingly. "You're still a handsome man, Alfred Barker. Perhaps not as sprightly as you were in '63. Bit more wrinkled, bit less hair. But then you could say that about all of us."

"And you're still a handsome woman, Faith. I've never stopped loving you, you know."

She pushed him gently in the chest and said: "Go to bed now. I'll see you in the morning." But, as she went down the stairs, she was already thinking: "Gettysburg – why not?"

In the room, Simeon took off his shirt, trousers and boots, scratched his chest, clambered into bed in his woolly combinations and socks and promptly fell into a deep sleep, snoring gently.

Jim neatly folded his clothes, as he did every night, and climbed into bed, but as he did so he saw Alfred sitting on the side of his bed, head sunk, gazing apparently at his boots. Jim said: "What's the matter, Grandpa?"

The old man looked up and by the light of the gas flame flickering in the lamp on the wall, Jim could see that his cheeks were streaked with damp. "Oh Jim-boy," he said. "I should have married her."

"Why didn't you?"

Alfred was silent for a long moment and then he said: "Oh, I don't know: prejudice and fear, I suppose. It was all my fault. What I told you about Mr Gardner forbidding us getting married wasn't strictly true."

There was another pause, as if he was making up his mind what to say, or screwing up the courage to do so. "Well, it can't harm now, I suppose. The fact is, Jim, I got her pregnant. The first time we, well we canoodled together after a Sunday walk. We couldn't stop ourselves. I knew it was wrong, but we did it anyway, couldn't stop ourselves...that's why I want you to be careful, because of what happened to me. See, we didn't have things like I've given you in that packet in them days."

He sighed and said wistfully: "It was lovely, you know. A few weeks after we got back from the battle of Gettysburg – I suppose that's what gave me a feeling of urgency, seeing all those dead young men who'd never had a chance to....that and animal instincts. And she was lovely, you know, Faithie.

"We only had a chance to do it the once. A few weeks later Mr Gardner hands me this letter she'd given him to give to me: come at once, you know? And so I goes to see her that evening and she says, Alfred, I am fearful scared that I might be, well, you know, with child. And it became true – she was, with my babby. A few weeks more and you could see the bulge growing...a little beating heart. My babby!

"Well, Mr Gardner calls me in and says to me: 'What are you going to do about it Alfred? Are you going to marry her?' And I knew I couldn't, not then. I wanted to, but she'd already told me her father would never give me permission: see, she was Catholic Irish and I was Protestant Irish and they just don't mix – it'd have been like me marrying a black woman. We could have gone ahead anyway, I suppose and told him afterwards, but she didn't want that. She didn't want to be estranged from her family. And all the time the babby's getting bigger and we couldn't make up our minds.

"In the end Mr Gardner says: 'I don't think you can delay any longer, Alfred. She's getting larger and you'd better make up your minds: marriage, or get rid of the child. Otherwise I'll have to let her go: I can't have a pregnant housemaid. She'll have to be sent away….' Mark you, he said, 'if you want to get rid of it, I know a doctor who can help.'

Alfred sighed again. He was scarcely talking to Jim now, more to himself. "See, in those days getting rid of a babby before it was born wasn't a crime. It wasn't such a stigma. You didn't get punished for it, except by the Church. Many and many people did it, fashionable ladies as well as housemaids – the only ones who didn't were those who needed to most, the ones with ten kids and no money. It was much worse to have an illegitimate babby…then you'd lose it anyway, to an orphanage, or the nuns. Be good as dead to you. Not that that makes it any better.

"So, we went to see this sawbones, across in Georgetown and he takes Faith in and, I don't know what, the babby goes. And I paid twenty dollars, which was a lot of money in them days. And she goes off to Mrs Surratt, as a fallen woman, to the only woman who'd employ her. And we missed our chance…."

He looked up: "You know Jim, I've always regretted that child. There's not a week when I don't think about what he might have turned into, even now. I think about him as a boy, and that's what I like to think he would have been, but I don't know…I've even given him a name sometimes. I call him Jonathan, you know – after King David's friend in the Bible: one in spirit with my own soul. He'd be seventy four now – perhaps we'd be going to Gettysburg together. P'haps he'd of been president…."

Jim had tucked his knees up under his chin as he sat up in bed listening to this. He felt almost as if he was an interloper in his grandfather's most secret thoughts. He had never heard him speak of any of this before. How different his own life might have been if Jonathan had lived. How different his grandfather's too. He wondered whether Faith had felt the same: perhaps he could pluck up courage and ask her one day when he knew her better.

He said: "So, how did you come to marry grandma?"

Alfred sat up. There were no tears now. "Who? Oh her, Sarah Jane…well, that one wasn't a lovematch, for sure. Since I'm telling you all this, I suppose I'd better go on. See, after the war, Mr Gardner's business got rocky – no war pictures any more. He and Tim O'Sullivan went off to the West to make their fortunes. Jim Gibson took me up to New York to be his assistant for the gallery he planned to open up there. And that failed too.

"I kept in touch with Jim, of course. One day, he comes to me and says: 'Alfred I'm in trouble. I've got this girl, Sarah, pregnant. What am I to do? She don't want to abort and I can't marry her, can I – what would my wife say? '

"So, do you know what I did – I went to see her and I agreed to take her off his hands, make an honest woman of her. I dunno why I did it – guilt, I suppose, over what happened between me and Faith. It wouldn't even have been my child.

"See, it was all a big mistake – I didn't have anything in common with Sarah Jane. We didn't even like each other all that much. I said to Jim: 'But she's only a little-bitty girl,' and he said: 'But she's a hard worker. She'll look after you in your old age…and she's a good cook,' – he was wrong about that too and perhaps he knew it!

"So, out of a misplaced sense of loyalty to Jim Gibson, I go down on one knee and I say to this Sarah Jane: 'I've come to rescue you, to save your shame and make you my wife…' And she says – you know what?: 'I suppose you'll do.' 'I'll have to,' I says, 'No one else'll have you now.' And that's what happened.

"She said: 'You'll have to get an honest job, or Father O'Flynn won't marry us,' – she was a good Catholic girl, or, well, considering everything, not good. And so, I said to Jim: 'I want to go back into photography and you've got to help me.' He paid for my camera – it was cheaper for him than an abortion.

"So it was a business deal, Jim, that was all – and do you know what the worst of it was? We got married and a fortnight later she lost the babby anyway naturally! So I needn't of done it – we got hitched for nothing and there we were, stuck with it! What do you think of that? We was stuck with each other and had to make the best of it…

"And then, in due course, years later, your mother Mary came along, a new babby, and that was that. We stuck it out, till death us do part. And Sarah died when you was a babby yourself, and then your father. So I had to look after your mother all over again, and you too. That's been the story of my life and now you've had it all. All the salient details, anyway. What is it, that opera? – The Slave of Duty! That's me…all because of a wrong choice, years ago. And now here I am, back with Faith to make it right. The wheel has come full circle. You won't begrudge me this little bit of love, Jim, will you?"

"No, grandad," said Jim, sleepy now and exhausted from Alfred's revelations.

"And you won't ever tell your mother, will you? That's why we couldn't bring her with us. It's got to be our secret, you and me...."

CHAPTER THIRTY-TWO

Jim was already dropping off to sleep when he became dimly aware of a commotion from the other side of the room. It was his grandfather who was still thinking about the Lincoln photograph. He had been muttering to himself: "We got the greatest photograph of the war, the most historic, the most unique, the most precious of all the pictures ever taken in America and we had no use for it. What do you think of that? It wasn't worth a spit in the box under my bed all these years. But one day, who knows? Stanton's dead and gone and we've got no obligation to him anyway. It'll be worth *hundreds. Then,* our ship'll come in."

But suddenly a thought occurred to him. "Darn and saize it, it's still in the car! Wake up Trumper! Move yourself – we've got to get the box before some Philadelphia sneak-thief makes off with it."

He launched himself across the room and gave his sleeping partner a sharp poke in the chest with his walking stick. Trumper, baffled and half-asleep, shook himself awake and stumbled unquestioningly down the stairs after Alfred to rescue the trunk and carry it into the hall.

The next Jim knew, it was morning and an elderly, stooped black man was knocking at the bedroom door and politely asking whether they would like hot water for washing. Then the man returned a few minutes later, bent with the weight and effort of carrying a large pitcher of steaming water up the stairs.

He peered closely at Jim and said: "My name's Lionel and ah'm sure pleased to meet you at last. I knowed it was you from that portrait downstairs in the hall. You looks jest like it's come to life, yes sir. Sure it must be you I been lookin' at all these years!

"Well, breakfast's cookin', with Mistress Brittan in a rare tizz, so come on down when you're ready. Sure is good to meet you after all them years lookin' at your picture…Your intended young lady is already down."

Jim said: "That picture was my grandfather, over there in the bed, when he was a young man, not me at all. And Annabelle's not my intended." But the old servant simply smiled knowingly and left the room.

Alfred himself dressed in his Sunday best to go down for breakfast. He had put a collar and tie on and his rough attempt at shaving had left several cuts on the side of his face from which small trickles were inching downwards. As they went into the parlour, he said to Jim: "I think she's going to come!"

Trumper had not made quite the same effort as the previous day and, if he had not slept in his clothes, he had clearly wrestled them about a bit. "Smarten yourself up, man. We've got a lady coming aboard," said Alfred.

Mrs Brittan was already ready. She was in a neat dark print dress that reached to her ankles, had a woolen shawl around her shoulders and a straw bonnet almost as ancient as she was already tied around her head. She came in bearing fruit and was followed by Lionel, the old servant, with the coffee pot. He was chuckling as if at some immense private joke.

"I've decided to come to Gettysburg," she announced. "Annabelle here persuaded me this morning. She clearly needs a chaperone and some female company."

"That's right," said Annabelle as she cracked a boiled egg. "I don't want any of these veterans getting the wrong idea. And I obviously can't be left alone with my intended." She smiled sweetly at Jim.

Mrs Brittan turned to Lionel and said imperiously: "Now, I am leaving you in charge and I shall give you a key. However, you are to take down the sign outside and admit no one to stay the night while I am away. Except possibly Mr Roosbridger, my commercial traveling gentleman. If he calls, you may let him stay but no one else, you hear? And I have taken an inventory of the food in the larder-store, so don't go helping yourself. You are just to keep the house clean and aired. Do you understand all that? I shall return in a week or so. Now – none of your tricks, you hear?"

Lionel seemed to be more amused than affronted to be patronized in this way. He continued chuckling and nodding and smiling like he was used to it and winked conspiratorially at Jim when his employer mentioned tricks. He had been in Mrs Brittan's service for many years but he was still not trusted with the key to the door when she was present.

Turning to the rest as if he was no longer there, Mrs Brittan lifted up her white-gloved hand in resignation and said: "You can never trust what the servants will be up to when you're away. They're just like children. If I didn't look after him I don't know what scrapes he wouldn't get into."

Lionel winked at them again and, with a final nod and a chuckle, quietly left the room.

The old men didn't seem to notice this little vignette. They were more intent on demolishing the bacon, ham and eggs as if it was the last meal they would have all day.

A few minutes later they emerged into the gray morning. Jim was ordered to help Trumper retrieve the box of photographic plates from the hall and they staggered down to the car with them.

Mrs Brittan clambered aboard the Model T with some effort and a helpful push from Alfred, explaining that she had never been driven in a motor vehicle before. She had armed herself with a carpet-bag of clothes and a faded green parasol and also carried a small bundle of provisions in a brown paper bag. The back seat was growing crowded, with the two lovebirds and Annabelle sitting morosely between them, the men's bundles of clothes, the box of plates, and Alfred's camera and tripod but at least if the cargo shifted now it would slide against something soft. Bony but soft, in the case of the old lady.

Trumper turned the starting handle and then climbed up beside Jim. As the car took off he caught sight of Lionel standing alone on the porch, waving sadly as they rolled away. They turned the corner and Jim looked back to see him starting to descend the steps, still waving absent-mindedly but no longer looking, getting ready to take down the sign. In the back seat, Alfred was leaning over the luggage and crooning softly to Mrs Brittan, his moustache tickling her ear: "*You are my sunshine, my only sunshine...* "and she was giggling and telling him to stop all his nonsense.

The day did not begin with much sunshine; it was hot and sultry with a leaden sky that offered the prospect of thunder later. Jim had no idea where they were going next. He knew Gettysburg lay somewhere west of the city, but had not a clue how to get them there. Neither did Alfred or Mrs Brittan. They had not troubled to buy a map.

They pulled out into a main thoroughfare and, anxiously keeping his foot pressed to the accelerator to prevent stalling the engine, Jim decided to follow the flow of the morning traffic. This was more sedate driving than they had experienced in New York but it was still alarming experience because the road was straight and featureless and entirely without indicators of which way they were going. They drove past rows of suburban housing, neat bungalows, all on their own narrow rectangular plot with a path leading straight to the sidewalk down the middle of the front lawn. Then there were some grander, two storey houses with porches and swinging chairs suspended on chains. Stars and stripes fluttered from little flagpoles in readiness for the Fourth of July. Women sat on the stoops reading the morning newspapers over their cups of coffee and elderly men in shirtsleeves tended to pots of geraniums. Through open windows came the sound of radios broadcasting dance music. Here and there small boys were playing knock-up games of softball, as men in business suits and straw boater hats scurried past on their way to work. The city was waking up to the morning and already the day was getting stifling. It would be hot and close.

They were in the flow of traffic and following the direction of the crowd. Soon taller buildings loomed ahead and the houses gave way to factories. Along the side of the road, and sometimes overhead, an elevated railroad track cast its shadow, the occasional roar and rattle of the trains causing them to jump.

After an hour's driving, they cleared the city. By now the weather had turned very sultry. The sky was a steel-gray color and the air was heavy and still. Jim could feel a trickle of sweat coursing down the middle of his back as he sat in the driver's seat. There would soon be a thunderstorm.

The air grew heavier and stiller and there was a rumble of thunder. Within seconds the sky grew very dark and great splashes of rain started to fall. Jim and Trumper leapt out of the car and started to fix up the roof with its awning. It had not so far been tested and came up on its wooden struts with reluctance and a grinding noise. The rain came down torrentially and soaked them through

Jim started the car again and they slithered onwards, skidding over the wet surface of the road and slewing to avoid parked cars. The Model T had no windshield wipers and driving was like trying to see through an opaque shower screen. Alfred wrapped Mrs Brittan in a bedding blanket and held his hat across her face to shelter it from the raindrops. Trumper folded his arms close across his chest and lowered his hat firmly over his forehead and Annabelle huddled against Alfred for shelter..

The water was bouncing off their shoulders. The car was becoming as difficult to steer as a bucking horse and their pace slowed to a walk. The awning was loose and flapped noisily. Little puddles were forming in the hollows and drips were beginning to seep into the car, rebounding off their knees.

It was hot and steamy and miserable but the rain stopped as suddenly as it had started and the sun came out. Everything around them was newly washed as if they were in a world that had been cleansed then battered into silence. The road gleamed with a silvery sheen and the trees beside it dripped as if shaking off the water like a dog. Nothing was moving. They had a purified world to themselves.

"We must get dry at once or we'll all catch our deaths of pneumonia," said Alfred and he clambered creakily out of the car, reaching back as he did so to extend a hand to Mrs Brittan, who was starting to shiver.

They stood by the side of the road, clothes dripping and the water forming puddles at their feet. Trumper climbed onto the running board and started rummaging about, pulling out the blanket wrapped round the box of photographic plates.

It took some effort and the box slid heavily against the back of the front seat as he did so. Alfred opened his mouth to shout a warning but shut it again as the box came to rest. The blanket had a more urgent purpose now. They placed it around Mrs Brittan's shoulders and he fussed about; rubbing her vigorously and hugging her close to him as if to squeeze the water out like a sponge. It was almost as if the rain had given him an opportunity for intimacy that he had not had for half a century and he was determined not to let it pass. At intervals he swept off his sodden hat and waved it as if to fan the dampness away. At each wave a spatter of water spun from the brim and dripped onto the sidewalk.

Trumper found a grubby shirt wrapped up in his newspaper – the one that he had been wearing until his illness at the roadhouse – and was toweling it around his face and hair. Jim and Annabelle jiggled up and down in the road, hands in pockets. Neither fancied Trumper's shirt or Alfred's embrace as a means of getting dry.

They were in the middle of nowhere with no houses in sight, just fields and scrubby copses of ash and birch trees all around. This was no place to stop. Mrs Brittan appeared to think so too. Her shivering had stopped. "Do leave off, Alfred. Stop fussing like an old hen," she said and climbed back into the car as if she was returning to her roost.

Trumper and Jim lowered the canopy and they started off down the road again. There were no signs on the road and the only buildings were the occasional battered and apparently deserted barns stuck in the middle of fields. They suddenly seemed to be far away from Philadelphia.

The shacks were made of corrugated iron and rusting tin advertising signs; the jubilant, rubicund white faces on the advertisements contrasting incongruously with the squalid shelters into which they had been turned. Some were so broken down and caved in that it seemed no one could have lived in them for years. And yet outside one or two, black children had come out after the rain and were sitting in the dirt or running about playing and squealing with pleasure.

The morning was now fine and they drove on towards Lancaster past fields of ripening crops. Now the countryside was richer and they passed neat, brick farm houses.

A farmhand was plodding along the lane and Jim slowed the car to call out to him: "Which way to Gettysburg?" The man scratched his head and said: "Where they had the battle?" as if it had happened just over the hill the previous week. Then he added: "I don't rightly know. I ain't never been there. I guess you should go on into town. All roads lead there from hereabouts."

They rattled onwards, but it seemed to Jim that the car was not running as smoothly as before. It seemed to be spluttering and coughing more than usual. They had not gone more than another two miles when a grinding noise started from the engine and then steam exploded from under the hood. The car rolled gently to a halt by the side of the road.

Once more they had stopped in the middle of nowhere. There were fields of sweetcorn, head-high, stretching away into the distance in all directions, hemming them in like a thick forest. Under the car, a large pool of dark liquid was spreading. It looked as if it would never move again. Trumper lifted the hood and peered inside, sucking his teeth and making little chuffing noises as he gingerly poked and prodded. Finally he said: "She's bust. I don't know…"

"What do you mean bust?" said Alfred, who had descended from the back seat and was standing beside him, his coat slung over his arm. "You were brought along to be our mechanic. You can't let us down now. Try a bit harder, man."

With a groan, as if he was remembering his long tramp for gas outside New York, Trumper sank down on the running board and mopped his forehead. "There ain't nothing I can do. Something's broke. She won't move. Can't push her. We'll have to get her towed," he said.

"Well this is a fine to-do," said Alfred. "How are we going to tow her in our condition? You'd better get moving Trumper. I hold you responsible for this mess."

Heavily, Simeon dragged himself to his feet. He was just opening his mouth to complain when Mrs Brittan, still sitting upright in the back seat of the car, shouted: "Look!" and pointed down the road.

In the distance, coming on slowly, was a horse and cart. They all stared at it. It was not like a farm cart of modern times. It was high sided and had big spoked wheels keeping it high off the ground. The carthorse pulling it was large and heavy and was wearing blinkers to keep its mind on the road ahead. But what was most remarkable was the appearance of the man holding the reins. He too was large and heavy, with a beard that curled around the line of his jaw, and he was wearing clothes that might have been more common in the days of the Civil War; thick black breeches held up with galluses, a simple loose shirt and a wide-brimmed straw hat.

As he came close, he stared at them as if working out whether he should stop or not. Then, as Alfred waved at him, he pulled up next to the car. The man looked at them and said: "Was ist los?"

Alfred turned to Jim and said: "What did he say? I couldn't quite make out his accent."

The man repeated himself and added: "Probleme?"

From the back of the car Mrs Brittan exclaimed: "Amish! He's Amish! You won't get any sense out of him. He's German."

A grin came over the man's face. "Ja, Deutsch…Amish," he said and then added: "Warten sie hier," and spurred the carthorse on down the road.

Alfred grunted: "Well, he's no good to us. On your way Trumper, as fast as you can, there's a good fellow. And no whining."

Mrs Brittan said: "That's the last we'll see of him. The Amish don't mix with ordinary folks. He'll be off hiding in a field somewhere till we clear off."

Mr Trumper reluctantly started down the road but he had scarcely begun when there was a cry from behind them and the man with the cart trundled up. This time he had another, younger, man with him, also wearing homespun clothes. There was a second carthorse trotting along behind the cart too.

As they drew level and reined in the horses, the younger man jumped down from the cart, raised his hat and spoke. He had been fetched because he had some English – though not very much.. "Hello, Nice Day," he said, very deliberately, as if trying to remember his words. "Are You in Trouble? We Could Help, Maybe."

Alfred said: "Our car is broke. We need help. Can you take us to town?"

The two Amish circled the car, scratching their heads and talking together in German. When they got to the back both put their shoulders to the Model T and pushed in unison, but the car scarcely budged. Then the first Amish went to the front and looked at the fender in front of the hood, giving it a hard tug. This too did not move the car, but he nodded and said something to his friend who turned to Alfred and said: "We can pull. To town. Maybe, there is help."

So it was that they found themselves being towed into Lancaster by wagon. The two Amish hauled a length of rope from their cart and tied one end to the fender of the Model T and the other to their cart. Then they hitched the second horse up to the front. Alfred and Mrs Brittan were helped up into the back of the cart where they sat on a heap of straw, like old country folks on a summer day's outing. Jim sat behind in the car, steering it and ready to apply the brake if it ran forward too fast. Trumper had watched from a distance and as they drew up to him he scrambled aboard. "Thank goodness for that," he said.

The journey into the town took most of the rest of the morning, for it was several miles further on. The two Amish sat together at the front of the cart never turning or speaking to the old couple in the back. They did not even appear to speak to each other either, or if they did, they managed their conversation without moving their heads. Alfred and Mrs Brittan did not chat to each other either. The old man eventually stretched out on the straw for a nap, while she remained sitting upright, ramrod straight, sheltering from the sun under her parasol.

They pulled into the town of Lancaster about lunchtime. As soon as they saw a garage quite near the edge of town, the Amish stopped the cart and unhitched the car. They all got down.

"I can't thank you enough. Will you take some lunch with us? Or can we pay you?" said Alfred, stretching out his hand to shake theirs.

The two men started away as if they were being offered something unclean. They ignored his gesture. The second Amish started winding the rope around his arm to form a coil and the first turned the horses and the cart around. The second man climbed aboard and, finally, raised his hat. "God Be With You," he said. "No Thanks is…Needed. Have a Nice Time." And they clattered off down the road at speed as if to avoid further contamination with the modern world.

Alfred murmured something about not even being able to thank anyone any more and turned his attention to the garage. It was little more than a corrugated iron shack, set back from the road, with a couple of tall, pillar-like gas pumps set into the yard outside. By the door a man in overalls was sitting reading a newspaper. He had not troubled himself to look up and continued idly turning the pages until Alfred was standing right in front of him, casting a shadow over the paper.

Alfred said: "Excuse me, my man, but do you mend cars that are broke?"

The mechanic slowly looked up, as if peeved to be interrupted, and then glanced in the direction of the Model T. Slowly switching his gum from one side of his mouth to the other, he squinted up at Alfred and said: "That old thing? Naw. I doubt it."

"Get up man," said Alfred, prodding the man's knee with his walking stick. "See here, we need to get to Gettysburg for the great reunion and we need the car to get there. So run along and help, please."

With infinite lethargy and muttering about his lunch break, the mechanic got to his feet and strolled over to the car. He lifted back the hood and stared at the engine inside, tutting and shaking his head as he did so. Slamming the lid back down again, he said to the world in general rather than them in particular: "What you got here is a cracked engine. Radiator's bust too. Could be done, but it'll take time and it'll cost you. Best see the boss."

"Where is he?" said Alfred. "Come on, man, we're in a hurry."

"Lunch," said the mechanic laconically. "He'll be back in an hour or so."

There was nothing for it but to wait so they went across the road to a diner to work out what to do. It seemed a shame to be so close and not able to drive triumphantly into Gettysburg after all their travels. Alfred seemed particularly distracted and kept looking out of the window in the direction of the car and the garage. He could see that the mechanic had resumed his seat by the door and was reading the newspaper once again.

Just as they were finishing their cherry pie and ice cream, Alfred leapt up and pointed. "That's him. He's back," he said. Across the road they could see the mechanic getting to his feet as a man parked his car beside the side wall of the shack. They could see the mechanic gesturing to the Model T and saying something.

Alfred was nearly halfway across the road before the rest of them had put their spoons down and by the time they joined him a few minutes later he was standing with the man beside the Model T, interrogating him closely.

"See here, we've got to get this car moving so we can get to Gettysburg today or tomorrow at the latest. It's brought us all the way from New England. Can you fix it? How long will it take? How much will it cost?" he was saying.

"Did you keep the oil changed?"

"No, why?" Trumper asked.

"Well, this here thing is the breather pipe," said the man, pointing to a round gadget down near the bottom of the engine. "Ya gotta keep the thing lubricated or it all gums up. You're supposed to do it every fifty miles in these old Ts – pour in more oil. How far d'you say you'd come?"

"From Massachusetts," said Alfred and he rounded on Trumper: "It's all your fault Simeon. I thought you said you knew about these things!"

"I didn't know you needed to do that. You don't normally on cars," Simeon replied defiantly.

The garage owner leaned over the engine and shook his head. "That's just what you had to do with these old jalopies in the early days. Not any more. People forget. The thing is," he said. "What you have here is a major problem. It's all seized up and that's bust the radiator through over-heating. You been speeding?"

He eyed them shrewdly and straightened up again, dusting his hands off. "I can fix it if there's nothing else wrong but you can never tell with these old sisters. Might take a day, two days, three days, could be a week, time we get the parts an' stuff an' I set Lenny here to get it going. Could cost you, thirty to forty dollars, maybe more."

Then he added: "Tell you what. I see you're in a hurry. I like this old car. Don't see many about but you can always do with the parts. I'll take it off your hands for scrap – thirty dollars. There – you'll be better off by sixty than if you'd had to pay for it to be repaired." The man had a calculating look in his eye, as if he was weighing them up.

"Nothing doing," said Alfred. "If it's worth that much to you for scrap, it must be worth much more if you can get it going. I want it repaired. Now, young man, here's what I'll do. Is there a railroad station in this town that'll get us to Gettysburg? Good, then we'll take it. You've got a nice car – you can drive us down there with our baggage and make sure we get on. And then after the reunion we'll return to collect the car and drive home. There – your Lenny will have all weekend to mend it in. Looks like he could do with some overtime to keep him occupied."

"Now, see here…" said the man, but he was quelled by the old man's glare. "You wouldn't have us miss the reunion because you just wouldn't run us down to the railroad track would you?" Alfred said.

Within a few minutes they had loaded all their belongings into the trunk of the garage owner's saloon car and squeezed inside. They were clearly not welcome guests. He turned and looked at them: Alfred and Annabelle next to him, Trumper, Jim and Mrs Brittan squashed in the back, all holding their dirty washing to their chests. The garage owner sniffed and said: "Guess we'd better keep the windows open. Don't want to have to fumigate the car afterwards."

"You do that, sonny," said Mrs Brittan tartly. "We'd hate to have you smell us out on such a warm day."

Lancaster was a fine old town with many big and ancient buildings and an attractive central square, but they barely registered these before the car pulled up at the railroad station, which itself looked like a lofty Victorian mansion, with Grecian pillars and a stone portico setting off the dark brickwork. The garage owner could not wait to get them out but, at the prodding of Mrs Brittan's parasol, was persuaded to find them a porter for the luggage and, groaning mightily, he helped haul the box of photographic plates onto a trolley.

"I am sure glad to help you folks. Is that all you'll be needing?" he said finally.

"No," said Alfred. "We'll be needing our car by Wednesday. Think you can manage that? We'll just stop by and collect it then if it's all the same to you. And it had better be working. Otherwise you'll be driving us back to Massachusetts yourself."

With a shudder, the man started his car and drove away. They went into the ticket office, followed by a porter hauling the luggage.

"There's five of us for Gettysburg. Three veterans and two companions," Alfred announced at the window and this time without argument or asking for proof of identity, the clerk behind the glass handed over the tickets without demur.

"How much is that?" Alfred asked.

"There is no charge sir. The fare is being met by the state of Pennsylvania," said the clerk.

"That's the first good news I've heard today. Well, I'm a veteran, you know," said Alfred, puffing out his chest with pride.

"Yes, sir. I can see that."

They went out onto the platform to wait for the train. It was a hot, still afternoon and they were the only passengers. The end of the platform shimmered in the haze and the only other man in sight was an old black man in the distance sweeping the dirt. "You're in good time," said the porter, tipping back his cap and reaching into his top vest pocket for some cigarettes. He nodded to a platform board. The train was due in twenty minutes.

"Hear tell there's a powerful lot of you old boys goin' " he added. "I read in the papers they're expectin' about two thousand of you to turn up. Can you believe it, after all this time? They're comin' from all over; every state in the Union is sending someone. Don't know what they're goin' to do with you all…"

"I never thought of that," said Alfred, suddenly at a loss. "Do you suppose there will be somewhere to stay? I was just calculating on finding a little boarding house…"

"…With a feather bed, remember?" Mrs Brittan butted in.

"Or lying out in a field, like the old days," said Alfred, ignoring her. "We been doing enough of that recently."

"I guess they'll find somewhere for you, even if it's only a tent. I think they got the army in to do something," said the porter.

A few moments later the train drew in, hissing steam, the big brass bell on its engine clanking. Every carriage was full of old men. Some leaned out of the windows and waved their hats, others just peered out through the glass, smiling gently and nodding. They were as excited as little boys on an outing. From the carriage opposite as the train pulled to a stop, an old man gestured insistently for them to get aboard and join him.

The porter placed a stool on the platform beneath the entrance to the railroad car and helped them up with their things, receiving a quarter for his trouble from Mrs Brittan and a handshake from Alfred. There were three seats around the old man who had waved and the old folk piled into them, while Jim and Annabelle stood in the aisle between the seats. This was no hardship to them; they had been sitting for so long on the journey, a chance to stretch their legs was what they needed. Jim had never been on a train before.

Along the platform, the train conductor stood in his uniform, his buttons gleaming, flag in hand. Then he cried: "Aaaaall Abooooooard!" and the train began to jolt forward.

"Are you a veteran too?" asked the little man they had joined. He was a small, wizened figure, with a creased and weather-beaten face and a white moustache. He was dressed in a gray, high-buttoned coat and black hat.

"I had that honor, sir," said Alfred stiffly, eyeing the other's uniform.

"Blue or gray, may I enquire, sir?" said the little man smiling and nodding his head to encourage the conversation along.

"Blue, blue, always blue."

"Ah good!" said the man, clapping his hands and chuckling with laughter. "Then you are just such a person as I always wanted to meet. Please shake my hand, sir. It's good to know you!" As he opened his mouth Alfred could see he had no teeth, making his enunciation slur. His laugh was a cackle and erupted at unsettling moments.

"I myself served the gray as you can probably detect, though not at Gettysburg," he continued. "And in all the years since, down in Carolina, I have never met a Yankee. I wanted to come just to see what you all looked like. Whether you really got horns or not! Ain't never been this far north before. Ain't that something to do on your own at ninety-five?"

"Don't you have a companion?" said Mrs Brittan.

"Oh no ma'am, had to leave my old woman at home to feed the hogs. Cain't both of us leave the old farm," he said. He was clearly delighted to be away and rocked back in his seat, cackling again.

"I wanted to meet you because I aim to be reconciled and to express my regrets and condolences for the late unpleasantness. I sure am pleased to make your acquaintance. I just knowed you was a Yankee when I saw you standing there on the platform," he said, extending his hand again.

"Likewise, I'm sure," said Alfred uncertainly.

"Ain't this fine?" said the little man. "I been traveling two days up from South Carolina and seen sights I ain't never seen before. Washington, Richmond, Baltimore. All my service was way down south, y'see. Never got to fight a proper battle. My name's Homer T. Graves. From Warm Spring, South Carolina. What's yourn? If we're to sit together we got to be pally."

Satisfied that Alfred was a real Yankee, Graves leaned forward once again and beckoned him to come closer. "You'll never guess," he said. "First night on the train they tried to get me in them night clothes things. Attendant come up to me and he said: 'Here, try these-here pajamas, sir.' Black man an'all! And do you know what I said? What d'you think? I said: 'No sir, I ain't a gonna put them things on. My wife put these clothes I'm a'wearin' on me when I left home and she'll take 'em off when I get back home again.' What do you think of that, hey?"

The old man rocked back and forth, gurgling with laughter at this. He evidently thought it was the most natural thing in the world not to change while away from home, even though he would be gone for more than a week, and he assumed Alfred would think so too. After all, they were all old men together, used to the privations of earlier times.

Alfred smiled and twitched a nostril. "I wondered what it was," he said. "Well there's a thing."

The train moved slowly through the afternoon, crawling through the cornfields of Pennsylvania. At every railroad station, the engine blew its whistle and rang its bell and along the carriage the old men would stick their heads out of the window and cheer, a reedy, high-pitched whoop. Sometimes there were small groups of people waiting on the platform and they would wave and cheer back.

"Mostly rebs' in here," confided Graves. "That's the famous Rebel Yell. The boys just want to let the Yankees know they're comin' back...peaceful this time of course." And he cackled again.

Jim's exhaustion was catching up with him and the rocking motion of the train made his eyes droop and then close as he nodded off while still leaning against a seat back. He was woken by the sound of raised voices. His grandfather was saying heatedly: "What nonsense you do speak! Your cause was the worst a man ever fought for!"

Graves continued smiling benignly as if he had not heard properly. "Well, the Northerners came down and wrecked our country anyway. There wasn't any call for that. Afterwards, they did not leave us a stick or a cow to call our own. We still feel it sir, we still feel it," he said.

Alfred glared at him. "You didn't have to rebel. It would have been better if you never had. Better men than you would have lived to raise the stock of American manhood. You couldn't treat darkies like dogs…"

Graves heard that, or at least detected the tone and he rapped his cane on the floor of the carriage. "Darkies! What do you know about darkies?" he shouted, suddenly passionate. "I've lived with 'em all my life. I never had no slaves, no more than anyone in my family, ever. But they was happy with us till you all came down and busted up the plantations. We looked after 'em, see? Made sure they come to no harm."

"Harm!" shouted Alfred, really angry now and oblivious to Mrs Brittan's restraining hand upon his arm. He had woken her up too. "I suppose keepin' them in slavery, as property, as things, not people, wasn't no harm to them? Buyin' and selling people, separating them – men and wives, children from parents – sendin' them away never to see their kin again, then workin' and beatin' them to death, wasn't harm? Don't talk to me about harm! You southerners are all the same, whinin' about your rights and not noticing them you enslaved."

"You don't know anything about it!" shouted the other old man. He was angry too now. "'Course they was cared for! What nonsense you talk! They was property! Stands to reason we'd look after them – they belonged to us! We had a responsibility! Not like afterwards – folk couldn't care what happened to them afterwards. They could go hang – or we'd hang 'em! You ask any old nigra who remembers the old plantation whether he wouldn't rather go back to it than stick in some tin shack pigsty an' see what he says! They *respected* us then, in them days…they was like our livestock – or our children."

By now the raised voices had drawn the attention of other old men in the carriage and they were standing up, stretching to get a look. Some were leaning over the back of their seats, cupping their hands behind their ears to hear what was being said. One old man, standing next to Jim, turned to his equally old friend and asked: "What's that? Have we got some darn Yankee in our car? What's he doing here?"

"See here mister," said one of the old men leaning over the seat behind Alfred and poking him in the back, "You didn't ought to say those things round here. There are men who lost everything because of you and your damn philosophy and they won't like it."

Alfred was beyond caution. He turned to face the new speaker. "Lost everything, damn it! Lost your freedom to enslave other people and treat them like hogs, you mean! Didn't lose your plantations! Still had your property – just didn't know how to farm it properly without slaves! Lose! What did you ever lose?"

The man moved his position slightly and waved his right jacket sleeve. It flapped, open and empty. There was no arm below the shoulder. "Lost this at Petersburg. That enough for you?" he said. "I never had no slaves or a plantation either. You imagine hitchin' a mule to plow your field with one arm all these years."

Alfred snorted. There was no compassion in him. "Well then you shouldn't ever have fought, should you? It warn't your quarrel. Teach you a lesson."

The man who lost his arm seemed scarcely to notice. He was in full flood now too, rehearsing an often-told bitterness. "Lost my arm in '65 just two weeks before the war was over," he was telling the carriage in general and no one in particular. "Just eighteen and with a widowed mother back home on the farm! I didn't want to fight. The gentry's sons *they* didn't fight, just sent the rest of us off to be cannon fodder. Give me ten dollars to enlist 'stead of them! Ten dollars and left with no arm the first time I was ever in a fight. It's bin with me ever since…"

"Well there you are, more fool you," said Alfred ruthlessly. "Don't wave your stump at me, ya damned rebel."

Suddenly there was a shriek from Graves and he hurled himself at Alfred, thrashing at his head with his cane. His face was red and there was a gurgle in his mouth as he shouted. "Darn Yankee! Show some compassion," he was yelling.

Alfred was taken by surprise at the suddenness of the assault and raised his arm to deflect the first blow, ducking his head as he did so. The cane slid down his arm and landed squarely on Mrs Brittan's head instead of his. It was a heavy blow. She winced and cried at the unexpected strike and started rubbing the bruise.

"Damn rebel! Look what you done – assaulted an old woman!" shouted Alfred struggling to his feet. "That's about your mark isn't it? Should've known better than to sit with you! You beast!" And with that he raised his stick to retaliate. Then, just as the whole carriage seemed to be seething together in battle, walking sticks raised, the train juddered and stopped without warning. They all piled into one another and lurched in a heap against the forward seat, pushing Alfred and the old man snarling together against it. They were still trying to free their arms to hit each other as several old men, Trumper, Annabelle and Jim fell on top of them.

After a pause, the train slowly moved forward again. Jim picked himself up, then helped Annabelle and Trumper to their feet. The other veterans slowly unpicked themselves from the heap, leaving Alfred and Graves entwined together on the bench, their chins bristling, breathing angrily a few inches from each other.

Alfred pushed himself up from the other's body, straightened his jacket and shirt and said: "There. Let that be a lesson to you not to tangle with a Yankee."

Graves righted himself too and, ignoring his opponent, leaned across solicitously to Mrs Brittan who was still groaning and feeling her battered head. A small trickle of blood was running down from her gray hairline and a bruise was rising on her forehead.

"Ma'am, I am so sorry. I ain't never struck a woman in my life. I was provoked but I didn't mean it, let me help you," the old man said, offering a grimy handkerchief from his coat pocket to staunch the blood. Mrs Brittan just groaned.

"Take your filthy hands away!" shouted Alfred. "If there's any tending to do to this woman, I'll do it!"

Mrs Brittan looked up at him and said witheringly: "Well you don't seem to be making too good a fist of it so far, Alfred!"

Just then, the conductor appeared at the end of the car, followed by an elderly man also dressed in gray like so many of the others on the train. He was a veteran but he carried a doctor's bag and was arriving in search of a patient.

"What's this? What, what?" he said officiously, looking at the glowering elderly men and the old woman rubbing her head.

None of the veterans had any breath left as they sat wheezing on the banquettes, so Annabelle said: "Excuse me, sir, it was just a small difference of opinion. All right now."

The doctor said to the old men: "Dear, oh dear and we haven't even got to Gettysburg yet! Do you want to kill yourselves before it's even started?"

Then he turned to Jim and added: "My name's Dr Bushrod Radford of Savannah. Allow me to treat the lady. I have some experience of these things." Without waiting for a reply he opened his bag, drew out a brown glass bottle and a wad of gauze, poured some liquid on it and applied it to the wound, leaning low over the patient as he did so. Mrs Brittan winced and gasped as the pad was applied, while the doctor made soothing noises. Then, holding it in place with one hand, the doctor searched his bag and pulled out a bandage, which he wrapped tightly around her head. He ordered Alfred to hold the end while he looked for a safety pin.

Dr Radford stood back to admire his handiwork and said: "I am afraid, ma'am, you will have some bruising and perhaps a black eye. Alas, your evident charms will be a little hidden at Gettysburg, for which I apologize. As for you, sir," pointing at Alfred, "kindly keep your old conflicts to yourself, for you may never know where they will end, or who they will hurt. Innocent people can get bruised when they get in the way. Never forget it as a principle of the conduct of war. By rights I should be charging you for this treatment but I won't, in the spirit of comradeship, even if you are a Yankee."

Alfred started to protest that he had not hit her, but the words died on his lips and he dipped his head in apology instead. The conductor smiled at him and Graves and, turning to the rest said: "Party's over for now gentlemen. Don't you go rough-housing any more, or we'll have to put you off the train and that would never do. You all have a good time now when you get to Gettysburg, y' hear?"

Muttering and with hard looks towards Alfred, the old men shuffled back to their seats. Still standing, he ran his hands down the front of his jacket to straighten it out. He felt for the knot of his tie which was askew and then, clear that honor had been satisfied, sat down next to Mrs Brittan, crossed his legs and blew out his cheeks in a self-satisfied way.

She closed her eyes and placed her head back against the banquette, passing her hand lightly over the bandage, wincing as she did so. She looked pale and a tear ran down her face. After a while, still with her eyes closed, she said: "I should never have let you bring me, Alfred. It's been nothing but pain and sorrow. Please let me go."

"Go where?" asked Alfred, concerned at last.

"Back home. I was happy there. Why, oh why, did you ever come knocking after all this time?" she said. "Why was I such a fool as to listen to you?"

"Now Faithie, you're with us for the duration now," he said. "We can't send you home in this state. I am sorry it hasn't worked out as I wanted, but we can't go back. After coming all this way we'd miss the reunion and now Trumper has let us down over the car, it's not an easy matter to get back to Philadelphia. You'll just have to make the best of it. It's only a little bump."

Mrs Brittan removed her hand from the bandage and turned her head towards him. Her eyes were pale and watery. "That's how it always was with you, wasn't it Alfred? You never thought of anyone else if they got in your way. I can't bear it. You haven't changed a bit in seventy-five years. Thank God

I never married you."

Alfred looked stubbornly straight ahead. Finally he said: "I am going to Gettysburg. It's my last trip and I wanted it to be a good one. I didn't count on you coming along, Faith, but since you said you wanted to, I am glad you did. Perhaps it was a mistake, but you made a mistake when you wouldn't have me. We could have had a good life together and it's your fault that we didn't. I've tried on this trip, goodness, I've tried, but some people just complain whatever you do."

There was silence again as both old people wrestled with their self-righteousness and then Faith placed a placatory hand on Grandfather's arm. "You do make it hard for everyone, Alfred," she said gently. "You are such a stubborn…old…man. I know, I know, this will be our last time together. Let's not argue about what's past."

Graves, still sitting opposite and listening, suddenly butted in: "Bravo! Well said, madam," he said. "Life's too short to bear enmity…"

"Who asked you?" roared Grandfather.

At that moment, just as hostilities threatened to break out again, the train whistle blew and it shuddered to a stop. Men started craning their necks to look through the window and the cry went up: "Gettysburg! We're here!"

It was true. Through the glass they could see brick buildings adorned with bunting and flags, and people standing outside waving up at them. Their journey had reached its goal.

CHAPTER THIRTY-THREE

Hundreds of people were milling around the station. There were the ancient veterans, some still hale and upright, moving with the gingerly grace of very old men, others much less mobile, bowed double with walking sticks or held up by crutches, still more in wheelchairs, pushed by young soldiers in khaki uniforms, ranger hats on their heads and riding breeches tucked into shining tan boots.

Most of the old men wore clothes in the colors of their former sides: Confederate men in gray suits and frock coats with brass buttons, Union veterans the same in dark blue. Some had dug out the kepis of their youth and stuck them on their heads as if they were nineteen again and others had their trilby hats decorated with their veteran association badges: GAR, for Grand Army of the Republic for the Northern men, UCV for the United Confederate Veterans of the South. Many had sewn their old rank insignias onto the cuffs of their coats. All wore their medals pinned proudly if haphazardly across their chests.

And everywhere there were greetings as the old men recognised each other, or saw fellow comrades in arms. They looked rejuvenated as they joshed each other, slapped comradely backs and shook friendly hands: seventy five years rolled right back. Some waved their sticks in the air in sheer exuberance. Here and there cheers broke out and guffaws of laughter; the more sprightly tried out quavering dance steps in their excitement, the most alert told their old stories for the umpteenth time to those around them. There were elderly black veterans there too, just a handful, greeting each other and being largely ignored by the rest of the crowd.

There were also boy scouts, in ranger hats, looking like small versions of the military. There were attendants, younger men who had come along to help elderly relatives There were nurses. And there were tourists and townsfolk. Somewhere, a brass band had started up playing military tunes, Confederate and Union in turn: *John Brown's Body* and *When Johnny Comes Marching Home*, *Dixie* and *the Battle Hymn of the Republic.*

"Well," said Alfred, standing up to peer out of the carriage window. "They've sure turned out to meet us," and, without waiting for the rest, he started roughly elbowing his way past the Confederate veterans, down the aisle to the door. Jim and Trumper gathered up the rest of their belongings, except for the box of plates, and followed the throng to get out.

"Cantankerous old devil you got there," one of the other veterans said genially to Annabelle. "Looks like he don't want to miss the battle…"

"No," she said. "Not like last time…he's got an old war wound. It makes him kind of cranky in the afternoons…"

Alfred had surged out into the middle of the crowd and waved his stick when he saw the rest coming down the steps from the train. "Over here!" he shouted. "Where's the box? What have you done with it?"

Jim explained that it was still on the train and that they needed a hand and Alfred wheeled round to confront two passing boy scouts. "You here to help?" he said. "Well, go with my grandson here and help him get something precious off the train will you? There'll be a nickel in it for you."

The two boys saluted him and followed Jim back into the railway car, which was already deserted. It was strewn with old newspapers, some empty bourbon bottles, sweet wrappers and orange peel and it smelled stale and sweaty; the distillation of a hundred elderly men wedged closely together for several hours. There was the box, sitting where the porter had placed it, against the carriage's end wall.

They could barely manage to get it to the door, but outside were two troopers who sprang to help. One grinned: "Here, let me give you a hand with that," and made as if to take it over for himself. Then he realised how heavy it was. "Godfathers! What have you got in this? Cannon balls?" he said.

Alfred watched the maneuvers with concern. "Don't drop it! That's come all the way from Massachusetts. Find a porter!" he cried.

A small boy scout approached Alfred and tugged at his coat to gain his attention. When the old man looked down, he saluted and asked whether he would like a wheelchair. "No boy. Do I look as if I'm half dead yet?" he told him.

"Actually, I could do with one," said Mrs Brittan. The parade, now grown to include two troopers, three boy scouts and a porter, walked through the station, to two lines of tables outside. One was for Confederate veterans and the other for Union men. A cheery young man in shirtsleeves and spectacles sat behind a sign pinned to the front saying: States M to R. There was already a small line of old men waiting, some even saluted as they approached him. He smiled genially and gave a mock salute back, before ticking off their names on a sheet of paper, searching in a box file and handing out registration cards marked with their name and the number of their tent, then pointing them towards a line of buses waiting nearby.

Then it was Alfred's turn. He did not salute but marched up to the desk and said gruffly: "Alfred Barker, Springbridge, Massachusetts. Here for the reunion."

"Well, hello, Mr Barker. I sure am pleased to see you. Welcome, on behalf of the great state of Pennsylvania," said the young man agreeably. "Now, have we got you on our list? Which association are you from?"

"Ain't from an association."

"Well, which regiment were you with? Did we know you were coming?"

"No, guess you didn't. Served with a New York regiment though. And I am a veteran. You can see that."

"Oh, of course. New York you say? Which regiment?"

"Ah, now, that poses a difficulty," he said. "It was the Irish Brigade, but I don't recall the number…"

"Oirish is it, bejabers?" said the young man looking at another list and then another. Finally he said: "I don't see a Barker listed."

Alfred was getting huffy by this stage, but before he could say something he might regret, the young man smiled and said: "Well I think we can resolve all doubts. My colleague has a book," and he called over another young man bearing a large, blue, bound volume. They pored over it together, turning the pages in sequence and running their fingers down the lists on each. Then they both looked at each other and at Alfred.

"Er, sir, there is an Alfred Barker listed here, born 8.4.1841, but it says you died at the First Battle of Bull Run…in, er, 1861…"

Alfred sighed deeply and tapped his stick impatiently on the ground. Then he addressed a point some way above their heads, as if to speak to them directly was beneath his dignity. He said: "See here. That's got my date of birth wrong. I'm not as old as that, though I may have pretended as much when I enlisted. I was at the Battle of Bull Run but, as you see, I survived. Here I am, large as life and twice as natural.They must've made a mistake."

The young man blinked. "Did you serve after that, sir? It's really not important…it's just that we want to put you with your old comrades…And we don't want to create any bad feeling with imposters, or people who shouldn't be here. Not that you, of course…not for a moment."

As if he had scarcely heard, Alfred continued to address the air: "I did serve. I am a veteran. I was at Bull Run, Antietam, Gettysburg, Spotsylvania Court House, Cold Harbor, Fredericksburg, Petersburg and Appomattox. Not necessarily in the ranks…"

A cloud passed over the young man's face. He did not want to deny the old man a pass, but it was more than his job was worth to hand out a special ticket to someone who did not deserve it.

Then, the veteran standing behind Alfred rashly intervened. An elderly man with a long white beard, he tapped him on the shoulder. "Trouble, partner? Care to stand aside for a second? I've been waitin' and I've come all the way from Nebraska."

"No, I would not care to stand aside," said Alfred. "I'm rightfully here and no one's going to take that away from me." This was Springbridge railroad station all over again.

And at that moment, as if on cue, a familiar figure loomed into view. It was Colonel Putnam, in a tailored, dark blue frock coat with silver buttons, his chest gleaming with medals and ribbons and a Homburg hat perched smartly on the crown of his head. "Ah, Barker. Still trying to worm your way into the veterans?" he said. "This man is a cheat and a liar. He never served. Throw him out, sir."

The young man looked from Alfred to the colonel and back again and then at the veteran from Nebraska, as if he might sort it out. "I have had enough of this," said Alfred angrily and reaching down for the trunk of photographic plates, he pulled his key chain from his trouser pocket and unlocked the lid. There, resting on the plates was the old, faded folder of paper prints. Muttering to himself, he started to shuffle through them until he found the one that he wanted and pulled it out with a grunt of triumph.

He thrust it down on the table and said: "There you are. There's your proof. You reckoned I was dead at Bull Run. Well, look there, you'll see me dead at Gettysburg!"

They all craned forward to see. It was a picture of a group of rocks with dead men littered all around it. Two men stood in the foreground looking down somberly at the corpse nearest the picture, their hats off in a mark of respect. The young man on the ground lay at a stiff but theatrical angle; his arms splayed out and one knee drawn up towards his body. Looking very carefully they could just make out his features: light hair, wispy moustache, eyes tight shut, smile on face. It was definitely Alfred Barker as a young man.

The man behind the table seized up the picture and, holding it close to his eyes, examined it carefully, turning it this way, then that, to look at the dead man's face. Then he looked up at Alfred and squinted again as if to erase the lines and wrinkles of seventy-five years. Meanwhile, the colonel chuntered and muttered beside him, craning his neck to catch a glimpse even as he tried to pretend he was doing no such thing.

"Yes," said Alfred. "It's a remarkable likeness. I look quite well for someone who's dead, don't I?" Reaching into his coat he then produced his pocketbook and pulled out a small, much creased and faded card. "That's me as a young man. My carte-de-visite from Mr Brady's studio. You can see we're the same."

The young clerk held both photographs up and looked from one to the other. "I don't understand," he said.

Alfred sighed as if overwhelmed by the tedium of having to explain the obvious. "Young man, what you have there is a photograph taken on the field of battle, only not quite what it seems. I was a photographer of the war. I worked for Mr Alexander Gardner – surely you've heard of him? No? Extraordinary! Anyway, after I left – after my period of army service ended – I accompanied him to the battles to take portraits of the war.

"Isn't it self-evident? With battlefields you need corpses, otherwise it's just a field. But you couldn't always find corpses where you wanted them, if you was late, or if they'd already been carted away and so you'd, um, just... get someone to play dead for a while. Help the picture, you know. 'Tweren't no deceit – there'd been real dead bodies there, or thereabouts, before. You was just helping the *verisimilitude*. We didn't do it all the time... Mr Gardner just asked me to do it round the rocks over yonder. So I was here, you can see it. Now give me my ticket..."

The colonel reached for the photographic print shouting: "Let me see it," but Alfred's cane shot out between him and the young man.

"Take your hands away, Putnam. They're not yours. That's something you can't buy," he said fiercely.

"There you are. He's admitted he's a fraud! Throw him out," said Putnam.

"Well I never heard the like," said the aged veteran from Nebraska.

Annabelle, who had been shielding herself behind Jim, stepped forward. "Hello Grandpa," she said. "Fancy seeing you here."

Putnam spun round and his jaw dropped. "Annabelle-Lee, what the devil are you doing here?" he exclaimed.

"These kind gentlemen have given me a lift," she said sweetly. "And I think the least you can do is thank them and don't be so rude."

The colonel shook his head in disbelief. "I thought you were with your friend?"

"I am. You've met Jim. And this is Mr Barker, who you know. And Mr Trumper, who you probably know and Mrs Brittan who you don't know at all. She's from Philadelphia.

"I just decided I wanted to see the reunion. And to see you of course. And these people have been very kind to me. They have kept me safe. They didn't leave me all alone in Springbridge. Please don't be angry grandpa…"

"No, no, of course…"

"Good," said Annabelle. "In that case that's all settled and you can stop making a fuss. Mr Barker is here as of right and you mustn't be a bore about him."

The colonel's shoulders drooped and he sighed. "I don't know what's happened to you Annabelle-Lee, mixing with these people. I would never have allowed it. But you are here now and I can't do anything about it," he said. "Very well, I withdraw my objection. But you can't make me like it. And I don't want you seeing this youth again." And he turned away.

The clerk was still looking judiciously at the photograph and showed it to his colleague. Then he stared at Alfred and chuckled: "I never heard a tale like that before," he said. "I guess you're a veteran alright, though I'm not sure what of. Perhaps you're the only dead person ever to come back for a reunion. Here you go, sir."

He handed Alfred the photographs and wrote something on a card that he also gave to him. Then he gave Jim a ticket too, to be his grandfather's attendant.

"It is alright, sir. I'll look after him." This time it was Alfred and Jim's turn to be surprised as Jim's mother appeared beside them.

"Mary," said Alfred. "What are you doing here? I thought you were in Springbridge…"

"For all your help, I might have been," she glared at him. "But when you left me in the dust like that, in the middle of the road. I decided to come here anyway and surprise you – and I am very glad to say I've done that. Oh you – you – old *bastard!*"

Mary flung her arms around Jim's shoulders and started sobbing. "Why did you let him do it, Jim? Why did you leave me all alone?" she cried.

"I am sorry Mom, I didn't mean to…I didn't know," said Jim, welling up too.

Alfred stood silently, leaning on his walking stick. "That is *disgraceful* language to use to your own father, Mary," he said. "I don't know what you are thinking of."

Mrs Brittan touched his sleeve. "Aren't you going to introduce us, Alfred?" she said. "Hello, my dear, my name is Faith Brittan. You possibly have not heard about me, but I used to know your father a very long time ago and we've just bumped into each other again."

Mary looked baffled. "Jim will tell you," said her father abruptly. "Now we must find our tents. We don't want to make a scene. Come along."

Mrs Brittan said quietly: "Haven't you forgotten something, Alfred? Mr Trumper and I need somewhere too."

"Damn, yes, I'd forgotten," said Alfred, turning to the clerk. "My companion here, Mrs Faith Brittan, also needs some place to stay. She was a nurse in the war, so she's a veteran too."

The young man eyed the bandage around her head and said: "She looks it." But he wasted no more time in verification and gave her a ticket too and one to Mr Trumper, to be her attendant. "Next gentleman," he shouted. "And no more corpses, please."

They turned towards the buses but Colonel Putnam barred their way. He pointed his stick at Alfred. "That was a neat trick, Barker, but don't think you'll get away with it," he said. "I don't know how you managed to seduce my granddaughter. There may be a case of kidnapping a minor, or transporting Annabelle-Lee across state lines for immoral purposes and if there is, you can be sure I'll get you for it and see you in jail. Do you hear?

"In the meantime, I shall have words with the Grand Army of the Republic about you. I'll get you thrown out yet. You're not a veteran."

Alfred retorted: "Put your stick down, you silly old man. I've proved I was here in the war. I've shown it to their satisfaction. And your granddaughter came of her own accord. You may not wish to have her name dragged through a court – just think about it. Now Putnam leave me alone and we'll get on just fine. Here Annabelle – take your grandfather away before he does himself a mischief."

Alfred doffed his hat and courteously stepped round them, leaving Mary and Jim and Faith and Trumper to follow him onto the coach.

Gettysburg was a small, unpretentious rural town, without skyscrapers or tall buildings, just modest brick houses with white shutters and tiled roofs. From every one there hung lines of colored light bulbs and red, white and blue bunting and American flags. Every telegraph pole and lamp-post had round signs saying: "Gettysburg 75th Anniversary", with the Confederate and Union flags hanging together, separated only by a Roman symbol of an ax and a bundle of rods. The town looked as if it was getting ready for the county fair and the sidewalks were crowded with people.

On the edge of the town there was a city of tents, row after row, block after block, stretching nearly as far as the eye could see, in neat lines, separated by wooden walkways. It was as if an army would be camped there – which, of course, it was; an army of old men and ghosts.

The first stop was at a line of tents kept slightly separate from the rest and the bus driver got up to help Mrs Brittan out. She was followed down the steps by Mary and Annabelle. It was where the women were staying and Faith was helped to a wheelchair by uniformed nurses. Elderly ladies in long dresses and summer straw hats gathered round to greet her and find out where she came from. Trumper might have been her attendant, but he was not going to join her. He stayed on the bus with Alfred and Jim. As it rumbled on, Alfred blew a kiss through the window and waved and Faith, despite herself, waved back.

Further on, the bus stopped by the end of one of the lines of tents in the men's camp. "Here you go," said the driver. "Row N, New York boys – your tent'll be somewheres down that line," and they all trooped out.

They were assigned a tent together at another registration table and Jim had to sign for the iron cots, bedding and mattresses that were already waiting for them.

"Is there still a photographic studio in town? Are Tysons, or Weavers or Tiptons still here?" Alfred asked one of the troopers helping to carry the photograph trunk. "I must find whoever it is. I need them to print off copies from these plates."

The army tents were all identical: rectangular, white canvas and regulation issue. They had plank boarding down the middle, which ran right up to the central boardwalk that stretched like a street between the lines. Each tent was big enough for a couple of men – three at a squeeze. The front of each tent was wide open, so the veterans would have no secrets from each other.

The Union lines had streets with numbers and the separate Confederate tent city had streets with letters. There were big mess marquees for eating, tents with latrines and others with first aid stations. They had set up an army field hospital at the college – more than they had had at the battle itself – there was a post office and telegraph exchange and there were drinking water fountains set up along the lines.

"Well, this is mighty fine," Alfred said, gazing around the tent. "Better than some places we've had this trip. Let's get some food and get to bed. I'm fair exhausted with all this excitement."

As they made their way back along the boardwalk between the lines of tents, towards the mess, other old men were emerging too, stretching and waving to each other and croaking greetings, like a line of blue-coated frogs. Some were sitting out in their canvas chairs, their faces turned blissfully upwards towards the evening sun. One little group had even set up a card school as if taking up where they had left off all those years before.

After supper, Alfred retired to bed, stripping down to his combinations before slipping into the crisp, white cotton sheets with a sigh of happiness. Within moments he was fast asleep, grunting benignly to himself.

Trumper and Jim sat on their beds as the twilight drew on. Outside, electric lighting illuminated the boardwalk. "I never knew that about playing dead for the photographs, did you?" said Simeon.

Jim said: "No. Isn't that the strangest thing? That people should want photographs of dead bodies and not care whether they were dead or not?"

"Well, that's what they thought they were. I thought the camera never lied. You know, some of those folk maybe bought them photographs thinking they might show their own kin and wishing all the time that they was still alive, not dead and cold. And yet really they were – not relatives, but still alive. What a strange thing to do, lie down and fake to be dead."

Jim said: "Even worse if it was your relative you saw and you thought they were dead and they weren't."

Outside the tent there were the murmurings of elderly men, chatting to each other and getting ready for bed. In the distance, through the warm summer's night, an owl was hooting in the trees. Occasionally someone walked along the plank walkway, stick tapping on the wood.

After a while, Trumper spoke again. "Jim, will you help me with something? I want to find the cemetery before we leave. It's not important – don't worry about it. Just thought I'd say."

"Yes," Jim said.

"You're a friend. Thank you," said Trumper.

CHAPTER THIRTY-FOUR

Izzie finally got through to Gene on the landline at the Photographer's House, which had previously always been engaged or on answerphone when she had tried. She was vaguely surprised that he answered this time, so brusquely and in a rush: "Thephotographers'housebedandbreakfast. How may I help you?"

"It's me," she said. "I've been trying for days but I haven't been able to get through. What's been happening?"

"Oh I'm fine. Been very busy – got guests coming tonight. And I've got an article to write, up against a deadline. When are you coming home? Three or four *days*? Does it have to be that long? I could really do with you back here," he said.

"Well we can't get back just like that – we're only just getting to Gettysburg," Izzie had said. "I'm sure you can manage."

But Gene couldn't. The previous evening he had had his first houseful: a nice couple from New York, two gay Episcopalian clergymen heading for New Hampshire and a retired dentist and his wife on their way from Portland, Maine to visit their daughter in New Jersey. They had been no trouble at all, unlike Mr and Mrs Lincoln, but there were more guests coming that evening and he had had to change all the sheets, replenish the soaps and clean the bedrooms on his own because there had been no sign of Shardonnay and Champayn. He had rung them up, but they had been out and never returned his calls.

And he still had that thumb-sucker article to write on rising tensions between the Administration and the State Department. There were always rising tensions between the Administration and the State Department – he had to write the same story three times a year, whoever was in the Administration – but he had to do 1,500 words by this evening and he had had absolutely no time to ring round his old friends and contacts in DC to check it all out and get the off-the-record quotes to give the article at least some semblance of credibility.

If only they could see him now, he thought bitterly, wrestling with the duvet covers and trying to understand how to operate the Kirby vacuum cleaner, so that it sucked up the dust rather than blew it out – why the hell did they give you a manual a hundred pages long, it was just a sweeper for God's sake? There was just three hours to do the whole lot. He really resented the housekeeping chores.

He could always busk the article – he knew what his friend, the former ambassador, would say. The old boy would just murmer: "You always know what I think Gene, and you'll express it better than I could myself, so just go ahead and say it, but don't put my name anywhere near it". And he knew what the line would be from the White House too: "There is no problem, there is absolutely no tension, it's all just Beltway gossip and tittle-tattle," but he really ought to make the calls if he could, in the gaps between cleaning the baths and showing people to their rooms. It really was too bad that Izzie was not there – it was her job to do the B&B and his to earn the money from the journalism. That is what they had decided: he really was not cut out to be ironing sheets and making beds. He couldn't be expected to do this, dammit.

Downstairs the doorbell rang and he looked at his watch. It was only half past three, no one should be arriving yet. He'd thought he would have another hour at least.

The bell rang again, more insistently this time and Gene ran downstairs, composing his brightest, most relaxed and welcoming smile as he did so. "Hello. Come in!" he cried cheerily, flinging open the front door.

It was Shardonnay and Champayn. "Hi," they said as his face fell. "We got your message. Sorree…."

Behind them as they trooped over the threshold came two adolescent youths in jeans and shirts bearing gruesome images of skulls breathing fire and two more girls, one wearing a t-shirt carrying the slogan: *"If It Ain't Stiff It Ain't Worth A F**k."*

"It's our friends," said Shardonay. "They want to see your gruesome photos of dead bodies…"

This was all Gene needed. He started to say: "You can't…" but they were already trooping into the lounge where the glass plates still lined the floor.

Now they were picking up the plates in their grubby hands and squinting at them, trying to decipher what they showed. The two youths started giggling and showing each other the plates they were holding.

Gene decided he needed to be placatory. “Now guys, please put the plates down, they’re very fragile. I can show you the paper prints, which are clearer. You’ll be able to see them better. It’s very busy today so perhaps you could come some other time?”

The youths ignored him. They were still chuckling. “But they’re here now…” said Champayn.

“Okay, okay,” said Gene, getting desperate now. “Just a history lesson. These glass plates shouldn’t be handled…”

“Why not?” said the girl with the t-shirt. “You musta moved them to get ’em in here. What’s wrong with having a look?”

Then Gene lost it. “Look, I’m extremely busy today. I can’t spare the time for you to see them. You can come back some other time, but I’ve got guests arriving and a hell of a lot to do.” His voice was rising now. “So just do what you’re told and put them down!”

One of the youths grinned at him, slack-jawed, and spoke for the first time: “What, like this?” And he let the plate drop onto the floorboards where it shattered, sending shards of dusty, tinted glass skimming across the room.

“Oh dear,” said Shardonnay. “There goes our job. You didn’t oughter done that, Troy.” She bent down to start picking up the pieces. “Perhaps they can be stuck together again,” she said helplessly.

Gene was convulsed with rage. He knew he had a baseball bat somewhere, but he daren’t leave them alone to go look for it. Shaking, he said: “Just get out and stay away, you stupid morons! Don’t you realise…don’t you care about old things?”

There was a silence and then the other youth said, menacingly: “Who you callin’ moron?”

Then the doorbell rang again. “That’ll be the police,” said Gene, his voice quavering and unconvincing.

“Better go,” said Shardonnay. “Out the back way….” And they all barged past Gene and rushed down the hall and out through the kitchen.

The bell rang again, echoing in the silence, and he slowly went to answer it. “Hello,” said the nicely-spoken middle-aged couple on the doorstep. “Orville and Mertylle Naughton. We believe we have a reservation with you for this evening?”

“Yes, yes! Yes, of course, come in,” Gene was almost shouting with relief.

"You are most welcome. I am sorry, I just had a little accident…"

The article he wrote that evening after the Naughtons and the other guests had gone out for dinner, was much tougher and uncompromising about the panty-waists and liberals in the State Department than it would have been had he had the chance to write it earlier in the day. The Administration was right to talk tough and react strongly to terrorists and infiltrators. These people were bringing anarchy into the world and they had to be stopped before they undermined the American way of life and wrecked everything. Militant Islam, the Taliban, Al Qaeda had no compunction about mindlessly destroying the world's heritage – look what they'd done, blowing up the ancient Buddha statues of Bamiyan. They were all the same these people: they needed to be stopped and Americans needed to do it! Donald Rumsfeld and Dick Cheney were right – he had never thought he'd ever write that. Goodness – he was laying it on strong! The article would quite shock his editors. It was not what they would have expected from him at all: but then, he thought, a conservative is only a liberal who's been mugged.

Nervertheless, in bed that night, he lay awake worrying. What if Troy and his little friends came back to finish what they'd started? They could smash every picture and wreck the property – and Shardonnay and Champayn knew where everything of value was! They might bust the whole place up, burn the house down with him in it. It would be like some horror movie, with ghoulish figures in macabre t-shirts leering through the windows….he couldn't stand that.

Maybe he should get a gun? Take them out before they took him? He had always sworn he would never have a gun, because he would never need one – see what effect these bloody people, these two-bit punks were having on him! God! He wanted to shoot them right now….

Suddenly, there was a noise downstairs. They were here! He could hear someone moving about. Cautiously, Gene slid his slippers on and tiptoed across the room to collect his dressing gown from the hook on the door, taking care not to step on the floorboard with the creak. He had armed himself with an old walking stick he had found, which would have to substitute for the baseball bat.

Slowly, he crept downstairs. There was a light on in the kitchen, shining through the crack at the foot of the door. His heart was beating fast as he reached out silently to turn the doorknob. He drew himself up to his full height.

"Aha!" Gene cried as he sprang into the room, brandishing the stick.

The figure by the refrigerator turned round with a guilty start and the milk bottle he was holding slipped from his grasp. "Oh hello," said Orville Naughton. "I am sorry, I just needed a drink for the night."

CHAPTER THIRTY-FIVE

In Gettysburg, after Trumper had lain down on his bed and gone to sleep, Jim put on his jacket to go in search of his mother and, more urgently, Annabelle. He made for the women's camp, only to be stopped at the entrance by a guard. Male youths were not allowed and a girl guide was sent to find his mother.

A few minutes later, Mary bustled up. "What do you want, Jim?" she said.

"I wanted to say sorry," said Jim. "I didn't know granddad's plan. I wish you'd come with us."

They sat down on two folding chairs and told each other their stories of getting to Gettysburg. Mary told him about her encounter with the Rev. Godley, but played down being saved by Colonel Putnam. After she had arrived a couple of days earlier she had volunteered to be a helper with the veterans, which meant that she had been given space in a tent in the women's camp. Then Jim told his mother about Faith Brittan. When he had finished, his mother said: "Well, I never knew. That explains a lot."

Her son thought she took it all quite calmly, but as she lay on her bed that night, Mary was thinking of her mother Sarah Jane. Blighted lives, she thought, why had she ever married Alfred?

It all made sense, the coldness between them when she was a child, the lack of kisses or embraces, if it had never been meant that they should marry, if they were putting up with each other on sufferance, if Alfred had felt trapped by the baby that never was, then the lack of love between them was explicable. But how was it that she herself had come along so many years later? What caused that – one drunken night of passion? One lucky conjunction? But there also lurked a dreadful, unbearable thought: was she perhaps someone else's baby, the product of someone else's liaison? Or even worse, the outcome of a liaison by one of her parents: but, if so, which one? Nothing in her life seemed settled any more and the fact that she was so far away from home, just made her feel more vulnerable somehow.

She turned her face to the wall of the tent. Some alternatives did not bear thinking about, perhaps that she had been looking after a man who was not her real father all these years – and he'd let her do it. The selfish, selfish *bastard* – there, she'd used the word again. What other word was there when she felt so strongly?

Where did she really come from? She would have to confront him about it, get him to tell her the truth without evasions for once in his life. No more secrets now. They should have done this years ago.

She gulped as she thought of Sarah Jane and a life that had spun off-track because she had got pregnant by the man Gibson, who could not marry her, and been hawked off instead to a man, Alfred, who did not want to marry her, but felt he had to out of misplaced loyalty to his friend. Jesus, what a mess! Poor Sarah…why did she allow it to happen? She had always seemed so firm and resolute, so staid and serious. Why did she not have any say?

There was a rustling by the bed and a hand touched her shoulder. It was Mrs Brittan.

"I am glad I found you," she said. "I just wanted to see whether you were alright."

Mary was acutely aware that her eyes were red and her cheeks streaked with tears. She was embarrassed to be found like that, by a stranger and it was made worse that the old woman knew more about the whole story of her father than she did herself. She raised herself in the bed and wiped her face with her hand, then she gestured Mrs Brittan to sit down on the bed.

Faith smiled and gently squeezed Mary's hand. "I am so sorry we made our acquaintance like this," she said. "I'd have wanted to get to know you in better times and in a better way. Did you not know anything about this?"

Mary shook her head. Faith said: "Well, it was all a very long time ago, so I suppose he saw no need to tell you. It's a shame, but it doesn't surprise me. He was always very closed up."

Mary said: "It explains a lot about our lives, I guess. I don't even know how much my mother knew about you and him."

"Oh, she knew quite a lot about it all – you see, she was my sister."

"What?"

"Yes, Alfred married the sister he didn't want, after making the sister who he did want pregnant and then losing her and their baby forever. Sarah knew that and he knew that she knew. So, you see, I've always known about you, from when you were born, because my sister told me. And that's how Alfred knew where to find me in Philadelphia."

"So I was Sarah's child?"

"Yes, you were, but maybe not Alfred's, I believe. But he'd better tell you about that – if he's got the courage to. Poor old Alfred! For such a selfish man he's had to take responsibility for an awful lot of loose women in his life!"

"You weren't that and neither was my mother...."

"No, I don't believe we were, but conventional morality says so. We weren't the first women to have our lives blighted in this way and we won't be the last. I wish things could have been different for me – and for that poor baby. How altered my life would have been if she'd lived – she would have been a she, you know. I was told that at least. These choices we make....I didn't know then that she would have been my only child and maybe she wouldn't have been, if I'd got wed.

"Sometimes I have thought I should have married Alfred, but this week's taught me it wouldn't have worked. The worst thing is thinking you might have been my child. I should have loved you and I missed my chance."

Mary felt a wave of affection wash over her, for her aunt. "We've found each other now, anyway," she said. "We can be friends. We can catch up. You can come and visit..."

Faith shook her head sadly. "I don't think that is going to be possible. I am exhausted. This trip has tired me out. But I am glad we've met at last. I am so glad you are here."

Before she left to find her way back to her own tent a little while later, they embraced each other and wept a little.

Across the camp, Jim had given up looking for Annabelle for the evening. They had refused to call for her at the entrance to the women's village and he had not bumped into either her, or her grandfather on his way back to Alfred's tent. When he got there, both the old men were sleeping soundly, heads flung back and mouths wide open. Alfred had piled his clothes up neatly beside his bed and resting on the top were his dentures, the teeth extracted from a dead soldier three quarters of a century before. At least they had made it back to

Gettysburg for the reunion.

As he lay in bed, Jim was pleased that he had made it up with his mother and told her about Faith. From the tents all around he could hear the grunts and snorts of old men sleeping. They sounded like a chorus of frogs on a summer's evening.

CHAPTER THIRTY-SIX

Jim woke early the following morning, to find his grandfather already up and stumbling about putting his clothes on. "I was too cold to sleep, Jim," he explained. "Want to make an early start to get these pictures seen to." He made his way off to the wash tent to clean his face.

Jim lay in bed a little longer. Through the flap he could hear the sounds of men getting up and wandering about and there were moving shadows on the canvas wall beside his bed. Chattering could be heard and bursts of laughter, but indistinctly, as if a long way off.

He wondered whether any of these men had been moving about like this, getting up in camp that same morning seventy five years before. He imagined them as young men scurrying about at the sound of bugle calls, strapping on their belts and webbing, pulling on their boots and ramming on their kepis as the orders came for them to move up fast to Gettysburg, where the rebel army was massing in great strength. He could imagine the orders being shouted: "Double up! Double up!" and the same men who were now hobbling about, leaning on their walking sticks, running to get on parade.

Robert E. Lee's mighty and victorious Confederate army, on the march up into Northern territory across the Pennsylvania state line, had surged towards the little town, foraging for supplies, not realizing that a full Union army was massing further south, between them and Washington. The two sides had barged into one another unawares and opted for battle: 65,000 men on the

Confederate side, 85,000 for the Union and by the time the fighting was over three days later and Lee started his retreat, 43,000 of them were dead, wounded, or missing. It was the mightiest battle of the war and, although the South did not surrender for another two years, after the first three days of July 1863, the tide was ebbing away from them. They would never get so close again.

Some of these old men would have been there then, Jim thought. They would have heard the drums and bugles and been deafened by the cannons' salvos and the shouts and screams of the wounded and dying, watched General Pickett's 13,000 desperate Southerners march line abreast across the fields towards the Northern line in a desperate charge on the last afternoon and be sent stumbling back, raked by artillery shells and rifle volleys, confounded, shattered and defeated. These old men had seen all that, or lived through it anyway, and survived for another three-quarters of a century when men standing beside them on that far-distant afternoon had died on the spot.

Alfred's shadow fell across the opening of the tent. "Aren't you fellows up yet? You'll miss all the fun," he said and moved inside to prod Trumper who was still fast asleep. There was no chance of lying in any longer.

In the wash tent, a queue of men was waiting to shave. Jim saw that the veteran at the next basin had only one arm. He was wiping himself down with a towel, reaching up right behind his neck, while the stump of his right arm swayed out from his body to equalize his weight. Jim watched as he took out a bowl of shaving soap and foamed it up with a bristle brush before getting out a cut-throat razor and scraping his face and chin, left-handed. The old man eyed Jim and chuckled: "Used to it, boy, after seventy years. Could never write as well as I did though."

Alfred was desperate to leave, even without breakfast. "We must get to town and find a studio to show my plates to," he said and strode off to find a trooper to carry the box and commandeer a taxicab.

In the town, shopkeepers were drawing out the awnings above their windows. The cab drew up outside a photographic shop – the best in town, the driver said – and Alfred was out immediately to knock on the glass door. Inside, it was dark and a notice said the studio was not due to open for another half an hour, but he ignored that and kept knocking. Eventually a man appeared on the inside and reluctantly unlocked the door. Alfred was through it almost before the bolts were drawn.

"Good morning, my good man, are you the owner?" he asked, raising his hat, and when the man said he was, immediately launched into a full sales pitch.

Alfred said: "Then you are a very fortunate man. My name is Alfred Barker, an associate of the late Alexander Gardner, the famous photographer. I had the honor to assist him and Mr Mathew Brady in the war and I wonder if I can interest you in a little partnership over my photographic prints of the late battle here, taken at the scene within three days of the fighting. All genuine and in good repair. Sold at twenty-five cents each, these reproductions could represent an historic opportunity. Allow me to show you…"

"Not interested, Mac," said the man. "I only take modern photographs here."

Alfred continued as if he had not heard: "These are most interesting and historical documents. I have the original plates with me. The dead of Gettysburg exposed on the battlefield immediately after the fighting…where the action was…" his voice trailed away as the man continued to shake his head.

"No sir," the man said. "These are no good to me. I cannot sell your pictures. After next week who will care to see them? Who wants pictures of dead men? I am too busy. Now, if you will excuse me, sir…"

It was the same at another shop they tried. The woman at the counter looked at Alfred's prints and shuddered. "We couldn't sell these," she said. "They're not…tasteful. I have children coming in here. We have no facilities for this."

At a small bookshop, the salesman was more interested: "This is fascinating material, but you should have been here last week. There is no time to copy them properly," he said.

They spent a fruitless morning. Trumper and Jim trailed after Alfred, hauling the box between them. Simeon had to rest every few yards as his fingers needed to stretch. The box grew heavier with each stop. They tried everywhere, but nowhere would take the pictures and Alfred's shoulders sank further with each rejection.

Finally, they found a bench on the sidewalk and he sat down heavily. Alfred leaned forward, resting his walking stick between his knees, twirling it between the open palms of his hands. "I don't understand it. These photographs are important documents – my best work – and if I can't sell them here, what's the use of them?" he said. "I thought they'd be interested, especially now. People just don't want to see the past. They want it all prettied up. They want it clean and reverent, like a movie, not like it really was. Just gallant heroes, that's all. No place for blood.

"'Course, I should've known. They all went bankrupt after the war…Brady, Gardner, Gibson. Nobody wanted the pictures then. Even the government wouldn't buy, or tried to beat down the price. So much for historic documents! What a fool I was to think anyone'd be interested in my pictures. Dragging them half way across the country – should have left them under my bed…"

Jim put his arm around his grandfather's shoulders. He said: "Don't worry. I like them. They're valuable to me…people just don't know how to appreciate them. It doesn't matter what they think."

He shook his head and his shoulders drooped more. "We should never have come. I might have known it would be like this. It always has been with me," he said.

They sat silently in a line of misery for a while, Alfred shaking his head occasionally. At last he said: "Well, I guess now we're here, we'd better enjoy it, see the reunion and then go home and forget it all."

Jim said: "Perhaps the veterans will be interested to see your pictures?"

He shook his head dismissively. "No, not them. They only want to remember the good things. Don't want to be reminded of the bad. Look at them – they're just all old pals together now. All good fun. At each other's throats for four years and now you couldn't separate them! What was the war about if you all make up afterwards and nothing changes? Look how them southerners treat black men. And that's decades on. No, you just wonder what it was all about. Whole thing was just a nasty accident, I suppose. If it was such a rotten cause, why do we celebrate it so much? We ought to forget the whole thing."

Trumper said: "If you've finished trying to sell your snaps, do you think we could go and see the cemetery now?"

"In a minute," said Grandfather. "Let's take this box of junk back first." And he kicked the trunk.

Back at the camp, they wandered into one of the mess tents for lunch and found themselves sitting opposite a veteran with his arm in a sling. He leaned across and offered his good hand to Alfred. "James Hamaker. I'm ninety-five. From Texas: Aledo, Fort Worth – know it?" he announced, exposing a mouth entirely without teeth. Then he gestured towards his injured arm: "Look at this. I didn't do this in '63. Jest fell out of my bunk on the train coming here! What d'you think of that? Too damn excited for an old 'un! Fell right on my old war wound too…"

Alfred said nothing and Hamaker, not noticing his silence, went happily on. "Yep, caught a Minié ball in the same shoulder in 1863 and now, damn me, if I ain't stupid enough to fall on it again, jest when I'm comin' back! Good job I was on the lower bunk otherwise it could've been my neck," and he broke into a cackle.

"Pity," said Alfred gruffly.

"Do you know what I want to do, now I'm here?" said the old man equably.

"I was shot near a tree in '63 and I want to find it now. I came all the way to Gettysburg to find that tree. All I want to do in this world is to find it and when I do, then I'll be ready to die. I told some newspaperman that. I told 'em in the hospital too when they put this bandage on me. Just want to see that tree! What do you think of that?"

Alfred looked at the old man for the first time. "Do you know how many trees there are round here, man?" he asked, his voice near contempt. "Look at them all. Can you count 'em? What sort of tree was it? Big one or little'un? Leafy one or spiky one? Do you even know where you fell? How on earth do you expect the self-same tree to still be here after all these years? I think you must've fallen on your head back in the railroad train."

"Don't care. I guess you was a Yankee, 'warn't you? Thought so," said Hamaker placidly, as if this explained everything.

After lunch, they returned to the tent, where Alfred insisted he would take a little sleep before supper. Jim agreed to go with Trumper to the cemetery.

They set off at a steady pace, marching through the town, Trumper with his good hand cradling the injured one, looking neither right nor left and taking no notice of the bunting and the crowds all around. He had dressed up for the occasion in a suit, wearing his old black tie.

The afternoon was still warm as they climbed the rise to the cemetery and went through its brick archway; still pock-marked from stray shots during the battle. The cemetery itself was quiet. There were groups of veterans and a few visitors moving peaceably about in the distance, but the site was mainly undisturbed. Jim and Trumper walked through neatly trimmed grass and pine trees, along paths lined with white gravestones, small plinths and obelisks. In the middle of the cemetery stood a circular pillar mounted on top with a stone soldier, on the site where President Lincoln gave his famous address four months after the battle.

Trumper seemed to notice none of this. Instead, he darted about among the graves, peering at the names on the stones, mouthing them to himself and shaking his head. Jim asked what he was doing and who he was looking for but he just muttered: "Wait a minute…wait a minute…. just coming…got to see," before dodging off to the next line of tombstones.

Finally they reached the far end of the cemetery and Trumper ran his good hand through his hair in desperation. "It ain't here," he said. "Oh Jim, it ain't here. What am I to do?"

"What ain't here? Who are we supposed to be looking for?" asked Jim.

Trumper looked at him as if he was a stranger. "My father, of course. Who else would it be?

"I ain't never seen where he's buried before. Never come this far south in all my life," said Trumper looking wildly about him. The reason for his wanting to come on the trip was suddenly starkly clear.

"I never knew him, see," he went on. "He died at this battle right here when my mom was carrying me and I was born seven months later. He never even knew I was on the way. I never had a chance to say hello."

"We must find someone at once," Jim said. "The cemetery will have records of where he lies."

In the cemetery office, the woman behind the desk asked Simeon for his father's name. Even that simple request seemed to surprise him, as if he expected that she would be bound to know it already. Then she asked what regiment he had fought with. He didn't know that, but thought it must be one from Vermont because that was where he had come from. "He was jest a country boy, ma'am," he told her by way of explanation.

The woman hauled down a series of volumes from the bookshelves at the back of the office. "Well," she said, "this could take some time. You boys happy to wait?" and she gestured to a couple of chairs in a corner. Then, with much ostentatious effort, she opened first one book then the next, sticking her tongue out to assist her concentration and running her finger down the pages. She wanted them to know precisely how much effort it was costing her.

Simeon was too nervous to sit. He paced up and down, occasionally going up to the woman and peering at the books upside down, as if he might be able to spot his father's name quicker that way. Then she would look up at him and he would skitter away with a cough and a touch of his hat. A few minutes later he could contain himself no longer and would be back, going through the same process again.

"I really think this will be quicker if you just wait over there," she said eventually, looking sternly at him through her spectacles.

"Yes, ma'am. Certainly, ma'am. Sorry ma'am," he said, taking off his hat and squeezing it in his hand. But he made no move to retreat.

"Well, go on then."

"Oh, yes," he said distractedly. Then: "What, ma'am?"

"Go over there. And wait," she commanded, pointing with the ruler she had picked up to assist in scanning the book.

Trumper sat down next to Jim, but almost immediately he got up again. He had not taken a pace towards the desk before the woman glared at him, so he wheeled round and started reading the notice of cemetery regulations on the wall. Still he could not help looking over his shoulder every few seconds to see how she was getting on.

At length the woman looked up again and said: "Is this the man? There's a Cyrus Trumper here, in the 1st Vermont Cavalry. He died alright. But there does not seem to be any record of where he is buried. Could be here, could be someplace else…."

Trumper was already beside her as she spoke. He peered down at the book, his nose getting closer and closer to the paper as if he could almost smell his father at last. Maybe he just didn't have his glasses with him. Finally he gasped as if in recognition. "That's him, that was his name, I do believe," he said. "But are you sure he ain't in here?"

The woman sighed and said: "I don't know. He might be. Could be he wasn't identified and so he's in an unmarked grave. Listen, sir, that's the best I can do for you. I haven't got more information than's in here and if it doesn't say, I can't tell you." She closed the book with a gesture of finality.

They re-emerged into the sunlit cemetery and wandered back towards the monument at the top of the hill. Simeon seemed to have shrunk a little. "I kind-of thought there'd be some memorial to him, that I'd be able to see a grave, something I could recognize," he said.

There were many small white gravestones marked for unidentified US soldiers and, as they paused, uncertain where to go, Jim had an idea. "Why don't you pick a marker and imagine that is your daddy's?" he said.

Simeon thought about it in silence for a bit and then nodded. A little further on he left the path and wandered off down through the gravestones on his own, coming to a halt before one slightly whiter than the rest under a fir tree. There, he took off his hat and held it in his hand before him, scrunching it round and round. Then he dipped his head and screwed his eyes tight closed, mouthing a silent prayer.

Jim stood beside him, thinking of his own father whom he had never known either. Instinctively, Trumper's fingers reached out from his side, Jim stretched out his and they squeezed hands in mutual support.

After a while he sighed and, placing his hat back on his head, looked up once more. There were tearstains running down his face and he pulled out his handkerchief. "I'm sorry, Jim," he said. "Don't know what came over me. That done me good though. My Daddy…my daddy. I ain't ever been close to him before an' I just wanted to tell him who I was. Have a little chat…say how I'd turned out, you know. That's what I done jest now."

They walked silently back to the path and down the hill. After a short way, while the grave he had selected was still in sight, Simeon stopped and turned round to look at it again. Then he said, almost to himself: "See, I don't know what I'd have been like if I'd had a Daddy. Maybe I'd have growed up better, not had such a wasted life with him to show me an example. Maybe made something of myself. If I'd only knowed him. Who can tell..."

A little further on he stopped again and added: "Mom said he was a brave man, killed in a charge or something. And he was a handsome young man in his uniform and all. I don't know. I ain't never even seen a picture of him. They weren't married, you know, but they would'a'been if he'd known I was comin'.

"Next time he come home. He'd have seen her right, I am sure of that. 'Course his folks didn't tell my Ma when the word come through that he was dead. They didn't even know she was his sweetheart, see. They was fine folks with a big house and a farm. My Ma found out that he was gone just from overhearin' what people was saying in the street. That's some way to find out, isn't it?

"She never told no one who the father was, so you can imagine we had a hard time of it. She was too proud. Folks didn't want to know a woman who warn't married, with a child. You know what that made me? I been one all my life. Never had no money, never inherited the farm or the big house. I only knew about what happened, when she was dying, see.

"That's when I changed my name, after that, to his'n. That's why I'm Trumper like him, not Ryan, my mom's name, like I was all my childhood. I wanted to be *associated*, is all. Too late then...I don't even know what he looked like...This is the first time it's like he even existed for me. I sure hope that grave was his and I weren't talkin' to the wrong chap."

They walked on a bit more. Jim did not know what to say and so said nothing. He thought of his father instead. At least he knew what he looked like, from the photograph of him being held as a baby. "I'm sorry, Mr Trumper," he said eventually.

Simeon said: "Don't tell your grandfather. I don't think he'd understand. But this little walk's done me a power of good, I reckon. I'm easier in my mind now."

Jim left Trumper at the edge of the tents in order to go and find Annabelle. It took more than an hour, but eventually he saw her by chance as he wandered through Gettysburg. She was sitting at a seat in the window of a drugstore drinking a milkshake and she gestured for him to go in, so he joined her.

"I am really sorry about grandpa," she said, sucking noisily on the straw. "I guess it was the shock of seeing us all that made him so rude yesterday. He's very excited and he went over the top. I've told him he ought to apologise, but

I don't know whether he will – he's stubborn like that."

They decided to go for a walk and made their way out across the battlefield, past the line of regimental and state memorials that had been erected marking the spots where particular units had fought. The monuments were scattered about like a well-spaced Victorian cemetery: large statues of generals on horseback, triangular piles of cannon balls and granite freizes of soldiers in lifelike combat, running at the charge, rifles at the ready, frozen in time. Groups of veterans were wandering about, admiring the statuary, seeking out the places where they themselves had fought amid the neatly mowed lawns along the sides of the road. Although all around were fields of ripening corn, reclaimed by the local farmers to resume their peaceful purpose, the battle lines themselves, preserved for ever, remained heavy with the oppressive weight of the battle of 1863.

Jim and Annabelle's path took them along the crest of Cemetery Ridge, the Union front line, from which the massed charge of General Pickett's men had been repulsed. Then, after a mile or so, as the monuments began to thin, they started climbing up through the woods to the conical hill known as Little Round Top. This had been the scene of ferocious hand-to-hand combat on the second afternoon of the battle as Alabamians and Texans tried unsuccessfully and at bloody cost to eject troops from Pennsylvania, New York and Maine from the summit. Had they done so, the Confederates would have dominated the end of the Union line and the North would have lost the battle.

The afternoon was sultry and Jim and Annabelle sat down on a large, flat-topped rock to rest and admire the view across the battlefield, stretching out below them, over the corn fields to the woods beyond and, in the distance, the blue hills on the far horizon.

Down the slope, ant-like figures were wandering around but up at the summit there were few people about and shortly Annabelle lay back, stretching her arms high behind her head. She was wearing white rimmed sunglasses and her summer dress was taut across her breasts and riding up above her knees, exposing her thighs. Jim took off his jacket and tie, undid the buttons of his shirt to the waist and lay beside her. The rock was warm and the covering of lichen softened its hardness. He could smell her perfume and, as he turned his head towards her, he could see she was gazing up to the sky, open-mouthed, with a secret smile on her face as if she was enjoying some private pleasure. He leaned over and kissed her and her arms came up to embrace him. He caught his breath and felt himself erect as their bodies touched. Next, he was caressing her breasts and her hands were reaching down inside his trousers. They rolled over and Jim became conscious that the edge of the rock could not be too far away. They squirmed backwards and he was kissing her neck as her head leaned backwards and her back arched. "Let's do it," he whispered in her ear.

Annabelle said: "No, not here. Let's go off a bit...somewhere more private. I don't want to do it on an old battlefield." So they scrambled frantically, urgently from the rock, clutching their clothes and made their way down the far side of the hill, where the trees and the boulders were thicker and there was no likelihood of being interrupted by anyone else.

They made love to each other there for the first time, urgently and clumsily, lying among dead leaves under a canopy of scrub oaks, surrounded by the peaty smell of soil and leaf-mould and afterwards they lay back breathless and happy, watching the clouds through the branches of the trees and listening to the calls of chickadees and wood thrushes high above. Then they made love again, more gently and slowly. They felt it was wonderful and they were exalted, as if they were the first people ever to discover the exciting sensation of love-making.

It was not until the light was beginning to fade in the early evening that they decided they had better go back to the camp and they slowly dressed and made their way through the woods, around the side of the hill and back down to Cemetery Ridge.

They could not stop smiling and hugging each other. Life had changed for them both, and they really could not care who guessed it. It was as if they had become grown-ups that afternoon and, at the age of eighteen, had finally left childhood behind. They felt that they were different and sensed that the world could see it too. "Look at them lovebirds!" said an old soldier to his companion as they sauntered past and Jim squeezed Annabelle's hand triumphantly.

They parted at the edge of the camp, so as not to be seen by her grandfather, promising to meet again in the morning and Jim made his way back to Alfred's tent, where he found the old man sitting on the edge of his bed, having just woken up.

Alfred said: "Hello, son. Have you had a good afternoon? I am raring to go again now I've had a good long nap. Whatever have you been doing to your hair? You've got bits of leaf in it."

Before Jim could answer, Simeon Trumper appeared at the tent flap. It seemed he had been hurrying because he was quite out of breath. "You better come quick," he said. "I think Mrs Brittan's dying."

CHAPTER THIRTY-SEVEN

Izzie and Annabelle drove into Gettysburg and booked into the Robert E Lee Guesthouse ("an authentic welcome in the heart of the town that made America great!") which at least allowed Isabelle to cast an appraising eye over the facilities with a view to comparing them with The Photographer's House.

It was a chastening experience: the Meade Suite into which she had been booked had tired décor and cheap, chipped furnishings to set off against the pink roses of the wallpaper and the bathroom had one miniscule shrink-wrapped bar of soap – enough to wash your hands once, she thought – and one thin plastic sachet each of shampoo and shower gel of the sort that you only discover you cannot open after you are already drenched. The picture on the wall overlooking the bed had a doleful cheap modern illustration of a group of charging Confederates and the only channels obtainable on the television were Fox News, the History Channel, home shopping programs and pornographic movies. The view through the drapes was of the rear parking lot. We have to be able to do better than this, thought Izzie, at two-thirds the price. At least their pictures would be of real soldiers, not prettified, imagined ones. She hoped Eugene was getting them printed up and framed in her absence.

Through the thin wall she could hear Annabelle settling down to the home shopping in the next room and she imagined her boiling the kettle to make herself a polystyrene cup of tea with real powdered kreemer. Izzie could almost feel the water boiling and felt sure that if the kettle was overfull and the water spurted out when it boiled it would be enough to dissolve the wall. Why have these pleasures alone, she thought, and went next door.

Annabelle, actually, had not been boiling the kettle, but getting ready to go out. She had tied a straw bonnet around her head, put on her pedal pusher slacks and was just searching out her sunglasses, when Izzie knocked. "Oh good, dear," she said. "I am so glad you've come. I was just heading in search of something I can remember from all that time ago. Do you want to go too?"

It was a late Spring afternoon and the town was closing down for the evening as the tourist buses pulled out from the coach park by the battlefield museum. Annabelle was adamant that there was some hill she wanted to see, with big rocks on it. The man at the reception desk had suggested they try a place called Little Round Top at the far end of the park and drew them a map showing how to get there.

Ten minutes along the road out of town they drove up the twisting narrow lane snaking to the wooded summit of the hill. Annabelle gazed about beadily all the way, screwing up her face hard to try and recognise the site she was looking for. Near the top, they parked in a layby and wandered along a path to the top of the hill. Izzie had no real idea what Annabelle wanted to see and tagged along behind her like a dog owner following a pet bloodhound.

The old lady skipped between the rocky outcrops studying the flat surfaces of each carefully and showing no interest in looking at the statues and monuments, or reading the signboards detailing what had happened in the battle at that spot. They left the path and Annabelle finally said: "I think this is it." She turned to Izzie, puffing along behind her and said: "It hasn't changed at all! This is the rock that Jim and I sunbathed on when we came to the reunion in '38. It's still here."

Izzie looked at her quizzically. It was hard on a chilly Spring evening to imagine them lying on the rock in the sun all those years before. The view had not changed however, the battlefield had not been built upon, of course, for it was sacred ground and the farm buildings dotted about in the far distance were ones that had been there in 1863. The woods were growing hazy as the light began to fade.

But Annabelle had not come for the view. She was already walking fast down a track leading through the trees to the far side of the hill. In a clearing, she stopped silently for quite a few moments, then shook her head, smiled and said: "That's it. I've seen what I came for," and marched determinedly back up the slope towards the path.

"What was all that about?" Izzie said, but Annabelle replied obliquely: "Oh, just remembering my past youth and the wrong paths taken through the woods. I'm ready to go home now."

That evening, they dined together in a diner in town. It had home cooking and table booths with blue check table cloths, its decor seemingly unchanged from the 1950s. As she tucked into her lime pie, Annabelle said: "Where we went in the woods…that's where we first made love, you know, that week, before we found out stuff about each other. It was heart-breaking really. That's why I left Springbridge I guess – didn't want what had happened to Faith Brittan to happen to me. I'll tell you about it sometime.

"Now dear, have you made contact with your husband yet? How's he getting on?"

Izzie sighed. "Not well. I think it's getting a bit much for him. He nearly hit one of the guests last night."

Annabelle said: "In that case, dear, I think we had better go home tomorrow. I can do without taking the full battlefield tour."

CHAPTER THIRTY-EIGHT

"Oh my Lord," said Alfred when Simeon broke the news that Faith was ill. "I'd quite forgot about her. And there's us just sitting here chatting without a care in the world."

Leaving the photographic plates scattered around the tent, they followed Simeon over to the women's section of the camp. It took only a few minutes, with Alfred muttering half the way about the damned southerner who had hit her.

There were far fewer tents for women than for men, of course – just a single line – so they soon came up to Mrs Brittan's tent. She was lying in her cot-bed wearing a pink nightdress to the top of her neck and a net on the top of her head to shield her gray hair. On her forehead was a bump that stood out proud from the surface and a livid blue and red bruise that ran down to her left eye and then on to her cheek. Her eyes were closed but she was not asleep and, as they came in, she opened her left eye, then rapidly closed it again, as if the light was too strong for her.

"Dear, dear Alfred, you shouldn't have come. I told Mr Trumper," she murmured. "Haven't been feeling too strong today, after yesterday. Just want to rest..."

Alfred sidled up to the bed and grasped her hand tenderly. "I am sorry to see you feeling like this, Faithie," he said. "Has any one seen you?"

"No Alfred. I don't need a fuss, just a rest. This trip has been too much for me altogether. I am sorry to be such a drag on you – you boys go off and enjoy yourselves and I'll catch up with you in a day or two."

"Well, if you're sure my dear…" he said doubtfully.

Simeon beckoned Jim towards the tent flap. "I reckon she needs to go to hospital. It's not right at her age, is it?" he said. "I don't think the old bird can take much more. I was right to call you wasn't I?"

"Quite right. I think we should get her to hospital. I'll fetch a nurse," Jim said.

Within a few minutes the nurse, a scowling, middle-aged woman, dressed all in white and wearing a small frilly cap on the top of her head, bustled up to examine the patient. "My dear, however did you do this? You need some treatment," she said, becoming solicitous after only the most cursory of glances. "We must move you to the field hospital at once."

Within a short time two troopers arrived with a wheelchair and Mrs Brittan was wheeled off down the boardwalk to an ambulance. Insisting he was her chaperone, Alfred hitched a lift inside with the patient, while Trumper and Jim, having gathered up her belongings and placed them in her carpet-bag, followed behind on foot.

The hospital across town was modern and clean. They squeaked across the polished linoleum floors and sat outside the private room where the patient had been placed. It had been set aside for female veterans at the reunion, but Mrs Brittan was the only occupant.

Through the round glass window in the door of the next room Jim could see another, larger ward filled with very elderly male patients: veterans who had got as far as Gettysburg before succumbing to age or infirmity. They lay flat and catatonic in their beds as if they had arrived in a waiting room for death. Jim pushed the door open a little and stood just inside the threshold. The room had subdued lighting and was still and quiet except for a low moaning and coughing that seemed to gain contagiousness as it floated down the length of the room.

A nurse came and smiled expectantly at him and Jim explained he was waiting for the doctor to come next door to visit his grandfather's companion. She grinned again and jerked her head: "Look at all these old boys. You've got to admire their spirit. Most of them are down with heat exhaustion. Thought they could still get out there in the sun and fight the battle all over again!"

There was a noise in the corridor. A young doctor in a white coat, with a stethoscope around his neck, had arrived to examine Mrs Brittan, accompanied by a flock of nurses, all in white, their shoes clattering on the floor.

Alfred came and joined Jim and Trumper outside the door while the consultation took place. They sat silently in a row, none of them liking to think too closely of their complicity in Mrs Brittan's plight, or their responsibility for it.

The young doctor came out again. "This poor lady's had a bad time," he said. "She should have been admitted yesterday when she arrived here and I am surprised that none of you gentlemen suggested it. There is a case of concussion, exacerbated by the heat, and she will have to remain here for several days. At her age such a shock can be very difficult to get over, but I guess she will have seen worse things. Now, gentlemen, my suggestion to you is that you go and enjoy the rest of the reunion. You may return to see her each day, but don't expect to tire her. I am not sure yet when she will be able to return home."

Alfred meekly muttered his apologies and, as the phalanx of nurses disappeared down the corridor behind the doctor, he poked his head around the door of Faith's room and slipped in to see her. Through the round window in the door, Jim could see him squeeze her hand gently and bend over to kiss her softly on the forehead. She winced as the bristles of his moustache touched the bruise but looked up at him kindly and smiled. Her ancient face suddenly looked radiant and the creases slipped away and Jim could suddenly see the beauty that had endeared her to his grandfather. Her gaze towards him showed that after all those years and all that had happened, she loved him still.

"Hmmm," said Alfred as they walked down the corridor to the exit. "That's made me quite hungry."

Coming towards them, in a wheelchair pushed by a trooper, was old Mr Hamaker, who had injured himself on his old war wound falling out of his bunk on the railroad journey. He waved his stick cheerily in their direction.

"Found your tree yet?" grunted Alfred.

"Yes indeed I have!" said Hamaker. "Do you know, it was just where I left it? I recognized it at once – bit bigger these days, of course."

"You don't say!" said Alfred.

"Coming in to have my dressing changed," Hamaker chirruped. "What're you boys doing here?"

"Silly, old fool," said Alfred as they made their way down the corridor. "Some of these old folks ought never to be allowed out on their own."

The following days were full of military parades and marching bands, reunions and gleeful old men shaking hands. Each day, Alfred and Trumper visited Mrs Brittan in the hospital but Jim did not go with them. Instead, while they were gone, he would go in search of Annabelle and they would slip away into the woods beyond the battlefield. They made love each afternoon, under the trees, stroking each other's soft, downy body, kissing, their tongues thrust deep inside the other's mouth, and entwining their bodies lasciviously together.

The other events happening around them seemed to be taking place unimportantly and far away in a distant haze. They could hardly bear to be apart, they thought about each other all the time and when they met they ran into each others' arms, barely able to contain their desire and desperate to make love to each other again. If they could have stripped there and then, in the street, in front of everyone, they would have done. The prophylactic that Alfred had given Jim remained forgotten in the detritus of his pockets.

Annabelle sat on the side of her bed in the Buford suite at the Robert E Lee Guesthouse, under another modern print, this time of a Union general falling melodramatically off his horse. She was thinking of those days. They came back to her quite clearly, she could see in her mind's eye the dress that she had worn and feel the texture of Jim's shirt.

If she thought very hard she could remember the feel of his body, even as she could not exactly remember now what he had looked like, or what he had said. The snapshot she had of him did not do him justice: it was faded and out of focus, leaving only the impression of his smiling, open face. She tried to remember what he had sounded like, but could not: a pleasant, soft voice, but no more than that.

She could remember the love-making very clearly, but not, properly, the person. The sensation remained sharp, but the image went in and out of focus. That's strange, she thought, when I have been thinking of him and what happened so much recently. But then she thought of her three husbands and realised she could scarcely remember them at all, or what making love to them had been like, except rough and cursory. No sensuousness there, she thought, not like in the woods round here, and she clambered into bed and turned out the light.

CHAPTER THIRTY-NINE

There was one event that Jim and Annabelle did not miss. On the Sunday afternoon, President Roosevelt himself arrived in Gettysburg for the veterans' reunion. He was there to inaugurate a great concrete memorial pillar, thirty feet high and topped by a burner with an everlasting flame.

Jim, Alfred and Simeon were joined by Mary to see the president, while Annabelle went separately with the colonel. The ceremony was to be the focal point of the whole reunion. They were way back in the crowd though and did not see much of the president – just being there would be enough: it was not every day you saw a president, in pictures, or in the flesh. There was just a glimpse of a big white fedora hat, the tilt of a cigarette and a glint of spectacles as he swept past in his big open-topped limousine with the presidential seal on the door. On the running board and trotting alongside were police agents; men in sunglasses and trilby hats, with their hands in their vest pockets and two-tone shoes on their feet.

When the president got to the podium, he was helped into position by men in uniform. He made stiff-legged lurching movements toward the microphones.

"My Lord!" whispered Trumper. "He's drunk as a skunk. Can you see? He can't even stand upright."

"No, Simeon," Jim whispered back. "They say he's had polio and can't walk properly."

"I think I can recognize a drunkard when I see one," retorted Trumper as the people around them hissed them to keep quiet.

Whatever his infirmities though, the president's voice was strong and clear and his honeyed expressions of brotherhood and peace echoed across the huge crowd and, through the loudspeakers, far out over the battlefield.

"What's he sayin'?" said an elderly Confederate veteran sitting next to Jim, his hand cupped behind his ear. "Hush, Grandfather. He says you all won," whispered the fat middle-aged man sitting next to him. "Well, he's a liar then," the old soldier replied, "We just got *beat*, but that's a different matter. We was not whipped – we was perished to death."

Afterwards, as Jim and Alfred made their way back towards the tented village, a young man holding a microphone stepped forward. His hair was brilliantined and his moustache neatly trimmed. He smelled of perfume.

The man accosted Alfred: "Excuse me, sir, are you a veteran? A few words please, for the Mutual Broadcasting Network..." The old man looked at him suspiciously.

"Did you enjoy what the president had to say today?"

"Is this being broadcast on the *raddio*?" said Alfred. The young man nodded and pointed silently to the microphone.

"Well sir, my name is Alfred Barker of Springbridge, Massachusetts. I am ninety-three years of age and I would like to send best wishes to my daughter and my sweetheart in hospital. Is this really being broadcast with this funny thing here?"

"Yes sir, it is. This is a microphone. Now, the president's speech…"

"Well, I thought he spoke mighty well and I hope his legs get better soon. But I think he ought to be thinking about us oldsters a bit more and paying us for fighting for our country as we did all those years ago. We need pensions. Some of these veterans have done all right but there's many in abject poverty and that's a scandal. But that's true of the whole country isn't it? I'm a Republican, see? Is that enough?"

"Are you proud to be here, sir? What memories does Gettysburg hold for you?"

"I was here in '63 of course and it seems to have changed a bit. 'Course, still too many damned rebels around for my liking, yellin' and screaming and showing off, but then there always were. In my view, their cause was lousy…" Alfred was into his stride.

"Thank you so much for speaking to us," the man cut him off hastily. It was not what he wanted to hear on such a day.

"Pity," said Alfred as the man moved away. "I was just getting going and now they'll never know what I thought. Did you hear me? I certainly put him straight, or I would've done if he'd not stopped me."

Alfred was in a good mood that evening. He had enjoyed his joust with the radio man and kept repeating what he had said as they made their way back to their tent. Still chortling, half-believing his remarks would shake the nation, he went inside to have a sit down and to change his shirt.

As the others waited outside, Jim had an idea. He said: "Simeon, would you do me a big favor? This evening when we are with all the others in the meal tent, could you ask him to show you his photographs?"

"Why?" said Trumper, equably. Although they had hauled the trunk all the way to Gettysburg, he had never shown any interest in its contents before.

Jim said: "Oh, you know, I think it would just be nice. No one's asked him about them all trip and I think he'd like to show them round. It would please him."

"Alright," Trumper replied. "Do we have to carry them again?"

They decided to leave the trunk in the tent and collect it when the subject had been raised, so as not to give Alfred any prior inkling of the plan. A few minutes later, at the sound of a distant triangle being struck to say food was ready, the men and Mary made their way to the mess tent. Alfred had dressed in all of his best clothes. He looked smarter than Jim had ever seen him.

The canteen tent was a big marquee with fly mesh drapes hanging down the sides. Inside were rows of trestle tables with plastic tablecloths. Soon everything was a bustle of scurrying white-jacketed black waiters and a clatter of plates and metal serving dishes. The old men seemed unperturbed by the sounds around them. Most of them had dressed to look smart, in suits, collars and ties, for the president. Their medals gleamed on their chests and, just like Alfred, they all kept their hats rammed tight on their heads. There were to be no concessions to informality on such a solemn day.

Soon their attentions were focused solely on their plates. As food was placed before them, they tucked in hungrily, eating while they could as if fearful of having to rush off to battle once more. They did not wait for anyone else to be served and the clatter of plates was replaced by the sound of old gums masticating. There was a sort of wallowing, chomping sound like a herd of hogs at a trough. Most of the veterans tucked their napkins inside the top of their shirt collars to catch hold of any dribbles and spills.

They were in a high state of excitement that night. They had seen the president, and watched the parades and soon, tomorrow or the next day, they would be heading home, finally, definitively, soldiers no more, leaving their old comrades for the last time. As the plates were cleared away, the tent became full of chatter and buzz and tobacco smoke from a hundred pipes and cigarettes began spiraling upwards.

Jim, Alfred, Simeon and Mary had taken their places at a table near one end of the tent and the aged veteran sitting next to them companionably turned to speak: "Well, boys, what did you think of that? Wasn't that something out there today?" he said in a friendly way, sucking his teeth as he did so to remove the last morsels of food.

"It sure was," said Alfred, thawing in the company of a Union man.

"I ain't never been a Democrat, not since they backed the wrong side in the Civil War, but I take my hat off to the president," said the old man. "Nor I ain't never seen a real live president in my whole life before. Made me proud to see him. I didn't know he'd had his legs took off in the war though. I come from Knob Fork, West Virginia. Ever been there? Name's George Washington Walker, what's yourn?" he added conversationally.

Alfred said: "I don't think I've ever had the privilege of seeing Knob Fork."

"Oh, it's a grand place, been there all my life. Say you fellows, what do you think of the food here?"

Alfred murmured something non-committal and the old man leaned forward, almost into Jim's face, cupped his hand around his mouth, and breathed hard and pungently: "Terrible swill, ain't it? They give us vegetable soup for lunch. Just a few vegetables! Well, I don't eat 'em. Never have and never done me no harm.

"That's no meal to give a starvin' man, is it? I hadn't any idea they'd be so short of meat round here. If I'd thought they was as bad off as this, I'd have brought up some pork from my smokehouse back home! I come here all by myself – no one to bring me – and they give me vegetables! Well! That's not how I've kept going all these years. I said to them, ain't never had no call for vegetables in all my life and I ain't goin' to start now. What do you think keeps me goin'? Heh? Have a guess!"

The old man was clearly going to tell them anyway, but Alfred hazarded a suggestion: "Pork?"

"Yep! How'd you guess that? Eaten it every day for seventy years and I come here and they give me vegetables! You know what else? Moonshine! That's my remedy. Give me a little out of the old still every night and that sure keeps the cold away. Brought some with me just in case…want to try some?"

He reached down to his feet and brought up a large earthenware pitcher. Walker chuckled as he poured the liquid into their cups: "Distilled it myself, for seventy years. All through prohibition and they never caught me once. Brought two pitchers with me just in case, so there's plenty to spare – I still got one left," he said.

The moonshine was pure alcohol and tasted like varnish, but Trumper and Alfred drank theirs back and soon the conversation was flowing more freely between them and Walker. As he sat listening, Jim felt his hand being squeezed. It was Annabelle, sliding onto the end of the bench beside him. She smiled at him conspiratorially, as if to suggest they should escape while they could, and Jim would have done so, had it not been for Mary who had seen the whole movement and was eyeing them both.

"Yessir, I was here," Walker was saying. "Served at Gettysburg, all three days. Nearly didn't get away with it though. See this?" he lifted his hat and pushed his skimpy gray hair away from his forehead with his hand. Across the hairline was a livid white line, running right across the front of his head like a streak of lightening leveled by a ruler. The scar contrasted with the grimy weather-beaten tan of the rest of his face.

"They nearly got me that time. Bullet went straight across. Reckon if I'd been half an inch further forward, it would've killed me stone-dead. You know what I did? Picked up some mud and smeared it across. Then I took up my gun and carried on fighting. What do you think of that? Dun't leave much of a mark – couldn't even see it when I had more hair."

Gradually the conversation turned to what Alfred had done in the war. For once, he did not try to cap the other old man's experiences. Perhaps he thought he couldn't, or perhaps he was too tired to pretend. "I took photographs for Mr Brady and Mr Gardner," he said simply.

This seemed like the right moment and Jim said quickly that Simeon and he would go and fetch the trunk. They both sprang up from the table before Alfred could say anything and were back carrying it within a few minutes. It was placed on the table, which groaned and lurched beneath the weight. Alfred unlocked the box and carefully put on his spectacles.

First he pulled out the folder of prints and, laying them out in a pile in front of him, began to describe them as if he was showing a family photograph album to a stranger. Mr Walker leaned across to look.

The first pictures were landscape views of the battlefield. Gradually, as he talked, a crowd gathered around the table. There was a press of elderly men peering over their shoulders, trying to see. Alfred had found his audience at last.

His voice rose. He was telling the story of the expedition. "See here, this is old General Meade's headquarters. This was taken within three days of the battle. Mr Gardner and me, we got there first, before the dust was settled," Alfred said, beaming ecstatically at the interest. A collective sigh ran through the growing audience. More men were coming up every minute. There was quite a group now. With every fresh photograph, there was a murmur of recognition and excitement.

Then he moved on to the photographs of dead men. This only seemed to enhance the audience's interest. Some had struggled up onto the next table and its benches to get a better look. As he spoke, a sort of spellbound silence fell all around.

Then, he produced a striking picture of a beardless rebel soldier lying across the end of a rectangular piece of ground. The space was boxed in at its sides by large rocks, maybe the height of a man standing upright, and at its end by a line of smaller rocks, which had clearly been deliberately placed there like a wall. The soldier was very young and very dead, though he looked as natural as if he had been asleep; eyes closed and mouth slightly open. There was no sign of a wound. The young man had been handsome, with clear, regular features. His right arm was at his side and his left hand was on his stomach. His legs, slightly bent, stretched out in front of him. His uniform tunic was undone, showing his shirt beneath. Next to the body, leaning against the wall, was the prop rifle. It was a strikingly clear and vivid picture and the audience murmured in appreciation.

"This poor young man, a teenager I'd guess, was found by us near the Devil's Den just by the Little Round Top," Alfred said. "He was a sharpshooter and clearly he laid himself down to die once he'd been hit. Goodness knows how long it took him to pass over. Just curled up and waited for the end, I expect.

"This portrait is illustrative, gentlemen, of the tragedy of war. That young man could have been any one of us – wrong side of course – but he died in the bloom of youth instead of living to a ripe old age as you or me have been fortunate to do. Who can say if the shot that killed him had been aimed just an inch to one side, he might have lived a productive and happy life, with kids and all, and been standing here – in one of the tents across the way – even today, instead of dead and cold this three-quarters of a century. Just an accident of fate…."

There were nods and murmers of appreciation among the old men. Alfred's rhetoric was flowing freely now. It was as if he was giving a lantern slide lecture: "I wonder who he was? Did his family ever know what happened to him? Did his old mother weep cold tears for her son? Did his father ever look up from the plow in the family fields down South in Alabama to see if he could see him coming home down the highway after all? A journey he would never make… Who can look on this picture and refrain from asking these questions?"

The crowd the old man had drawn was hanging on his every word. "Let me tell you gentlemen a very remarkable story. Mr Gardner and I returned to Gettysburg four months after the battle, in November 1863, to photograph Mr Lincoln's inauguration of the cemetery. And my boss and I were wandering the field and came upon the Devil's Den once more. And we looked for this quiet little space, where we had seen the young man. Do you know, *his body was still there!*"

There was a gasp. "Yes, gentlemen. Neglected and unburied! The uniform as you see it, the gun rusted by his side. And just a skeleton lying there, quite decomposed. He'd been missed when they cleared the battlefield, his last resting place known only to us. Forgotten and alone!"

The old men gasped. Jim was just working out that the gun could not have been rusted up if it still hung above his grandfather's bed when there was a stifled sob beside him. An old Union veteran was wiping away a tear. "Terrible things…terrible things happened in that war," he was saying to himself.

Alfred said: "You may see an account of this discovery gentlemen in Mr Gardner's *Photographic Sketchbook of the War*, which he published afterwards."

Then he paused for a moment for effect and, in the silence, there came the sound of a single man clapping, slowly and ironically. It continued for several moments and the old men craned their scraggy necks round to see where the noise was coming from.

It was Colonel Putnam. He was standing on the edge of the crowd, flapping his hands together languidly and contemptuously. Once he had the veterans' attention, he moved forward into the space that had formed across the table from Alfred. Jim felt Annabelle stiffen as she sat beside him.

Putnam said: "You know that's really very good. Very affecting. It almost brought a tear to my eye, that performance, Barker. The only thing is that it is not in the least bit true. Not a word. It is an unscrupulous fabrication, gentlemen, from beginning to end."

The colonel had their full attention. He seemed to fill the space beyond the table. He was dressed in his blue frock coat, on which the brass buttons and medals glistened in the light. The crowd paid him respectful attention. Some heads bobbed with deference towards the old officer.

"I know what happened that day because I saw it," the colonel continued. "I caught this man here and his colleagues rearranging this poor man's body for the picture. He didn't die there – they carried his dead body to that spot! I saw them dragging it about on a blanket. Despicable! And I remonstrated with them, gentlemen, I remonstrated with them!

"I recognise that picture as if it happened yesterday. It is a fake, obtained by crookery!"

"So it was *you,*" said Alfred, groaning. There was a murmering from the old veterans.

The colonel had the light of retribution in his eyes. "Yes, Barker, I saw you and your friends. It was a desecration. I saw you, because I was in charge of a burial party over the rise. And do you want to know why I saw you and marked what you were doing? Why I've never forgotten it?"

Annabelle clutched Jim's sleeve. The colonel was roaring now: "It was because it was my own brother!"

"*What?*" said Alfred, aghast.

"It was my little brother, Peter, who'd gone south to learn the cotton trade before the war," said the colonel. "I knew he'd joined the other side and I was on the lookout for him. Never thought I'd find him dead though. I'll give you credit for one thing, Barker, you helped me find my brother's body! You used him though. After death, you *used* him. You exploited him."

Annabelle was sobbing softly and Jim put his arm around her shoulder to comfort her, but she squirmed away as if she could not bear his touch.

Alfred was regaining his composure now. He pointed across the table at Putnam and roared: "I didn't exploit anyone all those years ago, you liar! We made a beautiful photograph, with respect. We were reverential. We were doing nothing wrong, just improving the composition. And we created an image which can move people even now! Can't you see? It was no lie!"

Putnam roared back: "You should not have done it! You made a story which was not true! And all that guff about finding him months afterwards… well, it's rubbish: I had him buried myself. He's lying even now in the cemetery with his comrades."

He turned to the others for support. "Look, look, you can see it's true," he shouted, the pent-up emotions of seventy five years spilling out. He pointed to the next print on Alfred's pile. "Look at this other picture of a body lying in a field – you can see it's Peter, where he fell. The creases in his uniform, the formation of his legs, the coat undone! *It's the same man!* My poor brother. They took his picture twice!"

Old Walker leaned forward to examine both prints, his spectacles on the end of his nose. His eyes went from one image to the other, then back again and back again. "By George, you're right," he said at last. "How do you explain this, sir?"

Alfred appealed to the crowd: "I don't have to explain. The man was dead. He died in the battle. We didn't make him up, or pretend he was dead when he wasn't. Mr Gardner was just pointing up the horror of that civil war, is all. Can't you see that? It's as authentic and true to what happened in that battle as I'm standing here. You know that – if Putnam hadn't stuck his oar in, you'd be none the wiser!"

"But I did, didn't I?" said Putnam nastily. "I've exposed you as a fake and a fraud. This picture is not true. You can even see the blanket under my poor brother's head! What man puts his blanket down to lie on and die comfy in the middle of a battle?"

He turned for support to the crowd. "This man has no right to be here! He is a scavenger on the backs of decent men. He did not fight like you gentlemen, but was a jackal, scavenging the corpses of nobler, braver men to make a profit from their misfortune! He should not be here!"

There was a muttering from the other veterans and a ripple of applause. Alfred had sunk, crestfallen, to his seat, surrounded by the photographic plates and their prints. Jim felt hugely sorry for him as the crowd turned. Then he saw his grandfather's fingers drumming on the table.

Alfred's voice rose and the veterans fell silent. "Now gentlemen, I must apologize. We have all done things that we're not proud of in our lives, me as much as any man who has lived so long. When things went against me, I always thought it was because I was just the little man, being crushed by the high and mighty banker, this Colonel Putnam here, the biggest man in our town, a man who could crush people who crossed him like flies, but now I know there was a reason for him bearing down on me and my family and I am sorry for it.

"But I am not going to apologize for this photograph. A few minutes ago you were admiring these pictures. They chimed in with your recollections of what it was like, didn't they? They did not tell a lie that you could see, did they?

"Yes, we did move that poor boy's body a few yards. So what? If he'd run a few more seconds, that's where he might have ended up anyway. We didn't kill him, or drag him to another battlefield, did we? We didn't prop him up against a board, or put a cigarette in his lips, or steal his clothes, or his dignity. We never took his boots. We even made him famous in a way, more famous in death than he ever was in life, poor man. What we did, gentlemen, was turn that picture into poetry. Put a face to an enemy – the pity and pathos of war. It's a beautiful, dignified thing. And it was a very little deceit."

As he paused for breath, Putnam burst in: "People did not need to see such things. It was best for them not to know about them. You earned money and fame from my brother's death, a poor young man, just as if he had been a prize hog, carted round the county fair for everyone to gawp at at five cents a go."

Alfred said: "Oh Putnam, don't be silly. We were recording a historical event! No one paid us to go there so we had to charge – it was a matter of commerce. But we had a mission: in a few years' time we'll all be dead and no one will know what the Civil War was like. All they'll know is the lies people will tell them about how noble and wonderful it all was! All good heroes together! Let's go and do it all again! We know different, don't we boys?"

He was winning them round. Now he got to his feet again and addressed Putnam directly, urgently, across the table. Alfred said quietly: "Anyway, you and I know the real reason for your enmity, don't we, eh Putnam? It's nothing to do with the photograph of your brother, if it was your brother, was it? It's only the presence of my daughter and your granddaughter that prevents me saying anything. But don't push me too far, Putnam, you louse."

Putnam went white. "You wouldn't dare!" he said. "Would you?"

Alfred glared levelly at him. One or two of the old men were turning back to their food, then Old Walker broke the silence by tapping him on the sleeve and saying gently: "You got any more of them photographs we could see, sir?"

Jim let out his breath. The danger had passed. Beside him, Annabelle still sat rigid with fear about what might happen next. He patted her thigh encouragingly, but she flinched again. Looking up, Jim saw Mary's face etched with anxiety. She was staring at her father.

Alfred turned once more to the trunk and Jim saw him pull out the plate wrapped in a towel. He was going to show them the dead Lincoln picture. He held it along the edges, balanced between the palms of his hands and gently held it up horizontally to the light until it was level with his face, almost as reverently as if it was a communion wafer at Mass. Alfred peered closely at the surface and gently blew a spot of dust away. "Jim," he said, "Get out the print would you please?"

Jim reached in the box and held up the print of Abraham Lincoln lying in his coffin. There was a gasp from the crowd.

With the air of a fairground barker, Alfred raised his voice again: "Look at this gentlemen. You won't ever have seen this before. Look and say that this is not a part of history. This, I assure you, is the only *authentic*, true photograph ever taken of President Lincoln after he was assassinated. I helped to take it, so I know. It is a portrait made in the White House on the day after he was shot.

This is no fake, gentlemen!"

The old men squinted up at the glass, screwing their eyes up to try and focus on the image. Some took their hats off in a gesture of reverence, as if they were in the sacred presence of the dead president himself. One old man, carefully and gently took the plate from Alfred and, holding it by the tips of his fingers, gazed closely at it. Then it was taken from him and another man looked with wrapt attention and then another. One by one, the plate was passed around the group of old men, adjusting their spectacles and holding their breath as they stared intently at the image. Then they looked at the paper picture and that went round too.

"That's him," said one. "Sure enough. I seen him once in Washington. It's like he was just lying there…"

There was a snuffling and coughing among the old Union men as they strived to control their emotions. Finally, the plate was handed back to Alfred. "Thank you gentlemen," he said. "You see? Historic, important work."

Putnam had been watching this beadily and now he spoke, his voice high-pitched with emotion. "You see? He's done it again and this time with the president himself! Show some respect, damn you. Who gave you permission?" And he suddenly seemed to go quite mad and launched himself at Alfred across the table, trying to reach the glass plates and thrashing at them with his walking stick. "Grandpa!" Annabelle shrieked.

The move caught Alfred by surprise and he grabbed at the print of the dead president just as the colonel seized it from the other side. There was a brief tug of war and then the paper tore in half with a great ripping sound. As it did so, the table itself started to collapse, under the pressure of the two old men clawing at each other and the weight of the tin trunk. Slowly, as the table tilted, the trunk and its contents started sliding inexorably across the surface. "Stop it!" Alfred cried. But it was too late and with a great crashing of glass it all hit the floor, landing on top of the Lincoln plate and crushing it to smithereens.

Alfred picked himself up and rising to his full height, brandished his walking stick from the bottom end like a club. "You've done it this time, Putnam!" he roared. "You bastard! Take that – that's for seducing my wife!" And he brought the stick down on the colonel's head.

Mary screamed. "Father!" she shouted.

Putnam was trying to rise now, a trickle of blood seeping down from the top of his head. He held up the torn half of the photograph and laughed, tearing it into small pieces as he did so and tossing them into the air. "Yes," he shouted. "I got your wife and you got the child!"

He had seized a table knife and fork to defend himself and launched himself at Alfred, stabbing at him with the cutlery, aiming for his neck. The fork stuck just above the collar

Alfred leaped at him again, but this time as he brought down the stick, the colonel flinched and it struck him on the shoulder. He subsided with a sigh. All around him the elderly veterans scrambled for cover, crunching the fragments of glass underfoot.

Waiters, soldiers and attendants rushed forward to grapple with the fighters and Jim saw his uncle, standing proud, laying about him with his stick, shouting in triumph and hitting Putnam again as the colonel slid to the floor.

Alfred was finally brought down under the weight of the onrush of attendants, crowing as he did so. Jim rushed to his side. The old man looked up at him from the floor, the fork still hanging at an angle from his neck. "I showed him, Jim boy. I showed him," he said and closed his eyes.

CHAPTER FORTY

Far off, in the distance, as Jim knelt over his grandfather surrounded by the broken glass, he could hear Putnam's voice saying: "I insist, sir, that you throw that man out. He's an imposter." The colonel was sitting up by now, dabbing at his cracked head with a handkerchief spotted in blood. Annabelle was kneeling beside him.

Old Mr Walker was telling one of the troopers: "It was the colonel who started it. He went for the photographer."

The trooper shook his head. "My God, I don't know what they do to the enemy, but they sure frighten me. Didn't anyone tell you boys that the war is over?"

The aged doctor who had inspected Faith Brittan in the railroad carriage stood over Alfred this time. "You again!" he said as he stared down amid the wreckage of Alfred's Civil War career. All around him there were shards of photographic plates, depicting pieces of bodies and fragments of military men, carpeted across the ground in all directions.

They took Alfred to hospital in an ambulance but the colonel insisted he did not need treatment and left the tent with Annabelle holding his hand. She ignored Jim's attempt to speak to her and did not look in his direction, so he was left, standing with Simeon, in the now-deserted tent. Jim bent down to see if the plate of the dead president was salvageable, but it had been utterly smashed. Finally, seventy five years late, Mr Stanton had got his way.

With the glass crunching under their boots, they shuffled across the debris to pick up the paper prints and put them all back in their folder. Some of the plates were undamaged and others had just cracked across so might still be saved.

Jim and Simeon walked through the still crowded streets, full of excited people chattering about seeing the president. The red white and blue coloured lights were all on now and music was playing everywhere in the hot evening air. *"I Wish I Was In Dixie"* and *"John Brown's Body"* competed with each other once again, but the revelry seemed oppressive and inappropriate to the two men as they headed once more for the hospital.

It was becoming a familiar place and they made straight down the main corridor to the ward of old men that he had looked into a few days before. Just as they were passing, the nurse came out of Mrs Brittan's room. She started when she saw Jim, recognizing him as one of the old lady's visitors.

She said: "Are you Mrs Brittan's relative, sir? Don't go inside, just yet, I will fetch the doctor to speak to you," and clattered hastily off down the passage.

Jim peered through the porthole in the door. Mrs Brittan's bed was empty and the ward was silent. The bed had been remade. They could hear the young doctor bustling along the long corridor long before they saw him, because in the silence his shoes were squeaking across the linoleum of the floor, accompanied by the rapid tapping noise made by the nurse, scurrying to keep up with him.

The doctor stopped beside them and cleared his throat: "I am sorry to be the bearer of bad news, but your, your...relative passed away this afternoon..." he said.

"It was quite peaceful," said the nurse, butting in. "She had her lunch and settled down for a little sleep and when I went in to check that she was alright, she'd just...slipped away, all alone. She must have been ever so peaceful...it was a good way to go. Really."

Jim nodded sadly. He did not know what to say. He felt he was almost a relative and yet they had scarcely been acquainted. It was no more than a week since they had met. "I think that's how she would have wanted it," he said. "I think she was a very unassuming person. She wouldn't have wanted to cause any trouble."

The doctor said: "No. Well. Would you like to view the body? We will of course make arrangements to ship her home to – er – Philadelphia." As he did so he was checking the time on his watch as if anxious to be on his way. "I think you will need to sign some forms but it will be routine. You are, I take it, next of kin?"

Jim nodded again. He guessed he might be. They took his silence for grief, but it was grief more for Alfred than for Mrs Brittan.

Jim said: "I need to find my grandfather. He's in here somewhere too. There was a little accident at the camp just now and they've brought him in."

"Of course, just as soon as we have sorted this one out," said the doctor, scarcely paying attention. He only wanted one problem at a time and was thinking more of his paperwork than of patients."Well, there it is," he said with finality before moving off in a businesslike way to attend to easier tasks elsewhere.

Finally Jim got to see his grandfather in the ward. He had been dressed in hospital pyjamas and placed behind screens in a corner, but he was already sitting up and arguing with the nurse. There was a large sticking plaster on the side of his neck, where the fork had dug in and a bandage round the top of his head to cover the bruise caused when he and Putnam had toppled over the table.

"Ah, Jim, Trumpy! Tell this lady that I need to go home at once," he said without preamble. "I don't need to be here and I want to get back to Springbridge with Faith."

"There is no question of that for a day or two," said the nurse, but Alfred ignored her. He was thinking of the scuffle in the tent. . "I showed him tonight, didn't I? I landed such a crack on that Putnam's head, didn't I? Do you know what's happened to him?"

Jim said the colonel had gone off with Annabelle and his grandfather retorted: "Well I don't want to see him. Have they said anything to you about Faith? I must get out and visit her."

Jim ignored the question. It was too difficult for him tonight. Instead he said: "Anyway, how are you Grandpa?"

"I'll be fine. I'm just so damned tired. Been overdoing it, I guess. I don't know what came over me – got too excited, silly old fool. All we need to do is get out of here and then get Faith and pick up the car and head for home." Alfred lay back in the bed, wheezing for breath.

There was a pause, then he said confidentially, as if letting Jim into a great and unexpected secret: "You know, I am rather sweet on her, even after all these years. I guess we might even settle down together…I think she would."

And, to seal the relationship, he lifted his head from the pillow slightly and began to sing in his thin, high, reedy voice. It was the old Eddie Cantor number that he had once liked so much:

"We'll have that cottage you've been wishing for;
We'll have the roses rambling round the door;
When my ship comes in…."

The voice rose higher. The other patients were beginning to stir and a nurse farther down the ward was looking up to see where the noise was coming from. Jim tried to shush him up. There was no possibility of telling him about Faith now.

"Hush Grandfather, you'll wake everyone up," Jim whispered in his ear. "Go to sleep now. You need some rest and I'll come to see you in the morning."

Alfred gazed up at his grandson like a child and smiled. The singing ceased in a bout of coughing. "Yes Jim, you're right," he said. "I'll see you in the morning…."

Jim said: "Oh Grandfather, you do get into scrapes. Was that all true what you were saying?"

Alfred smiled. "What, about the corpse in the rocks? Well, a little poetic license maybe…"

Jim started off early for the hospital the next morning, picking up his mother along the way and telling her the bad news about Faith. He had not been able to sleep for worrying what he would say to his grandfather. Mary said: "You'll just have to tell him, is all. It's a shame – I'd sure like to have known her better and found out some more family secrets." She offered Jim no words of advice and he made his way through the nearly empty streets rehearsing to himself how to break the news.

In the hospital, Alfred was sitting up in bed arguing once more with the nurse. "Ah Jim and Mary, I'm glad you've arrived at last," he said as if he had been waiting all day. "Can you tell this lady that I have an appointment to see Mrs Brittan in the next ward? She will insist that there is no one of that name in here."

The nurse looked at Jim pleadingly and backed away. He would have to tell him unaided. It was the moment he had been dreading and he did it badly.

"The fact is, Grandfather, that you just can't see Mrs Brittan, not now or ever again. You see she's dead. She died yesterday in her sleep, the doctor just told me. I am sorry. They've taken her away already."

Alfred collapsed back on his pillows. He seemed at that moment to deflate. Then he closed his eyes, said simply: "Oh no, not that too," and fell silent.

Jim and Mary sat with him for the rest of the day. The old man was exhausted. Alfred dozed a little but when he woke he said unexpectedly to Jim: "I'd like you to give my prints to your sweetheart. They'd show her that her grandfather was wrong, once and for all. You can always get some others printed up from the plates for yourself if you want."

Jim said: "I don't think that will be possible Granddad, they mostly got smashed in your fight, don't you remember?"

"Oh yes, bother," the old man said. "Well, give them to her anyway. They're no use to me any more."

Jim said he would, but he was in truth not sure that he would be allowed to see Annabelle again after what had happened. He sensed their relationship had ended with their grandfathers' fight in the tent.

A little while later, Mary reached forward and stroked the old man's hand on top of the bedclothes. There was something she needed to ask and sensed it could not be left, so there was urgency in her question.

"Father," she said. "Faith told me about her being Sarah's sister, so I know about all that now. But what did Putnam mean about seducing your wife and giving you a child?"

Alfred stirred. His eyes opened wide. They stood out, watery blue in his parchment-coloured face against the white of the pillow. He was wide awake now and startled. Mary and Jim could sense him gathering his thoughts and his strength.

"Oh Mary, I hoped to spare you that. He didn't need to say that, the bastard – excuse me saying so. He was getting his own back on me. Help me up."

They propped him upright against the pillow and he turned to look her in the eye. "The truth is, Mary, that you are not my child. You know your mother and I, well, married in haste and did not get on too well. Never a love match.

"Well, the fact is that I bored her and annoyed her for some reason and she resented me, especially when I sent her out to work to earn some money to help us both out. Well, she went as a daily help at a big house…and the master seduced her. She went to bed with him, you know? And she got pregnant, but he wouldn't do anything to help her.

"I think Sarah thought he might marry her – divorce me, you know? – but of course he wasn't going to marry a servant, was he? She didn't tell me about it for a long time, until she had to – scared I would find out, I suppose. And then, well, I wouldn't agree to an abortion, not after what happened before. So she had to carry the babby all though – I made her. I felt it was like God was saying to me, now this one's yours, it's your turn: you've got to look after it this time! And so I have, all these years – that's you!"

He was exhausted after his long speech and short of breath, but Mary, in tears now, said: "But who's my real father then?"

Alfred's eyes were closed, but he said: "Can't you guess? It was Putnam."

"Oh my God!" she said, putting her hand in front of her mouth.

Alfred said: "I didn't mean ever to tell you and you'd never have known. It's only me and him does and he's never done anything to help till now. But he knows who you are…I'm sorry you've had to find out. You're my child, really."

Mary's shoulders were shaking now and huge tears were rolling down her cheeks and splashing onto her lap. Jim put his arms around her and kissed her. "It's alright Ma," he said. "It doesn't matter. You're still you. It's alright.

"Oh Father," she said. "You *are* my Father. And I love you!" But Alfred's eyes were still closed and she could not tell whether he had heard her or not.

The old man slept most of the afternoon, but occasionally he woke up and looked at them. He didn't say much but from time to time he stretched out, reaching for their hands, and smiled. As the day wore on, he grew increasingly gray and sunken in. Once, Jim thought he saw a tear trickle down his face. He did not speak again.

As evening drew on, Alfred's breathing became more labored and intermittent. It came in deep pants, irregular and shallower each time, and then gradually stopped altogether. After a few moments, they realized he had died. When Mary reached up to kiss the old man's forehead it was already cold and hard, like marble.

CHAPTER FORTY-ONE

"Two dead relatives," the young doctor had said. "You have not had much luck have you? I guess the effort of getting here was just too much for them. OK, now there's more paperwork: would you like to do it madam, since your son did it yesterday?"

After Mary had completed the formalities, she and Jim wandered back into the ward to collect Alfred's clothes. His body was still in the bed. Somehow it seemed shrunken and empty, not just of life, but also of all trace of his spirit, except for one thing: his face had a slight smile, as if he had come out, finally, ahead.

They walked back together through the town, which was already starting to return to normal. There were still a few straggling veterans, their coats and kepis dustier and shabbier than they had been during the reunion. Workmen were beginning to take down the bunting and the lights.

Mostly Jim and Mary were silent with their thoughts, but as they approached the camp, Jim said: "I must go and find Annabelle and tell her what's happened, and give her granddad's pictures."

Mary said: "I suppose you do realise you can never be her intended now, don't you? You're cousins and I must be her aunt. You'll have to tell her."

It had not occurred to Jim and it struck him almost as hard as his grandfather's death had earlier in the day. He was not sure he could cope with that as well.

Fortunately, they made it easy for him. He found Annabelle and her grandfather sitting outside the colonel's tent, waiting for a taxi cab to take them to the station. She turned her head away defiantly as he approached. "You keep away from us, young man," growled Putnam.

Jim stopped in front of them. He had throught what he was going to say: a second rehearsed speech of the day. "It is alright," he said. "I won't come any closer. I was just asked, by my grandfather – my *late* grandfather – to give Miss Annabelle these pictures. They were precious to him and he thought you would like them as a keepsake…I can get some more made."

He handed the file of prints to Annabelle, who opened them with a look of disdain and ostentatiously tossed them aside onto the grass.

"What do you mean, late?" asked the colonel.

"Oh, he died in the hospital a few hours ago. I think he was worn out by all the stress."

"Good," said Putnam.

"But he told us all about you and my grandmother before he went," said Jim. "About how my mother was your daughter. And how he brought her up as his own."

The colonel shifted uncomfortably. "That's all stuff and nonsense and lies," he said. "Don't you go spreading that, or you'll have hell to pay."

Jim wandered back to his tent to pack up. He was glad he had said what he had to Putnam, even if it did him no good at all. He wanted him to know that he knew. And he wanted Annabelle to know too. He had been pleased to see her staring quizzically at her grandfather as he turned to go. What he did not see was her quietly picking up the file of photographs after he had left and putting them away in her suitcase.

The next day Mary, Jim and Simeon Trumper started the slow, melancholy journey back to Springbridge. Alfred's body accompanied them in the guard's van, in one of the coffins the organizers of the reunion had provided for just such an eventuality. They did not trouble to get the Model T Ford as they passed through Lancaster: Jim wrote to the garage on Simeon's behalf when they got back home, to say that he had decided to accept their kind offer to buy the car; but they never heard back.

At the same time, Jim wrote to Mrs Brittan's address in Philadelphia to tell Martin and Lionel what had happened and to advise them to find a lawyer to sort out her affairs. Some weeks later he received a laboriously-spelled letter, attached to a large package, through the post. It said:

"Dere Mister Barker,

Thanks yew for telling uz about Mrss Brittans death. We are off course very sad for she *was good to us all these yeres. The lawer sa she leff her properte to thee hospitale but she want uz to hav 100$ each for ourseln, for ar servis over the time we wuz wiv her. That's mighte kind. We thought befor her things went, yew wod lik this piktur ov yor granpap. He lok a mighte fin man an we iz sad yew loss him to.*

Yors sinserly,

Martin an Lionel

Inside the package was the photograph of the young Alfred that had hung in Mrs Brittan's hallway, so carefully wrapped in old newspapers and brown paper that the glass had not even cracked.

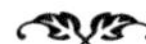

It was one morning in the Fall four months later, that there was a knock on the front door as Jim and Mary were having breakfast. It was Annabelle, as if they had never parted.

"Hi Jim," she said and gave him a peck on the cheek. "Can we talk for a minute?"

Jim led her into the parlour and they sat, chastely, in the armchairs on either side of the wireless set. There was an awkward pause. Annabelle fiddled with the strap on her handbag and Jim sat waiting for her to speak. Then they both spoke at once.

"How are you doing?" he said.

"I'm moving away from here," she replied. Then she burst into tears. "I've got something to tell you. My grandpa said I shouldn't come here, but I had to. I thought you should know. I've had a problem…you made me pregnant at Gettysburg. And I've had to do away with it."

"Why?" said Jim, aghast. "We could have worked something out…I could have married you. Has it been done yet? Why didn't you say while there was still time? Oh Annabelle!"

Annabelle tilted her head defiantly. "No. That's what I wanted. It wouldn't have done for me to have the baby. Not now and not with you, I am afraid. I couldn't let it hurt my future career and I didn't want to blight your life either, by marrying someone out of duty. That's had to happen too often in your family hasn't it?

Jim said: "But I love you. We could have had the baby. We could have worked it out…Got married."

Annabelle got up to go. She was not going to have an argument. "No Jim. It's done, over and we can get on with our lives. Anyway, it would never have worked, would it? Cousins....I'm leaving for Hollywood at the end of this week, so you won't see me around."

Jim walked her to the front door. He felt numb. On the threshold, she gave him a peck on the cheek and said: "Don't worry, dear. It's all for the best." Then she went down the steps without a backward glance.

CHAPTER FORTY-TWO

"It had to be done, you know," said Miss Annabelle as she and Izzie drove back to Springbridge sixty-four years later. "I had to make a clean break of it. And I never forgave my grandpa for what he had done to that family."

"You were pretty ruthless," said Izzie.

"Yes, dear, I suppose I was, but there was such a tangled relationship between our families that I felt there was no choice. I didn't want to get married to Jim then. We'd had a lovely summer together, but I didn't want the baby. And I'd *had* him. It would have interfered with my career – little did I know what *that* would amount to! So it was a good job, as it turned out. But I often think of it, you know, especially now. That baby would have been my only relative. It's a regret."

"Do you know what happened to Jim?"

"Yes, I do as it happens." Annabelle was looking away from Izzie, out at the view as they roared along the Merritt Parkway in the afternoon sunshine, so that the younger woman could not see the pain on her face. "I found out years later, after I came back here to live. He fulfilled his ambition: he did become a war photographer during the Second World War. They had smaller cameras then, of course, they could get closer to the action, didn't have to take one picture at a time. That just made it all the more dangerous. You remember that battle in Belgium at the end of the war, in the snow, in the woods – what was it called? Bulge, Bulge-something. Well anyway, he got caught apparently and the

Germans shot him as a spy.

"Poor Jim. I expect he was just standing around, waiting for something to happen as usual. Or thinking he was back home in the woods round here, waiting for the Confederates. I expect they just lined him up against a tree and – rat-a-tat-tat – just cut him down, all alone in the slush. I don't even know where he's buried."

"That's terrible," said Izzie. "I am so sorry."

"It doesn't bear thinking about. Poor boy. Well, there it is. I'm sorry too. I've started thinking a lot about him again since we met up, and the baby. You're the only other person who knows all this. But it would never have worked out, you know. No use crying about it."

Out of the corner of her eye, Izzie saw Annabelle's face had set firm as she stared fixedly straight ahead through the windshield. Her jaw jutted out and her mouth pointed down, but her eyes were wet.

Then she said: "At least you have got the photographs now, dear. That's something. Pity about the ones the old man took to Gettysburg. And that one of the president in his coffin. That might have been worth some money by now."

At the end of that summer, Gene and Izzie put The Photographer's House up for sale. They had not really been able to make the business work and it was true that they had not enjoyed strangers tramping through their home. It had all been too much effort. And, actually, they missed Manhattan.

The country life – and especially the house itself – was just too melancholy, especially as the dark nights drew on. Sometimes, now she knew the story, at night on the upper corridor, Izzie would get the creepiest feeling, as if she had missed somebody turning the corridor, just out of sight, beyond the corner of her eye. It was all nonsense of course, but it wasn't helped by Gene's decision to hang some of the Civil War photographs on the walls along there. They weren't the pictures of corpses on the battlefield, but the bright eyes of young men now long dead seemed to gaze out levelly at her and follow her as she walked past.

George Montgomery Price of Bijou Memories had agreed to buy back at reduced rates some of the antiques Gene and Izzie had bought from him nine months before. They did not regret seeing the escritoire and the mahogany sideboard going, nor even the Currier and Ives prints.

Joshua Butterfield IV gave them four hundred dollars for the glass plates, though Izzie kept one, showing a young soldier lying dead against a dry stone wall. "Pity about the Lincoln photograph," Butterfield had said, when Izzie told him the story. "That would have been worth some thousands. I wonder there's not a copy somewhere in the government archives…"

And so they drove off, back to the big city. But as they took one last look round, Izzie was struck by the old rocking chair that they had decided to leave behind for the new owners, as a sort of small inheritance to go with the house. It was gently swinging to and fro in the early winter breeze, which was sending the leaves swirling on the gravel drive. She could almost have sworn she heard music playing in the distance. An old Eddie Cantor song:

"You know, I hate to hear you sigh,
But you get blue and so do I,
Because our ship of dreams,
Is lost at sea, it seems,
But though it's very far away,
It will return some day….
When my ship comes in."

POSTCRIPT

Many of the events in this story, large and small, really happened: not just the battles of Antietam and Gettysburg of course, but the capture of Congressman Ely at Bull Run, the Confederate orders wrapped round two cigars, even the aged veteran who wanted to find the tree where he had been shot 75 years on.

Many of the people were real too: Mathew Brady's name was only the most prominent among dozens of photographers who covered the war, a tribute to his showmanship but also the technical brilliance of many of the photographs that he and his employees took. The work of men like Alexander Gardner, Timothy O'Sullivan and James Gibson is increasingly appreciated today, particularly as the difficulties and hardships under which they labored are better appreciated.

Millions of pictures were taken during the war, one of the first events to be covered extensively by photographers, using technical innovations that had only very recently been developed at that time. Many of their glass plates ended up as garden cloches, but others still have an immediacy and quality that remain breathtaking, 150 years on, as accomplished and vivid as any photographs taken today. With a change of clothes, many of those depicted in their pictures could easily pass as contemporary Americans.

Remarkably, the 75th anniversary reunion of veterans at Gettysburg in July 1938 – as far away in time in 2013 as the battle was from them – attracted more than 1,700 old soldiers, coming from 47 of the 48 states then in the Union –

only little Rhode Island sent no representatives. Of the 1,359 Union veterans and 486 former Confederates who were able to be present, out of about 12,000 still then living, it was thought that 65 had actually fought in the battle. The oldest veteran attending was a black former soldier called William Barnes, who was said to be 112, the youngest was 85. Three old soldiers died during the reunion and six passed away on their journeys home.

Abortion was relatively freely available in mid-19th Century America, so Faith's termination would not have been unusual: it has been calculated that as many as one in six pregnancies in the US Civil War era was ended by an abortion – though that must surely remain a speculative figure.

Anyone who writes about American Civil War photography is endebted these days to the work of William Frassanito, a Gettysburg resident and former intelligence analyst in Vietnam, whose dogged and intensive forensic study of the battlefield photographs enabled the dates on which they were taken and many of their locations to be identified. It was his work that definitively established for the first time after more than 100 years that the body of the Confederate soldier in Gardner and O'Sullivan's famous picture *The Home of a Rebel Sharpshooter* had been moved 72 yards from its original location – and it was this insight, in his book *Gettysburg: A Journey in Time*, which I bought on my first visit to the town in 1980, that first stimulated my interest in early photography and the journalism it spawned. Other fine historians such as D. Mark Katz and Bob Zeller have also developed – pardon the pun – this fascinating and rewarding field of research.

ABOUT THE AUTHOR

Stephen Bates is a British journalist and author who has been fascinated by the American Civil War and the pioneering Victorian photographers for many years, and this story combines his two enthusiasms. He lives in England but knows the US well. This is his first novel.

OPEN ROAD
INTEGRATED MEDIA

CPSIA information can be obtained at www.ICGtesting.com
Printed in the USA
BVOW02s1007180215

388285BV00001B/72/P